DIPLOMATIC TANGLE

TIM ENRIGHT

Diplomatic Tangle
Published by Birch Forest Publishing
Alexandria, VA

ISBN: 979-8-9851415-3-5 (Hardcover Edition)
ISBN: 979-8-9851415-4-2 (Paperback Edition)
ISBN: 979-8-9851415-5-9 (eBook Edition)
FICTION / Thrillers / Political

Cover and interior design by Victoria Wolf, wolfdesignandmarketing.com; Publishing management by KLR Literary Management. All copyrights owned by Tim Enright.

*With thanks to my children, whose curiosity
and love of adventure enriches my life.*

*For Emily, without whom I would never have begun
writing. She makes my life better, and I look forward to
many decades of adventures around the world with her.*

Other works in this series

Proportional Response

CHAPTER
ONE

THE BUREAUCRAT TRUDGED DOWN one of the State Department's many long hallways, stretching the length of a building that encompassed two square blocks of prime Washington real estate. He took his normal path, noting the color-coded stripes painted near the ceiling. He once heard that one secretary of state, frustrated by an inability to easily navigate these corridors of power, mandated that each corridor be painted a different color. *As if that would make navigating these corridors any easier.*

The man ruminated on news updates he saw on television, grimacing at the thought of additional international problems. If only people would listen to those like him, experts whose experience enabled them to shape policy effectively, then the world would be better. *But no,* he grumbled, *the administration decided to hand out ever more political appointments, robbing me of the opportunity to lead my own team.* As he approached his office, he noted with envy and renewed anger that his boss's name was so much bigger, or perhaps his name was just *significantly* smaller.

Robert James Prescott Morgan III, Deputy Director, the office sign read. It looked good. He, however, could not ignore the larger name above: Jonathan Mells, Director. He swiped his ID card and entered the suite, looking morosely around the bland office, lights activated by motion sensors. Usually, their office management specialist, Tammy, was already at her desk when he arrived, offering a kind wave and an inquiry about his day. Robert missed serving overseas, where the locals opened doors and he had unfettered access to a driver. *But serving in DC matters because this assignment will springboard me to even better opportunities.*

"Good morning, Robbie." The voice came from the large office to the right. Robert rolled his eyes at his boss calling him Robbie, seemingly as a joke. He choked down an insult, as he had done since this political appointee took over just weeks before. Summer in DC was always sweltering, never more so than in late July, when only morons didn't escape inland to cooler temperatures. Robert took off his suit jacket, revealing a carefully pressed white button-down shirt, and trod towards his boss's office.

"Good morning, Jon," Robert replied, poking his head in to see Jon's desk in a state of constant disarray. There were candy wrappers on the credenza, stacks of papers strewn about the desk, and the requisite bag of donuts and enormous cup of coffee near the computer. Everything about Jonathan was sloppy and borderline disgusting, but White House staff seemed to ignore the mess and treated him like some sort of European politics god.

Looking down at his own perfectly tailored custom Italian suit and meticulously polished Italian leather shoes, Jonathan reflected that there were career Foreign Service officers better qualified who should be in that director position. He was embarrassed to serve as number two to such a dolt.

"How is your morning?" Jon asked absentmindedly, looking up from his computer but not even really expecting a reply.

Jon claimed he could multitask, but Robert seriously doubted it and always wondered how this buffoon ever gained the attention of people senior enough to make him a political appointee office director. Everything about Jon annoyed him. It wasn't fair that this guy, a think tank guy who spent much of his career on Capitol Hill, had *his* job. Just two months ago, the previous director announced suddenly that he would transfer early and someone needed to take over for him.

Everyone agreed Robert was the obvious choice, giving him needed experience, but then some moron from the seventh floor suggested a supposed expert fill the role instead. For once, the stars aligned, and Jonathan's hiring took less than a month—which meant Robert was not given the chance to take the chair for even a day.

If he was honest with himself, Robert was more annoyed that the promotion boards passed him over again after doing so last year. Robert dreamed of joining the most senior ranks of the Foreign Service, like becoming a military general. He needed the money that came with the more important jobs, especially the way his wife bought clothes and shoes.

He met her during his first assignment in the Foreign Service at Embassy Kyiv while he served his consular tour. She was a translator at a local nonprofit organization and helped him break up the drudgery of daily visa interviews, but he also significantly improved his Russian language skills while they dated. He still thought of her as his long-haired dictionary.

By the time Robert finished his first tour, he had married Ludmilla, scored advanced reading and speaking in Russian, and his career at that point felt limitless. Yet here he was fifteen years on and only the deputy director of the regional office for European political-military affairs. He could not even score the deputy director job in the prestigious Russia office. He always gave his all to the Department, reporting on important issues, but was always overlooked. He served in Chisinau, Moldova, Paris, France, Riga, Latvia, and finally in Yekaterinburg, Russia, before coming to DC for this assignment.

Years ago, he wanted children, wanted to get in the special club of parents with kids at the fanciest international schools. However, Ludmilla wasn't interested in ruining her figure for a kid. Now, he liked that his wife was still as hot as when they first met, while so many other colleagues' wives were fat from eating too much cake at children's birthday parties.

Looking morosely out his office window, Robert looked across the courtyard to the sixth and seventh floors. He applied for staff assistant positions for senior officials in the Department but was passed over in favor of people he knew were not of the same caliber as him. *They will never be as smart as me or give advice as well as I do.*

Robert sat at his desk and looked around his office, which, like everything in his life, was immaculately clean and organized. He logged into his workstation, carefully typing his password. While the computer loaded, he used a pressurized canister to spray dust out of his keyboard, wiping the debris with a wet wipe from his top desk drawer. Robert believed cleanliness was vital. Having been a sickly child, he privately feared getting sick and never recovering. He scanned his inbox, focusing on grammatical errors in an email the legislative office sent listing upcoming Hill briefings, observing several in his area of expertise where Jon would seize the spotlight only to bring Robert along as a notetaker.

Removing his planner from his satchel, which he never let out of his sight, Robert saw that he was scheduled to meet later that week with security experts from various embassies in DC. He opened the invitation in his inbox and searched the agenda for the list of partic-ipants at the end. He knew his job would be to represent the Bureau since Jon refused to attend meetings like these, so he wrote a memo in his planner describing what suit, tie, and shirt he should wear. He noted one name in particular—a man he met the year before, with whom it would be interesting to talk. *It never hurts to exchange ideas, and nothing I tell him is all that sensitive.*

THE LITTLE GIRL ON THE BOAT sat huddled in a mass of people, all of them freezing from the water. *Father still hasn't told me why we need to cross the Mediterranean Sea.* She heard the Turkish men who demanded more money from the men in their group explain that the pitch black and rough weather would be the safest conditions to cross.

Narisa thought of the onions her grandmother chopped for dinner, their layers reminding her of how the families arranged themselves. The adults took turns holding the children for the first part of the ride, but soon, her mother had to let go to shift her lanky frame. *Her belly is getting so big,* the girl observed, remembering with sadness the loss of siblings she had never met but hoping this time for a baby sister. Her feet touched those of the other children, one who was crying, but Narisa remained quiet.

They were all from the same village, so none of them were strangers. Their fathers spent nights discussing the need to leave their village, where their families lived forever. *Why couldn't we have stayed home?* the girl wondered, unable to understand the effects of war at her young age. She loved her home, with trees she could climb. *I hope they have trees in Germany.* She held tight to her doll, her most cherished possession in the world. *The trees in Iraq reached to the sky.*

The Turkish man steering the boat tried to ignore the crying Iraqis. *Why can't they just shut up?* he thought, careful to keep a scowling eye on the approaching shoreline. There were many islands in this part of the Mediterranean, though with waves of immigrants fleeing the Middle East, the wretched Greeks and their European partners increased their patrols. *And that's why we're out in this awful weather,* the man thought, keeping his feet apart as he guided the boat towards the distant shore.

This weather is against us, the Turkish man grumbled to himself minutes later as the waves slowed their journey. He had lost count of the number of times he drove his boat in these waters. Usually, he did so for tourists, but the money from the desperate refugees was too good to pass up. If they didn't make better progress in the next hour, the best-case scenario was they would have to return to Turkey. *Then I'll have to try again, only this time for free.* Still, that was better than the alternative.

He shivered involuntarily, not from the freezing water but from the thought of dumping his fellow Muslims overboard. He'd done it before, forced to toss them all into the water to flee the Greek coast guard, hoping Turkey's historic enemies would fish them all from the sea. The screams of children drowning haunted his dreams and caused him to drink raki more frequently than he ever admitted to his wife. *I'd rather die than abandon these Iraqi families,* he reminded himself, refusing to kill again.

After another half an hour, the boat was quiet, the families dozing. *Anyone would be hard-pressed to fall asleep with so much water in the bottom of the boat,* the Turk noted. In the distance, he saw the nearing shoreline, sighing with relief and taking a moment to crack his knuckles and rub the water from his face. He picked the wrong moment, especially for one family.

As he lowered his hands, the Turkish man felt the boat lurch to the side, too focused on the distant shoreline to see the wave that crashed into the boat. The men, women, and children all slammed into one another.

Narisa's doll slipped from her grasp as water drenched her clothes. *I need to get her,* she thought, refusing to part with the most beautiful gift she had ever received. Narisa saw her mother in a tangle of people and her father reaching to help get everyone back into place, all of them struggling against the rocking boat. Crouching carefully, Narisa got her feet under her, proud that she didn't fall over, and took a tentative step towards the side of the boat, where her doll lay in a pool of water. She didn't realize she was so far from everyone else, which was her first mistake.

I have her, Narisa cheered silently, grasping her doll tight before making her second mistake.

Without thinking, as is so common for four-year-olds since time immemorial, Narisa stood and turned to rejoin her family. However, she never saw the wave that struck the side of the boat behind her, catapulting her into the air, over the people staring wide-eyed at her, and into the churning sea.

The powerful man let go of the child, dropping the youth into his mother's waiting arms, and without thought, hurled himself over the side of the boat, following his daughter. He felt waves crashing over him, one after another. Everyone on the boat peered at him, and his wife's mouth opened in a scream he could never hear over the roar of the storm. A lifelong swimmer who, despite his bulk, could beat any man in a race, he turned on the spot, effortlessly kicking his legs. His lifejacket kept his head above the water despite the meter-high waves.

There! The man observed an orange lifejacket in the near darkness and reached out of the water, quickly eating up the distance with powerful strokes. Though he swam away from the boat, he was confident he could retrieve his daughter and get back. Edging nearer but still unable to see anything, he triumphantly reached out and brought the orange vest to his side. *She's not here.* He held the empty vest between his strong hands, a sense of powerlessness washing over him with each successive wave.

So caught up in his grief at the loss of his daughter, the man never saw the boat that plowed into him, the bow digging deep in the water and catching him in the back. The pain of the hard surface shook his body, though still his mind refused to accept that his daughter was gone. "Where are you, Habibi!" he shouted as hands reached to drag him into the boat.

Ten meters below the surface, the girl clung tight to her doll. She was terrified, struggling to hold her breath, yet the pounding waves prevented her from reaching the surface. Feeling lightheaded as her brain screamed for oxygen, the girl inhaled deeply, the rush of water overwhelming her. She fought for a moment and cried, *I want to live!* But then her body went limp and was carried away by the waves. Even in death, as the water embraced her, she clung tight to her beloved doll.

"FUCK! HOW THE HELL COULD THIS HAPPEN TO ME? On today of all days!" Brent Paulson wondered aloud, though no one could hear him with his office door closed. It was also the lunch hour, when everyone escaped into beautiful Budapest to enjoy the excellent local cuisine. He arrived at the embassy a year ago, full of hope and promise. At first, it was all amazing. But the past year had been nothing but pure hell. The ambassador in his first year, Don Felter, was his mentor, an amazing family man who took him to lunch, provided advice, and promised to help. Then came Alan Richards, who from day one treated him like an errand boy, not the political and economic chief of an important European country.

Although he had never previously referred to ambassadors without respect, Brent knew Richards deserved no respect. He bullied his staff into biweekly poker games and then cheated, taking money that first- and second-tour officers could barely afford. The man worked his staff too hard and screamed at anyone he didn't like. Brent was often his favorite target.

The worst part was that the deputy chief of mission, Paul Finnegan, seemed more interested in continuing to serve as a political officer than actually running the day-to-day affairs of the embassy. Paul spent most of his time at the foreign ministry chatting with various senior officials and practicing his Hungarian. The man loved foreign languages but also seemed intent on being out of the embassy as much as possible.

The entire embassy was dysfunctional, but all problems started at the top, with the executive office. The ambassador was a narcissistic asshole, while the DCM was never around. Brent could have forgiven a political ambassador for these mistakes, but Richards was a career Foreign Service officer. All of his subordinates could tell he rose through the ranks by stepping on others to get ahead.

The past few weeks had been miserable, with increasing problems developing between Brent and his wife, Stacey. She could not possibly understand how hard Brent worked to get ahead and provide for his family. Life in Budapest was bankrupting him with Stacey constantly wanting to take trips to Paris and Milan on the weekends. She insisted on staying in four- and five-star hotels, eating in restaurants she saw on celebrities' Instagram accounts, and buying designer purses. He was the man of the family, as his father reminded him constantly, and it was his job to provide.

The other stress had been bidding, which was always so easy, but this year, he faced a headwind in the form of his ambassador. Richards previously served on the seventh floor as a staffer for the deputy secretary, so he personally knew the director general of the Foreign Service as well as many senior staff in the European and Eurasian Bureau.

Brent was convinced Richards screwed him on bidding, going out of his way to scuttle every opportunity to remain in Europe. London fell through, as did Yerevan, and now this email detailed how his backup assignment of Budapest fell through. This meant he might have to accept one of those war zone posts he loathed; he always told his colleagues that real diplomats shouldn't have to wear body armor. Sure, some FSOs liked that work, but those were broken toys who could not hack it in the real Foreign Service. There was nothing to being a diplomat in a war zone where you dealt with warring tribes. It took real diplomatic skills to work with cultured people, those who understood the nuances of foreign policy and were not trying to kill one another all the time.

Right then, he wanted a double whiskey and did some quick math to figure out how many hours until he could pull out the bottle from his bottom desk drawer.

It was all too much, Brent thought as he massaged his forehead. The headaches kept coming, and he knew he should cut back on the booze, but everything was going wrong, and nearly every night for the past three weeks, he had slept in their spare bedroom. Stacey refused to talk with him, though perhaps he should not have been so mean to her. She was a big girl, and all he had said was she should spend more time at the gym and eat less. When they met back in college, Stacey had been a fit cheerleader, but now it seemed she would just not stop eating. She had never been less attractive to him. If he was going to kill himself to support his wife and three children, the least Stacey could do was keep up her appearance.

Resolving to deal with his bidding problems directly, Brent grabbed his jacket and walked through the various doors to reach the executive suite, too distracted to realize that he forgot to lock his computer. He already exchanged multiple emails with colleagues and friends in neighboring posts, who all told him that he needed to man up and confront his boss. "I know the ambassador is in his office, I'll just go in to see him," Brent said in passing, not even stopping to talk with Janine, the ambassador's secretary.

"I wouldn't go in there if I was you," Janine called out, but Brent ignored her.

Finding the door unlocked, Brent entered, as was his right as political and economic chief. He demanded—*required*—unfettered access to the ambassador and knew the man would lock his door if he did not want to be disturbed. As he entered, he scanned the giant room, not seeing anyone, until he noticed movement on the couch.

"Hello," Brent called out, seeing two heads pop up, one Ambassador Richards, the other belonging to his wife. "Stacey," he stuttered involuntarily, so shocked to see her naked and with the ambassador that he couldn't say anything else.

"Don't look at him," the ambassador said to Stacey, pulling her back to him as she tried to stand.

"Brent, I think this is as good a time as any to tell you that I blocked your bidding on any other European assignments." Brent was shocked, both by the words he heard and at seeing that the ambassador continued making love to *his wife*. "The reality is that you don't have the temperament or the willingness to do whatever it takes to get the job done."

What the hell is this? Brent contemplated, unable to tear his eyes from the motion on the couch.

"The only thing keeping me from kicking you and your family out of the post for gross incompetence is the services your wife has been providing me these past weeks."

Brent's eyes bulged and he found his mouth as dry as cotton. He wanted to scream, say anything, but only watched as they writhed in passion.

"I will arrange for you to get an assignment in a war zone, leaving your wife here for a year to tend to my needs. The best thing would be if you died there, but we likely won't be that lucky."

Brent felt like he was having an out-of-body experience and couldn't stop himself from walking to where the ambassador and his wife moved in tandem on the couch. He reflexively grabbed the nearby pitcher of water and poured it over both of them, then smashed the pitcher to the floor, ignoring their screams as he walked out the door.

"You son of a bitch, that was a valuable gift!" Richards screamed. "I will have your ass for this!"

Brent walked in a daze, not even stopping to return to his office, and instinctively patted his pockets for his wallet, phones, and keys.

Leaving the Chancery, the most secure part of the embassy that housed offices for the ambassador, the deputy chief of missions, the political and economic section, the regional security officer, and others, Brent headed for the pedestrian gate. Knowing his first stop should have been to see the security officer to report the incident, he instead felt guided by an invisible hand as he donned his sunglasses and ignored everyone around him.

The city was divided in two, Buda on the west and Pest on the east. The Embassy was in the East, in the city's fifth district, and he called that place home since 1935, when it took over the property from the Hungarian Royal Postal Savings Bank.

Expertly navigating the city, he entered a hole-in-the-wall bar where he had often been spending afternoons when he should have been working. It was only a twenty-minute walk from the embassy, though he walked quickly, so he was confident no one would find him unless they purposefully followed him from work. Inside, using his near fluent Hungarian, he ordered a double of the local spirit, Unicum, and bellied up to the bar. The entire area smelled of stale smoke and various male odors, none of which Brent even registered after growing accustomed to Hungarian bars as he got comfortable.

After three drinks, one after the other, Brent relaxed and slouched on his bar stool. He looked around, shaking his head to try to erase the image of the ambassador doing *that* to his wife.

They had been married nearly twenty years, so long, in fact, that he couldn't remember any of the women he slept with in college before he met Stacey. They had always been in love. She willingly followed him around the world, but in the last year, things changed when she let herself go, and they fought about everything.

Brent shook his head, realizing someone was speaking to him. "Can I buy you a drink?" the man asked again, and this time, Brent focused on the man who spoke to him from a nearby table.

"No," Brent responded, "this should really be my last."

"Are you sure?" The man switched from Hungarian to English. "You look like you've had an awful day." He spoke with a pronounced accent, but it was perfectly understandable.

As if some invisible floodgates opened, Brent felt all the emotions wash over him. "Are you kidding me?" He slid off the barstool and sat at the table. "Today has been the worst day of my entire life."

Without taking his eyes off the man, and never quite cognizant of the fact that the man kept buying him drink after drink, Brent proceeded to talk about every problem he had faced over the past several months. *I shouldn't be telling this complete stranger all of this,* Brent thought, but he merely shook his head. This man listened, nodding sympathetically and expressing horror when Brent detailed walking in on the ambassador with Stacey. Brent looked absent-mindedly out the window of the bar and saw a group of migrants walking but shook his head and focused on his own problems.

"Worst of all, no one at work seems to care." Brent tucked his badge into his dress shirt pocket, not realizing until that second that it hung from his neck, his lanyard proclaiming his affiliation with the US Embassy in Budapest, Hungary.

"That is terrible, my friend," the man replied sympathetically.

Brent felt so relieved, like someone was *actually* listening to him for once. For months, he kept going, never feeling heard. He was on autopilot, like a robot. He wiped away tears, realizing how unmanly it was to cry.

"I'm sorry." Brent cradled his head in his hands. He cried for his career, for his wife, for all the bad things that happened to him. *What did I do to deserve any of this?*

"Not at all. You sound like you are exhausted and alone."

This man said all the right things. The sympathy was something he craved, yet a voice inside cautioned him to be vigilant to threats. Reluctantly, he forced himself to obey his training.

"You haven't told me anything about yourself," Brent said cautiously to the man. "Not even your name."

"My name is Radek, and I am pleased to meet you." The man smiled and poured another glass of the dark liquid Brent had already consumed in massive quantities. Brent raised the glass to his lips, feeling better after taking a giant gulp.

"It's nice to meet you, Radek."

WALKING THROUGH TOWN, THE MOROSE GROUP of Iraqis marveled at the clean streets, the working shops, and the general normalcy of Budapest. The men led the way, trailed by women and children uniformly huddled in gaggles as they looked around at this metropolitan area. The men darted their eyes everywhere, surveying for threats. Though skinny from their travels, the men all appeared strong, especially the largest of their group, who lumbered along the street. They appeared out of place in the city, instead seeming better suited to carrying weapons and seeking enemies.

Hassan led the group, displaying more bravery than he felt. He was unwilling to let his wife, the other men, their wives, or their gaggle of children see fear. He was the most worldly of the crowd, having traveled previously to Turkey and even once to Cairo.

They were middle-class Iraqis, the ones able to afford the

exorbitant cost smugglers charged to transport their entire immediate families from Iraq to the West. Hassan was a trader back home who imported electronics from other countries. He was well-educated and a fiercely patriotic Iraqi who hated the Americans for invading his homeland in 2003.

Looking around, Hassan knew his country, the cradle of civilization, should be the one welcoming refugees rather than him, his close friends, and their families seeking shelter.

"Look at how well everything functions here," Abdullah said, careful to keep his voice low. He was their engineer, the man best suited to handling anything mechanical, and his help had been invaluable during their long trek across Turkey and then the Balkans. They had stopped temporarily there in Hungary. His wife, Nasreen, and their two children followed behind, earning dirty looks from passersby because of their ragged and dirty clothes.

"Yes, but I can tell everyone here hates us," Nasser commented to no one in particular, fingering the prayer beads he inherited from his father. Nasser previously worked at a bank, an honorable job involved in monitoring foreign transactions of government money, but fled with his family when he realized his children could have no future amidst the chaos of Iraqi politics. He carried their life savings, protected by his bulk and covered by shabby clothes.

Hassan dared anyone to try to rob the largest and strongest member of their group, who he trusted as if he were one of his brothers. His wife, Aisha, a mathematics teacher at the university back home, strode confidently behind with their three children clinging tight to her skirts.

"How long will we stay here?" Ali asked. He was the youngest of their group and the best with foreign languages, as he had worked at a foreign hotel before selling all his possessions and traveling with his friends. His new wife, Sahar, walked behind him, exhausted from their journey but staying with the crowd.

"We will stay as long as is necessary, then continue on to Germany," Hassan replied testily to the same question each of the men had asked. "But for now, we must stop here in Hungary to rest." He also did not want to stop, weary of the hostile looks they all received wherever they traveled, but he knew they could not continue at their current pace without one of them getting sick. "We are lucky to still have enough money and rest at all, though for a long time, we will continue to share one house."

"Have we ever not shared a house?" Malik asked, holding his side. He was nearly crippled when the boat slammed into him when they crossed from Turkey to Greece in the dead of night. He hadn't been able to recover because they pushed themselves to travel as quickly as possible through the Balkans.

"This is a big city with many foreigners," Malik continued, sweeping the area expertly. He had served in Saddam's army, then switched to fight for resistance groups to punish the Americans and other Westerners for invading their country. He was the only one of the men to serve longer in the military than the mandatory eighteen months of service. He had served more than ten years. "We will blend in here and be able to rest."

Malik's wife, Aliyah, trailed along like a zombie, still grieving the loss of their daughter during the crossing. Her husband injured himself trying to save Narisa, who was only five years old. Aliyah knew her husband still blamed himself for not better securing the lifejacket to their daughter. It was too large and had slipped over her head when she fell into the water. As an added trauma, the shock of the waves aborted Aliyah's early pregnancy, another cruel attack on their family. Aliyah wished she could have died with her daughter in the seas, but for now, she dutifully followed, uninterested in exploring the city where she felt they would stay for some time.

The five men and their families had been thrown together when they were formed into a larger unit within *Keta'ib Hezbollah*, an

Iranian-affiliated Iraqi militia that fought using guerilla tactics against American and Western forces who invaded in 2003. They continued their day jobs, earning meager pay while receiving stipends from the Iranian Republican Guard Corps (IRGC), field operatives who sought to inflict pain on the Americans. The five of them were what remained of their larger group. All others were killed during fierce fighting over the years.

Each of them knew how to handle weapons. The most proficient killer of them all was Malik, who used to slit the throats of his victims with his Kukri knife even after riddling their bodies with bullets from his Kalashnikov. The Kukri was a ten-inch knife carried by Nepali Gurkhas, who fought for British forces in Iraq, and hand-forged in Nepal. As he told the story, Malik bought one from a Gurkha in Baghdad who he met in a bazaar, then drew first blood with it when a fool tried to rob him at gunpoint. Since then, he used the knife as a weapon of vengeance against invading forces. As they walked, the men instinctively flexed their hands, which over the years grew accustomed to holding weapons, all well aware that they were unarmed and relatively defenseless in this new city.

The Iraqis were under no preconception that they would easily find work or that their lives would be easy, but they hoped they would be able to provide better lives for their children. Like parents around the world, the men and women of their group simply wished for their offspring to enjoy more comfortable lives than they ever did. It was painful to admit, but their once powerful nation was now a hopeless mess of civil war. They had no choice other than to leave to give their children a chance at a better future.

Turning a corner, they saw a line of buses and trams but continued walking, none of them permitted the luxury of riding anywhere in a vehicle. Their limited resources were reserved for emergencies, such as when one of them required medical care. The adults often went without more than one meal per day, and the women long since stopped experiencing their monthly periods due to malnourishment.

After walking for hours, with dusk approaching, the group came to an area where they were directed to shelter by Hungarian government officials. Their middle-class backgrounds rebelled at the thought of living in such squalid conditions, but the men knew they would search for work the next day and could soon afford to rent a room. They entered the building they saw earlier, the one they refused to enter when first showed, which was why they all walked into town. The children explored the house, their mothers following cautiously to ensure none got lost.

"Leave them," Nasser growled at his wife. "This space is small enough that they won't get lost." He looked across at Hassan, who also surveyed the small dwelling where they would spend the foreseeable future. Their eyes met, the five men wordlessly agreeing that they would do whatever it took to move their collective families out of this hopefully temporary space.

"At least we have food," Hassan's wife called, unloading a bag of food provided to the refugees by a religious organization.

The children played, keeping an eye on their mothers, who busied themselves preparing rice with beans in the provided pots. As they found places on the floor, everyone with plates overflowing with food, they each thanked Allah for bringing them safely to a place where they could all eat their fill.

CHAPTER
TWO

BEN SAT BACK FROM HIS COMPUTER, shaking his head at the intelligence he read. The Iranians were at it again, breaking their commitments not to develop nuclear weapons. *It all feels so surreal,* he thought as he stood and stretched. *Just a few months ago, I was in Herat, Afghanistan, saving the world.* He longed for those days out in the field, though he was happy to be back in a place that had more comforts and food options. He still thought about his encounter with the Grand Ayatollah, recalling that as exciting, and wished he had been able to better disrupt the attack in North Dakota, which claimed the lives of thirteen.

His current job was to provide foreign policy advice to Senator Cavanaugh, but Ben realized he did more than that. The Senator had served in Congress since before Ben was born, so he did not need anyone to tell him what to think, especially not an early thirties mid-level Foreign Service officer—a man to be respected, a war hero everyone admired for his willingness to stand up for his principles. One who volunteered to serve in Vietnam, an infantry officer who earned the admiration of all his soldiers for never asking them to do anything he himself wasn't willing to do. The Senator was all those things and more. Ben was proud to work for the man, even if it meant long hours of fighting with people at the State Department and the interagency over topics far beyond his control.

Looking at his watch, Ben shook his head. *Is that the right time? My God, I have been at it for hours without a break.* Checking his planner, Ben saw a clear schedule for the night. Realizing his luck, he opened the door and walked the short distance to lean against the nearest open door.

"Hey, Marty," he called to the man seated at the cluttered desk. "How are things going?" Ben looked around the room, realizing this man had been there for some of the most important events in the past twenty years. He didn't look like much, but Martin Santos had served the Senator for decades, starting when the great man moved from the House to the Senate.

"Geez, Ben," the tired man replied, taking off his glasses so he could rub his eyes, "it almost sounds like you care about me." Ben laughed at Marty's dry and sarcastic sense of humor. They got along well, though at the start, things had been rocky. Marty was resentful that the Senator made a personnel decision without input from his chief of staff.

"Listen," Marty said, smiling to convey a sense of encouragement he knew all people needed, "the past few days have been a nightmare of paper and politics." He watched as Ben did some twists, envious of the younger man's ability to stretch and instantly feel better.

He examined Ben, still amazed that this guy, really just a kid in his view, had pieced together a terror attack without any support from the intelligence community. An American soldier's misguided attempt at revenge started a chain reaction that led to a deadly attack by Somali terrorists in North Dakota. Records proved that Ben tried to share a warning with all agencies that he pieced together while working as a junior political officer in Afghanistan. Had they listened, the Minot Massacre could have been avoided, or at least minimized.

One of the few Capitol Hill officials entitled to hear the entire story, Marty knew Ben never would have been so successful without his British girlfriend, Kate. He didn't know the entire story surrounding Kate but knew her father had a title and she worked for the Foreign Office. Or at least that was what Ben said. Marty suspected there was more to the story but didn't push.

There was also that dish of an FBI agent, Jennifer, who also attended the private ceremony at the White House for the president to recognize their important work. They were a team of junior officers—just kids, really—and yet they had been able to piece together one of the most significant attacks on US soil since 9/11. It was too bad they didn't get more public credit for their heroism, but then notoriety could be a burden for young professionals aiming to make a career in government service.

"Ben, we have nothing happening tonight," Marty said. "No receptions. No last-minute foreign policy initiatives requiring you to stay late. Nothing." He stretched, trying to mimic Ben and hoping it might work. It didn't and his back now hurt more. "In fact, the Senator left about an hour ago and flew back home, so you could even skip coming to the office tomorrow and start your weekend early without feeling guilty." He tried pushing Ben to enjoy downtime back in the States, including taking breaks to get out of the Beltway and travel along the eastern seaboard.

"Well, it is seven o'clock already, and I could absolutely use a break." Ben stretched again. "If you are sure there is nothing, I will head out."

"Good," Marty said in mock anger. "Get out and don't come back until Monday!" He grinned, knowing that leaving at a normal time meant Ben could salvage a night out.

Marty's row home on Capitol Hill meant he could walk back for lunch if he wanted, which he rarely did, especially since his wife decided to teach at a small Midwestern college rather than support his career. He could not blame her and would do the same in her shoes, proving that Marty was more married to his job than his wife, just as she had said since their first year of marital bliss. She came to visit more often than he deserved, their marriage only holding up because they needed one another.

Ben whistled as he collected his things, then waved goodbye to the remaining staff in the office, the ones who had not yet left for happy hours or receptions across town. During his first month, Ben had taken advantage of invites to get out and meet people, but unlike most of the staff working for the Senator, he continued to receive his full Foreign Service salary, complete with DC locality pay. The interns working on the Hill were either rich and able to buy a place without a second thought or worked night shifts at nearby bars and restaurants, unable to afford to live in the district on a staffer's dismal salary.

Never able to afford to intern in DC while at university in Minnesota, Ben admired the people who sacrificed so much to work on Capitol Hill, especially the ones without family money. He stopped at the men's bathroom down the hallway from the Senator's office suite and changed into his biking gear.

Outside with his bike, Ben navigated the streets of DC with care. It was peak rush hour, drivers edging through the streets to arteries that would carry them home, but once on the National Mall, Ben made excellent time as he cycled past Smithsonian buildings and national monuments. As he passed the Vietnam Veterans Memorial, Ben considered how lucky he was to work in his nation's capital. *Still,* he thought as he pedaled towards Old Town, *I hope Kate is enjoying a quiet work trip.*

CROSSING THE STREET AMIDST the chaotic traffic of Tehran, Kate forced her hands to stop adjusting her headscarf. *Despite all the time wearing one, I still can never get it properly fastened to cover my hair.* The morality police were especially active in Tehran, watching for girls and women who showed any of their hair. *This is why I'm fighting against this regime,* she reminded herself, loathing the elderly Iranian religious leaders who thought they knew everything there was to know, including about women's bodies. She hated the ever-present oppression of women in current Iranian culture.

She crossed the street, moderating her speed so she avoided bumping into other people, notably Iranian men. More than once, men leaned against her and pressed their hands against her curves beneath her long coat. On one occasion, when the man thought no one else was looking, he pressed himself against her. She saw the looks of disgust and pity on the faces of the other women but then surprised them when she effortlessly shoved the man into the side of a bus. She allowed herself a smirk at the thought of that incident earlier today, especially the sight of the man's surprised face, but then concentrated on the matter at hand.

Arriving at the other side of the street, Kate neared Francis, an MI6 officer assigned in Tehran to analyze security threats to the embassy, notably Britain's intelligence operations in Iran. He was there because he knew Tehran's streets better than anyone and he had diplomatic immunity in case anything went wrong. No one mentioned that Kate's father insisted she always have backup whenever she operated on Iranian territory.

"We're tracking two of the men," Kate confirmed in Farsi, "based on intelligence from our MFA contact that they will meet at this mosque in ten minutes and both be wearing watches on their right wrists." She was thankful she didn't need to address the needs of that asset and could use actionable intelligence to track down the

Immortals network. She thought back through everything she knew about the group, including patronage by a senior Ayatollah. *I would authorize serious money for real information about the group.* Everything she collected was based on rumors from sources, plus unexplained deaths around the globe that benefitted the Iranian regime.

"You need to go to the women's section of the mosque to pray," Francis reminded her gruffly in the same language. He didn't want to be out here, especially not with as tall an obviously foreign woman as Kate Sinclair. She fit with the crowd, her hair darkened to a light brunette, so she blended, yet her nearly alabaster features were too fair to accurately pass for a Persian woman. He, on the other hand, fit in seamlessly because his grandfather emigrated to London in the 1950s and ensured everyone in his family spoke Farsi at home. His father then broke family tradition by marrying his mother, who, originally from Scotland, was also darker skinned than the English. *I blend, she doesn't.*

They crossed the large square, approaching the grand entrance to the mosque. As they approached, Francis kept a step ahead of Kate, projecting a willingness to ignore her as one would a younger cousin. Halfway across the square, Francis grimaced inwardly as he saw two women step in front of Kate. *The morality police.* He steeled himself, wondering what Kate did to attract their attention.

"You," the older woman said, stepping up to face Kate. In an attempt to avoid inflaming the situation, Kate averted her eyes.

"Yes, auntie," Kate answered demurely, her eyes flickering hesitantly to the older, shorter woman's face, then looking around nervously before again looking down.

She really is an amazing actress, Francis thought, seeing that Kate even wrung her hands exactly as any younger Iranian woman would in the same situation.

"Is this your husband?" the older woman inquired while her younger colleague stood back, watching them carefully.

"No, this is my cousin on my mother's side." *Go away,* Kate screamed in her head, wishing the busybody would find someone else to harass.

"You tell her mother she needs a husband," the woman from the morality police lectured.

"Of course." Francis smiled, relieved that this busybody was merely bored and wanted to harass someone to feel important. These same women lived in countries around the world, yet in Iran, they wielded fierce power and were never afraid to use it. "I will also tell her that I need a wife." She turned to address this comment to the younger woman from the morality police. She blushed.

"You do that," the older woman snapped, then turned her back to shoo away her young partner, who stared unabashedly at Francis. "Go now and pray to Allah the Merciful for guidance." With that, the two women rushed towards a group of young women, several showing their hair.

"Let's get out of here," Kate growled. "People are staring at us." They rushed from the spot, blending with several groups also going to the mosque.

As they approached, Kate slowed and stepped to the side to withdraw her mobile phone. Francis saw her and stopped to confirm their plan.

"You'll stay outside, then?" he asked, not expecting an answer, more because they rehearsed their lines and wouldn't deviate while in public. *You'll stay outside to take photos of any likely matches for your mythical Immortals,* he told her the night before while talking through the plan. He didn't believe any group remained a secret for so long and refused to accept Kate's hypothetical group as fact.

"I need to check in on my mother." Kate put on her oversized sunglasses that matched those worn by nearly every other woman in the city. They hid her features and permitted her to watch other people. She stepped back and took a seat on a bench, enjoying the shade in the heat of the day, and focused entirely on her phone, ignoring Francis.

"I'll go, then." He walked to the front of the mosque, removed his shoes, and put them on the shelf, satisfied that his shoes were nicer than most others but Iranian manufactured so no one would mark him as a foreigner. He walked inside to find many men assembled for prayer, all their carpets facing in one direction. As he settled into his spot near the back, he scanned the room. *What is the likelihood I'll find two men wearing watches on their right wrists?*

The men collectively performed their prayers while the imam called out to the assembled. Most men moved automatically, having performed the prayers five times per day their entire lives—most since they were old enough to mirror their fathers, uncles, and grandfathers.

With their prayers concluded, the men collectively stood. Some stood in groups to talk, but most went to collect their shoes. Francis stayed behind to scan men's wrists. *There.* The man on the right swung his wrist, and Francis again saw he wore his watch on his right wrist, unusual in a country when most men wore them on their left.

Francis moved forward, unsure whether to believe his luck, when he saw a flash of the other man's wrist. *It's also on the right wrist. Kate might be right!* He calmly followed the men, staying three meters behind, but he locked his eyes on their collarless shirts and concentrated on the color combinations. *One target wearing blue, the other light gray,* he mentally noted.

After retrieving his shoes, Francis put them on, chancing to look up and find the two targets standing opposite him. He abruptly stood and, with apologies to the men around him, wove through the throng to get outside. Exiting, he turned to where Kate sat under the tree and relayed in coded words that he identified two targets by watches on their right wrists and the colors of their shirts. Then he moved away so he and Kate wouldn't both be burned if identified.

Kate kept her phone in front of her, the recording function active as she panned across the faces of men exiting the mosque. She searched for the two men in the different-colored shirts with watches on their right wrists. *What could wearing their watches on their right wrists signify?* Kate wondered for the hundredth time.

Kate and Francis saw the three men together at the same time. Their targets were walking with another, shorter man between them, the three conversing intently. Kate waited an extra ten seconds, always believing she needed that extra time to analyze the details so as to not miss anything. Then she noticed two men trailing behind, both concentrating on the shorter man and appearing to watch the crowd for threats. She saw bulges beneath their jackets, marking them as obvious protection, likely for the shorter man walking between her targets.

Everything next happened at once. Francis began to move, and she realized he hadn't taken the time to notice the trailing security guards. She watched in horror as Francis followed their targets. *It's not his fault he doesn't see the security guards, but they're going to see him!* As if she held a crystal ball, Kate watched as the two security guards, in fact, zeroed in on Francis, dropping back like true professionals as Francis trailed his two targets.

Unable to do anything to disrupt the events unfolding, Kate zoomed in on her phone camera and focused on their two targets, hoping they would turn around. *Just one of you turn around, damn it!*

As if on cue, the trailing security guards seized Francis from behind, pinning his arms to his sides and propelling him forward. Francis was the same size as them but expertly dug in his feet, letting the two guards' inertia propel them forward. As if he had exercised it dozens of times, Francis reached behind and slammed the two men's heads together before turning to sprint left.

The crunch of the men slamming together must have alerted the targets because all three stopped and turned. They spun on their heels to stare first at the men on the ground, then at the fleeing figure. Kate zoomed in to get video and photos of each face. Neither wore sunglasses, so she was able to get decent pictures. For good measure, she even took a picture of the man standing between them, who screamed for his guards to get off the ground.

Realizing she had already pushed her luck, Kate held her phone to her ear and talked animatedly in Farsi while walking in the opposite direction. She fell in with a group of women, smiling at two of them as she rolled her eyes and pointed to her phone, eliciting their laughter. Kate wasn't in Iran on a diplomatic passport, or under her own identity for that matter, and as an illegal would be quickly sent to Evin prison and executed as a spy.

Even with all the dangers inherent in sneaking into Iran, which she'd done several times before, her three days in the country weren't wasted because she got pictures, which she could use to piece together more about the Immortals. As she flagged a taxi to return to her hotel and then on to the airport, she wondered what Ben was doing at that moment, hoping to talk with him after she returned to London.

THE FOLLOWING MONDAY MORNING, Ben sat in the back of the conference room, lost in thought during the Senator's morning senior staff meeting. He kept his notepad and pen at the ready, but they mostly covered domestic issues, which were not his focus. Ben was just wondering what Kate was doing at that moment when he heard a thunderous pounding on the table and was jerked to attention.

"No, damn it, if I've said it once, I've said it a hundred times," the Senator thundered. "How can those idiots at State or at the White House even begin to trust the Iranians?" Everyone looked down at their folders stamped with classification markings that detailed the administration's plan to proceed with negotiations with the Iranian government. "I don't care what this administration thinks, but any negotiations with the Iranian government will be a mistake."

Everyone focused intently on the Senator, all knowing that he was about to begin one of his regular speeches about the dangers of the Ayatollah and the ramifications of the Iranian takeover of the US Embassy in early November 1979.

"I remember watching the events unfold, people," he said, "and I refuse to endorse going down that path again. It is foolish and misguided to believe the Ayatollah and his men will do anything but continue to threaten the free world."

More than a month into the job, Ben was already familiar with the Senator's views on Iran. The Senator routinely interacted with members of an Iranian opposition group, soliciting their opinions on how to best fight the Iranian regime. Ben had spoken with the Senator and Marty, expressing his unease at meeting with members of the group while they remained on the terrorist watchlist. They respected Ben's position as an employee of the executive branch, so he excused him from those meetings. While Ben suspected the Senator would continue speaking about the dangers of Iran for a while, he was surprised when he heard his name spoken and saw everyone turn to face him.

"Ben," the Senator said, "I would, of course, never bundle you in with the State's bureaucrats running the nuclear deal negotiations with the Iranians." Ben's gaze shifted from Marty and settled on the Senator, and he flashed his boyish grin, which he knew always put people at ease.

"Of course not, Senator," Ben responded. "I would never once include myself in the group of folks over there who are putting our national security at risk."

"Now, son, don't think you can charm me by miming my own words back at me," the Senator attempted to say sternly. But then he broke into a wide grin and said, "Yet you're coming along nicely with your worldview. We'll make a politician out of you yet!"

The entire room chuckled as one. This was why the Senator routinely brought in fresh blood, claiming that he liked to shake things up. Ben fit the mold. He wasn't too ambitious, yet he was an accomplished diplomat who could speak authoritatively on many countries and regions.

"Ben," the Senator said, calming the laughter with a wave of his hand, "I would like you to brave the muck that is Foggy Bottom and speak with your colleagues on the Iran Desk."

Ben looked down, not liking this assignment because he knew what would come next.

"And while you are there," Marty said, picking up like the veteran political operative he was, "you could perhaps toss in a few of the Senator's concerns with these negotiations going forward." Marty leaned in and the Senator leaned back, proving Ben's suspicion that Marty would ask Ben to do the dirty work. That kept the Senator's hands clean so he wouldn't have to make that request.

"You must understand, Ben, the significance of these negotiations. If they move forward as proposed, they will endanger all that we have accomplished. Through decades of pressure, we are finally seeing results from our sanctions. The Iranian economy is splintering under pressure. I'm sure the Iranians will seek a lifting of our moratorium on them receiving payments for their oil shipments to Asia."

Ben knew the statistics, the intelligence community raising

alarms throughout DC about Iranian support for terror groups around the world, all funded by Iranian exports of a virtually unlimited supply of oil and gas.

After meeting Grand Ayatollah Shirazi in Afghanistan only a couple of months before, Ben had to agree with the Senator's views. He knew full well the dangers of Iranian power in the region and how it undermined fledgling democracies throughout the Middle East and competed with US foreign policies.

"You should also know, Ben, as should everyone else in this room, that I intend to personally observe any planned negotiations between the administration and the Mullah's representatives." He turned to Marty, everyone's gaze following, and asked, "When did they say the negotiations are?"

"I believe in late winter, early spring, Senator," Marty responded, then he addressed the crowd. "I must stress that the Senator's planned travel to observe these negotiations, along with a potential staffer or two"—he zeroed his focus on Ben—"is a classified secret, so no talking about this outside this room, folks."

He didn't mention that the Senator had already raised his concerns with the president. Repeatedly. The president finally conceded to the Senator's request to observe the negotiations. That gave State bureaucrats a fit, but they were already quietly preparing for the likelihood of the Senator's presence, hoping his visit would fly under the radar and not disrupt their goal of reaching a nuclear deal. The room was silent following that admonishment, everyone understanding the threats to the Senator's safety, especially when it came to as dangerous a foreign government as the Iranian Republic.

Wanting to be responsive to the Senator, Ben decided this was as good a time as any to chime in.

"Of course, Senator, I'm happy to trek over to the Truman Building and anywhere else you need me to travel," Ben said, knowing his job was to share what he learned on the Hill with respective offices and gather what information he could.

"Perhaps I could make a day of it tomorrow, roaming the halls, as it were, and keeping my ear to the ground." Then, as what appeared an afterthought, Ben added, "As it happens, one of my friends is now working on the Iran Desk." The Senator smiled like a Cheshire cat, and Ben continued. "I'm sure he can give me some insight that will be helpful." Ben smiled back, knowing that just by sharing the Senator's concerns and confirming details already shared by the NSC, he would have earned his keep for the next month.

"Ben, you are the star of the show today," the Senator said, reflecting the politician's tone of voice reserved for those who earned his appreciation and affection. "Hell, Marty, even for the week. Perhaps after Ben focuses on this for the week, he could get a bit of time off to visit his girlfriend in London." The Senator tossed this final tidbit of information in to prove he knew more about his staff's lives than they assumed, always keeping them on guard.

The single women of the office all perked up. They viewed Ben as an eligible bachelor, but Ben had been clear from the beginning that he had a girlfriend. He hadn't shown off any photos, despite them asking, but several of them secretly hoped Ben's long-distance relationship would fail and they could get him to ask one of them out.

"That would be great, Senator, and I would appreciate the chance to dust off my passport and take a trip across the pond."

After the meeting wrapped up, Ben grabbed his notebook and pen and returned to his desk on the other side of the office suite, feeling some of the staff staring at him but ignoring them.

When he first arrived, every one of the single girls in the Senator's office aggressively flirted with him, unsubtly and annoyingly informing him they were available for dinner or more, prompting him to share with everyone that he was in a serious relationship. Ben knew as he logged into his computer that he was as committed to Kate as he ever could be to another person. He thought about her before he fell asleep at night and wondered what she was doing when he woke in the morning.

At that moment, he walked outside to call her. It was their agreed-upon time to call, right after Ben's staff meeting and before Kate went into late afternoon meetings. The miracles of modern technology meant he could call her using internet-based voice apps on his phone.

"HULLO, BEN, IS THAT YOU, LUV?" Kate asked as she walked through the streets of London. She timed her walks outside headquarters to speak with Ben because trying to arrange a time for him to call or for her to call him would have been impossible. She worked for the United Kingdom's Secret Intelligence Service, better known as MI6, and was quite literally born into the service. Her father was the current chief, something she never wanted to admit, yet anyone intelligent enough to work in the UK government could deduce that there would be few with the surname Sinclair who were unrelated.

"It is marvelous to hear your voice, my love," Kate half whispered, having looked forward to Ben's call for hours. She always considered calling him earlier, hoping to speak with him more than their guaranteed once a day, but she knew both had jobs to do.

She and Ben met at a bar in Kabul the year before, and almost instantly, she knew he was the one she wanted to be with. He was funny, smart, and independent, the opposite of so many men she knew in London. Although her father had given up on overtly setting her up with anyone, he remained on the fence about her budding relationship with an American.

"How was your commute?" she asked. Neither spoke much about their work, acknowledging the difficulty of working for different governments, so they always shared with one another details of their commutes, meals, and what they loved about their cities.

"It was a good ride," Ben replied. "You were right to push me to buy some of that equipment, because it makes for a more comfortable ride."

On the other end, Kate beamed, having asked her colleagues who biked for suggestions on what kit Ben should buy. She wanted him to be safe and comfortable.

Unbeknownst to her father, Kate was working secretly with her current supervisor to arrange an assignment for her for at least two years in Washington to be near Ben. The distance made their relationship difficult; despite that, they met in France shortly after Ben departed Afghanistan. They spent a marvelous two weeks at a villa owned by one of her friend's parents, who were happy to lend the house in August.

Those two weeks had been magical. The two of them drove through the countryside, spent long hours together, and told one another everything they could think of. Ben was gorgeous, she admitted to herself, and she hadn't wanted to share him with anyone, not once she had him away from the prying eyes of his embassy in Kabul. His government treated him so poorly when he tried to tell them about the plot to stage the attack, but she was so proud that he doggedly pursued the truth, sharing information with her to disrupt the attack that killed thirteen people.

"What does the rest of your day look like?" Ben asked, eager to learn more about London.

"More meetings," Kate answered. "Though tonight I plan to order a pizza from a new restaurant near my house." Ben always suggested she try new foods, but she remained unwilling to eat pizza with pineapple on it.

"Do you have any travel planned?" he asked, having already thought through what it would mean. Ben knew their romance had been rushed, with most wartime romances failing because the two could not make it work. However, Ben promised himself that he would go the extra mile for the intelligent, sexy, and accomplished woman on the other end of the phone line, even if it meant having to meet her on the moon.

"No plans at the moment," Kate responded, knowing instantly that Ben was planning a visit to London by the way he asked the question. "Are you considering a visit?" She paused long enough to bounce on the balls of her feet, which she did when she got excited, but only when she was not in the field.

"What if I was? Would that be okay with you?"

"Ben, you can visit anytime. I'll give you a tour of the city you won't soon forget." She could not hide her excitement at the prospect of finally introducing him to her friends in the city.

"I was thinking that while I was in town, perhaps I could meet your parents. I'd even spring for dinner for the four of us if you help me get a table at a suitable restaurant." Kate took a deep breath, and Ben continued. "But if they're unavailable then, I'd be happy to meet some of your friends."

Kate had been after him to meet her family, who were anxious to meet the man who captured her heart. Ben was secretly nervous about meeting Kate's family, who all had titles, while he did not have much left in the way of family. At least not family he spoke with anymore.

"Oh, that would be lovely, my darling," Kate replied with as even a voice as she could muster, but she failed to hide the cracking of her voice. She felt a bit overcome with emotion, fighting back tears because she knew—*no, felt*—that Ben was the man she wanted to spend the rest of her life with. She stopped by the railing overlooking the Thames. "My parents mentioned they still haven't met you."

"Only once or twice, right?" Ben asked as nonchalantly as possible.

He knew Kate was under tremendous pressure from her family, which is why he decided now would be the time to meet them.

She grinned. "Yes, they have asked after meeting you just once or twice." *Try hundreds of times since I returned home,* she mused. If her father was insistent, then her mother and grandmother were positively inquisitorial, calling at any decent or indecent hour to inquire when Ben would visit.

"Well then," Ben said, "I cannot wait to see your beautiful smile, and more, when I arrive at Heathrow next week."

On the other end of the line, despite walking at a brisk pace back to her office, Kate felt her entire body glow, anticipating being reunited after months apart. "My darling, you have no idea what you are in for, but I love you and cannot wait to see you. I will speak with you again tomorrow."

Kate ended the call, walked the short distance to her office building, and locked her phone in a locker inside the lobby. She rushed upstairs to her desk, foregoing the elevator in favor of the stairs. If she was meeting Ben next week, she needed to focus on maintaining her perfect body to be ready for all the cardio exercise they would do together.

Opening her chat function, Kate noticed a message from Charlotte, with whom she had gone through training upon entry to the service. Charlotte, also from an upper-class family, shielded her from the prying eyes of her fellow agents who viewed her as a topic of gossip. Assigned to Washington, Charlotte had also agreed to check in on Ben every so often. It wasn't that Kate didn't trust Ben, but after several years working for MI6, she didn't really trust anyone. During her time, she met people who seemed like saints, only to discover they lied, cheated, and would murder anyone they could, all for their own ends.

How are things in Washington? Kate typed, curious about life in the city. She had always fought any assignment to such a boring posting but was willing to do most anything for Ben.

Quiet, as always, Charlotte responded. *You will also be happy to know that your boyfriend is a* portrait of commitment.

Kate involuntarily leaned in, always looking for validation that she was making the right choice with Ben, and continued reading.

Out with friends from the staff at a popular bar in Old Town on Saturday night, I happened on a gorgeous man meeting your lover's description.

Kate smiled, knowing that Charlotte had come across Ben several times over the two months since he returned to Washington. She appreciated her descriptions because it confirmed that her Ben was a man other women wanted. Just so he didn't want them back.

You will be happy to know that several women approached lover boy, but he deftly and expertly steered each wayward lady to the men in his group. This hottie must have quite the heartache to refuse the advances of such women.

Kate flinched, feeling remorseful when she realized Charlotte likely sent several women to hit on Ben. It boosted her confidence to know that he remained committed to her, but she realized that she needed to wave Charlotte off future tracking.

It sounds like this beauty is committed. I hear he will come to this side of the pond soon, so you can cancel any further tracking.

Kate knew that Charlotte would track Ben through the country, if asked, using her freedom to do whatever she wanted, but she didn't want any further tracking of her boyfriend.

Are you sure you don't want me to accompany him on the plane to London, to avoid a repeat of the Edgar Affair?

Kate jumped when she read the last bit, feeling the drop in her stomach as she thought about her boyfriend Edgar, who claimed to date her exclusively, but secretly maintained his membership in the Mile High Club with his flights across the Atlantic.

I'M SURE, Kate wrote. I trust my handsome.

Okay, Charlotte responded, getting the message. Is there any other news from your end on the move? Updates on when everything will be approved?

Nothing yet, Kate replied, but I'm hoping once my parents meet my love, then I can broach my move with the man upstairs. Have to run, love to you and Chester.

Kate switched her status to away, not wanting Charlotte to respond. She wondered if she ever should have asked Charlotte to track Ben, but her past experiences made her wary. She thought for months about Ben, examining him from every angle, and concluded that he was the real thing. If he asked her to marry him, she would say yes, and travel anywhere around the world with him.

Thinking about the numerous discussions she endured with her friends in the City, she acknowledged that their romance was rushed, but viewed that more as a matter of the operating environment of Afghanistan than anything about them. She heard repeatedly about couples who met in war zones but quickly fell out when they could not remain committed. She lifted the mat beneath her keyboard to reveal a photo of Ben she took in France of him smiling contentedly at her.

Running her finger over his face on the photo, Kate knew she was making the right decision in doing whatever it took to be with Ben. Her career was already off to an excellent start, having received accolades for her work in Afghanistan, both piecing together the plot and several sources she recruited to provide information for Her Majesty's government. Besides, Washington was not exactly an unimportant post, but more focused on liaison work than actual intelligence collection.

Looking over her schedule, she blocked off time at the end of the week, deciding that she needed a good shopping trip to update her wardrobe ahead of Ben's arrival. He would send her his flight details as soon as he booked, not wanting her to search the incoming passengers list using her contacts at MI5, the Domestic Counterintelligence and Security Agency. She threatened that once, in a moment of arrogance, when he teased her that he might sneak into the UK and surprise her. Deciding that perhaps she should get the next phone call over with, she dialed a number on her desk phone from memory, unsurprised when the person on the other line picked up after only one ring.

"Yes, who is calling, please?" the beautiful, stately voice asked.

"Hullo, Mum, it's Kate." *And we're off,* Kate thought, preparing herself for the conversation.

"Kate, my love, wonderful to hear from you. To what do I owe the pleasure?" Kate knew her mother suspected something, so she decided to give in and share the news.

"Ben is coming to visit and—"

"Darling, that's wonderful news. Where will he stay? Would you both like to stay with us while he is in town? We, of course, *must* meet him the moment he gets off the plane."

Kate felt a headache coming on, one only her mother could elicit. "How about I come for dinner later this week to talk through Ben's entire visit?"

Kate heard a scream of excitement on the other end. It sounded as if her mother was prepared to begin wedding preparations today. She sighed, bracing herself for the coming onslaught. The only positive of this was that bringing Ben would infuriate her sister. She did not notice the smile that spread across her lips at that thought. Their sibling rivalry had continued over the span of decades.

CHAPTER
THREE

IN BUDAPEST, THE MAN BRENT KNEW as Radek, but whose real name was Ramin, sat in his office pondering the report he typed based on their meetings. The American had met him several times since their seemingly chance encounter in the bar. Radek always listened, provided enough alcohol to slow down a rhino, and kept track of any tidbits. The American was a virtual goldmine of information, sharing details about the various members of the embassy, usually with little more than gentle prodding from Radek.

For an intelligence officer, an unhappy diplomat was the jackpot, especially one with such wide-ranging access as this American. Radek knew the Teacher would share his findings as needed with other Iranian intelligence personnel, though mainly the Teacher collected information to be used to advance the cause of the Iranian revolution. His expenses were racking up quickly, especially on food and drink, but the Teacher was clear in their previous communication that this information was of great importance to the Grand Ayatollah himself.

A member of the Immortals, Ramin knew his efforts would pay dividends for Grand Ayatollah Shirazi, who sought to guide the Islamic Republic through these troubled times. Their group was small with six operatives total, each assigned a geographic area. Several months before, for the first time ever, all six Immortals traveled to America to protect the Teacher during an operation, one of personal interest to the Grand Ayatollah. Mahmoud led that operation and used his years of expertise to ensure their safe exfiltration from the enemy's territory.

Comparatively, things were easier for Ramin, his country friendlier with Iran, which ensured that he could disappear to a neighboring country if anything went wrong. He used to stick out because of his dark skin, but years before, his features began to lighten to blend with people in Eastern Europe and Russia.

That afternoon's meeting with the American was particularly useful as the drunken fool let slip the Teacher's long-held suspicion, namely that the Americans intended to send many high-level delegates to Budapest for the nuclear talks with Iranian representatives. Many months ago, Ramin secured an apartment in the city to serve as a base of operations in anticipation of the negotiations. The Grand Ayatollah strongly opposed negotiating with the Americans, but members of the IRGC successfully lobbied the Supreme Leader to grant his support, aimed at reducing sanctions against Iran's economy.

He was lucky because the Immortals operated outside of formal Iranian government channels, so at least he rarely needed to interact with the bureaucratic fools at the Iranian Embassy. Embassy staff would aid an Immortal in a true emergency, but the Teacher was clear that was a last resort. As such, Ramin hadn't even visited the embassy since arriving in Budapest. He always secured information through the Teacher, whose sources within the IRGC and *ettela'at* guaranteed the Immortals were always better prepared than any other Iranian government official.

Ramin considered the challenge of Iranian embassies, where IRGC personnel and the *ettela'at*, traditional intelligence officers, wielded the power. Iranian embassies, by their nature, were small operations, each diplomat holding many roles.

The news of the American Senator's intent to attend the talks was sure to cause a stir within Tehran. This was one of the reasons Immortals were so valued: Ramin and his brothers discovered morsels of information no other could secure. Ramin knew this Senator, whose failed campaign for head of state made the news a lot, was a constant thorn in the side of Tehran. Especially his alliance with the hated *mujahideen*. That group had been trouble for decades, agitating the Islamic Republic. As he typed up his report, Ramin guessed at the Teacher's response.

On the one hand, he knew Tehran would do anything they could to discredit, injure, or even kill the Senator. During their conversations, the American extolled his hatred for his ambassador, vocalizing his desire to see the man dead. At the end of the report, more by instinct than any other reason, Ramin added a personal comment, this one an operational suggestion.

Ramin's time in Budapest, particularly listening to gossip within the diplomatic community, provided a perfect recommendation for those to undertake an attack. A small group of Iraqis recently moved to the city and were living in the slums of the capital. Able to pass himself off as a businessman from any number of countries, Ramin attended events throughout the city and slowly gathered what information he could about the Iraqis to formulate his plan.

Thanks to information provided by the Teacher, Ramin learned that these men had been members of *Keta'ib Hezbollah*, an Iran-affiliated Iraqi militia known for their fighting skills and willingness to kill. Friendly diplomats reported that the Iraqis were unable to find anything but meaningless and poorly paid jobs. Ramin assessed they would be open to employment.

Providing a list of options from which the Teacher would recommend a plan to the Grand Ayatollah, Ramin suggested a plan that he hoped could kill the ambassador and the Senator, derail talks that would never benefit Iran, and ensure no one ever tracked the attack back to Iran. He was confident no foreigner knew of the existence of the Immortals, who operated exclusively to protect the Grand Ayatollah's vision of Iran.

IN WASHINGTON, ROBERT CHECKED his itinerary one more time before looking through the partial collection of printed documents stacked neatly on his desk. Under the pretext of claiming that he could not connect his computer to a printer, Robert asked the most junior staff on the desk for help. They were always so eager to please and never questioned his requests. He now had forty-five printed copies of the most detailed reports, all classified, but none with his name related to them. Some were hidden under his desk at home, where Ludmilla would never look, while the remaining few sat in front of him.

It had not been difficult to request the reports over the span of weeks. He carefully marked them off his list before locking the remaining pile in his safe. He then transported them home only a few at a time, cautiously at first but growing surer of himself each day.

Back in the days before he began speaking with Andrei, Robert would have cringed at the thought of building so tall a tower of classified documents or ever taking them from his office. Nor would he ever have contemplated sharing classified information with a foreign government official, leastwise one from the Russian Embassy. However, things changed, mostly for the better, when he unburdened his soul and began speaking honestly with Sergei.

From the start, Sergei listened and understood, plus took precautions that made Robert feel special. It especially stung to not see his name on the promotion lists. At home, Ludmilla constantly reminded him of his failings by bringing up her friends' more successful spouses, their larger houses in more desirable neighborhoods, and their country club memberships. When he complained about credit card bills exceeding his monthly salary, she shot back that he should be more successful so his salary wouldn't be so low.

Sometimes he worried that she would leave him, even though he was an excellent husband. He had never been unfaithful to Ludmilla, at least not in the same town where they lived. Going by the mantra that he should never engage with a girlfriend or mistress near where he lived, Robert always kept his liaisons away. Work trips were ideal for breaking up the monotony of married life. Sergei promised him a surprise during his next trip abroad, all a result of documents Robert promised to pass.

The question on his mind while he blankly looked out his office window was how he should properly transport the documents to Europe. There was no question of putting the pages in his suitcase, since he never knew when some over-zealous airport security official might inspect his bags and tear through everything in the hopes they would be the next hero to save the republic. Sergei provided a new suitcase with special compartments between the lining, which looked very ordinary but under his close inspection was quite special. He calculated that the forty-five pages would weigh just under two and a half pounds, meaning he just needed to be careful how he carried the bag.

After pocketing his printed tickets, checking his safe, and ensuring the last of the pages were secreted deep inside his briefcase, Robert began his exit from the building. Tammy was at her desk, and he gave her a small wave as he draped his coat over his arm, unconsciously protecting the secrets he intended to smuggle from the building. As he walked the halls of the State Department, he thought he saw people following him, just as he had the other several times he brought these illicit documents home. He willed himself to take deep breaths, knowing that no one would ever suspect *him*, a trusted member of the State Department, of stealing classified information.

His heart thumping rapidly, Robert exited the elevators and walked towards the exit gates in the C street lobby. Sergei recommended that Robert always exit through the front door when carrying any documents because security personnel reportedly paid more attention to people leaving from side exits. The security guards—uniformly tall, muscular men in their twenties and early thirties—stood around the large hall. Flags from every nation lined one wall, plaques with the names of diplomats who died serving the United States overseas at either end, with great banks of windows letting in all the sun possible.

Robert walked calmly, reached for the badge tucked in his dress shirt pocket, and walked up to scan out. He inserted his card into the reader, but it returned a red light and a message. *Access denied.* Why wasn't his badge working? Did someone suspect him of treachery and not want him to exit the building? He tried again, only to see the same message, and his heart threatened to thump its way out of his chest.

"Sir," the uniformed guard called out to him. But Robert couldn't bring himself to acknowledge the young man, so he willed himself to calm down, knowing that if he engaged, they would see the fear in his eyes and smell his treason. "Sir," the guard repeated forcefully, raising his voice and attracting the attention of everyone nearby. Several people stopped their conversations and turned to stare at him.

Finally, painfully, Robert raised his eyes to meet the guard's hard eyes, wondering if this was the end. *I haven't actually given any documents to Sergei, have I?* No, he reassured himself, they could suspend his clearance pending an investigation, assuming they even discovered the documents cached in his briefcase.

"As I was saying, sir," the uniformed guard said, approaching him, "that gate is not working, so you should use the one immediately to your right." The guard, whose badge read Spencer, pointed to the gate to Robert's right.

Robert let out a laugh of relief and shuffled to the right, inserted his badge, and was gratified to see the light flash green and the gates open. Realizing the eyes of every security officer in the hall were on him, Robert gave them a cool look, held his head high, brushed his lapel, and walked out of the building.

These so-called guards were all incompetent, one more thing to disdain about his workplace. Other countries were guarded by true police and competent security professionals, while the State Department guards were a joke. If one of them called in sick, they could be replaced with a Tyson's mall cop, and no one would know the difference.

Outside, Robert decided to take a walk along the National Mall, hoping to calm his pounding heart. These walks were another precaution Sergei suggested; something about ensuring no one followed him. Robert took deep breaths over and over again, but he couldn't suppress the sudden feeling that he was invincible. Someday, when he assumed his rightful position of power, he would fire all of those moronic guards. Today's deception was simply research for tomorrow's improvements.

Walking to the mall and basking in his success, Robert didn't realize he unwittingly fell victim to multiple aspects of MICE, the intelligence community's acronym explaining why people spied: Money, Ideology, Coercion, Ego. The emotions he felt were pure ego, feeding his already inflated sense of self-worth. He felt on top of the world, untouchable. There was also the money Sergei provided, with the promise of more to come with the delivery of the documents.

As Robert walked through the October splendor of Washington's monuments, he realized that if he could get these forty-five documents out without much trouble, there were others that Sergei would find even more interesting.

What could he ask in return? He contemplated that for a moment, not minding the weight of his briefcase, and slowed while he thought. Perhaps an apartment in Paris or Bern where he could live in retirement? He dreamed of traveling as often as he wished, eating at the best restaurants, and never having to worry about money. Knowing his government pension would never give him that kind of financial freedom, he hefted the briefcase. What type of documents would it take to get a place in one of Europe's finest cities?

Robert knew the last report the third-tour officer printed for him that afternoon would catch the Russian's attention because it detailed arrangements for planned talks between the US and Iranians, including the likelihood that a prominent Senator would participate on the margins. One thing Sergei repeatedly pressed for was more information on the extent to which America would push its eastward expansion of NATO. Robert paused at that request, realizing that topic hit on *real* national security information. He still considered himself a patriot, so he was as yet unwilling to share any more on that topic, but peace with Iran was a joke and not a genuine possibility. Who cared about those meaningless talks in Budapest?

Robert learned throughout his childhood how he needed to fight against the Russians and worked for years in embassies to advocate against Russian influence. He assured himself he could give *some* information to the Russians, but not all that they wanted, controlling the situation. He instinctively knew this was like holding a tiger by the tail because if he let go, the tiger would eat him. Yet he was different because he was smarter than the Russian, better able to keep control of the situation. He didn't think about the apparatus working behind his Russian contact, making the timeless mistake of overestimating his abilities and underestimating those of the opposition.

He looked around, seeing only regular people, and felt confident he was safe. He focused on crossing Memorial Bridge at a steady pace, only slowing several times to transfer his heavier-than-normal briefcase from one hand to the other.

FIFTY METERS BEHIND THE DUPLICITOUS AMERICAN, on the other side of the bridge but within easy view, Sergei ambled along with his hands in his pockets. He was confident the diplomat, who craved money almost as much as recognition, held in his briefcase everything he needed. In a few days, they would meet in Europe, far away from the prying eyes of FBI counterintelligence experts.

Robert James Prescott Morgan III was the best asset he recruited in his career, senior enough to have access to valuable intelligence and angry enough to give it away without a thought. For relatively few dollars and a few flowery compliments, Sergei owned a goldmine of information. If the American delivered even half of what he promised, they would have him for life, able to force him to continue getting information for the Russian government through coercion. Sergei could tell the American thought he could walk away at any time. *He is wrong.*

Offerings of money were easy, especially when such simple men dealt in relatively small sums, and the Russian state was blessed with a bevy of beautiful women, many who worked in the security services. They would provide companionship on command—had done so in the past with men far worse than this American. The diplomat would never be swayed ideologically because he was too brainwashed into believing in the American dream. Still, coercion was the motivation that would sink the Federal Security Bureau's claws ever further into him. The American could make most any request, provided it was not too messy, and Sergei believed Moscow would support the action to keep their asset happy.

EXITING THE BUILDING AT MAIN STATE, Ben thought about his meetings over the past two days. He bought lunch in the cafeteria for several of his colleagues, enjoying the company of people he worked with in years past. Sitting in either of the two main State Department cafeterias, either at Main State or at the Foreign Service Institute in Arlington, Ben knew he was guaranteed to see half of the Foreign Service walk by, enabling him to see old friends. Networking was as important in the Foreign Service as anywhere in Washington, especially when one aspired, as Ben did, for bigger things. He learned back in Minnesota to be humble but knew there was no harm in dreaming about becoming an ambassador someday.

His first stop at the Department, an unwritten one, was to check in with his counterparts in H, the Bureau of Legislative Affairs, who oversaw FSOs detailed to Capitol Hill. Brenda, the political appointee who kept regular communication with FSOs on the Hill, was disappointed that Ben, a rising star, opted to work for a member of the opposition party. When the assistant secretary called her in two months ago, she explained the special nature of this FSO's detail to Capitol Hill. She did not approve, believing someone who provided such a service should work for a member of her party, yet she wisely kept those thoughts to herself. Her position was ostensibly apolitical, but the reality was that politics pervaded every aspect of life in Washington.

During that meeting, Ben detailed the Senator's major priorities, and Brenda took copious notes, promising to share these insights with others in the building. The Senator was powerful and influential, so having Ben on the inside to provide insight into the man's priorities was beneficial. Ben left to walk the halls, his next social call to his colleague serving on the Iran Desk.

Ringing the buzzer, Ben entered, instinctively flashing a grin at the secretary at the reception desk, and inquired after his friend, Nick. They were close, having overlapped several times over their careers, though never for long stretches of time. Nick served as an Iran Watcher in Berlin, tracking the German government's complicated relations with the Iranian government, while Ben worked as a political officer in Afghanistan.

"Ben, how the hell are you?!" Nick yelled across the crowded office. Some were startled, while others were apparently accustomed to his big personality and booming voice.

"Not bad," Ben replied. He offered his hand but was drawn into a bear hug that only Nick could pull off in an office setting. They walked through the rooms and arrived in a small conference room where two people sat waiting in the cramped space.

"Ben, I want you to meet Susan, our director." Ben nodded to her while she kept her seat. "And Joey, our deputy." Ben shook the deputy's hand. Ben took his seat and checked his pockets, thankful he hadn't brought his phone or any electronics into the secure room.

"So, how are things in the Senator's office?" Susan asked.

Getting straight to the point, aren't we? Ben thought.

"Things are going well." Ben pulled out his notebook, prepared to provide the requisite brief on the Senator's opinions.

"Is the Senator still in regular communication with the mujahideen?" she asked. "You know they are designated on the US terror watchlist."

"He does speak with the mujahideen, if that is what you mean," Ben replied coolly, nearly as protective as any of the Senator's staffers even after only a couple months working for the great man.

"Perhaps you could give us insight into the Senator's views on the upcoming talks?" Joey asked, without any of Susan's attitude. Ben saw Joey's attempt to bring the conversation back to a friendlier topic, thankfully blunting Susan's attacks.

"Yes, I would be happy to…" Ben began. He was ready to read from his notes, which included which parts of the agreement the Senator approved of as well as those that met his disapproval. Ben was unsure Marty would have approved of providing such inside baseball information, but he decided he would ask forgiveness later, opting instead to trade his information for what the Senator badly wanted, which was insight into how things would proceed.

"No, damn it," Susan said, pounding her fist on the table, which reverberated throughout the small room. Ben wished the door hadn't been closed because then the sound would not continue echoing in his ears. "I want to know," she said, rising slightly and wagging her finger at Ben, "what the Senator intends to do to disrupt our plans for a nuclear deal and possible peace with the Iranians."

Ben gaped, unsure he heard correctly, but out of the corner of his eye, he saw Nick and Joey both scrutinizing their notebooks as if nothing was more important than the blank pages before them.

"My job is to serve as a foreign policy advisor to Senator Cavanaugh, one that I perform to the best of my ability." Ben tried to keep his voice calm, but he wished he could have fired back at her with some of the rhetoric that constantly originated from the Senator's speechwriter. *Do you mean reckless talks with a terrorist state that held fifty-two American diplomats hostage for 444 days?* But saying that would be like declaring war on the woman sitting in front of him, who far outranked him and could cause major problems for his career.

"I can tell you that the Senator intends to attend the talks in Budapest to exercise his legislative prerogative of oversight of foreign policy. He plans to be there but understands the executive branch takes the lead on foreign affairs." He said all of this calmly but resented the way he felt she attacked him. He was proud, especially of his service, but also because he took a personal interest in every one of his assignments. He remained frustrated with people who attacked him for opinions, whether he advocated them for work or personally. Also, her malicious tone struck a chord within him, reminding him, for some reason, of how Marsha Hunter treated him back in Afghanistan.

Across from him, Susan smiled smugly, not at all pleasant, but more the way a poisonous toad would smile if able. "It appears," she said, writing quickly in her notebook, "that you are doing your best to remain a bipartisan FSO representing the Department's interests on Capitol Hill." Ben noted that her statement dripped with sarcasm. "I hope you will not permit your personal allegiances to cloud your ability to see the merits of the administration's top priority."

She slammed her notebook shut, which cracked like a shot from a rifle, and abruptly stood and walked out of the small conference room. Ben realized as she opened and closed the door that she must have purposefully selected the chair nearest the door.

"Am I the first person to receive her barrage of artillery fire?" Ben asked, looking at Nick and then Joey, hoping to get a sense of how he walked into a trap.

"Well," Joey said, "Susan recently completed a detail for the National Security Council. She made senior Foreign Service, owing it to her time at the White House."

Ben sat back, having forgotten that FSOs' general liberal attitude lent support to Democrat administrations, especially after eight years of Republican foreign policy advocacy.

"Does she realize that I was here sharing insights into what the Senator does and does not support with regard to the Iran negotiations?"

Ben asked the room, not expecting a response and realizing that his good intentions meant nothing. "I didn't know I was the enemy. Never thought I'd walk into such a shitstorm."

They spent the next hour going over the Senator's concerns, things he and others on Capitol Hill supported in the draft agreement. Joey and Nick were a good audience, asking astute follow-up questions and even sharing snacks while they spoke. Others in the office poked their heads into the conference room, all, without exception, friendly to Ben.

Finished with their talk, Ben shook Joey's hand, and Nick offered to walk him out. In the hallway, after Ben collected his phones, Nick suggested they continue walking. After taking numerous turns through several corridors, Nick stopped when he seemed confident that no one was nearby.

"I won't apologize for Susan, because I don't apologize for other people's actions," Nick said, "but you should know that this was a setup." He looked around hurriedly, double- and triple-checking no one was around. "She just went up to PDAS Hunter's office after she screamed at you to confer with her mighty mentor."

"Hold on," Ben said, leaning in conspiratorially, "do you mean that Susan's mentor is Marsha Hunter? How is she a principal deputy assistant secretary? I didn't realize the Department created a Bureau of Paranormal Affairs, dealing with people who were looney toons."

"Yeah." Nick laughed, continuing to look around the empty corridor. "Those two are thick as thieves. Hunter arranged her detail to the NSC. And Susan watched Hunter's cat while she was in Kabul." Nick looked at Ben, a connection sparking in his mind. "You never crossed paths with Hunter in Afghanistan, did you?"

"Well, I wouldn't say I worked with her." Ben tried hard to keep the sarcasm from his voice because Nick was doing him a solid favor by filling in the gaps. "But she did not approve of my work in Herat."

Ben stopped there. Not everyone in the government, or even the State Department, was privy to everything associated with events leading to the Minot Massacre. Or even activities undertaken afterwards. Ben wished he could confide in Nick, but they were not in a secure area. Plus, he thought it tacky to brag about his accomplishments.

"Listen, Ben," Nick whispered while checking his watch, "I need to return to the office, but I wanted you to know that you did nothing wrong." He paused, checking around again. "Though spouting the Senator's rhetoric played right into her hands. You will not be popular with anyone advocating for these Iran negotiations, especially not after Susan sees all her friends throughout town."

"Thanks for the heads up," Ben said while shaking Nick's hand. "And next time we meet, let's try to keep things less hostile." Ben grinned, and as he retreated to his final appointment, he heard Nick chuckling.

CHAPTER
FOUR

 Ben reflected on
the whirlwind of briefings with the Senator and select senior staff
after his meetings at State. He learned enough to make the trip from
Capitol Hill to Main State worthwhile, also picking up a list of useful
reports for the Senator's staff. The Senator read things but only when
printed out, never on a computer.

Ben made a point of describing how Susan, the office director
for Iran Affairs at State, would be a formidable opponent, especially
in tandem with pressure from the White House for the talks to
proceed. The Senator seemed intent on drawing out all details about
the encounter, touched by Ben's loyalty yet wanting to know what
resistance he faced.

On Ben's way out the door Friday afternoon, Marty handed him a
business card with the contact information for a restaurant in London,
including the maître d's direct line. "It's the Senator's favorite restaurant
in the UK, which is saying something considering how many times he
visited, and this is"—Marty cleared his throat, affecting his best British
accent—"the poshest restaurant in all the Queen's realm." They shared

a laugh, Ben mentally calculating how much it would cost to take Kate's parents out for dinner there, then bid Marty farewell.

Walking down the gangway, Ben checked his pockets, always slightly disoriented after a trans-Atlantic flight, though he did use miles earned during his time in Afghanistan to upgrade to business class. That was a treat, especially for a small-town Minnesota boy who grew up dreaming of the glamour of working in Chicago, never imagining he would travel the world for work.

Navigating Heathrow, Ben felt the strangest sensation that someone was following or watching him. It reminded him of serving in Moscow and Jordan, where he knew people monitored his movements, and of Herat, where he always suspected the Iranians were tracking him. *But I'm in London's main airport,* he told himself, calming the instinct to check his six for a tail.

The counter-surveillance training he took before serving overseas flooded back into his brain, and he thought about what to do before taking a deep breath and reminding himself that he was on friendly territory. *What is the worst that could happen*? Ben considered the question, realizing that serving as a diplomat overseas, especially for a country with as many enemies as the United States, put him forever on alert for threats from anywhere.

Just then, he noticed movement to his right as a figure swooped in and grabbed his arm, pulling him into a hug.

"I surprised you." Kate grinned, leaning in to kiss Ben.

ROBERT WALKED PAST THE COUPLE AS THEY KISSED, not approving of the public display of affection. He remembered seeing the guy on his flight and vaguely thought he had seen him around Main State. Well, he realized, the Department was a huge bureaucracy. It was not beyond the realm of possibility that two State employees sat on the same flight to a transit point like London.

To be cautious, Robert moved to the left, cutting across the flow of people, to stop at a kiosk and look at a magazine. While doing that, he surreptitiously looked around, searching for the tell-tale signs that someone followed him or stopped to observe him. He took basic counter-surveillance training before deploying overseas yet was less on edge in London than he was in Washington. Whereas at Dulles International Airport, they could have stopped him at any time, now he was on official travel, more able to wave his diplomatic passport and bypass serious inspection.

Continuing to the luggage claim to collect his bag, Robert did not realize how little he knew about surveillance and counter-surveillance, nor that Russian intelligence invented many of the tricks he believed originated in the United States. His handler, Sergei, dressed in baggy clothes and sporting a hat and fake moustache that would have concealed him from his own mother, walked ahead of where Robert stopped. *That fool thinks he is smarter than anyone else,* Sergei concluded.

Knowing the documents he craved so much were just dozens of feet from him, encased in a suitcase he provided to the arrogant American, Sergei arranged to ensure he secured the documents, no matter the contingency. Even if someone stopped the American, Sergei had three additional men conducting surveillance, all within twenty yards and prepared to steal the American's bag if the need arose.

The three couriers all held diplomatic passports and, worst case, would be prohibited from transiting London in the future but would never see the inside of a jail. *It's worth the risk,* Sergei concluded, *to ensure we get our hands on those documents, especially if we can answer Vladimir Vladimirovich's personal request. I will be a hero, rewarded beyond my wildest imaginings.*

AFTER DISENTANGLING, BEN STARED AT KATE, shocked by her airport surprise.

"Should I ask how you gained access to Heathrow's main terminal, or should I be more surprised that you discovered I booked an earlier flight?" He grinned at her, folding her hand tight in his, as they walked together joyfully towards the baggage claim. "I was planning on being the one to surprise you."

Kate smirked. "In fact, my father called to send me out here."

Ben nearly stopped at that, almost causing a pileup of people behind them. He would have had Kate not tugged him along, never letting go of his hand.

Propelling himself forward and guiding Kate back to his side so she no longer pulled him, Ben wondered whether he should have done more research on Kate's family. She had told him precious little about her background, admitting that her father was very senior at MI6, but his research confirmed that he was, in fact, the head of MI6.

He knew this was a touchy subject for her, having her father as the head of her Agency, so he let that pass. He also knew that her mother and grandmother were very involved in her life and would remain so, but he knew next to nothing about her two siblings. She had one brother and one sister—that was all she admitted to him during their stay in France. He recalled how she silenced all further questions with a proposition to join her in the shower that he didn't refuse.

They exited the airport to a private parking lot, and Kate led him to her car. "One of the perks of the job," Kate explained, loading his bags into the boot, as they called the trunk there. Ben walked to the right side, what he thought was the passenger seat, until Kate reminded him with a quick kiss that the driver sat on the right side in the UK.

Expertly shifting through the gears, Kate drove her Range Rover Sport faster than he imagined an SUV could go, accelerating quickly as she navigated the service roads to the expressway into the city.

They chatted about Ben's flight and recent news out of Afghanistan throughout the drive. Kate turned on the radio while Ben watched the countryside pass by. After what seemed a short drive, they pulled into the underground garage, and after she put the vehicle in park, he kissed her passionately.

"Only a little bit longer," she whispered through kisses, then turned off the car and rushed around to drag him upstairs. Ben realized he loved the cadence of her accent, that it aroused in him a longing for her that he never knew existed.

Reading her mind that they would return for his bags, Ben followed her to the elevator, embracing her as they rode up to her apartment. Inside, their two forms melted into one embrace, and they stopped missing the other.

"BRENT, HOW ARE PREPARATIONS GOING for my Iran negotiations?"

Brent Paulson sat in the senior staff meeting, people around the table in a secure room, and read from his notes. He knew he had to respond to the ambassador's request. Still, despite continuing to do his job as best he could, he harbored nothing but resentment and hatred for the man before him. He never before knew he could wish someone was dead.

In the months since he caught the ambassador screwing his wife in his office, and after learning that was a barely kept secret by everyone but him, Brent had taken to working, drinking, and sleeping on the couch. He tried to remain a good father to his children but could not even bear to look at his wife, much less speak to her. Not after seeing her in that compromising position. Every time he saw her in the apartment, he found a reason to leave.

Detailing the proposed plans, Brent talked through attendees from the US side, from European partners, the Russians, the Chinese, and, of course, the Iranians. He saw Ambassador Richards salivating at the thought of so much attention on *him*. Clenching his hands, Brent wished he had the strength to punch the ambassador in the face, in the nuts, or anywhere.

Thinking about his humiliation, Brent realized that his only friend was Radek, the mysterious businessman who always met with him. Brent knew he was telling the stranger too much sensitive, even classified, information, but he had long since stopped caring.

After seeing the ambassador with his wife, he tried getting support from another senior embassy officer, but that spineless so-called friend refused to engage with him. He, like everyone else, was worried about the ambassador retaliating. *I would normally do anything for you,* Brent remembered hearing, *but I need to get promoted and stay overseas. You understand, don't you?*

Of course Brent understood. No one looked out for anyone but themselves, so now Brent was looking out for himself and seeking his revenge. He realized that he was not, and never had been, a violent man, slight of build and not physically strong. But he was smart. *Yes,* he consoled himself, *I am smarter than the man in front of me, and I will get my revenge.*

After a few drunk conversations, Brent eventually began applying common sense to his encounters with Radek, taking precautions to learn what he could about the man who had become his confidant. After learning his new friend's last name, which he suspected was fake, he asked the foreign ministry and learned that the man was, on paper at least, some sort of businessman.

Proving that who you know is as important as what you know, Brent called in a favor from his friend at the foreign ministry. The friend shared copies of the pages from Radek's passport, which Hungarian immigration took surreptitiously when he entered. Over drinks, Alexandru explained that when they wanted more information, they would claim their booth scanner did not work, taking the passport book to a back room. Alexandru confided that airport officials were now so adept that they could photocopy all the pages in any passport in less than a minute, never raising suspicion with anyone but Chinese diplomats.

The pages proved that Radek traveled regularly but little else. Faced with the prospect of losing the one person in whom he could confide, Brent ignored the warning signs in his head. It felt good to complain to someone, to have someone listen to *him*.

Who is Radek? Brent asked himself. The ambassador was speaking again, going on about how important it was that the talks be successful, but Brent was no longer paying attention. *I just want someone who listens to what I have to say. I'm entitled to that, right?* He was doing this with the best of intentions, he assured himself, because everyone needed an outlet. What could go wrong?

HASSAN LOOKED AROUND THE ABANDONED WAREHOUSE, then at the men huddled around the fire. Despite weeks in Budapest, they remained strangers in an unwelcoming land. The men's steeled glances tried to hide the pain and despair they felt, each staring at the pitiful fire that burned from trash they stole from a garbage can.

While they all found menial jobs with local companies, the type of low-paying work no local would willingly do, such as cleaning buildings and backbreaking work outside, they relied on charity to feed their families. The most demeaning thing was each man had skills that should be of use to businesses, yet the Hungarians were a racist people who hated anyone who was not from their country, especially non-Christians.

Looking around the circle, he watched as Abdullah morosely stabbed at the fire with a stick, trying to prod more warmth from the smoldering embers. He applied for jobs, but his lack of Hungarian and inability to speak any language but Arabic and Farsi meant the only job he could find was as a janitor at a construction firm. Hassan knew his friend could run that firm, if only given an opportunity, yet every door seemed closed against them. "Everyone hates Muslims," he grumbled softly.

Next was Nasser, the banker-turned-falafel salesman. He complained the least, willing to accept any work so he could feed his wife, Aisha, and three children. Aisha took on the responsibility of educating the children in their extended family, spending their dwindling money on necessities such as paper, pencils, and a chalkboard. Hassan remained in awe of her, unable to deny her assertion that they were better off poor but educated than rich with stupid children.

"At least we are each finding work," Ali remarked, though none of the other men even deigned to look up at his remark. As the youngest, he seemed the most determined and optimistic, even though they all privately admitted there was little hope for optimism in this city. Indeed, likely on the European continent. His wife, Sahar, found work in a café serving food to wealthy foreign tourists, using her foreign language skills, while Ali convinced a hotel to hire him on a trial basis.

"If only we could move on to Germany," Malik said morosely, though his lower back remained too injured to work more than a few hours each day. He suffered the pain without complaint, pushing himself too hard, yet still, his body continued to grow stronger. Hassan knew that within a matter of weeks, Malik would be back to full strength, given the work he did in the construction yard and the exercises he performed every morning as he ran around their neighborhood, willing his body to health.

His hands flexed as he thought about the repeated embarrassments he and the others experienced in the weeks since they arrived. Were they not proud men who sought to provide for their families? Was it not every man's right to give his family a better future?

Silently, each of the men fumed, angry with their situation but powerless to change anything. Privately, they consoled themselves with the knowledge that at least they were earning some money, even if only a pittance.

I would kill for more money, Malik realized, staring at the pitiful fire. He looked to his left, seeing the threadbare carpets each used for their required prayers. These were not true prayer carpets but scraps torn up so each man could hold his head up with some dignity.

"Surely Allah will not leave us here in the depths of hell," Malik whispered.

"We should pray for Allah's blessings," Ali suggested. "If not for us"—he paused, looking down to examine his hands—"then at least for our wives and children."

As bidden, each walked to their scrap of carpet, knelt, and prayed with their foreheads to the ground, all facing towards Mecca and pouring their tormented hearts out in prayers of supplication.

CHAPTER

FIVE

EXITING THE CAR, BEN MENTALLY READIED himself. He enjoyed an amazing afternoon and night with his girlfriend, pausing their time together only to eat, drink, and feed one another chocolate. They professed their love for the other in Afghanistan after only months of knowing one another, yet Ben knew this was real love, not the crap he thought he had experienced in the past. He once again considered how quickly they fell in love and how living and working in Afghanistan made him painfully aware of the fragility of life, and now he didn't want to waste more time. Ben was done with games and ready to get on with life.

"Are you ready for the onslaught?" Kate asked, grasping his hand as she handed her key fob to the valet before they entered the Highlands Club. As nervous as Ben might or might not be, Kate admitted that she was downright terrified. She spent years training for and living in stressful situations, but terrorist attacks paled in comparison to the nerves she felt now as she led Ben to her parents.

As they entered, Kate caught herself straightening Ben's tie and jacket so he would make a perfect first impression. They approached the maître d', who merely gestured to Kate to the center of the dining room. Her father's favorite table was guaranteed to provide as much privacy as a table in the middle of a football pitch. Though the average British citizen could not pick her father out of a lineup, Arthur Sinclair was known to everyone in the dining room.

She knew he loved the way other diners discreetly looked his way when he entered. On nights like this, with his beautiful family in tow, Kate suspected that her father loved to sit in the middle of the room and attract envious looks. Her father was the ultimate authority figure, Kate reminded herself as he inspected Ben. She wanted to protect Ben but let go of his hand so she could introduce two of the most important men in her life. Watching them size up one another, she realized everything just got more complicated.

"Father, this is Ben, my boyfriend." Kate scrutinized her father's reaction, disappointed to see that Arthur took her statement in stride, gripping Ben's hands in his rather than expressing any dismay.

"A pleasure to meet you, Ben," Arthur Sinclair replied. He secretly dreaded this moment but steeled himself ahead of time on the drive over from the house and betrayed no emotion. Arthur examined Ben, comparing what he saw to what he knew from his conversations with his chiefs of station in Washington and Kabul, as well as his American counterparts. The young man presented himself well, standing erect, and had a firm grip.

Ben moved around the table, shaking hands with Kate's mother, then politely kissing her grandmother's hand, following Kate's instructions. Dame Elizabeth Sinclair, unaccustomed to an appropriately polite American, correctly suspected that her granddaughter provided pointers to the man for whom she professed true love and did something truly surprising to everyone gathered around the table. She stood up and hugged the young American.

"Benjamin," she said, embracing him, "we are so pleased to finally meet you in person." She withdrew and took her seat, to the astonished stares of her son and daughter-in-law but to the adoring look of her granddaughter. "Now that you are here," she said, waving for the hovering waiter, "we shall order drinks and proceed with the inquisition."

Ben chuckled, embarrassed, then took the proffered seat between Kate and her grandmother, directly across from Kate's parents. There was one empty seat, between Kate's father and grandmother, and Ben realized Kate was staring, surprised that their table was set for six.

"In case your sister graces us with her presence," Kate's mother, Angela, commented, picking up the menu to study, despite that she always ordered the same meal, which the chef would have begun preparing when she walked in.

Kate was instantly angry, positively pissed off, and glared at her mother. Her mother, with an elegance Kate hadn't yet mastered, studiously ignored Kate in favor of the menu. *This is my damn night,* Kate fumed, *and my bratty sister will do nothing but derail the conversation with her pompous monologues and attempts to be the prettiest in the room.* Kate's thoughts skidded to a halt when she realized this was why her mother had not responded to any calls or messages since yesterday. She narrowed her eyes, studying her parents, while her father stared back, willing her to say anything.

They sat in silence, Ben realizing he needed to say something to break the ice. After all, he intended at some point during this trip to ask Kate's father for permission to propose but knew he needed to get to know the man first. Ben believed in himself, but sitting with her family, he suddenly felt like a villager trying to date a princess. The waiter arrived with drinks, breaking the silence as he delivered each cocktail in turn.

"Lord Sinclair," Ben began, ready to ask about the finer points of cricket, a game he knew from Kate that her father had played since university, but Arthur Sinclair cut him off.

"Unless you intend to quiz me on the happenings at headquarters," Arthur said curtly, "you need not address me with my title." He took a sip from his gin and tonic, steeling himself to press on. "Before we get too far," Arthur said before Ben could speak again, "I should like to know what your intentions are with my daughter."

The reaction around the table was absolute silence, except that Ben unexpectedly drew strength. Never knowing what drove him to be so honest, Ben took a healthy drink from his glass of gin and tonic and responded.

"Sir," Ben replied with as much strength as he could muster, "in short, I love your daughter."

Arthur Sinclair sat back in his chair, taken aback as if Ben had dropped a bomb on his world.

"I've loved her since we went on our first date, to be honest."

Another explosion rippled through Arthur Sinclair's carefully constructed universe, one where he was the most important man in Kate's life. He knew his daughter undertook dangerous activities for her country, but he took pains to not interfere in her work life, respecting her independence. It was just that he still saw her as his little girl, his oldest child, and had some trouble accepting the fact she was making these decisions on her own.

"And I wanted to do this in person, to be honest with you…" Ben took Kate's hand, kissing her knuckles before continuing. "I'd like to ask for your permission, when the time is right—"

"Before we jump into that serious a discussion," Arthur interrupted, controlling the conversation, "perhaps we could get to know you better? And you could get to know us?"

Ben sat back, nearly carried away sufficiently to ask Arthur Sinclair for his permission to marry Kate. *We're meeting for the first time,* Ben reminded himself. *As much as I want to rush things, I need to respect that I might be going too fast for Kate's family.*

Kate exhaled, caught between relief and disappointment. It sounded like Ben was ready to ask for her father's permission to propose, which made her want to cry. *At the same time,* she thought, *that might be taking things a bit too fast.* The room glazed over, Kate realizing she was tearing up, emotions flooding her as she considered Ben's words. *He just met my family,* she conceded, *and they need to get to know one another.* She took a sip of her drink, pleased that her Ben was brave enough to speak his mind to her father, who intimidated so many other men.

Across the table, Angela was disappointed that her husband interrupted Ben's admission of love. *He was about to propose,* she fumed, knowing it would do no good to revisit the discussion until they got to know her daughter's boyfriend. She realized that Kate had finally picked the right man for herself. Not for anyone else, least of all for her family, but for herself. She saw in Ben a fierce love and loyalty to her Kate that made her proud of raising a daughter whose judgment proved impeccable. *I'm patient.*

Meanwhile, Elizabeth Sinclair admired the man who very nearly proposed in front of their family. *He would have impressed Alistair,* she admitted, smiling at the thought of her late husband meeting this young American. Taking the long view, she saw well enough into the future to know her granddaughter and this young American would make a good couple.

Good Lord, Arthur Sinclair thought, his world momentarily frozen in time, *this is real.* He looked at Ben, whose resolve shone like a candle in a hurricane, and then to his little girl. He could never claim to love any of his children more than the other but felt a kinship with Kate as she had gone to his university and then followed him into the Queen's service. His other two children were more of a mystery to him.

Arthur was not ready for Kate to build a new life with a new family, so he was thankful he interrupted Ben before he took things a step too far. *No,* Arthur realized, *I'm not ready for this yet, especially since I know so little about this young man.* And then, keeping his face a mask, Arthur's real feelings shone through. *Why does it have to be an American?*

Out of nowhere, oblivious to the awkward silence blanketing the table, a younger version of Kate's mother, slightly shorter and more intense, approached the table and settled into the empty seat.

"Hullo," she said, looking at Ben before snapping her fingers and, with unwavering focus, pointed to wordlessly order the same cocktail as her mother from the hovering waiter. "I'm Beatrix." She beamed. "Kate's younger and better sister." She smiled, expecting attention from everyone. Taking a beat, she looked around the table.

Beatrix's arrival broke the spell of silence that had settled for several minutes on the table, each person absorbed with their own thoughts.

"My dear, you are punctual as ever," Angela declared, accustomed to her younger daughter's lack of adherence to any schedule but her own.

"You happened to miss Ben's profound admission of love for your sister, followed by your father's insistence that we all get to know one another better before Ben asks a certain question," Elizabeth stated, enjoying the needling of her immature and slightly superficial granddaughter. It wasn't that she had a favorite, though Kate following in Arthur's footsteps, as well as her husband Alistair's, certainly made it easier to understand her. Beatrix worked in finance, singularly focused on making money in the city, certainly an honorable profession followed by others in the family.

"How the absolute bloody fuck did I miss so much already?" she fumed aloud, angry that she was late arriving from the office. *I always miss everything.*

IN BUDAPEST, RAMIN WALKED THROUGH the streets towards his appointment. Per his training, he left plenty of time to ensure no one, either local security services or hostile foreign intelligence services, followed. Today was the culmination of days of effort, including multiple phone calls from the Teacher to senior IRGC personnel to force the Iranian Embassy's intelligence officer to give up his contacts within the Iraqi community. The challenge, when normally none existed, was the IRGC officer at Post was related to a senior IRGC officer, who in turn was married to the daughter of a Grand Ayatollah, who viewed Grand Ayatollah Shirazi as operating far outside the acceptable structure of the Iranian revolution.

In truth, the complexities of Tehran's political and religious elite, not to mention of Qom, Isfahan, and other important Iranian cities, were beyond Ramin's comprehension. He knew the Teacher gave him and his brother Immortals assignments, all designed to advance the Islamic revolution. It was not his job, the Teacher reminded him routinely, to understand but merely to trust the wisdom of those above.

During his years overseas, he killed, stole, and destroyed lives, never really comprehending an end goal. In one operation, he took an incriminating video of a visiting Islamic scholar, one critical of the Grand Ayatollah's vision. The *ahund* preferred drinking, smoking, and engaging in deplorable acts with prostitutes. Ramin noted with satisfaction, after the scholar returned to Iran, that he vocally supported the Grand Ayatollah's goals. Ramin later admitted to the Teacher that he wished he could have killed the scholar for his treatment of women.

In a rare display of empathy to an Immortal's conscience, after the scholar publicly endorsed the Grand Ayatollah, the scholar met his untimely death on the mean streets of Tehran in an apparent mugging gone wrong. The circumstances, reported by newspapers, bore the hallmarks of the Teacher and exhibited a violence that terrified police investigators.

Ramin circled the blocks in random figure-eight patterns and gazed into shops until he was confident no surveillance had gotten ahead of or remained behind him. He conducted the ritual operational cleansing to make sure he could meet safely with the Iraqis. He found them, as arranged, in an abandoned warehouse, gathered around a fire for warmth.

In the space were narrow strips of carpet piled carefully to one side. *However low may be their situation, at least they treat guests well.* The Iraqis offered him tea and, as a gesture of goodwill to supporters of the Iranian cause, he handed them the two bags of groceries with bundles of 500 euro at the bottom of one bag for each of the men.

Noticing the cash, the men silently agreed that the man before them commanded respect. Without another word, they shifted and offered the best seat to their visitor. This seat, which Ramin felt as he sat, was made of wood, felt broken, and smelled of burning trash. It was so uncomfortable that he would have preferred to stand, but he did not want to offend his new friends.

While the men sized him up, Ramin looked at each and recalled perfectly what the reporting said about their backgrounds. Each fought well and valiantly against the Americans' continued control of Iraqi territory, setting roadside bombs and conducting attacks on foreign convoys.

He knew what the Iraqis truly wanted was for their country to be left alone, yet conversely, the five found themselves stuck in one of the Western countries they hated. He knew from the IRGC reporting that all hoped to make it to Germany, where they heard tell of promises of a warm welcome and plentiful jobs. For now, they were stuck in Hungary until they could gather the resources they needed to continue west.

Ramin knew giving the men too much money now risked them absconding to Germany, whereas 2,500 euro between the five families would never be enough to smuggle themselves across borders.

"I seek to employ your skills and expertise," Ramin began in Arabic. It was not one of his best languages, but it was the one he knew all five spoke. "I have a stationary target in mind." He paused when three women entered bearing tea and small plates with treats. Looking to where the women entered the room, Ramin saw several children standing, staring at them. The five men, having adjusted bricks to be used as makeshift tables for their tea, waved the women away quickly after they deposited refreshments.

After the women and children exited the room, Ramin examined each man as he explained what he wanted, testing their resolve over the night fire. None looked away, accepting the job with the hardened resolve of veteran fighters. He remembered this look from when he fought for eight long years against Saddam Hussein. He paused, momentarily lost in thought as he realized that back then, Iraqis had been his enemy. "With sufficient preparation and material, which I will supply"—he paused again, realizing he needed them to succeed—"we will strike the Americans."

Their eyes lit, all eager for this assignment. For the Iraqis, the operation gave them the opportunity to continue their life's work—attacking the Western forces that had destroyed their homeland. Also, he would pay them more than enough to move on to Germany and start comfortable lives.

None of these men have a clue how much they will be feared, hated, and belittled when they reach Germany. Though his responsibility was Eastern Europe, the former Communist bloc countries, Ramin traveled routinely to support his brother Immortal, Farrokh, often enough that he understood Europeans' small-mindedness.

Europe succeeded where others failed, using their money and

technology to dominate the world stage, yet now, wave upon wave of immigrants were taking over the continent, forever changing Europe's landscape. As minarets dotted the skies of Europe, towering over the unused Christian buildings and serving as a beacon for lost souls to follow the teachings of the Prophet Mohammed, Ramin knew the continent would change. *We are accomplishing through migration what those in the past failed to do through war. Slowly, we are replacing the Christians.*

"*Kam althaman?*" the oldest of the group, ostensibly the leader, asked. *How much?* The man wore a simple jacket and hat against the night chill, but Ramin could tell that the others trusted him.

I have them, Ramin silently cheered, unable to betray emotion in front of them. Whether they knew it or not, these men were prostitutes, offering their lives to be used in service to his cause. Ramin would happily sacrifice these men, who were victims in any society, towards his ultimate goal of advancing anything the Grand Ayatollah desired.

Withdrawing a calculator from his inside pocket—he never wanted to make a mistake dealing with money—he typed in the number, showed it to the man, and said, "For each of you, 10,000 euro, plus half that amount to each man's family back home."

Realizing it would be unmanly to negotiate, Hassan al-Sadr, a distant younger cousin to militia leader Muqtada al-Sadr, nodded to his four companions. They would follow him anywhere, he knew. That was the stipulation they discussed before the Iranian arrived, bringing honor to their names. Each man could return to their families tonight with money for food and clothing, providing assurance that their families in Iraq would receive the promised support.

CHAPTER

SIX

"**THEY ENJOYED MEETING YOU, DARLING,**" Kate said as they sat in the taxi.

"I could have sworn a couple of those guys wanted to fight me, especially that guy David." Ben laughed, masking his unease at meeting Kate's university friends. All of them were so successful, some working with Kate in government, others in academia, and others working in London's huge private sector. Ben felt that he needed to prove himself to Kate's friends. He felt the same way when he returned to Minnesota, like he was an oddity. People were always intrigued by his overseas assignments, but it was clear they considered him as foreign as the countries where he lived.

Kate could not admit her complex feelings to Ben. She did not get along with all her *friends*, if that was what she called them. Alice had been her roommate at university, attending many of the same classes, yet she seemed more like a competitor. She worked at MI5, Britain's domestic intelligence service, and their services viewed threats very differently. Then there was Samantha, now a junior professor at the London School of Economics. David was a story unto himself, a man who, time and again, proclaimed his love for her, but she never felt anything for him. He should be a perfect match—he was a match on paper—but the chemistry was never there.

Kate did not want to admit it, but she often felt small compared to her friends, as if they had accomplished so much more in their lives. Knowing she was a great officer, Kate always felt like everyone assumed she got her job because of her father. Being with Ben made her feel strangely complete, him liking her because of their shared experiences in Afghanistan. She knew that was silly, because she was an independent and professional woman, and she shouldn't focus on others.

Kate desired more in her life than just work. She wanted a partner to share it with. Looking at Ben as he stared out the window, she realized how different their world views truly were. He looked out at a foreign land, while she saw home. She got excited every time she thought about adventures with Ben, knowing that being with him changed so much for her.

Suddenly breaking what felt like a magical moment, Ben's phone rang. It startled Kate. She was not accustomed to the melody, which she thought came from the radio at first. He checked, seeing a DC number, and decided whether to answer it.

"I suppose I should answer," he muttered. He was enjoying his time focused exclusively on Kate but accepted that carrying a work phone meant people could contact him any time.

Hearing the coughing of a lifetime smoker on the other end of the line before the caller said a word, Ben smirked and said, "Yes, Marty." After a short pause, he said, "Yes, of course I am having a wonderful time in London." He looked to Kate, who looked gorgeous in a skirt, blouse, and heels so high he was amazed she could walk in them.

"No," Ben said, "I haven't checked my email in days." He lowered his voice. "But will contact the pol chief in Budapest to ask."

Listening from her seat, Kate realized she couldn't listen to multiple things at once. At parties, she could stand in one place and listen to at least two conversations simultaneously, even in foreign languages. She once tracked three conversations, though when one switched to a new language, which she couldn't identify right away, she lost track of everything.

"They moved the meeting?" Ben asked. He ran his fingers through his hair, which Kate knew was one of his tells that he was stressed. "I didn't pack for a trip with the Senator." Ben was nearly shouting into the phone now, though resigned himself to his fate. "Could one of the staffers who lives in Old Town, perhaps McKenzie, grab a few things from my apartment? I left a spare key with my neighbor."

After he hung up, he said, "It appears I'll travel with the Senator to Bern to learn more about developments inside Iran, particularly in advance of planned administration-led discussions." He stared out the window, lost in thought, but Kate felt a surge of excitement, sensing an opportunity to get back into the field.

"Darling," she asked nonchalantly, "any chance I could join you in Bern?"

For work, Kate tracked Iran's support to Hezbollah and other groups throughout the region. They funded and armed terror groups throughout the region, particularly in Yemen, threatening stability within the Gulf states. Recently, an asset reported the existence of a mysterious group called the Immortals operating within the Iranian government. Allegedly, the group had operated outside government control for decades, with tacit support from a senior benefactor. *Someone close to the Supreme Leader,* she concluded. She was dying to get out of London and away from headquarters.

"Well," he replied, thinking, "I doubt there's a planned UK component to the visit, but I'm happy to put in a good word with the Senator." He chuckled, doubting the Senator would say no. He was more likely to jump at the chance to meet Kate. The Senator asked about her often, often remarking on his wish to see Ben happily married.

"We're here," Kate sang, happy that Ben agreed. She would have to talk with her supervisor about logistics, but that shouldn't be a problem since this trip could be beneficial.

Ben looked at the house. *No, mansion,* he corrected himself. It was an old, imposing building. The taxi dropped them off across the street in what seemed like the wealthiest neighborhood in London. As they approached the house, Ben noted nondescript vehicles and security parked out front.

"Hullo, Mark," Kate called out, waving to a man standing to the side of the front door. The man was fit, wore a tailored suit that seemed too bland for the street, and coolly analyzed every movement within one hundred yards of the house. He also looked familiar. Ben realized Mark was at a table near the front of the restaurant the night Ben met Kate's parents and grandmother.

"Good afternoon, Miss Kate." Mark stared at Ben and smiled, and Ben had the feeling he was being appraised as to the quickest way to kill him. He supposed that was the job of men who protected someone like his girlfriend's father. These were targets to much of the world, so Mark was someone trained to view everyone as a threat until told otherwise.

"I'm Ben," he said, unsure whether to hold out his hand or not. Just then, the door opened, the movement causing Mark to snap nearly to attention.

"Good heavens," Kate's mother said from the entryway, "are you having a party out here?" She smiled, looking very kind, and Ben wanted desperately to know the backstory behind how such a nice lady could have married a man so unsmiling as Kate's father. They had stayed up late discussing the drama during the dinner, laughing about the absurdity of it after returning to her place that evening.

"Ben," Angela Sinclair said, "this is Mark, one of Arthur's bodyguards. He hangs around the house incessantly." Mark nodded at Ben, grimacing slightly, and Ben felt he had received some stamp of approval. Or was it disapproval? Before he could give it much thought, Angela grabbed Ben's arm and pulled him into the house. This was the kind of house Ben only ever saw on the BBC, like something out of the Victorian era. He immediately felt like he did not belong.

"This is home," Kate said simply, and she went about taking off her coat but shook her head when Ben started to take off his shoes. They reached the point in their relationship where they could communicate without words, which was helpful because Ben often found himself confounded by British customs. Their cultures were supposed to be cousins, viewed in some parts of the world as almost identical, but after living in Kate's world for a couple of days, he realized how wrong that was.

"The family has owned the house for quite some time," Angela said simply, guiding Ben out of the entryway and into a giant library. Ben looked at the high ceilings and artwork throughout, with simple but expensive pieces hanging on the walls.

"It is a beautiful house," Ben said, "and I think my childhood home would fit neatly into this room." He laughed at his own joke while staring at a portrait of one of Kate's ancestors.

Out of nowhere, Arthur Sinclair walked into the room. "Ben, hullo there, welcome." He walked over to shake Ben's hand, then joined his wife and daughter in the sitting area by the fireplace.

"You commented, Ben," Angela inquired from the sofa, on the other end of which Arthur took a seat, "on your life growing up."

Kate, who sat in a loveseat near her parents, patted the seat next to her. Ben sat down, still taking in the surroundings, particularly row upon row of bookcases, all filled with books that probably belonged in museums. He marveled at the priceless artwork and imagined Kate's family diligently buying pieces over the centuries, passing everything down in the family.

"My childhood?" Ben asked, playing for time. He did not particularly want to discuss how he grew up, not in Kate's childhood home, a palace more than a house. "It was simple, a good childhood." He was uncomfortable but hoped these were his future in-laws, so he decided to be honest.

"I grew up in a small town where everyone quite literally knew everyone else." He grasped Kate's outstretched hand, grateful for her comfort. "My parents both worked, my father in the local bank, while my mother taught at the high school. Both of them were vibrant and intelligent. They gave me a great life." Now came the hard part, Ben realized, and he steeled himself.

"Both of them died in a car accident when I was just ready to start high school." He took a breath, thinking about when he got the news. "The whole town kind of came together to raise me. They never forced me to move out of my parents' house, but someone was always there to check in on me."

Neighbors on both sides constantly checked on him. Sven and Leena Carlson lived on one side, all their children grown up, so he ate dinner at their house nearly every night, grateful for the company. They ran a hardware store and volunteered at their church, and they taught him the value of being honest. On the other side, old Mrs. Darwitz lived alone. Her daughter had moved away, and her son was a casualty in Vietnam. She, along with the numerous veterans in town, taught him the value of respecting the sacrifice of those who fought and died.

"I have a sister, but we have not spoken in nearly twenty years, since my parents died." Ben realized he hadn't even told Kate about that. He didn't want to think about how his sister selfishly refused to return home to watch over him. He learned early in life to rely on himself, which made him a bit more independent than others, yet he believed that was a good thing.

Kate turned on cue, sensing the hurt, and jumped in to fill the void. "Thank you, Ben," she said, flashing a look of protective instinct at her parents that would have made a mama bear proud. Her mother understood the look, reaching out to hold Arthur's hand. He, on the other hand, seemed oblivious and wanted to know more about Ben's difficult childhood, though he was startled by his wife grasping his hand.

Ben's phone rang again. He pulled it from his jacket pocket. *It's the same number as before.* Ben excused himself to answer it. He looked around, realizing he had no idea where to have a private conversation. He pivoted with the phone halfway to his ear.

"You may take your call in the library," Angela said, pointing to a door behind Ben.

Wait, Ben thought as he strode across the room, *this room isn't the library?* He opened the door and then closed it, plunged into a semidarkness lit only by table lamps.

"Hi, Marty," Ben said, not waiting to hear the chief of staff's voice. He tried to find a place to sit. "How are things going there in Washington?"

In his gravelly voice, Marty asked, "Ben, how are you enjoying London?"

Sitting up straight in the overstuffed leather chair, Ben realized his mistake. "It is going very well, Senator, thank you for asking." He spotted what looked like a more comfortable chair near a window, which would surely give him better reception. "I apologize that I thought you were Marty, but you are calling from the same number."

"Not a problem, Ben," the Senator responded, calm as always.

"Listen, I do want to hear how things are going there, but we have a slightly urgent situation you need to understand."

Ben leaned forward. "I'm listening."

"The administration is throwing a fit about my opposition to their planned talks with the Iranians. Of course, we knew that in advance based on your briefing from last week. I owe you one."

Ben wondered what it meant for someone to be owed a favor by arguably one of the most powerful senators in Congress. The Senator described several political challenges involving other members who sought peace with the Iranian regime. Ben followed along because he knew it would be useful context.

"The end effect, Ben, is that I need your help setting up meetings in London, starting Tuesday morning. I don't want to involve the embassy," he emphasized, though Ben already knew the Senator's desire to avoid oversight by embassy officials. "Then we need to prepare for our meetings in Bern for later that week."

The Senator made the request with the confidence of a man who always got his way, much as when he invited Ben to work for him while they stood in the shade of trees in Kabul.

"Senator, if you can hold one minute, I think I can talk with my dinner hosts and make the request." Ben remembered Kate's request to accompany them to Bern and saw a solution.

On Capitol Hill, Marty hit the mute button, speaking for the first time. "It appears nabbing Ben to work for us paid off more than you ever could have guessed."

The Senator chuckled. "How long will it take Ben to ask his future father-in-law for this favor? And will Sinclair bite?"

In London, Ben felt nervous at the thought of asking his girl-friend's father for a favor, but he reasoned that he was asking for the Senator, not for himself.

"Lord Sinclair," Ben asked, then rephrased. "Sir, I mean. I have

Senator Cavanaugh on the phone. He would like to visit London for meetings en route to Bern and wondered if you could help arrange meetings."

Arthur stood. He had briefly met the Senator years before and knew from his daughter, as well as his station in Washington, that Ben worked for a powerful man who almost won his bid for the US presidency.

"Yes, Ben, I understand," Arthur replied, relaxing because he guessed what was happening. He knew that the Senator vehemently opposed negotiations with Iran over a nuclear deal, American politics effectively muddying international waters. The UK government also supported negotiations, while Arthur recognized that the Iranian government would never abide by any agreement unless it somehow benefitted them. He looked at Kate, who leaned forward with interest, momentarily no longer his daughter but instead a trained MI6 officer excited to seize an opportunity.

"May I have the phone, please?" Arthur asked, toning down his usual mannerisms since his daughter seemed to think things were serious with this man. It would do no good to scare him. Taking the proffered phone, he withdrew to the library, leaving Ben staring at his girlfriend, her mother, and her grandmother, who entered the room while he was in the library.

"So," Ben quipped, "if that is the library, what is this room called?"

Kate stood and stepped towards Ben, laughing as she hugged him. "Does this mean I'm going to Bern?" she asked, knowing she could hide nothing from her mother or grandmother.

IN WASHINGTON, ROBERT WALKED THROUGH the woods in Fairfax County Park, miles from his home, near Pentagon City. Beside him, Sergei walked calmly, confident that no one paid any attention to them. He used multiple officers from the Russian Embassy to canvas the park, ensuring no one entered without their knowledge.

Robert thought back to his trip to Europe, realizing that everything went off without a hitch, thanks to his careful planning. He even enjoyed the company of a Russian girl, Anastasia, on two stops of his trip. Robert loved Ludmilla but never saw that as a reason to turn down the liaisons that Sergei arranged for him. Sergei cautioned Robert to only ever refer to her as his girlfriend, yet another rule of their encounters. He gave some of the documents shortly after arriving in Paris, his first stop, knowing he needed to keep control of the relationship.

In Berlin, Robert provided another batch of documents between meetings with German counterparts. They were *his* documents, Robert considered, and therefore, he wanted to control how he shared them. Anastasia visited later that evening, encouraging him to hand over the remainder of the documents, but he was smarter than everyone. He ensured that he did not fall asleep after he and Anastasia made love so she could not search his suitcase for the papers.

Ultimately, it was only after Robert arrived in Estonia, his final stop on his trip, that he gave the last of the documents, ones he knew would be the most damaging if anyone ever discovered that he gave them to the Russians. Anastasia stayed with him those two nights, and Robert slept soundly; after all, there was nothing for her to steal.

Walking methodically, always on edge when meeting one of his agents, Sergei was initially annoyed with Robert. The games he played were *nekulturny*, but the American delivered important information, corroborating information other SVR officers learned in other countries. There was a source in London that the Kremlin valued highly, but Sergei now ran a State Department official who could corroborate all but the most sensitive reports.

The most challenging thing was Robert had an ego that could match that of the Russian president, a man who never accepted anything but complete success. Sergei praised Anastasia for her excellent tradecraft and for being able to keep their asset happy without causing any security problems. Anastasia performed skillfully, adapting well the last night when Robert unexpectedly demanded another lady to join their evening.

"So," Robert asked with nonchalant arrogance, "what is my code name within Russian intelligence?" He kept walking, never looking at Sergei, but they strode so close together that they could have held hands.

What is wrong with this American? Sergei mused, thankful this was one of the questions he discussed with leadership in Moscow. The FBI agent Robert Hanssen successfully avoided detection by American counterintelligence officials by demanding that his real name never be communicated, which prolonged his success at spying for the Soviet Union. Russian intelligence had since learned lessons, now giving master code names for sources that were shared with only the most trusted but then rotating sub-code names on a monthly basis. *There is nothing to be gained by lying,* Sergei considered and slowed to speak.

"Your code name is Apollo, for the Greek god." He did not elaborate further, knowing privately that American and other Western intelligence would kill for a peek into the office that controlled the assignment of code names. There was a system, one that Sergei barely understood. If he found a good intelligence source, his job was to recruit that asset, report fully to Moscow, and wait for them to decide.

There was always the risk of The Dangle, as intelligence officials called it, of a trained spy offering to work for the Russian government, only to provide garbage to misinform and wreak havoc. Sergei endured many sleepless nights while a team directed by a Moscow senior official followed Robert to and from work, ensuring that he did not lie.

"Apollo, huh," Robert mused, knowing Sergei was feeding his ego but loving the attention. He was in this for the money but also the opportunity to get back at people who thought him a loser. People who disrespected him. Like his boss.

"Listen, Se—" Robert started to say Sergei's name, stopping himself when the Russian looked at him intently, realizing he almost broke one of their cardinal rules. He was never allowed to say Sergei's name, at least not in the United States. It could be a disaster.

"I'm sorry." *Well, they need me, so I am going to ask.* "Listen, I have another request to make." He knew what he was going to ask next would cross a line. But he did not care. "I need a house on an island in the Caribbean, or perhaps a house by the water somewhere nice, but somewhere without an extradition treaty. And European passports for myself and Ludmilla so we can travel freely. Of course, I will need money to live the good life." He steeled himself further, delivering his final demand. "I gave you a lot on the last trip, and I need an exit plan, just in case. I am not going to jail for the rest of my life like Robert Hansen."

"We will consider your request," Sergei whispered, knowing the American's demands were unreasonable considering the information provided. *But you will provide so much more to us, whether you like it or not.*

"That is excellent," Robert responded enthusiastically, only caring that he would get what he wanted. Then another thought crossed his mind. "When can I see my girlfriend again?"

Robert ached for her, loving the feel of her youthful and athletic build. He didn't know she was an SVR captain who could easily kill him. He would not have cared anyway, because he sought to satisfy the carnal desires that first arose early in high school but which he could never fulfill because girls back then never gave him a second look. Or even a first look, for that matter. Well, now things were different. He was in control.

"Soon," Sergei replied, smiling inwardly. As his supervisor predicted, the American was following a path that would enable Sergei to pull strings for years to come. His intelligence would confirm reports from other people, and eventually they would task him with getting more sensitive information. This recruitment would guarantee him prestige and, more importantly, money to live a comfortable life.

BEN AND KATE WALKED ALONG THE BANKS OF THE THAMES, another of London's many bridges. *I am finally starting to get my bearings in the city,* Ben realized, and yet he would have to leave tomorrow for

Bern. He and Kate held hands, comfortable after spending several days together. The Senator arrived two days before and attended numerous meetings organized by Arthur Sinclair, some of which had been real eye-openers.

The British government still maintained an embassy in Tehran, never having broken relations, and so kept more insight into developments in Iran than the United States. It amazed Ben that the United States never reopened even just a presence post in Tehran, operating under the auspices of the Swiss, who represented US interests to the Iranian theocratic regime.

Although his clearance permitted him to attend the meetings, Ben knew they held back information they might otherwise have provided. The Senator sat on the Armed Services Committee, still seeing himself primarily as a Navy veteran who served multiple tours in Vietnam and years at sea.

Normally, the Senator would have traveled with a military aide, but he asked the commander who worked in the office to remain in DC. Ben knew Charles would be annoyed, though less so since the visit had nothing to do with the US military but with Iran. He and Charles got along well enough, having enough in common to justify beers out once a week to exchange notes when both were in DC.

With the Senator meeting with the ambassador at the US Embassy, Ben had the remainder of the afternoon off to spend with Kate. He loved seeing the city through her eyes, having learned to follow her lead because this was *her* city. They turned to cross the bridge over the Thames. *Which bridge is this?* Ben considered, still not able to quite keep them all straight. They turned from the walkway onto the bridge, and Ben saw the Big Ben and Parliament buildings ahead of him. *Westminster Bridge,* Ben realized as they strolled across along the walkway.

On their side of the bridge, the walkway was empty behind them.

There was a gaggle of young schoolchildren ahead of them moving slowly towards Parliament. Ben and Kate took their time, heading for the gardens on the other side of the river. Just then, Ben heard footsteps from behind them that sounded—*felt*—odd.

He walked with Kate on his left, and the man came running up behind him and looking at the group of children. He was oblivious to everything behind him. Ben noted he looked like most anyone else in the area, dressed in what he thought of as business casual clothes. Ben pressed into Kate, moving her closer to the bridge to give the guy plenty of space.

Just as the man came even with Ben and Kate, he whirled around. The flash of a metal blade sliced through the air directly at them. Reacting instinctively, Ben put himself between the man and Kate and shoved her towards the side of the bridge, then raised his arms defensively. The man wielded the knife like an amateur, screaming incomprehensively while slashing madly at Ben.

Kate was lost in thought, happier than she had been in years and staring without thought ahead of her at Big Ben when Ben pushed her towards the bridge. Without thinking, she scanned the area and saw a man attacking Ben wildly with a knife. *Not my boyfriend, you bastard,* she screamed inside.

Ben fended off the man's slashes, thankful for the business clothes he wore beneath his overcoat. The knife was tearing his overcoat and suit to bits. Before he realized what was happening, he saw Kate slam the man to the ground and scream, "Police, police!"

Pedestrians on the other side of the street watched the scuffle in horror as buses, cabs, and motorbikes continued crossing the bridge. The children ahead of them, urged on by panicked teachers, rushed forward to the other side of the bridge, breaking their sloppy lines and stretching the width of the walkway. A man on the other side began running towards the other end of the bridge.

Ben watched Kate calmly and quickly knock the man on his wrist, forcing him to drop the knife. Ben scrambled to grab the knife before the assailant could get away from Kate and get it back. He needn't have worried because Kate was now face-to-face with the attacker, throwing expert punches that flung the man against the bridge's railing.

Ben watched Kate pummel the man. *Mark better watch out if Kate decides to take over as her father's bodyguard!* Simultaneously, he heard screaming police officers as they ran towards them from the Parliament side of the bridge. Ben took several steps back and raised his hands. The police wouldn't know what was happening on the scene. Ben could feel that he was bleeding, but now was not the time to worry about that.

Kate, seeing the police approaching, punched the man several times and then rolled away, coming to rest with her ID held high. She knew the procedures for an attack such as this. The police would arrive at the scene keyed up but would be unable to distinguish the good from the bad guys. The attacker, ignorant of this, stood and screamed incoherently, backing towards the railing and searching for his knife.

"Get down!" the first officer screamed, three other officers quickly joining him. A tall officer stood near Ben with his weapon drawn, and one who appeared out of breath from running stood over Kate. Two officers cautiously approached the man against the railing, their weapons drawn. "Get down!" the two officers yelled simultaneously, yet despite their orders, the man grasped the railing, hoisting himself nearer the river.

Hearing screaming and two shots fired, Ben whipped his head around to see that the man must have jumped off the bridge into the Thames below. *Did he just Peter Pan into the river?* Ben wondered, but he was too aware of the officer standing over him. Two others looked over the bridge's railing and into the river.

Leaning against the railing and feeling lightheaded because he was losing blood, Ben kept his hands above his head. The officer stared at Ben with weapon drawn, but Ben thought he saw the man's finger wasn't directly on the trigger. *Thank God he hasn't shot me.* Ben knew it would have been a different story had this occurred back home.

The officer standing near Kate saw her outstretched hand and cautiously moved forward to examine the ID. "Sarge," the officer called, "we have a lady from Six here."

After he offered her his hand and helped her up, Kate noticed Ben on the ground, his hands still raised. His jacket was in tatters, but he was wisely leaning against the side of the bridge. Kate could not see how anyone could view her boyfriend as a threat, but she knew that in the heat of the moment, anything could happen. She also registered that the man who attacked Ben had jumped over the bridge, but she was now more focused on Ben.

"That is my boyfriend," Kate said calmly, pointing to Ben.

"One moment," the officer said, keeping her back. Just then, Ben's knees buckled, and he crumpled to the ground. Kate rushed forward, bowling over the officer to get to Ben.

"You, get down!" the sergeant screamed at Kate. But he had internalized the information that she was Six. His job was to safeguard her identity while simultaneously controlling the situation.

"He's bleeding out, you fucking idiot! Get an ambulance now, or I'll see to it that you are assigned to guard a beach in Scotland."

The sergeant hesitated, preparing to force her to follow his orders. However, something inside told him that he should reconsider. "Give me her ID," the sergeant demanded, "while you keep an eye on the injured one, and you two keep searching for the man who jumped." He paused, then lost his temper. "And how the hell did he get over the bridge so quickly!"

After mere minutes, the sergeant was thankful the situation was under control. One call placed on a secure police frequency with the ID number resulted in a flurry of vehicles heading to his location. Shortly thereafter, medics arrived from the nearby Parliament and began treating Ben.

The sergeant soon saw numerous helicopters in the air, including one that appeared to take off from the south and head straight for them, hovering overhead. Before he knew it, security officers flooded the bridge, approaching civilians on the other side of the bridge and escorting them away. Meanwhile, police on motorbikes moved traffic that stopped to gawk at the scene, threatening them with arrest if they continued to dither.

While that happened, the sergeant saw patrol boats approach, searching for the man who jumped off the bridge. *I wonder if he survived the impact,* the sergeant thought, *or if we'll find his body floating.*

Less than ten minutes later, as the sergeant relinquished command of the scene to one of his supervisor's supervisors, an imposing man flanked by numerous security officials approached from the other end of the bridge, where several vehicles with flashing lights waited. The man jogged forward, the men and women surrounding him rushing to catch up.

"Kate, darling, are you here?" the man called. He looked a true English gentleman, the sergeant thought, complete with clothes that screamed his wealth and privilege. Though his face was set impassively against the world, and his voice was quite under control, his eyes shone with concern. Here was a man not to be crossed under any circumstances.

The sergeant stood back and watched the events unfold. He felt like he had seen the man somewhere before. The woman from Six refused to leave the bleeding man's side. Even when he was transferred to a stretcher and tended by two medics, she clung tight to his hand.

"Father!" she called out. The sergeant watched the tall man rush to her and hug her fiercely.

"What on earth happened here?" he asked. As if on cue, a disheveled man trailed by three people trotted towards them from the other side of the bridge. His hair was fashionably untidy, and his suit did not look like it fit. There the mayor of London stood.

"My Lord Sinclair," the mayor called. "I rushed over as soon as I heard the news, especially of your family's involvement in this terrible ordeal."

"As I told the inspector just minutes before," Kate said, "the man came rushing up, and before I knew what happened, Ben pushed me away. He shielded me from the attack."

The inspector, a senior detective from Scotland Yard, stepped forward and began telling everyone what to do when he first arrived on the scene.

"Mayor, My Lord," he said, addressing each of the men in turn. "We already confirmed this young lady's story from camera footage."

"This is my daughter," Arthur Sinclair said through gritted teeth, struggling not to lose his temper. Before Arthur could say another word, a deputy commissioner stepped forward and seized control of the situation.

"Were it not for this couple's actions, I daresay the man would have attacked the sizeable group of children walking ahead at the time." The deputy commissioner felt he had the best overview of the situation. Also, he was politically astute enough to know that controlling this situation could benefit him. Greatly. "And your daughter, Lord Sinclair, according to officer reports, struggled with the man, incapacitating him long enough for officers to arrive."

Everyone seemed to relax at that statement, except Arthur Sinclair. "Unfortunately, the man managed to escape, yet our officers fired two shots and may have hit him. We have boats in the water and are searching for him now."

"And my daughter's boyfriend, how is he?" Arthur asked calmly, barely able to control his anger that this happened in the center of London. With *his* daughter involved. His security detail pulled him out of a meeting when they heard Kate's ID number over the police radio, and he immediately drove to Westminster Bridge. He arrived at a chaotic scene but refused to let anyone or anything get between him and Kate.

"Excuse me, ma'am," one of the medics said, gently separating Kate's hand from Ben's, then quickly pushing the stretcher towards a waiting ambulance.

Ben moaned in pain when he felt he was no longer holding Kate's hand and vaguely noticed he was moving. He looked up to see two people on either side of him.

"Ben!" Kate called, watching the medics wheel Ben away and jogging to catch up.

"Kate, wait," Arthur said, surrounded by security personnel who precluded him from racing after his daughter. He watched helplessly as she raced after her boyfriend.

Looking around at the scene, Arthur knew that extremism, if that's what motivated this attack, was an increasing problem in the United Kingdom. He saw Kate get into the ambulance, which quickly departed for the nearest hospital.

"Sir, are you ready to return to headquarters?" Mark asked, standing patiently but nervously near his boss. He didn't like being out in the open like this, always worried about an attack, especially considering the events of the past hour.

"I suppose Kate's American isn't such a bad fellow," Arthur said aloud, not expecting a response. His phone buzzed in his pocket, distracting him from the excitement.

The sergeant looked on from a distance, not understanding everything happening and hoping the injured American would recover quickly and that London's law enforcement would catch the attacker. He looked out on the Thames, wondering where the man was, and was thankful his only remaining task was a stack of dreaded paperwork waiting before he finished his shift.

CHAPTER
EIGHT

 as their plane taxied to the terminal in Bern, "I must say that you bring the notion of a cowboy to the twenty-first century." He eyed Ben carefully, worried that *his* staffer was pushing himself too hard after his involvement in the attack on Westminster Bridge two days before. However, Ben's wounds were hardly life-threatening, instead mostly superficial, yet the loss of blood kept him in the hospital overnight until they discharged him yesterday.

Kate had never seen her father quite as agitated. He promised he would see the attacker in jail for life. The police had caught him within an hour and, according to an intelligence report she read yesterday, he was a disgruntled, unemployed recent Bulgarian immigrant with severe mental health problems.

"I'm still annoyed about my favorite suit," Ben grumbled, rubbing the bandages covering his arms and hands where the attacker slashed with reckless abandon. Kate's father promised him a new suit, a gift from the British crown, but there had not been time. In reality, McKenzie did a phenomenal job packing clothes from his closet and sending them with the Senator as an additional checked bag.

"You're honestly lucky the police kept their heads, especially given the UK's increased terror threats. I heard from the security officer at the embassy that someone"—the Senator glanced at Kate—"knocked over a security officer, and the sergeant at the scene almost lost his head."

"Senator," Kate said, her worried eyes never leaving Ben's face, scrutinizing his demeanor to decide whether he was too tired. "I may have bumped into an officer on my way to assist Ben." She smiled now. "But I can assure you that I made my affiliation with Her Majesty's government clear enough that no one was in serious danger from those personnel."

Across the seat, Ben exhaled, closing his eyes as he rubbed his hands and arms. Kate was worried and felt she should have insisted that Ben stay in hospital. However, none of his injuries were life-threatening, and Ben was stubborn, so he signed himself out of hospital and threatened to check into a hotel if she did not drive him back to her flat.

While their plane taxied, Kate and the Senator individually considered the ramifications of the averted attack from two days before. Kate knew from her father that the PM considered the deranged Bulgarian a terrorist, yet Whitehall kept the entire affair quiet, security officials having successfully confiscated all recordings. Footage from nearby police cameras provided clear corroboration of Ben and Kate's stories, ending any official inquiries. London's mayor wanted to publicize the event, but the PM squashed that quickly given Kate's involvement and Six's desire to keep her identity secret. Kate was happy to put the event behind her.

The Senator, meanwhile, spoke at length with Arthur Sinclair, having bonded over drinks at a private club the night before. Arthur confided that Buckingham Palace heard about the incident and, since it involved children, the Queen was briefed. Her Highness was reportedly interested in a private meeting with Kate and Ben at some point in the future, fascinated after hearing about their involvement and history together. The Senator told the US Ambassador to the United Kingdom, a wealthy donor who helped bankroll the president's campaign, that these types of connections were invaluable and would further align the two countries' policies.

After their plane stopped, the three exited and went to the jetway, then walked through the arrival hall at the Regional Aerodrome Bern-Belp to discover two people waiting to meet them.

"Welcome to Bern, Senator," an American diplomat said, extending her hand as she stepped forward. "My name is Maria Cortez, and I'm the political counselor here. Welcome to Switzerland. The ambassador is only sorry she could not be here personally to see you."

"And from us, Senator"—a British diplomat stepped forward—"we are pleased to support this joint inquiry into events in Iran." The man beamed when he saw Kate and stepped forward to give her a pointedly un-British hug. As far as Ben could tell, Brits were not big into displays of affection, which told Ben that these two had a history.

"Albert!" Kate exclaimed. She hugged him back but then stepped away to stand beside Ben. "Darling, this is Albert Beckett, a friend of mine who will help smooth the way for us here in Bern."

Ben looked at Albert, a tall, brown-haired man who looked like a Ken doll. "Nice to meet you," Ben said. They shook hands as Albert closely examined Ben. During their long chats, Kate told Ben that anyone she referred to as a friend was, in fact, MI6, while anyone she said was a colleague was from the Foreign and Commercial Office, the State Department's Counterpart Agency. It was confusing, Ben admitted as they strolled through the airport to collect their checked bags.

The ride in the US Embassy's van went quickly. Ben and the Senator spoke with Maria, while Kate and Albert spoke about their scheduled discussions with the Swiss government. When they arrived at their hotel, Ben was pleased to find each of them was prechecked into their room, enabling them to rest before their meetings.

Later, at the Swiss Federal Department of Foreign Affairs, they proceeded to a conference room next to Karl Felber's office. He was the head of Political Affairs. They grabbed coffee and small trays filled with chocolate, then sat around a large table, joined by several staff. One gentleman arrived late and sat in the back of the room, though Ben thought he saw all Swiss staff prepared to jump to attention when he entered, halted only by a small wave of his hand. *Who is he?* Ben thought, noticing Kate also watching the man.

"Welcome to all of you," Felber began.

Ben tuned out the following description of relations between Switzerland, the protecting power for the United States in Iran, and the Islamic Republic of Iran. He knew from reports that the former US Embassy in Tehran was now a museum dedicated to educating every Iranian about the evils of the Americans.

"That is all very helpful," the Senator interrupted after some thirty minutes of briefing. "But I am particularly interested in learning more about the driving forces behind the Iranian government's desire for negotiations."

His remark stunned the Swiss diplomat, who appeared to have been prepared to give a lengthy presentation. Ben saw the sheaf of briefing papers and thought he detected a hint of annoyance at being interrupted. As if no one in Switzerland ever interrupted anyone else.

"Senator," the man in the back said, walking forward. "I would be happy to try to answer your questions to save all of us time." He stood erect, like a star cadet at an elite military school, and Ben thought he

saw in this man someone who would have been at home commanding regiments of soldiers into battle on the plains of Europe. He was
clean-shaven and the model of a Swiss gentleman, someone who
obviously grew up with wealth and power. The man mumbled some
words in what Ben realized must have been *Suisse-Deutsch,* the local
dialect. Ben grew up speaking German in his house as a second
language, but the man spoke so rapidly that Ben could not follow.

After half a dozen Swiss bureaucrats followed Felber out of the
room, leaving three standing beside him, the man said, "My name
is Johann Schenk."

Ben guessed that this man, who spoke with such authority, was
likely a Swiss intelligence official. The Swiss intelligence services
merged into the Federal Intelligence Service. He noticed Kate watching the man, obviously not expecting this turn of events. This conversation was about to get much more interesting.

"Herr Felber is quite knowledgeable about many things, but
like many diplomats, he goes on more than necessary," Schenk said.

That cinches it, Ben thought, *because intelligence folks never like
diplomats much.*

"First," Schenk began, taking his seat, "you should know that
the Iranians are only negotiating because they want your country to
remove decades of sanctions. They have no other motivation." Schenk
sat erect, not leaning either against the back or the handles of his chair.

Ben felt like he was lazy and instinctively sat up and straightened
his shoulders as he listened carefully.

"Second, the Iranian government remains in a state of chaos
following the 2009 presidential election, still recovering from the
people's response to what they saw as suspicious election results."
He paused for questions, then continued. "The hardliners emerged
stronger than ever, with Grand Ayatollah Shirazi encouraging the
Supreme Leader to suppress the protests."

Looking around, his eyes found Ben, and Schenk smiled, seemingly a painful act on his part. "I believe this young man even met the Grand Ayatollah some months back, correct?" It was less a question than an accusation.

All eyes focused on Ben. Obviously not everyone knew that Kate had also been there, clandestinely recording everything. He wasn't about to share that fact with anyone.

"Yes, sir," Ben said, willing himself to remain calm but remembering some of the stress from the chance encounter with one of the most powerful men in Iran. "The Grand Ayatollah had an aura about him, as if he radiated energy."

Beside Ben, Kate listened, comprehending that the Swiss didn't know she also attended the meeting in Herat. The purpose had been to return a Kalashnikov to Behzad Bashiri, the Afghan Minister of Counter Narcotics. But it turned into a shouting match when Ben, operating under orders from DC, declined to permit the Afghans to prosecute the soldier who shot three people, setting off a chain of events that led to thirteen dead Americans in North Dakota and an apparent roadside bomb that killed Bashiri's youngest son. She was grateful for the turn of events, even though tragic actions by a multitude of people left many dead. Without this terrible series of events, she and Ben might never have bonded and cemented their relationship.

Schenk managed another painful smile, then continued. "Third, the Iranian government desperately needs payment for the oceans of oil they shipped to China and other consumers. However, your sanctions effectively halt all efforts at renumeration, frustrating Iran's leaders. They need money to continue spreading their foreign policy throughout the region. And the world."

"But," the Senator asked, speaking up after listening carefully, "will the Iranians keep their word? Can we trust any deal they make with us?"

Schenk grimaced, which Ben surmised was the man's attempt to show amusement at the question. "Senator, I will respond to your question with two of my own. First, what can you possibly do to incentivize the Iranian religious leaders to keep their word when the world is forever changing? And second, how can you expect them to trust that you, or any other country, will keep your word when you give it to them?" But Schenk was not done.

"You must understand, Senator," Schenk implored, leaning forward on the table to make his point, "the Iranian people have held grievances against the United States and Great Britain going back to the fifties." He scanned the room, looking at Maria, the political counselor, then at Albert, and finally at Ben and Kate.

"Nothing you can say or do," Schenk continued, "will convince them that you do not wish to end their control over the Iranian people. Especially," Schenk whispered, which seemed to echo through the room, "when you, Senator, speak so regularly with the *mujahideen*, who seek to overthrow the Iranian religious leaders." He paused, as if tired from speaking so much, and the room grew quiet. The other Swiss officials sat watching, as they had throughout the conversation.

"In that case, our visit was successful," the Senator responded morosely. He stood, with Ben, Kate, Maria, and Albert all rising to join the most senior member of their group. It was an unwritten protocol that every government official learned on the first day: The most senior member of any delegation dictates whether to stay or leave. The Senator walked to where Schenk stood, inquiring in the directness that Ben knew so well, "Exactly which Swiss bureaucracy do you represent?"

"I represent the Swiss government's intelligence service, Senator," he said, rising to shake the Senator's hand. "But I hope you are not leaving quite yet," Schenk said, surprising the Senator.

"We have plenty more to share with you, and this evening, all of you will be my guests," Schenk announced. He smiled again, and Ben realized at that moment that Schenk reminded him of a mortician, someone comfortable with death. It gave him power that set him apart from everyone else.

"Plus," Schenk added, "I have questions for your young colleague." He stared at Ben, his eyes drilling in as if trying to read his mind. Ben wondered if he indeed might have that power. "Our diplomats in Tehran heard that Grand Ayatollah Shirazi was quite taken with Mr. Brownwell and was impressed with his language skills, ability to hold his own, and respect for the Persian culture."

Ben was shocked, never thinking that the Grand Ayatollah had registered his existence. He flashed back to that moment in Minister Bashiri's home, proud that he held his ground. Visualizing the elderly man surrounded by men in Revolutionary Guard uniforms, Ben knew he was one of a handful of people outside of Iran who had ever laid eyes on arguably one of the most powerful men in Iran. People at Langley and throughout DC questioned him for a week, many envious of the chance encounter.

"Well then," the Senator said, recovering quickly, as any good politician would, "we, of course, accept your offer and look forward to your hospitality." They resumed their seats, settling in for long discussions about the complexity of Iran. Ben took copious notes for the Senator, careful not to miss any gems from their host.

RAMIN WALKED THROUGH THE STREETS, his expert tradecraft ensuring no one followed him. He used the same techniques the Teacher taught him decades before, doubling back, pausing at shop windows, and walking around streets. His goal was to force anyone following him to make a mistake and show themselves. Satisfied that he was clear, he continued meeting with al-Sadr and his fellow Iraqis in the same abandoned warehouse. It was in a part of town rarely visited by locals, as it was now overrun by migrants fleeing devastation in Iraq and surrounding countries.

As he approached, Ramin reminded himself that these men were his tools, useful to send a message to the Americans. The previous day, he met with the American alcoholic, who remained frustrated in his job and longed for revenge against the ambassador. Per his training, Ramin reported everything securely to the Teacher, who offered suggestions to improve the operation. They communicated using an internet portal contained within a website that sold Korans to people around the world. That was an effective front, but clicking on a secret link buried within the pages enabled him to submit reports and chat with his fellow Immortals.

The Iraqis were in much better spirits then when he met them, as they had been in subsequent meetings since they could not feed their families. By the time they finished the operation, Ramin knew they would set off for Germany right away. In a separate conversation, he prohibited the men from sending their families ahead, knowing if he lost control of them, it would be impossible to ensure they completed the operation.

The Teacher questioned him earlier that day about how he would deal with them after the operation. He should leave no loose ends, yet he also raised the possibility that if they were successful and did not die in the attack, they could be useful in the future. *If they survive.*

"A salaam aleykum," Ramin said to the gathered men, entering the light emitted by the small fire. The man who stood sentry outside the warehouse followed him to the fire. He insisted on better security for all of them, not wanting to risk the operation.

"Wa aleykum a salaam," the men replied in unison, standing to greet their benefactor. Hassan, who spoke for the men, rose and gave the Iranian his seat. Ramin felt the fabric and, though he could not see the patterns, could feel the tight, irregular stitches that were likely made by these men's wives.

"We have made much progress in the past weeks since we first met." He surveyed them, pleased to see they were all sitting a bit straighter in their chairs, better fed and more confident than when they first met. Having a mission gave a man purpose in life, which is what these men needed more than anything. "You are all now familiar with and have memorized the operational details?" He searched each face, hoping to find no sign of weakness, which would guarantee that man would be removed from the operation. Indeed, he realized grimly, anyone who failed to perform would experience the harsh justice of the Immortals.

"We're ready," Hassan replied. He reminded himself that he was a member of the al-Sadr family, one of the most powerful in Iraq. Things had changed since the hated Saddam Hussein and his Baathist party lost control of the country, with the Shia taking control while the Sunnis were being put in their rightful place.

"Our next step," Ramin said, nodding his approval, "is some weapons training. I assume none of you have fired a weapon in some months."

"We are all familiar with Kalashnikov rifles and have no need to reacquaint ourselves with those weapons," Hassan replied, hiding sarcasm.

Ramin tensed when he heard the boasting rebuke from the Iraqi. He contemplated slapping the man for his disrespect but sat watching, letting the silence make the men uncomfortable.

Sensing he may have spoken too forcefully, judging by the Iranian's narrowed eyes, Hassan backpedaled. "However, we, of course, are happy to engage in refresher training. To prove that we are ready," he added. "No man is perfect, and all may require some practice."

"It's good that you are ready to train," Ramin replied, eliminating emotion from his voice. He wished he could have chosen other men for this mission, but these were his men. And they were expendable.

Little did they know, the Iraqi's insolence cemented in Ramin's mind his decision to adjust the plan ever so slightly. He knew these men were proud and had to seize control where they could, but he also could not countenance them acting or thinking independently. The money he paid them came from the Grand Ayatollah's foundation. If successful, it would be worthwhile, but if their foolishness cost him a victory, then he would get his revenge on each of these men. And their families.

Setting those thoughts aside, Ramin needed to remain focused. He gave directions and instructions for where they could meet next, in a forest outside of town. They would have to ride a bus, which was their problem to resolve, but it was a sufficiently secluded location where they could each fire several clips of ammunition, proving to Ramin that they had the skills necessary for the operation.

CHAPTER
NINE

" Nick said as they sat in the Iran Desk's conference room. "You are like a brother, and I will always be there for you, but you could have given us a heads up that the Senator was skipping off to Switzerland to speak about Iran." He paused, reading from his notebook. "Susan wants your head on a pike, saying that you are a hotshot who doesn't hold allegiance to the Department."

What a way to start November, Ben thought morosely. The door was partially closed, open just enough for others in the office to hear their conversation. As he spoke, secure in the knowledge that everyone was listening, Nick wrote on his notepad. He flipped the page, showing Ben, while continuing to read. *Susan instructed me to tell you this. Sorry, man.* The note meant Ben was not truly in trouble with his friend. Nick was only acting on orders. He understood that even if it hurt a bit to have to play this game with one of his oldest friends.

Ben listened to the tirade, mentally taking notes so he could report back to Marty and, by extension, the Senator. This told him that their meetings with the Swiss succeeded in conveying the

Senator's concerns, which Schenk obviously shared. Ben realized that under normal circumstances, in a secure room like this, he could have confided in Nick that Schenk regaled them with tales for hours that evening. Everyone left his club feeling positive that they had an ally who understood the true gravity of the situation, even if the political masters in Washington didn't.

After leaving Bern, they flew back through London, but the Senator insisted that Ben accompany him back to Washington before the start of the weekend. Kate was furious with the Senator for taking Ben away from her, especially when he was still injured and needed someone to tend to him. Her parents considered visiting the airport to see Ben off, but Arthur couldn't avoid a meeting with the Prime Minister. Ben was glad he had those last few minutes with Kate. Her parting words were "Don't you let anyone else tend to your wounds, or those will turn fatal." It was the best joke she could summon.

Now, he sat in the State Department's building on C Street, between 21st and 23rd Streets, a mammoth, sprawling building that housed thousands of employees on seven floors. The Westminster Attack, as it was publicized in Britain, was overshadowed in the US by the Occupy Wall Street protests. Ben's involvement in preventing the attack was never publicly known, though reports continued to circulate that an American was somehow involved. Ben and Kate did not speak quite every day, but when they did, he half expected her to jump through the line to care for him.

After a several-minute tirade, one that Ben could tell Nick was trying to tone down as much as possible, Nick winked and then stormed out. Collecting his bag, Ben walked through the office with his head held high. The fact was that Susan and others were taking a policy disagreement personally, which Ben knew was a mistake. *People take their jobs too seriously,* he reminded himself, *and need to realize the world is not necessarily a zero-sum game.*

Before leaving the office, Ben retrieved his phones and headed for the jogger's exit, a side door that would enable him to head back towards the Capitol and his desk. He knew that in the grand scheme of things, taking sides in a battle over Iran would not mean much, so he shook off his worries and set off along Constitution Avenue. He could have caught a taxi but decided walking was important, especially since tomorrow he knew he could take off his bandages and gain full mobility of his wrists.

After passing through security, waved in by the Capitol guards who by now recognized him and his tangle of badges around his neck, Ben sped through the hallways to the Senator's suite of offices. Adjusting his tie and smoothing the collar of his suit coat, Ben thanked the weather for being cool enough that he could walk twenty blocks comfortably.

"All hail the conquering hero," bellowed a voice as Ben entered the suite. Ben realized that the guards must have tipped off the Senator's staff, who were all milling around the suite's entryway.

"What is this?" Ben nearly shouted as staffers surrounded him with claps on the back. Blushing slightly, not accustomed to being the center of attention, Ben saw the Senator standing at the door to his office, beaming with pride.

"There is the man who single-handedly warmed the frosty relations between the US and UK," the Senator announced, and Ben was thankful he closed the door as he entered, else every office on that corridor would have known. "Come in, Ben, come in and let's talk."

It wasn't an invitation but more of an order from the retired Naval officer. His respect for the Senator grew each day.

"How are your arms healing, Ben?" Marty asked, taking a seat while several other senior staffers settled on couches in the Senator's spacious office. The space was already arranged, with Ben seated near the Senator, and he set his bag down, ready for the long haul.

An hour later, Ben exited the office suite, searching for lunch. The Senator retold how Ben bravely jumped in front of the attacker, wisely leaving out mention of Kate as anything but a "passerby," to the raised eyebrows of several staffers. Many had worked on the Hill for at least a decade, staying out of loyalty to a man who they respected more than the lure of K Street lobbying jobs.

They all viewed him with a new sense of admiration, perhaps even wary respect. It wasn't every day that someone could say they jumped in front of a foreign terrorist to protect a gaggle of school children. The military officers joined others in taking notes, prepared to share the story, which, as the Senator warned, was classified. That made it even juicier, a story that would be more fun to spread around the Pentagon or in the White House. In Washington, secrets were power.

Ben sidestepped tour groups, trying to avoid them as he walked through the halls. Truth be told, he was no hero, just someone who saw a threat to his girlfriend. *Anyone would have done the same in my shoes,* he reasoned, not fully comprehending that many people selfishly protected themselves, even over those they loved.

In the cafeteria, Ben saw the long line of staffers waiting for food, so he took a table and pulled a copy of *The Economist* from his suit pocket.

He exhaled loudly and started to read an article, then felt someone tapping him on his right shoulder. The last thing he wanted to do was talk with anyone, but as a denizen of the DC area, he knew it was always best to check who was there. He looked to his right, expecting to see a staffer, but instinctively slapped the latest edition of *The Economist* on the table, jumping to his feet.

"Mr. Vice President, sir, a pleasure to meet you."

"Ah, don't give me that crap, Ben." The vice president chuckled and punched the Senator's shoulder as he approached. The Senator was his longtime political opponent. "This isn't our first meeting." The VP looked at the Senator and explained, "I met Ben in September when the president awarded him for his role in disrupting the Minot Massacre from being far worse than it turned out to be." He waved Ben back into his seat and sat down in a chair opposite.

"Where can I get a cup of coffee around here?" he asked as the Senator and others joined them at the table.

ROBERT SLOUCHED IN HIS CHAIR and kept his arms folded across his chest. *I made a reasonable demand, dammit, and I expect them to honor it.* He wanted to be certain he would be safe, just in case he was found out. He crossed his arms, letting his displeasure hang over the table.

Opposite him, Sergei was in a serious bind. Moscow Center balked at the list of demands, deeming what the American delivered so far to be insufficient to merit passports, a promise of a retirement home, and the extravagant amounts of money this man wanted. They wanted more but did authorize him some token of their appreciation.

"Da," Sergei said, making a show of giving in. "You have given us good information." He smiled broadly, a Russian smile that ended at the eyes. "However, you must provide more information, especially that we consistently requested." *You bastard,* Sergei mused, *you will pay if you ever stop producing for us.*

"As a sign of our appreciation, here are photos of your and your wife's passports." He slid across two photocopies, knowing that the passports would be destroyed if the American ever got greedy. Even that step of procuring two European passports required significant approval because they required an expenditure of resources. Robert picked up the two pieces of paper, inspecting them carefully, and Sergei fumed at the need to be so solicitous to this fool. *But he is a fool with access.*

"We have this for you." He slid a brown leather satchel across the table, giving it a slight shove before letting go. Robert set aside the two photocopies of the passports he and Ludmilla would need to travel the world. Richard and Bethany Adams, the passports read but with their photos. He did not consider where Sergei procured such quality photos of them. They just needed to accede to his demands.

Robert's hands shook as he opened the satchel, finding small bundles of cash that could not total more than $25,000, as well as three credit cards. He held up the cards. "What are these?"

"Those are cards under your and your wife's names, into which we will deposit funds so you can, how would you say, *improve* your lifestyle. They are credit cards issued by a European bank that you can use for any purchase, but you must never spend more than $10,000 at any time." Sergei leaned forward. "If you stop providing us with documents, the cards will stop working." *And we will come looking for you,* he didn't say.

"That's great," Robert responded, oblivious to everything but wondering what to buy first. *Perhaps that necklace she wanted?* "And this one?" He held up a separate card.

"That's a card for your use in Europe. You must *never* use that card in this country." He stared at the American, who held the three cards and was mentally already spending money. All told, he just gave the American the equivalent of just over $50,000 but with the hitch that the Russian government could easily turn off the cards for nonpayment.

In the past, their sources always demanded cash, but in the modern world, the SVR discovered that giving cards and having that threat hanging over their heads worked as an added incentive. This way they would also know precisely where the American was without having to track him at all times, using valuable resources.

Robert looked up and smiled. "Thank you, I am pleased." Now it was time to deliver the goods. He had not provided any intelligence reports in at least three meetings, always claiming that he would give nothing until they completed the task.

He picked up his briefcase, but he was already thinking about Ludmilla. She wanted him to quit the government and enter the private sector to make more money. With the cash and cards he received, Robert could mollify her and continue with the Foreign Service. He loved the access to secrets and power; it was like a drug. With this money, he could make her happy and keep his career. The best of both worlds.

"Here," Robert announced as if expecting a standing ovation, "are documents I would have given you before, had you made up your mind earlier." He pulled from his briefcase a sheaf of photocopies.

Sergei picked them up as Robert watched on expectantly. His left hand clenched into a fist at the man's insolence, but he controlled himself. He was a senior SVR intelligence officer, a man whose reports the president himself had seen! He would control himself, taking out his aggression and exercising his demons later that night, as usual.

"*Nichevo,*" Sergei whispered, not believing his eyes. Robert watched as Sergei devoured each of the pages, reading through the detailed minutes of NATO meetings, reports on troops' movements in Europe, and, most importantly, talks about possible NATO expansion. *This is it,* Sergei realized as he gripped the papers tightly. *These are what we want.*

Looking at Robert, Sergei relaxed and set the papers down. "These are fine, just fine, but you see, we are still looking for ever more sensitive documents, ones about the sources and methods of collecting." He continued to lecture Robert for several more minutes, covering the same topics as before. It was the technique of not allowing the asset, *his asset,* to get too comfortable.

"Okay," Robert said absently, still focused on spending his newfound money, "but I'll only share what I feel comfortable sharing." He met Sergei's eyes. "I don't mind helping your government, but my wife feels passionately about Eastern European countries' independence." He smiled, then added, "Of course, I do too."

This is not going as I predicted, Sergei realized, *and this man's Ukrainian wife's ideas are preventing me from getting the material I need.* "When would you like to see your girlfriend again?" Sergei asked casually. He knew they needed to maintain control over their asset, which was best achieved with direct contact.

"Not now," Robert said, waving his hand dismissively. "She has been fun, but I want to enjoy this money with my wife." He stood and gathered everything back into the leather satchel, then put his coat back on. "I will keep working with you," Robert said arrogantly, "but on my terms."

They bid farewell, the American not comprehending how the Russian understood his last statement. Sergei took a circuitous route back to his car, always checking for someone tailing him. *The American's wife,* he grasped, *means we can never fully control him or exert true pressure to compel his actions.*

He thought about that carefully, absentmindedly hefting the briefcase with the documents the American provided in his hands. *Moscow will appreciate these documents, but they will want further results.* Sergei knew that the Tsar demanded immediate results and never accepted mediocrity. A plan began forming in his mind, one that would compel the American. The Russian government had done it before, but as always, he would need guidance and approval from Moscow.

BRENT SLUNK INTO HIS OFFICE, closed the shades, and withdrew a bottle from his desk. He had slept on a couch since the day he caught his wife screwing the ambassador and hadn't said more than five words total to her since then. *How could she? We have children,* he fumed. They had been married for so many years, and this was how she repaid him.

He thought about his latest meeting with the businessman, occurring regularly enough now because he seized on his *need* to vent to *someone.* The man asked questions yet never took notes, which at times seemed strange to Brent. *If I were a businessman looking to learn something, wouldn't I take notes if someone gave me good information?* It seemed almost casual how, over the weeks, Brent began bringing documents to show his friend, most sensitive but unclassified, a few classified. He needed to give back to the man who listened to him for hours.

Eyeing his computers, he logged on and sorted through materials, deciding what he would and would not share with the businessman. The man claimed to be from somewhere in Eastern Europe, but Brent deduced after numerous meetings that the man was likely Middle Eastern. *I'm not spying for anyone, just sharing information with a friend,* he thought, though, with guilt, he remembered the oath he swore to support and defend the Constitution. *I'm not really doing anything wrong, am I?*

He began mouthing the words as he scrolled through sensitive and classified documents, realizing he needed to be cautious. His friend offered suggestions for how he could undermine the ambassador, very astute ideas, and Brent realized that he would stop at virtually nothing to get even with the ambassador. However, he felt—*no, knew*—that he was in control of the situation. This was a friendship, where each side gave and took. *That makes sense, right?*

As he printed out documents, Brent made a point of ruffling the pages, never wanting them to appear he was printing them just to give them away. They would sit in his office for several days, as had others, before he would claim he shredded them. In fact, they would leave the embassy in his briefcase and go into the waiting hands of his friend Radek.

That one won't do too much damage, he mused, *but definitely not that one.* He wanted to show a shred of loyalty to protect information. Simultaneously, he wanted to get even with his cheating wife but stopped himself. *Stacey has been a good wife for a long time, and my children need a mother, even one who is a bad wife.* Where would they be without their parents? He did not want to think what would happen to them, with his family and Stacey's fighting for custody. He wanted them to live in a happy home, which seemed impossible now.

Lifting the shade to look out the window, Brent knew tonight was his night with the kids. He and Stacey did their best to make it seem he was busy at work, but he missed being around them. *Perhaps after I get my revenge on that cheating ambassador, we could reset. Maybe get back together,* he considered optimistically. A small smile spread on his face, the first in a long time, and on his drive back home, he stopped to buy gifts and takeout for the kids, as well as flowers for Stacey. It was a small step, but he couldn't expect anything from her. Not yet.

CHAPTER
TEN

LUDMILLA MORGAN EXITED THE STORE, her arms full of bags. She walked with a bounce in her step. Robert had been unhappy for years no matter how she tried to distract him from his frustrations at work. She was a good Ukrainian wife, grateful to her husband for providing her a life of glamour and travel, one she never could have imagined when she finished university.

Exiting the mall at Tyson's Corner, she was happy because Robert gave his blessing to buy whatever she wanted using the new credit card. Over the past several weeks, he paid more attention to her, real attention. He was not focused on his phone, or watching television, or reading work documents at home. He returned three weeks before with a present, a simple bunch of flowers and a bottle of wine, but for him, that showed interest. She cooked dinner that night, as she always did, but he stayed in the kitchen and talked to her about his day. It was as if they had traveled back in time to when they first met, when he found joy in life.

She smiled when she remembered finding him in the kitchen making breakfast for her. She almost screamed in surprise, because he had not willingly spent time in the kitchen since they moved back from their last overseas assignment. Not unless she was out. Still, she gratefully ate the breakfast, then was pleasantly surprised when he made love to her on the kitchen island, making him late for work. She giggled as she recalled that they forgot to close the curtains, so their neighbors caught them in the act. *But not before we both finished,* she thought smugly.

Since that first day, Robert was once again the man she married, no longer a stranger. A devout Catholic who spent her formative years in Western Ukraine on the Polish border, Ludmilla thanked God once again for her good fortune. And the return of her husband's happiness. Two weeks ago, he gave her a new credit card, telling her to buy what she wanted, within reason. She strode to her car, parked in the covered garage, and placed her bags inside. Not really paying attention, she hummed to herself, distracted by her happiness.

SERGEI WATCHED FROM A DISTANCE, thinking through his discussions with Moscow. They researched Ludmilla Morgan, delving into her background, and concluded she would be an obstacle to what they needed from the American. That she was a beautiful Slavic woman was beside the point. Moscow was elated at the documents the American provided, but that was three weeks ago, with no additional deliveries scheduled. He left numerous signs to schedule a meeting with the American and prearranged leaflets in his neighborhood, but the stubborn American ignored them.

Last week, Moscow ordered Sergei to bump into the American, casually, and apply pressure. The arrogant man's response—"I'm busy now but will make time for you soon"—was the kind of brush-off Sergei would not accept. *We paid you money! You owe us!* To make matters worse, the Russian government was feeling pressure because of increased tensions with Ukraine, as well as criticism from

Western nations for weapons sales. The general in command of his directorate, Konstantin Alexandrovich, approved action to force the American further into their control.

THE MAN STARTED HIS AGING VOLVO as the target stood staring into the distance. It had to be a Volvo because it was one of few cars made completely from steel, not from plastic or other composite materials. This vehicle could take the shock of slamming into another car at ninety kilometers per hour, without more than superficial damage, and still have the power to get away quickly. They searched for weeks for such a car, finding a model from the nineties at a used car lot and buying it with cash. Mechanics replaced enough of the engine that it purred when running, which was better than the clacking sound when he first started it for a test drive.

Get in your car, woman, the man willed, wanting to leave America and return to his beloved homeland and bees. He was a man of few pleasures, though he relished his bees and his small house. *Once I complete this mission, I will have enough money to buy my neighbor's land.* He smiled at the thought of expanding the small plot of land that his grandmother left him, one of the few possessions he truly prized. *I will grow pigs,* he thought suddenly, the idea coming to him like a light, and he smiled, excited at the prospect.

Now get in the car so I can finish my business. Then I can return home, where things are organized. He wiped a speck of dust off the dashboard, preferring order to disorder even though his special skill was creating chaos, applied for decades to aid his government.

ROBERT SAT IN THE SECURE CONFERENCE ROOM, in a far corner from the door, with no means of escape. The speaker droned on, reciting details he already knew about Eastern European military strength. It was another briefing by Pentagon officials about the need to defend against the Russians, else Europe would fall just like when the Iron Curtain went up.

Allowing his mind to wander, Robert thought about the past three weeks when he stopped obsessing over work and his lack of success to instead focus on Ludmilla. He romanced his wife. *And she responded,* he reflected. It made him happy to know he had his wife back as a major part of his life. *I never stopped loving her.*

She's getting older, his mind argued. She wasn't as young and lithe as when they first met. Didn't he deserve the most beautiful woman in the world? And yet, he found that their passion together was better than that which he found with other women.

Robert considered the numerous signals from Sergei, including the very odd in-person chance encounter last week. He dismissed the Russian's obvious agitation. *They will get more documents when I am ready,* he reasoned, feeling fully in control of the situation.

He and Ludmilla each used their cards to buy nice things—*which I earned with those documents*—and he would provide more material in the coming weeks. *They need me more than I need them, right?* He knew that with this money, his marriage would be happier, he could truly focus while at work, and he could score a better chance at promotion this year.

He looked at his notepad, lost in thoughts about his future, and without thinking wrote down the numbers listed off by the briefer. He examined her, sitting a bit straighter in his chair to see her full figure, and saw that she was quite attractive. *But she is not Ludmilla!*

Shaking his head, Robert fought to stay focused on the content of the presentation. Not the presenter, but the presentation.

Eastern Europe's Defense Against a Potential Russian Invasion.

LUDMILLA GOT IN THE CAR, her husband's Audi, and started the engine. Though it was only mid-October, she turned on the heated seats, relishing the warmth on her bottom. She looked in the mirror, pleased with the makeup she bought, and grinned mischievously at the thought of the lingerie that waited in the trunk. *Tonight,* she mused, *I will keep him too distracted to concentrate on the television.*

She backed the Audi out of the spot, then throttled it forward, as Robert taught her to drive. *You must be aggressive on the road,* she remembered him saying, *and this car will always keep you safe.* Working the manual transmission expertly, she exited the mall and turned onto Route 7 for her drive home. She did not notice the vehicle following her. Unfortunately, Ludmilla's unfamiliarity with her husband's car, and the lights being in her favor, meant she did not notice how squishy the Audi's brakes were. Unbeknownst to her or her husband, a trained mechanic broke into her car while she shopped that day and replaced the brake lines with a pair far beyond their service date for a car only three years old.

THE MAN FOLLOWED from a distance, trailing farther behind by two additional vehicles: one, a taxi driver who would ask no questions and transport the man directly to the airport; the second car watching curiously as the beautiful woman drove to her death.

Having studied his target over the past week, knowing which turns she took, Sergei watched as Valentin sped up as they neared the 66 interchange with Route 7, chosen especially because of the road construction and the gaps in the rail guards. In actuality, an associate last week destroyed a rental vehicle on that same stretch of road, guaranteeing compromised structural integrity of the rail guards.

The man sped expertly, machine-like, to catch the Audi. Though he would mourn the loss of the beautiful woman inside, his task was set, the time passed for him to deviate from his plan.

After turning from Route 7 onto 66 eastbound, Ludmilla slowed as she crossed the bridge. There were virtually no other cars around and, as surveillance determined, no cameras.

Okay, the man thought, speeding to drive parallel to the woman's car. As they approached the gap, he counted down before slamming on the gas and jerking to the right.

The second car's occupant watched from a distance, elated to see everything went to plan. The Volvo slammed into the Audi, and the car slid easily through the gap in the guard rails. The man driving the Volvo continued approaching from the left lane, speeding to avoid the cars that swerved to stop at the sight of the Audi disappearing through the gap. The man corrected his vehicle and, without looking back, sped to meet at the rendezvous with the taxi three miles away.

He will make a clean getaway and get on the plane before anyone ever finds his vehicle, the man in the second follow car told himself as he drove to his office. *The man is a true legend.* The taxi driver, a man who did favors without asking questions, had an associate who would firebomb the vehicle using high-octane fuel, ensuring nothing would remain but a charred hunk of metal.

ROBERT PERMITTED HIMSELF to look at his watch, bored to tears by the questions from the men and women around the table. *These people—these idiots!—are the reason why America is no longer as great as it once was.*

With a rush, everyone stared as the door to the secure conference room flew open, a rumpled woman in a knit dress and matching cardigan rushing into the room.

"Robert, where are you?" she yelled, searching the room for him. The presenters looked aghast, unaccustomed to people interrupting their presentation. The man before them was an expert from the NSA who specialized in satellite imagery, a man more comfortable with computers than people.

Robert stood. "Tammy?"

Everyone stared at him, sure nothing like this ever happened in their small world of intelligence. They looked from the man in his pressed suit to the woman in her knit dress and cardigan, wondering what to make of the puzzle before them.

"Robert," Tammy shouted, "your wife was in a terrible car accident. You must come now."

Rushing from his seat, practically climbing over people, Robert forced his way to the front, firmly grabbing hold of Tammy's arm as he dragged her from the room.

In a flood of tears, she cried out, "They think someone murdered her."

Even after Robert closed the door, everyone in the room heard him scream, "What do you mean? And why would you say someone killed her?"

THIRTY MINUTES LATER, ROBERT SAT in the back of an official vehicle from the Department's motor pool. Jonathan, his office director, arranged for a vehicle to take him out to the INOVA hospital in Fairfax, nearest to the accident. The Foreign Service took care of its own, and getting a taxi to navigate DC traffic would have taken so much longer. In the front seat, armed as a precaution, was a member of Diplomatic Security. Jonathan alerted them to the possibility that Robert's wife was murdered.

Speeding along the streets, with lights flashing, the professional driver took turns at nearly fifty miles per hour, confident he could make them with judicious use of the emergency brake. He momentarily looked in the mirror at the man who sat in shock, driving the way he would want someone to drive him if his wife was in the hospital. The flashing lights alerted local police that the federal vehicle rushing into Virginia's northern suburbs was on official business and, therefore, no one should interfere.

I don't even have my bag, Robert thought, *and I don't really care.* He sat staring at a framed photo of Ludmilla. He picked it up absently when he entered his office and never put it down. This photo, taken on their wedding day, traveled from post to post with him, always on his desk.

Careening into the hospital's parking lot twenty minutes later, twice as fast as anyone could legally make the drive, the Suburban screeched to a halt, the Diplomatic Security agent holding open the rear door and then rushing in after the man he was assigned to help.

Inside, Robert rushed to a desk, shouting his wife's name almost incoherently. Without realizing what he was doing, Robert began pounding on the desk, demanding to see his wife. *It cannot be true. I made love to my wife this morning, and she must return home so we can go out to her favorite restaurant.*

With the Diplomatic Security agent standing at his shoulder, a doctor approached and asked him calmly, "Excuse me, are you Mr. Morgan?" Robert nodded, momentarily mute. He wanted to scream, but he had to hear what the doctor said. "I'm so sorry," the doctor started, "but there was nothing we—" The doctor stopped when Robert dropped to the floor.

CHAPTER
ELEVEN

 as Ben walked the jetway into the terminal. The Senator and Marty sent him to scout out the location and engage with the ambassador ahead of the Congressional Delegation, or CODEL. Ben heard the ambassador was a blowhard. Looking up the name in the email system, he remembered that he previously met the political and economic chief at lunch a few times during language training several years ago.

The State Department's Foreign Service Institute, located in Arlington on a sprawling campus that once housed the predecessor to the National Security Agency, was one of the federal government's best educational establishments. Students could learn one of more than one hundred languages and could learn skills ranging from public diplomacy to consular tradecraft, as well as other professional skills.

During his time with the Foreign Service, Ben had spent years in those buildings, marveling at the people training for multiyear assignments. He studied Russian for a year before his first assignment, then Arabic for a year before his second assignment, and finally Farsi for a year before serving in Afghanistan. Most FSOs did not get so many languages so early in their careers, but he considered it one of the best perks of the job, namely that he could reach a level of real, professional proficiency, giving him marketable skills if he ever chose to do something different. Ben also spoke French and German, but never served where those were spoken as a primary language.

As he exited passport control, Ben saw a sign with his name on it. He strode to the sign's owner. "Hi. I'm Ben. Thanks for coming to get me."

"You're welcome," Brent replied, not really meaning it because this guy was an added pain in his ass. He heard enough from his desk officer, who heard from the Iran Desk, that this Ben Brownwell character thought he was more important than anyone in the same time zone. *I wonder how he and the ambassador will get along.* They walked together to collect Ben's bag.

"I'm pretty sure we overlapped at FSI a few years ago, back when I studied Farsi," Ben commented as they walked, searching his memory.

"Yeah, you're probably right," Brent said, though he wasn't going to treat the man screwing up his schedule any differently just because they spoke a few times at FSI.

Met at the exit by the waiting embassy driver, Brent trailed behind to watch Ben drag his own bag after refusing the driver's offer. *Well, at least he isn't such an asshole that he cannot carry his own bag.*

Their drive from the airport was painful because, as Brent expected, Ben asked about the city. In better times, Brent would have expounded upon the wonders and beauty of the city, pointing out landmarks. He was somewhat happier than a month ago because, after he brought flowers for his wife weeks ago, their relationship thawed. Even slightly.

Stacey was nicer to him now, or at least talking to him, and he noticed she no longer went out secretly at night as much as she did when he first caught her cheating. For the first time in months, they even ate dinner as a family, something they used to do all the time. They still could not spend time alone in a room together, Stacey always leaving whenever he entered to collect his clothes for the day, but at least they could stand one another when with the kids. *This is progress, I know it is. I will fight for her.*

The driver pulled up to the hotel, where Ben dropped his bag, and they drove to the embassy. Brent explained that the ambassador wanted to speak with Ben immediately.

For his part, Ben confirmed that he and Brent previously met, but the man was different than he remembered. Gone was the man who laughed and told jokes, replaced instead by a man of quiet intensity. As they passed through embassy security, then entered the chancery so Ben could collect a badge, Brent spoke very little but responded to questions.

"Welcome to *my* embassy," Ambassador Richards quipped, standing as Ben and Brent entered the office.

Ben braced himself for the conversation, knowing he had to deliver bad news to the man before him. Before departing, the Senator relayed that he agreed with the White House to not vocally oppose the negotiations so long as main logistics and control were handled in Washington. The Senator still vehemently opposed the negotiations but recalled too clearly a slight made by Ambassador Richards during his confirmation ceremony. Ben hoped the ambassador would not be too annoyed at the message he was about to deliver.

After they finished pleasantries and the protocol staff brought tea and coffee, they sat at a small table, the ambassador claiming a chair and Brent oddly sitting as far away as possible.

"You don't have to be here, you know," Richards said, startling Ben.

"Ambassador, I thought you wanted to speak with me about the negotiations," Ben replied.

"No, no, no, of course not you." The ambassador laughed. "I meant him." He pointed to Brent. "He can leave anytime he wants."

Ben was perplexed, not least because he knew the political and economic chief *had* to be in the room when they discussed substance. He missed a beat but jumped into the fray without missing a beat.

"Ambassador Richards," Ben interjected, seeing Brent staring at a curtain as if he wanted to be anywhere but in this office while the ambassador stared daggers at a member of his staff. "Brent, of course, must be here because he's playing an important role in engaging with the local government to make these negotiations successful."

Brent had not been listening to anything, pointedly ignoring the ambassador, but he registered what Ben said, especially the ambassador's response.

"How dare you, you insolent little peon," Richards nearly screamed, standing up and wagging his finger at Ben. "Say that this piece of shit"—he swung his finger to point at Brent—"does more work than me"—he swung his finger around to point at his chest—"in my goddamn office." He slammed his hand on the table.

Ben stared for a second, momentarily shocked at the man's behavior, but then indignation took over. As well as a strange excitement at sharing the news from the Senator.

"Well, Ambassador," Ben responded coolly, withdrawing a slip of paper, "you'll read in this letter, addressed to you from the Senator, that you won't attend the negotiations."

The ambassador grabbed the letter and read it. "What do you mean I won't get to attend these negotiations!" He stomped around, acting like a small child who didn't get his way. "The Under Secretary of State will be there, dammit, and so will I!"

As the ambassador leaned into his tirade and shouted that he would resign if not permitted to sit in on the negotiations, Ben looked over at Brent, who looked like a kid whose Christmas presents all came at once, months ahead of schedule.

"Get the fuck out of my office, you little bastards! Get out of my country!" the ambassador yelled.

Ben was thankful he only took those two pages out of his folio, else he would have had to scramble to collect everything before rushing out. Brent rushed ahead, never having even opened his notebook or taken his pen from his shirt pocket.

"That was the most amazing thing I've ever seen in my life." Brent gasped with the biggest smile on his face, nearly at a loss for words. "He tries to throw me out of the country on a weekly basis, so don't pay any attention to that. He will calm down." His smile took on a nasty turn, as if he could reach out and throttle the ambassador. "Eventually."

Ben was almost afraid when he saw the look on Brent's face, fearing something was truly wrong with this situation. "At a minimum, I need to report this to the Senator and others in Washington," Ben said as they walked into Brent's office. "And you should report this verbal abuse up your chain."

Brent slammed the door, oblivious to the looks of the two officers in the room outside his office, and gave Ben a giant bear hug. "Ben, I cannot ever begin to thank you for standing up to that bully in there."

Ben saw as he withdrew that Brent was crying actual tears. "My God, man, are you okay? Is everything okay? You look like death warmed over, and just now, I saw what it's like to deal with that man."

He was not wrong.

For the next two hours, Brent poured his heart out, or at least some of it. He told Ben about the ambassador blocking his bidding attempts, how he would soon be forced to serve in a war zone, and about catching his wife with the ambassador. He told Ben nearly everything, except about his friend Radek. He still felt somewhat uneasy with how much information he continued to share with the foreigner but reasoned that he could control the flow of data.

"Jesus," Ben whispered. He knew that since entering the embassy, he had missed at least a dozen calls from Kate and others, none of whom had heard from him since he landed. "I am so sorry you have gone through this, but you should know that the negotiations are on and will not be changed. It appears the Iranians agreed to hold them in April, after the weather turns warmer."

They both laughed, Ben at the absurdity of the situation, Brent at the thought of how angry the ambassador would remain. The man was proud—too proud to work in government—and Brent almost cackled with glee at the knowledge that his wife and the kids were out of town for a few nights, meaning the bastard would not get to take his aggression out on Stacey. He felt protective of her once more.

"How about dinner, Ben?" Brent said, standing as he grabbed his jacket. "I know a good place where we can talk and even have a drink or two."

Ben nodded, happy to get out of the embassy, while Brent promised himself that tonight, he would only have a drink or two but then really focus on cutting down his alcohol consumption. He was drinking too much lately, since the first time he caught Stacey in the ambassador's office, which made him feel terrible. Hell, he might even go to the gym tomorrow.

AVI COHEN STEPPED FROM HIS EMBASSY, located in a historic building in the center of the city, and turned left. Budapest once was home to more than one hundred and fifty thousand Jewish people, but only several thousand lived in the city now. He bemoaned the continuing decay of the old Jewish quarter, which at the start of the Second World War teemed with life. Now, that vibrant community was merely a hollow memory.

Today, the young Mossad officer was on the hunt for a reported Iranian, one he heard from his contacts in the local government and community was operating in the city. Though not close to the Jewish state, the Hungarian government still sought countries for trade and investment. Undercover as the commercial attaché, Avi met freely with people in the business community, offering him the opportunity to learn about developments around the country. His work involved talking with people, visiting trade fairs, and using the Hungarian that he studied before arriving in the country.

In addition to the Iranians, Avi also worried considerably about the migrant population from Iraq, Syria, and Afghanistan. These refugees brought with them an ingrained hatred of the Jewish state, one that threatened to turn a neutral country into a tinderbox for the remaining Jewish population.

The one piece of information Avi learned was from an apartment building owner claiming that a man of likely Iranian origin rented an apartment on a long-term lease but stayed there infrequently. Unbeknownst to the building's residents, the owner was from an old Jewish family that could trace its roots back centuries in Budapest. Usually, the owner did not take notice of individual tenants, since he owned many buildings in that part of the city, but his building manager raised the strange habits of the man, who listed his name as Radek on the paperwork.

In fact, besides the paperwork, it was one incident with another tenant that convinced the owner to bring the man Radek to Avi's attention. Despite no elevator in the building, there was a pulley system in place so the residents did not have to carry their groceries and other shopping up the flights of stairs.

On a Saturday afternoon, when old Mrs. Weinstein returned from the market, she was loading her bags onto the pulley's platform at the same time the man Radek walked past. He tried to slip by but jumped away from her when he saw the Star of David hanging from her necklace. Ever since, old Mrs. Weinstein claimed the man avoided her, as if afraid of catching something infectious.

After reviewing the paperwork, Avi asked members of the local community to keep an eye on Radek. The man came and went at odd hours, which was not uncommon, but his lack of background made him someone to investigate more fully. Avi reported this information back to his headquarters in Jerusalem, receiving a reply in less than an hour to make finding out who this man was a priority.

Paranoid about Iranian threats to the Jewish state, the Mossad sought to look into anyone who seemed to be hiding things. The Israeli Ambassador heard there was likely to be a secretive meeting to negotiate a deal between the United States and Iran, which would include other major powers.

Why would anyone want to negotiate a deal with a country that will never honor its commitments? Avi considered. He was a patriot, a man who loved his country so much that he accepted this assignment, even though it kept him away from his parents and sisters. He served his compulsory military time and attended university, but then his professor introduced him to a man who forever changed his life.

Avi saw he was on early, as his instructors demanded throughout his arduous training, and lingered in front of a clothing store. It was the perfect cover, offering him the opportunity to stay in one place for as long as he wished. He was dressed in slacks, a thin dress shirt, a bland tie, and a worn jacket, looking like another office worker on his lunch break.

There he is, Avi told himself, seeing Radek on the other side of the street. He knew the man walked in this neighborhood, but cursory surveillance showed that Radek wasn't all that he seemed. He could sense that the man was conscious of being followed, so Avi kept his distance, never getting too close. The benefit of knowing where the man lived was he knew where he could pick him up the next day. His instructors drilled into him the need to be patient, knowing that it took the other guy making only one mistake to create an opportunity for success.

Avi watched the man abruptly turn to his right. *Stay calm,* he told himself, recognizing these as trademarks of an intelligence officer, someone checking for a tail. *They could also be the habits of a suspicious person.* Yet Avi grew excited.

So much of intelligence work was waiting for things to happen. *I wait more than I actually do things.* He was excited when he did something real as a member of the world's most dangerous spy agency. His parents were proud of him—he knew that—yet they were also disappointed that he had not stayed in Tel Aviv and taken work with one of the many technology companies that offered a more comfortable lifestyle. As well as the opportunity to marry and have children. *That can wait.*

Avi patiently moved to the next storefront and watched Radek. *He must be Iranian or else he would never have such easy access to the diplomatic and business community.* He spoke with others in his embassy, one of whom remembered seeing Radek speaking in hushed tones at a diplomatic reception with someone from the Iranian Embassy. Perhaps as a businessman, that could be explained, but it was all the more reason to investigate the man.

The Iranian intelligence officer, *ettela'at,* was covered as a second secretary in the political section, so Avi guessed Radek was not of that service. *He could be IRGC,* he contemplated, which could make sense because those men were trusted enough to wander freely outside the embassy. Perhaps even to be an illegal operating in Budapest.

Bingo, Avi thought, congratulating himself on his patience. Radek completed a full circle of the block and appeared more relaxed, as if he was less concerned about someone following him. Avi stayed a full street behind, taking his jacket off, donning a hat, putting on and taking off glasses, and in general changing his profile so he never appeared exactly the same as they walked along the same busy street. He knew, as did every intelligence professional around the world, that you could only memorize so many faces before your brain overloaded. His tradecraft helped him stay behind the man for many blocks.

Unfortunately for Avi, Radek continued towards the southern side of Budapest, where the number of people on the street dwindled. It was then, when he knew he would be caught, that Avi backed off completely. This was the third time the man entered this commercial district, full of abandoned buildings and warehouses. Three times was enough to make a pattern. Confident in the knowledge that he had another piece of the puzzle to add, and not wanting to press his luck, Avi doubled back to stop for his actual lunch hour. Even spies had to eat, he reasoned.

As he sat at a table, enjoying a bowl of soup with black bread, Avi mentally drafted his report, knowing that the next time, he would have to ask for help from a colleague. Then he would have to pre-position himself in that warehouse district to get another clue as to what Radek was doing.

RAMIN/RADEK ENTERED THE WAREHOUSE DISTRICT, unable to shake the feeling that he was being followed. He was careful, completing three full circles of blocks to clean his trail, yet an unknown sense within him warned that some danger lurked out there. He turned around but did not see anyone, so he continued walking towards the warehouse where he regularly met the Iraqis. The men were coming along. After practicing with their weapons in the forest twice, each successfully hit targets.

He found the men better fed, more confident, and happier than when he found them months before. They had taken over the warehouse, claiming it as their own, and Ramin knew that they even made inquiries to buy the property. When they first met, the men wanted nothing more than to continue to Germany.

Now, however, Ramin knew they had settled in to the migrant community, their children attending school and making friends. The Hungarian people still did not love migrants, or immigrants for that matter, but they were less hostile than many in Western Europe. Ramin knew all too well the horror stories that reached the ears of migrants; they flew through a network with the speed of light. It had always been that way, the best and worst stories getting the most attention because they alternately inspired and scared people the most.

Scholars in Tehran, mathematicians, reportedly ran the numbers. If they were to be believed—which Ramin doubted because he never trusted people who thought too much—the European continent would be overcome by Muslims in the next one hundred and one hundred and fifty years. That may seem like a long time to some countries, with many being no more than three to four hundred years old, but to a member of the Persian Empire, that was a blip in time.

"*A salam aleykum*, my friends," he said as he approached, seeing that all chairs in the circle were comfortable, the broken ones used for kindling. Gone, too, was the drum that they previously used for the fire, replaced instead by bricks arranged around a fire. Looking carefully, as he knew the men wanted him to, he saw a structure surrounding a metal box designed to collect the ashes from the fire. He then saw more bricks piled around, leading to the fire itself, which had vents built in to allow for airflow. On still another level, he saw a tea kettle, as well as spaces for frying pans.

He looked around and saw clean prayer rugs rolled up in a neat row. The men spent significant time here, time that meant they had made this their home away from their families. He respected their collective instinct for camaraderie but resented them because he lacked that same fellowship of brothers. Pushing aside his anger, which always grew stronger the longer he was away from his fellow Immortals, he shared his delight with the Iraqis.

"My friends," Ramin said in wonder, amazed by their ingenuity, "Allah has truly blessed you with comfort and happiness."

The men beamed with pride. "It was Abdullah"—Hassan pointed to the man sitting straight in his chair—"who wrote the plans, collected the bricks, and designed this stove for us." The men beamed in unison, pride in their bearing and faces. "But," Hassan continued, "it was you who gave us this opportunity, who gave us the money to be more comfortable here."

Ramin listened as Hassan explained that each of the men's wives were either working or setting up businesses in the community. "My wife is cooking traditional Iraqi food, which is very good indeed," Hassan proclaimed to the group. They all clapped, Ramin joining in belatedly as he realized they were getting comfortable.

They caught up. Hassan explained what each of the men did, and then they spoke about world events. This was an important time for Ramin because it assured him that the men knew who they were fighting. Not all of them spoke any language other than Arabic, so they relied on the limited supply of Arabic newspapers, which they found only at kiosks downtown.

Turning serious, Ramin interjected at a lull in the conversation. "It is good, my friends, that you are growing comfortable here."

"Thanks to you, our families are all growing comfortable."

"But do not forget that we have a bargain, one for which all of you must be prepared when I give the word," he cautioned. The men all grew serious, as if someone put a blanket over the light. "I gave you money to perform a service, and I expect that service to be performed without question."

"Of course," Hassan responded quickly. "We will be ready when the time comes."

Ramin looked at each of the men, who before had been hungry and eager. *More like desperate,* a voice inside chided, which he quieted but listened to nonetheless. Now, he looked at each of the men, judging whether they would be ready to do his bidding. He scrutinized the faces, looking for the man who turned away, pleased to see that all of them accepted their fates.

"Well, my brothers," Ramin said after finishing his tea, sweet with cube sugar, "I must go." He set his cup down on a ledge available on the stove. He marveled at the construction, never realizing this man must have trained to be an engineer with such an imagination and knack for building things.

Going to each man, wishing peace upon him and shaking hands, he made his way around the circle. That done, he collected his bag and strode from the warehouse. As if a switch flipped, he once again took in every sound, every movement around him. It was late afternoon. *How did I spend two hours in this warehouse district when I spent less than an hour speaking with them?* Once again, the gnawing feeling returned as he approached the edge of the warehouse district, where he knew he would encounter more people.

On full alert for any movement, Ramin checked for signs of people following him. Growing more confident that no one followed him or could outwit his superior training, he relaxed yet continued looking around. He saw men and women in cafés, some reading, others looking out at those walking on the street. Ramin did not judge these people to be threats because they whiled away the time in the cafés every day with little else to do with their lives.

Nor did Ramin pay attention to the shopkeepers who watched him walk by, because those men watched every man go by. One such shopkeeper, an antique dealer whose shop coincidentally was on the main street, was a friend of Avi Cohen.

The shopkeeper noted down the time Radek headed into town, looking around him as if his head was on a swivel. *He is nervous,* the man wrote, *and suspicious of everyone.* This was exciting, the man thought, much more exciting than selling antiques. With the man gone, he returned to his Hungarian newspaper, beneath which he kept the latest copy he could find from a nearby hotel of *The Jerusalem Times.* He was not ultrareligious, but he was still a Jew and a citizen of the Israeli state. As such, he would do his work, helping those who fought to protect the homeland.

Ramin kept walking, deciding then that tomorrow he would speak with his American to get information, knowing that collecting as much as he could would aid his and the Teacher's planning for their operation. He knew Brent liked to keep to a routine, visiting certain shops with his children and sometimes with his wife. Ramin would stake out a location along the American's route, which he had long since plotted out, and surprise him. *Perhaps not a pleasant surprise for the American*, he thought with a smile, but it would definitely be enjoyable for him to show his upper hand.

WITH MERE HOURS UNTIL HE LEFT for the airport, Ben decided to get out of his hotel room, congratulating himself for delivering the Senator's message to the ambassador. He called back to brief the Senator after eating dinner with Brent. Ben knew that by providing a briefing of his encounter, as well as background only Brent could provide, the Senator would back him up if Main State came back to complain.

Following a tourist map the concierge provided, Ben walked through a downtown area popular with tourists. Though there were not too many tourists this time of year, given the colder weather, Ben suspected these streets were always filled with locals buying what they needed.

Taking a roundabout route, Ben wound through the streets, stopping once for coffee and to get warm in a small coffee shop just a block from the river. Exiting the shop, he looked left and right, orienting himself, and across the street saw Brent walking along with a woman somewhat shorter than him, as well as three children. About to call out to Brent, Ben instead decided to follow since he was heading that way and say hello to them when he caught up to them.

Trailing behind nearly a block, in no real rush, Ben watched as a man of medium build rose from his table and began following Brent's family. He didn't know why the man's movements attracted his attention, but it seemed like a staged move, as if the man had waited for Brent. Continuing to follow them, Ben kept far enough back to avoid attention; the man kept his attention fixed on Brent's family.

Wondering why the man stayed so focused on Brent, Ben was grateful that the vehicles parked along the curb and trees on his side of the street provided cover. With his sunglasses and hat, he doubted Brent could pick him out of any crowd.

BEHIND THE AMERICAN'S FAMILY by slightly more than fifty yards, Ramin walked slowly and waited for the opportunity to attract the man's attention. He never thought to look around him, convinced after following the American and his family so often that no one paid attention to this mid-level diplomat even though he possessed enormous quantities of information.

What if all mid-level diplomats were equally full of useful information? Ramin contemplated the thought, realizing he would have to raise that possibility with the Teacher, perhaps seeking to replicate his source of information in other countries. As the American turned the corner with his family, he glanced back and locked eyes with Radek. The Iranian smiled and gestured.

"HONEY, WHY DON'T YOU TAKE THE KIDS up ahead, and I will meet you in a few minutes?"

Stacey looked at her husband, whose eyes were fixed where they had just walked. She trusted her husband to look out for their family, just as he had at their numerous other posts.

"Of course, dear," she responded. Stacey didn't understand or care what her husband did at work. She studied in college to be a teacher and never wanted to live overseas, but her love of her husband and desire to give her children opportunities she never had brought her into this comfortable lifestyle.

Walking back to Radek, Brent wondered what could be so important but instantly tried to relax.

BEN WATCHED AS BRENT WALKED TO THE MAN. If the man, who dressed more like a local, wanted to speak with him directly, why hadn't he approached Brent while he was with his family? Ben stopped to check his map when he realized he no longer knew where he was going. Turning to the street, he found himself directly across from Brent and the man, seeing their faces clearly.

Ben's imagination temporarily went wild, wondering if perhaps Brent was spying. *Is that possible?* Ben dismissed the thought, reasoning that Brent was too smart to spy on his own country. Anyway, what would anyone want to know about the United States' relationship with the Hungarian government? The Hungarians weren't exactly friendly to US interests, yet they were solidly in Europe's orbit and appeared to be moving away from Russian influence.

After navigating back to his hotel, Ben arrived in time to grab his bags. Though he couldn't shake the feeling that something was wrong with the encounter he witnessed on the street, he knew he would remember the stranger's look of intensity for quite some time, as if determined to discuss something serious.

Outside, waiting for a taxi, Ben moved to the side as several large vehicles arrived, disgorging a sizeable group of men. The men exiting the first vehicle all spoke together in Russian, while men from the second and third vehicles spoke quietly. His ears perked up at the sound of a language he recognized, Ben listened as the officials spoke of their recent visit to the Hungarian Foreign Ministry.

Russia and Hungary enjoyed close relations, Ben read in cables and the news, but their hushed conversations indicated that they were visitors to Hungary, not permanently assigned.

Ben was so distracted as he averted his eyes and carefully listened to the Russian that he was surprised when he heard Farsi. It was difficult enough for him to switch between English and another language, but the shock of hearing Farsi right after Russian nearly overloaded his brain.

Looking up quickly, Ben saw two Persian-looking men walking from the third vehicle, surrounded by several others who Ben knew must be Russians. *There is a different ethnic look that is noticeably different between their populations.* Ben knew this after having worked in both countries. He also noticed the two men in their collarless shirts, a trademark of the Iranian culture that rejected collars as Western and embraced a style unique to that country.

Unable to force his brain to switch to understand Farsi, Ben instead focused on the Russian he heard. *I'll bet Kate would be able to switch more easily between languages,* Ben groused, proud of his girlfriend yet also annoyed with his rusty language skills. Playing in his favor was that the Iranians on the right spoke in Russian to the man next to him. *So the Iranians speak to one another in Farsi, but then to the Russians in that language?*

Listening for as long as he could and hearing the Russians respond with details about the forthcoming nuclear negotiations, Ben nearly dropped the bag he picked up as he walked to his arriving taxi. *They're talking about the negotiations that are supposed to be secret,* he realized. *Could there be more to this close relationship than meets the eye?*

Riding in the back of the taxi to the airport, Ben contemplated everything he saw and heard that day. *Who was the man following and speaking with Brent? What is a large Russian delegation doing here, especially one discussing upcoming nuclear negotiations? What are the Iranians doing here cozying up to the Hungarian government?* Ben thought about how to frame all of this, realizing it was a lot to digest, but he knew he needed to sleep on his flight back to DC.

CHAPTER
TWELVE

RUNNING ALONG THE MOUNT VERNON TRAIL, which ran twenty-three miles from Mount Vernon north along the Potomac River, Ben listened to music and thought through the past weeks. In Budapest, he visited the Hungarian government's proposed sites, getting a sense of what to expect. He also met with a few officials, always with Brent at his side, but the entirety of his trip steered clear of the ambassador. The man was still pissed at him for delivering the news, but their response was "tough luck." That was a simple answer for politicians who saw ambassadors come and go while men like the Senator represented their constituents for decades.

The biggest threat, as Ben saw, was from someone attempting to disrupt the negotiations. He still was not convinced that either side was right, at least not yet, but as he ran through the crisp autumn morning, Ben knew his boss wanted to monitor the negotiations, ensuring the United States did not give away too much to the enemy. Another concern that refused to go away was that of the presence of the Russians and Iranians in Budapest. Ben reported it following his return, but he poisoned the well of Richards ever taking anything he shared at face value. "We all know the Hungarians are close with the Russians," the Europe Bureau staffer told him when he stopped by their office, "but the embassy refutes any serious connection between Iran and Hungary."

The Senator is not your boss, a voice reminded him. *Senior State Department officials are your bosses, while you are merely on loan.* Ben quieted those voices, knowing his divided loyalties would eventually catch up with him when he finished his year with the Senator. He was already considering his options for his next assignment, a perennial issue that Foreign Service officers faced. Some wanted to stay overseas their entire careers, usually those with families, while others fought to remain in DC for as long as possible, usually those whose spouses worked but could not easily find jobs overseas.

Considering multiple assignment offers on the table, Ben knew he would have to make up his mind soon. The Senator asked him to stay on another year, which would give Ben stability, something he at times craved above all else. Ben lost out on the position at the embassy in London to a senior advisor to the Under Secretary for Political Affairs. Ben would have loved to be posted to London and be with Kate full time. He was loath to call in a favor, especially since someone else beat him out for the job, but he was disappointed because he thought, with his record, he should have beaten out the senior advisor.

As Ben approached Riverside Park on his left, he ran by a couple jogging in the opposite direction. He turned around at nearly the same time as the other two did and ran back to them.

"Jennifer, is that you!" Ben said, then hugged her. They once briefly dated, then cooperated in the effort to foil the Minot Massacre. He saw her in early September at the White House ceremony, but they had not spoken for more than a few minutes. The ceremony still pained Ben because, while Jennifer's family attended, he had been alone. Not even Kate was allowed to attend since their relationship was still a secret; at the time, Sir Arthur Sinclair was unwilling to be flexible. He set that thought to the side, knowing negative thinking would do him no good.

"It is wonderful to see you, Ben," Jennifer Adams exclaimed, meaning it. She recalled the president giving her a medal, watched by the FBI director and several other top officials. She remembered Ben being sad, likely because he attended on his own, only the Senator and one staffer standing with him. While Jennifer was hailed by her leadership as a hero for intervening directly in the attack, killing five terrorists and arresting another, the Foreign Service viewed Ben as a cowboy.

"Have you met Nigel? He's my friend," Jennifer said offhandedly. She watched the men size one another up. In truth, her relationship with Nigel burned bright as the sun for several weeks but then faded into a comfortable, if loveless, friendship. It was as if they got married, lived together, and got divorced without any formality. But there it was, and Jennifer was content with him in her life. He was someone who understood what she experienced. That could not be underestimated.

"No, we haven't met," Nigel responded, shaking Ben's hand, "but I believe we have some mutual friends." He knew, along with three other people in the embassy, that Ben was dating Kate Sinclair, the chief's daughter. Making friends with someone who had a direct connection to the head of MI6 could prove career enhancing, though Nigel was secure in the role he filled at the embassy.

"Are you doing anything this evening?" Nigel asked.

Ben smiled. "As a matter of fact, I arranged with several friends to meet at a pub called O'Connell's. Would you like to join?"

"That sounds lovely," Nigel responded, hearing the effect of Ben dating an upper-class English girl in the cadence of his speech. "Shall we meet you at O'Connell's around seven o'clock this evening?"

Jennifer watched this, amazed at how effortless the conversation was between these two men. Normally, Nigel, a fit and serious man, intimidated other men. She heard that Ben was seeing someone, but he evaded her question when she asked at the White House. As she and Nigel jogged back to their vehicles, she decided she would ask her questions tonight, getting an answer come hell or high water.

That evening, Ben arrived early to secure a spot at the bar.

"Seamus, how are you, my friend?" Ben greeted the bartender as he slid onto a bar stool in the nearly empty bar. *It is only 6:40.* Not too early to drink. "I'll have a pint of Harp, thanks."

Seamus was pleased to see Ben, appreciating that he was polite, would chat, and always tipped well at the end of the night.

While he waited for his friends to arrive, Ben's thoughts strayed to Kate, as they regularly did. Ben realized he should propose to her, knowing she would say yes and that he had her father's blessing. The question was finding a ring—*the right ring*—one that would signify how much he loved her. He hoped to get a ring made for her, using the one he borrowed from her. It slightly ruined the surprise, but theirs was an honest love, one that did not conceal from the other. Too many lies had been told in their careers to be anything but honest, at least with one another.

Others filed into the bar, mostly strangers, but Ben knew a few, who pulled up bar stools and ordered their own drinks.

"Thanks for holding these for us," Nigel said when they arrived, lifting Jennifer atop an open bar stool. Ben smiled, amused that these two lovebirds were together.

"I do wish you wouldn't do that," Jennifer whispered to Nigel, careful to continue smiling, but inside, she was fuming at Nigel's male bravado. They had not slept together in months, a mutual decision because he was unwilling to commit, yet still he pretended as though they were together.

Nigel dutifully ordered drinks while making small talk with Ben, but then a table nearby grabbed his attention.

"Who are you looking at?" Jennifer hissed, annoyed that he appeared more interested in the brunette than talking with her.

"No one, love," Nigel quipped, "just a mate from the UK Embassy who appears to be alone." He walked over to the table, and to Jennifer's surprise, the woman was not happy to see him. He asked her questions, but she was not answering them, and Jennifer smiled with satisfaction at the knowledge that Nigel's luck with other women was no better than with her. *I'm not the broken one.*

Half dragging her, Nigel walked the brunette over to the bar, introducing her to Jenny and then Ben.

"Hi, I'm Ben." He felt he had seen her somewhere before.

Charlotte was amused to find herself face-to-face with her friend Kate's boyfriend. *His boyish charm,* she realized, *is infectious and he's not bad-looking.* She shook hands and politely refused the offers of drinks.

Casually flirting with the bartender, who could not move fast enough to ask for her order, Charlotte instead kept an eye on the door. She noticed Ben looking at her from time to time and decided she was being too obvious.

I feel like I have seen her somewhere before, Ben thought, *but she is as different from Kate as anyone I know.*

An hour into drinks, Charlotte saw the door open and a lovely, flowing mane of blonde hair glide into the room. She and Kate had planned this for more than a week. Every man in the bar turned to the front door, stunned at the beauty before them. All except for Ben, who was ordering another drink.

"Is it at all possible to get service in this bar?" Kate asked, smiling at Ben. Dazed at hearing her voice and unsure exactly what was happening, he turned to her, wisely leaving the drink he ordered on the bar.

"Kate!" Ben exclaimed. He wrapped her in a giant hug, one she returned ferociously. "How could you surprise me like this?" He was unexpectedly overcome by emotion at the sight of the woman he loved.

"You have me at least until Christmas, perhaps longer," she whispered.

Without hesitating, the men around him backed up as they sensed something was happening. Ben got to one knee.

"Holy shit," Charlotte said.

Kate sat frozen.

"Kate, my love, I love you to the moon and back." He paused, taking stock of the moment. *I'm only doing this once.* "How about we make this official, even without a ring?" His voice caught slightly. "Will you marry me?"

"Yes, you bloody fool, I will marry you!"

The bar erupted in applause, and the owner, a towering Irishman named Michael, walked over to congratulate Ben and introduce himself to Kate. "Get these two lovebirds drinks to celebrate," he roared.

As people congratulated them, Kate rounded on Charlotte and Nigel, grabbing each by the arm. "I will bloody kill either one of you who breathes a word of this to my family." Both nodded, stunned. "I will figure out how to handle this unexpected surprise," she whispered so only they could hear, "but I need your absolute silence."

She watched Ben with mixed emotions. *I love the man, but this puts me in a difficult position, one that could make things complicated with my family.*

CHAPTER
THIRTEEN

MOSSAD OFFICER AVI ROUNDED A CORNER in Budapest, this time with more than a dozen locals ready to observe and report to ensure he learned the Iranian's ultimate destination. Headquarters was screaming at him to send in something useful, especially with reports flooding in from Israel's friends in Washington that the Americans had already set a date for their secret negotiations with the Iranians. *As if this is even a secret anymore,* Avi huffed, careful to position himself at the outer corner of a building inside the warehouse district.

Through careful planning, Avi found locations within the warehouse district where he placed watchers to move from building to building. His contacts within the local government secured him utility worker uniforms, which younger members of the Jewish community volunteered to wear. This was a team effort, and he was grateful he could rely on so many people. The Jewish community was small, numbering fewer than two thousand in all of Budapest, with several hundred forming a close-knit community.

Now comes the waiting, Avi thought morosely. He and his team had been staking out the warehouse district for two weeks now, since shortly after the Iranian last visited the men. It was November already, and the weather was noticeably colder, which made it more difficult to blend into the surroundings. He could not keep these volunteers outside indefinitely, never more than three or four hours at a time.

One of the younger community members suggested that they should just grab the Iranian. The others chuckled, but Avi quickly quashed that thinking. His small service relied on volunteers from the community to succeed, people who pitched in when necessary. If this developed further, he would get more resources and people to help, but until then, this fell to him.

UNBEKNOWNST TO AVI or any of the Jewish residents, Ramin was not alone that night. Shortly after reporting his suspicion that someone was following him, the Teacher unilaterally decided to send two other Immortals for support. Ramin was excited to see men he'd known since he became an Immortal.

The six of them were hand-picked by the Teacher, an elite force beholden only to Grand Ayatollah Shirazi. The Grand Ayatollah originally envisioned the men as secret soldiers tasked to spread the Revolution, but over the years, they developed into so much more. The men killed the regime's opponents, intimidated those seeking to obstruct the Grand Ayatollah's plans, collected information that not even Iranian intelligence agencies managed to uncover, and operated inside Iran to take direct action against the men who opposed the Grand Ayatollah.

The Teacher sending two additional Immortals seemed like overkill to Ramin, but he was glad of the company. For the first time that summer, the six men worked together. First, when they accompanied the Teacher to America to witness the attack by the Somalis, which was not necessarily a success, and second, when they accompanied the Grand Ayatollah to Afghanistan. The men were sworn to protect both the Grand Ayatollah and the Teacher, with their lives if necessary. None of the six would be alive were it not for those two men, though to be honest, even they were getting older.

Ramin walked through the warehouse, taking note of people watching him, but sure in the knowledge that Mahmoud and Farrokh were also watching. He cleared his trail, doubling back and circling blocks, as he agreed with his brothers. Still, the feeling that someone watched him never left, although people in the warehouse district appeared to belong there. Relaxing as he walked, he concluded that no one could have tracked him.

AVI WATCHED THE IRANIAN WALK THROUGH the blocks and wind through the rubble, avoiding potholes, as anyone would do, but continued straight to his destination. *Aha,* Avi told himself, *it must be that building.* He grew excited, knowing he could mark the building on his map and return later to explore, after the Iranian departed.

As the hours ticked by watching the warehouse and evening turned to night, Avi felt a chill. It felt as if a spirit passed him by but decided to let him live. *What was that?* He was terrified but held his ground. He tried to avoid looking around, keeping his gaze fixed on the warehouse, but could not control a glance over his shoulder.

The evening was starless, save for lights in the distance, and he knew anyone could hide in the dark if they were skilled at conceal-ment. If someone was watching him, he would be ready with the weapon he carried, even if it meant alerting the Iranian. He was willing to die for his country, but not while doing reconnaissance in a warehouse district in Budapest.

THAT MAN IN THE DARK LEATHER JACKET with dark, curly hair will live another day, Farrokh decided. He was but a short distance from the man, not knowing who he was but confirming grimly that someone followed his brother. Though accustomed to operating in European capitals, Farrokh was comfortable in the most squalid of conditions. He rose silently to his feet, feeling rather than seeing the path away from the man.

You are lucky, little one, Farrokh thought, *that my mandate was to track you but not kill.* The Teacher forbade them from killing unless one of them was in danger. Momentarily, Farrokh toyed with the idea of accidentally kicking a rock or just making noise to provoke a fight, but his training controlled his impulses.

Growing up in the poorest slums of Tehran, Farrokh had been alone his entire life. His mother abandoned him at the age of seven to the care of an aunt who already had too many mouths to feed. With no comfort at her house, young Farrokh set out daily, learning survival habits. He never experienced the pride of a parent doting on him and could not remember the warmth of his mother's embrace. *She had no warmth to give, but at least she gave me intelligence and cunning,* Farrokh reasoned. Those skills served him well on the streets, enabling him to fight and survive.

Only early in his teenage years did the police finally catch up with him and threaten to throw him in an orphanage if he did not find a stable home. He finally found a place with a distant uncle who served in the Shah's army but whose allegiance to Islam and the Revolution burned bright. When he turned seventeen, Farrokh joined the Revolutionary Army, prodded by his uncle, who left the Shah to support the Ayatollahs. His uncle's connections with the Ayatollahs secured him a place in a frontline unit, giving him real skills and a bright future. The army gave him a sense of belonging that he craved all his life, a feeling that he mattered.

Then came the dreaded war. It was a war of death—one that killed so many of his comrades who fought valiantly against the

Iraqis but died nonetheless. After his unit was ambushed by artillery fire, Farrokh woke in a tent, cared for by brave doctors and nurses. The Grand Ayatollah found him there, a broken man who had lost all those he loved. But the soldiers who fought with him mattered. They were his entire life.

Farrokh shook his head, returning to his thoughts of his life on the ground, ready to die. *I always think about those dark days when I kill or am about to kill.* He retreated to another building, still able to make out the shadow of the man who followed Ramin. *I could kill him, but the Teacher told us to collect information. We will act later.* Crouching on the ground, Farrokh wrapped himself in the large overcoat he wore and unconsciously rocked. Back and forth. Back and forth. It soothed him but did not dull his sense. It calmed his desire to kill.

ON THE OTHER SIDE OF THE STREET, where Ramin walked, Mahmoud watched. It was still early evening, and he was comfortable watching out for people monitoring and tracking his brother. Surveillance work was boring but provided vital intelligence. This side of the street was quiet, though he noticed several people who appeared to be busy but were doing a poor job at it, almost as if they, too, were static surveillance. The problem, Ramin had warned, was the difficulty of differentiating between a real and fake worker; most Hungarians were not very industrious and retained a Soviet-style mentality.

Mahmoud snorted at that thought, recalling when he and his brothers traveled to the Soviet Union as part of a military exchange program in the late 1980s. The Soviet intelligence officers thought them mere enlisted soldiers, dismissing them but providing the training, while the Revolutionary Guard officers were interrogated for information. He recalled seeing drunk workers throughout the city he visited, reinforcing the Teacher's message about the dangers of alcohol. The drug dulled a man's mind, and thus, he was less able to react. That, in his profession, was dangerous.

Hopefully Farrokh has better luck, Mahmoud lamented, *because I saw no verifiable surveillance.* He watched his surroundings, respecting his brother's operational decisions, but suspected Ramin grew lazy operating in a country where the local government was not necessarily hostile to Iranian interests.

Settling in, Mahmoud looked to the stars, pleased that at least there were not so many lights that he could not enjoy the peace and calm of the evening sky. After a while, he saw Ramin picking a path through the rubble and debris.

We will do this again in two or three weeks, Mahmoud considered as he clandestinely snapped photos of the men he saw, no longer quite trusting his mind to recognize the same faces. *If the same people return, we will deal with them.*

IT ALL STARTED WITH BEN'S VISIT. Brent silently thanked whatever divine being for that change in his life.

Since Ben's visit, Brent had gone to the gym, sometimes twice a day. He also made much more of an effort, both with his children and his wife. Being honest with himself, he knew it was partially his fault that she began sleeping with the ambassador. He had prioritized his career over his family. He was ashamed but determined to make amends.

In return, his children's lives returned to a sense of normalcy as he and his wife worked hard to shield their children from the tensions between them.

But the biggest difference was in Stacey, who once again reciprocated Brent's interest. He knew it would take time to repair their relationship, perhaps years, but they both agreed to try. That involved cooking meals together, going for walks with the kids, and in general spending more time together. The biggest condition Stacey demanded of Brent was for him to prioritize his family over his career. He agreed to that wholeheartedly, to the frustration of the ambassador.

As a result, Brent wasted less time at work, focusing so he could leave on time, as much as it was under his control. The ambassador seemed happy that Brent was more productive but still went out of his way to see Stacey whenever possible. For her part, Stacey avoided the embassy and anything to do with the ambassador, denying Brent's boss the opportunity to be in the same room with her. She admitted to sleeping with him because she felt lonely and ignored, not because she liked him.

It turned out the ambassador was one of the first men to pay attention to her, not treating her like a housewife but someone to be desired. Brent felt better understanding her motivations, yet the sting of her betrayal remained.

Workwise, Brent enjoyed being able to focus on the upcoming secret negotiations. Only a handful of people in the Hungarian government were aware of the preparations, though that would change about a month prior to the event. Brent proposed, and Washington fully endorsed, a plan to book the venue and hotel rooms under the cover of a large book convention. The ambassador was angry as a hornet, yelling at anyone who drew near, but for weeks, Brent managed to always place the DCM squarely between himself and the ambassador, never wanting to be in a room alone with that man.

The one remaining conundrum Brent wrestled with was how to deal with Radek. He knew now that he made a deal with the devil by sharing so much information that it would be difficult to stop. During one meeting, when Brent balked at sharing more information, Radek made it abundantly clear what would happen if Brent stopped cooperating. Photos of his wife and children placed on the table, as well as of the school his children attended, halted Brent's efforts to control the relationship.

In truth, the best Brent could do was share less and be less cooperative. He still retained a strong desire to get revenge on the ambassador, lest that man continue to make his own rules. Brent reasoned that it was too late to report his communication with Radek to the security office, assuming they would never understand how events unfolded. He once considered admitting everything to his Agency colleagues but opted against it because he feared being turned over to the FBI and spending decades in a federal prison.

CHAPTER
FOURTEEN

KATE SMILED TO HERSELF as the two of them lay in bed together. *I am so happy!* She returned to Ben's apartment after a night of drinks, dinner, and general merriment. Ben was stunned to find Kate's bags in his apartment, but then saw a note from Mrs. Johnson, his neighbor who held a key when he traveled.

Mrs. Johnson brought him cookies shortly after he moved in, and he repaired a couple of her leaking faucets. Her husband had served in the military and then elsewhere in the government for decades, though the older lady was always short on details and instantly changed the subject. That was normal in the DC area, where it seemed at least half of the people one met worked in jobs they didn't, or wouldn't, discuss.

It was a Sunday morning, and despite his desire to stay in bed all day, Ben wanted to show Kate around Alexandria. They each showered and, after minimally tense discussions, decided that Kate should unpack her things and put them in the closet in his guest bedroom. Ben's master bedroom was already packed with stuff and didn't have space for both of their clothes. It occurred to Ben that if

Kate stayed, perhaps they should look for a bigger place, especially if they wanted to host guests. His two-bedroom apartment was fine for him but not large enough for a couple with so much stuff.

After leaving his north Old Town building, Ben directed them towards the town center, leading Kate along quaint streets lined with historic rowhouses.

"Ben," Kate said casually after they walked in silence for several minutes, "did you intend to propose to me last night, or was that spontaneous?"

Ben slowed, unsure how to respond. He wondered where she was going with this but trusted that she had good reasons.

Sensing his hesitation, Kate added, "I am ever so glad you proposed." She kissed him, holding him tightly as they walked. "I only ask because this is going to take my parents a bit by surprise."

Bingo, Ben thought. Her family is always on her mind, a factor she must consider. He never really thought of how they would respond since he no longer had a real family. His sister was another story, one he mentioned by accident but then never brought up again.

"To be honest," Ben said, "I had no idea you were coming to town, so it was completely spontaneous." He stopped to kiss her hair, loving the smell of her, and they ambled slowly down the street. "I could not stop thinking of you, and it just seemed right." He didn't add that he had thought about proposing to her for a long while, even looking at rings, but nothing ever seemed right for a woman like her.

She laughed, amazed by Ben's honesty. She didn't yet have a ring on her finger, but she was now his fiancée. They agreed to search for a ring together because she knew what she wanted to wear for the rest of her life. *I am engaged,* she realized with excitement. But she tamped down those feelings.

"My darling, I am so happy. And of course I meant it when I said I want to marry you."

"Why do I sense a 'but' in there somewhere?" Ben asked. He started getting a bit nervous, which wasn't like him. *What if she isn't sure?* As an orphan, Ben lived so much of his life on his own, never letting many people get close to him.

"Well, you see, my family has a tradition that a couple get engaged with some family around."

This could go one of two ways, Ben realized, knowing that life was about options. *I can make this difficult or easy on her.* It wasn't really a competition between those options, so he responded right away.

"Then that just means I need to propose to you again, with your family present, right?"

Kate was bowled away by Ben instantly grasping what she thought. *He seems to read my mind, knowing what I want—nay, what I need—and doing it because he knows it will make me happy.*

"Ben, you are amazing," she said, in awe that she found someone who loved her enough to adapt his life to the demands of her family.

They walked in silence for a couple blocks, and as they approached King Street, Ben steered them to a Starbucks, where they fueled up for their busy morning. From there, he directed Kate away from the Potomac.

She was enjoying this exploration of the city. As they approached a church, Ben turned and asked, "Can we go in for the service?" She smiled and hurried in, noticing that this Christ Church bore a striking resemblance to churches back in London.

ROBERT WOKE IN HIS BED, not quite remembering events from the night before. In the weeks since his wife died, he operated in a dreamlike state. The police continued to search for the man who, according to witnesses, rammed Ludmilla through the break in the guard rails. It made the headlines for days afterwards, a major story that garnered attention because it appeared someone targeted her. The detective on the case questioned Robert numerous times, though he answered truthfully that Ludmilla had no enemies. It seemed an arbitrary case of road rage.

During moments when he was alone, Robert grieved for Ludmilla, painfully admitting that it was his fault because he had not been there to protect her. Jonathan gave him time off work and the freedom to work from home whenever he wanted, giving Robert time to think through his emotions. He did not realize how accustomed he was to her presence or how empty he would feel without her. For the first time in a long time, Robert regretted their lack of children. If they had a son or daughter, he would still have a piece of her.

As he stood in his kitchen, Robert stared at the island and remembered meals there, then turned to look out his window. *I don't want to leave the house today,* he fumed, yet he knew he needed to get out or go crazy. He found himself wandering from room to room, searching for something that he missed, and bemoaned all the times he opted to work rather than be with Ludmilla.

Ludmilla. Each time he thought her name, or saw her clothes, or smelled her perfume, his heart would break all over again. *I wish I could be with her,* he thought, then set that idea aside. He could never take his own life because there was so much to live for.

Subconsciously, Robert avoided any communication with Sergei, focusing instead on his rage and pain. He decided to go for a walk, just to get out of the house. After grabbing his jacket, he put on boots in case he walked a long distance.

Robert was so focused on himself that he did not see the vehicle parked across and down the street from his home. The man behind the steering wheel keyed his radio twice, pausing as he watched the American walk to the curb and turn left. He then keyed the radio again, this time three times in rapid succession, in a preplanned code indicating the American's direction. Done with that task and grateful the man finally left his house, he straightened in his seat, started the car, and drove off. *Three days I've been sitting here, and finally,* he fumed, knowing he could not question Moscow's instructions.

Robert walked casually, consciously heading for the extensive Fairfax County public park. Ludmilla used to love visiting the park for walks, never losing her Ukrainian love of the outdoors and all its beauty.

More alert as he entered the park, Robert reasoned that late on Sunday morning, the park would not be crowded, so he would not have to deal with the pathetic words of sympathy from anyone who might recognize him. Since losing Ludmilla, he lost so much of his drive, half deciding that he would stop working for the Russians because it wasn't worth the hassle. *Does it even matter anymore?*

As he pondered that question, Robert rounded a corner to find himself on an isolated stretch of the park, surprised to find he enjoyed the solitude.

"Good morning, Robert," came a voice from his left. Startled, Robert spun to the sound. Sergei was impeccably dressed, looking more like an affluent American businessman than a Russian spy.

"Oh," Robert paused, uncertain what to say. "Hello." He resisted the urge to use the Russian's name, knowing that would only antagonize the man. He resolved to break contact with this man, making a clean start and redoubling his efforts to serve his country.

Sergei motioned with his hand, gesturing towards a small clearing off the paved path. Hesitating, Robert looked around.

"You have nothing to fear," he said, drawing a bright smile. "No one is following you." After staring for several seconds, he continued. "I can assure you that we will have several minutes to speak privately."

Robert entered the clearing, staring up to the sky as his eyes followed the upward line of trees that circled the small open area.

"I never told you how sorry I was for your—" Sergei began, but Robert cut him off.

"Thank you for saying that," Robert said, "but you should know I decided that I can no longer give you information."

Robert watched the Russian carefully, trying to judge his reaction. He expected his statement to come as a surprise to the man he faced a mere few feet away.

"Don't be silly," Sergei retorted, barely pausing to collect his thoughts. He knew the weak American would try something like this and was grateful that he spoke through this with his supervisors in Moscow. Sergei had run operations for fifteen years overseas, so he knew all the tricks but was wise enough to know that talking through these scenarios helped him think through potential challenges.

"I'm not being silly," Robert protested, but Sergei raised a hand to silence him.

"We could stand here all day and debate what you say you will and will not do, but the fact is that you now work for us." Sergei waited for the expected outburst.

"How dare you suggest I have to do *any*thing?" he nearly shouted, no longer caring if anyone heard. "I am my own man." The last sentence was weak, almost an admission that even he didn't believe the sentiment. "Besides, my Ludmilla is gone." He spoke those words with a sense of dread, as if afraid of every new day to come. "There is nothing more anyone can do to hurt me."

"Really?" the Russian asked, smiling for the first time since they entered the clearing.

"Really."

"And who do you think eliminated your Ludmilla?" Sergei asked, feigning innocence. He did not know how the American might respond, but he liked surprises even less than the next man, so he was prepared for any eventuality. Feeling in his right pocket, he gripped the taser, ready to use it if necessary.

"You killed my wife?" Robert was too stunned to say anything else.

"Yes, we did."

With those words, multiple emotions flooded Robert's brain at once. He felt anger at the admission, sadness again at losing his beloved wife, rage at the man's callous attitude, hurt that he could never have foreseen this, and a measure of comfort at knowing the truth.

"How dare you!" he started, but again, Sergei's calm demeanor caught Robert off guard.

"You see, life is cheap. The only reason we care about you is because you can provide information to us." He took a breath, knowing this was the tricky part. "You traded your nation's secrets for money, which you spent at any number of stores for yourself and your wife." He watched Robert carefully, gauging his reaction. *I can push more. I must.* "We are now in the business of transactions, where you give us things and we give you things. For instance"—Sergei withdrew his hand from his left jacket pocket and handed a photo to Robert—"those in that picture could face the same fate if you do not cooperate."

Robert took the photo and saw the faces of his sister and her children. Once again, the sense of loss overwhelmed him. *I will not cry,* he willed. *I will not be weak in front of this man.*

"You wouldn't dare."

"If that is not enough, you are also quite expendable." He searched the American's pained eyes, knowing the man's weakness meant he would never want to feel pain. "It would be so easy for a vehicle, traveling at approximately the same speed as your vehicle, to abruptly slam your vehicle over the side of a bridge, killing you instantly."

Freezing involuntarily, Robert realized that Sergei's words matched almost identically the police report issued by the investigators. Robert opened and closed his mouth.

"Now," Sergei said, knowing he'd tightened the noose completely around *his asset's* neck, "you must begin returning to the office on a regular basis. We cannot have you missing more time in the office, can we?" Turning to grab Robert's arm, half dragging the man from the clearing, they resumed their walk along the path.

Unable to speak, Robert found himself again fighting multiple emotions at once.

"It will take you some hours, perhaps even a day, to process our discussion," Sergei said, no compassion in his voice. He knew now was not the time for the stick, which he already used to beat the American, but instead to offer a carrot. "I suggest that when you are ready to accept reality, you place a plastic bag with an empty box on the handle of your front door as a signal that you agree." He smiled at the world, reveling in victory.

"In return, when you are ready, we will arrange for further payments and"—Sergei stopped, turning to face Robert—"even a visit with your dear Anastasia." He eyed the American carefully, seeking the signs that the man fully capitulated to his plan. If there was any doubt, they would have to take more extreme measures. *This American has valuable information, and I'm not going to lose this source!*

"Anastasia would come to see me?" Robert asked. Overwhelmed with fear for himself and his sister's family, he clung tight to her name.

"Yes, of course, wherever you would like to meet her."

Walking slowly next to Sergei, Robert knew he would continue to grieve but could not do so forever. He considered his options. He knew this was a dangerous game. Ludmilla was already dead, which pained him every time he considered it, but nothing could bring her back.

What is the next logical step? He raged, emotions fighting reason. His thoughts flashed through his mind in quick succession. Seeing one image in his mind holding steady, Robert knew when to accept that the situation was beyond his control.

"When can I see her?"

CHAPTER
FIFTEEN

"MY FRIEND," RAMIN SAID, "you have been avoiding me." He smiled at Brent, whom he cornered in a small café. Ramin knew the American's schedule well, knew where he stopped and when, and knew well that the American was avoiding him. That would not do, Ramin told himself, because he needed more information to perfect his plan.

"Radek," Brent replied, failing to compose himself as he looked up from his coffee and croissant. He was surprised, though he also knew he was a terrible liar. His life was finally coming back together, and he wished he could forget he'd had anything to do with this man.

"Things have been so busy at the embassy. Busier than you can imagine."

This American is a terrible liar, Ramin realized, wishing Farrokh and Mahmoud were still in town.

They stayed for nearly three weeks to help detect surveillance, but whatever they thought they saw the first time disappeared by the second time. Farrokh swore he saw someone who appeared to be observing Ramin but wisely took no action. A dead body would have merely raised more questions, ones that would draw unwanted attention to his presence and activities.

"We made a deal." Ramin sat, fixing his stare at Brent to keep him still. "I am upholding my part of the bargain, including designating your ambassador the number one target when we strike."

In fact, there were far more prominent targets, yet he showed the Iraqis the photo of the ambassador enough times that they would not hesitate to kill him if the opportunity arose.

"But now," Ramin continued, leaning in, "I need more information from you about American plans for the negotiations." This was the point the Teacher made to him just yesterday, prodding him to action because other agencies struck out when they attempted to gain insight into American policies.

"I told you many times," Brent responded, failing to hide his irritation, "Washington has told me nothing about their negotiating position." He leaned in, not caring that his tie dipped into his coffee. "The fact is that no one in our embassy has seen anything about the substance of the negotiations, except perhaps for the folks at the Station." He paused, looking around to ensure no one paid attention to them, and continued. "You see, my work is focused on our bilateral relationship with the Hungarians."

Ramin tuned out the American, having heard this weak defense many times before. He considered Brent's mention of American intelligence officers, knowing they could be potential assets. *They will be much better trained than this weakling before me and will properly report any attempts to influence or contact them.* No. Ramin realized his only hope was to squeeze every last bit of information out of this American, who could at least give him the necessary details about the venue and other logistical arrangements.

After letting the American talk himself into silence, Ramin made a show of contemplating what he heard. "Okay, my friend. You are right, but I had to ask. You understand, I am sure."

Brent laughed, Ramin's apparent truthfulness breaking his anger.

"But it would be helpful for me to know everything you can share about logistical arrangements for the talks, anything on your side that the Hungarian government may have told only you. I need information if we are to get your revenge on the man who slept with your wife."

"Yes, yes," Brent said impatiently, getting angry at the thought of the ambassador. "I gave you photocopies of everything I received from my local foreign ministry contact."

"Fine, fine," Ramin replied, realizing he had pushed this meeting too long. "I will contact you again in January. Enjoy your holidays with your family. But"—he paused, grabbing and squeezing Brent's wrist—"I expect cooperation from you at that time. Or I will pay a visit to your home when I know you are at work." He released Brent.

Brent's eyes went wide, but he said nothing. He rubbed his wrist, surprised at the man's strength.

"Perhaps I could also arrange a visit to your children's school, the international school on the other side of town, right?"

Again, Brent's eyes popped. "There will be no need," Brent said, deflating. "I promised to help you. And I will help."

"That is good," Ramin said as he rose from his seat. He left the café knowing the American's eyes followed him the entire way. In fact, the Teacher already forbade going after the American's children, seeing that as a very un-Islamic move. Ramin was relieved, never wanting to target children for the sins of their parents.

AS NOVEMBER ENDED and December quickly disappeared, Ben's and Kate's lives took on a routine. Kate traveled each morning to the UK Embassy off Massachusetts Avenue, not far from the National

Cathedral, and continued the same missions as when she was in London, focused on Iranian targets. She discovered that she could take the train up near Georgetown, then jog the remaining distance up Massachusetts Avenue to the embassy. It required her to leave her work clothes in a closet in the office, but it was worth her exercising every morning.

Kate noticed Charlotte seemed annoyed, so she made more of an effort, eventually drawing out of Charlotte one night over happy hour drinks that she feared losing Kate's friendship. She assured Charlotte that being with Ben had not changed anything between them. After that talk, Charlotte spent the night in their guest bedroom and slept off a hangover. The next morning, her friend seemed happier.

Ben, meanwhile, continued to throw himself into work, always at the Senator's beck and call. Kate resigned herself to the Senator's hold over her fiancé, accepting this was his assignment, much as her assignments required her to make certain sacrifices.

Life is pretty good, Kate knew, yet they still had disagreements, much like any other couple. The main challenge was their living conditions. Kate, who grew up surrounded by wealth, was unaccustomed to living in a small place and could not see herself relegated to Ben's small apartment. Charlotte tried to convince her to accept an embassy flat, which would be more convenient to work, but Kate fell instantly in love with Ben's charming neighborhood.

No, she thought as she left her embassy late one afternoon, the answer was for them to buy another place, one where they could make a home together. It was a big step, and one that made Ben nervous because of the cost. This was another area where Kate had to tread carefully. She didn't want to throw around her family's money to solve the problem, which she fretted could make Ben even more uneasy.

Kate learned that in lieu of embassy housing, she could request a lump sum payment from the British government to find her own quarters. It would not be enough to buy a property outright, but it would be enough for a down payment, allaying Ben's concerns about buying a place for both of them.

In terms of work, Kate read reporting chatter that intelligence officers from around the globe were converging on Budapest in advance of the proposed direct negotiations between the US and Iran, as well as observing nations. *These negotiations are no longer a secret.* She laughed to herself.

She was particularly concerned about an increase in the number of officials seen entering and exiting the Iranian Embassy, based on reporting from the UK Embassy in Hungary. The officers there liaised with their Hungarian intelligence counterparts, securing copies of visa applications and entry information for everyone. That gave them names and identities, sort of, because everyone assumed that the Iranians used fake names and doctored photographs.

Looking through the scanned photographs, Kate realized she owed it to Ben to share what she could about this, though she needed to go through the proper channels. This was routine intelligence collection, but unless she shared it with Ben through the proper channels, he would not feel comfortable sharing it with the Senator or his aides. It was one thing Kate loved about Ben—he followed the rules and respected their professional boundaries.

Knowing she could solve this by simply swiveling her chair, Kate did just that, turning to face Charlotte.

"Char," Kate asked, getting her friend's attention.

"Yeah," Charlotte responded.

She appreciated that Kate and Ben were making an effort to keep her included, especially since this was the first time in years that she and Kate were in the same city together. She was a regular at their apartment, even keeping an overnight kit there, but she knew that when she stayed, she made Ben slightly uncomfortable.

Lover boy will just have to deal, Charlotte thought as she smiled at her friend.

"Two things," Kate said. "First, this weekend, we need to go look at townhouses together, without Ben, because I want to get a better sense of what is available."

"That sounds fab," Charlotte said, loving that she was party to a secret kept from Ben. "And the second thing?"

"The second thing"—Kate handed her the sheaf of papers documenting the Iranians who entered Hungary—"is if you could start the process to share this information from the Hungarians." Charlotte read through the documents while Kate continued. "I will help you fill out the paperwork."

"My, my." Charlotte smiled. She knew she would do this for her friend, but she wanted to have a little fun and determine if her hunch was correct. "This wouldn't happen to have anything to do with the fact that a certain Ben, *your fiancé*, will be in Budapest? Are you doing this, perhaps, because you are worried about the Iranians getting their hands on him?"

Leave it to Charlotte to see through me, Kate acknowledged that particular fear. She was not prone to hysterics, but she knew Ben was firmly on the Iranian government's radar after his open meeting in Herat with the Grand Ayatollah Shirazi.

Charlotte knew nearly all the details, learning so much after she snooped to find out more. Following Kate's return to London from Afghanistan, Charlotte flew back to care for her friend. Rumors had flown everywhere, and Charlotte threatened to sleep with whoever it took to know the deepest, darkest secrets so she could protect her friend.

Ultimately, it was Arthur Sinclair, who knew of Kate and Charlotte's close friendship, who authorized Charlotte to be read in on everything that happened. She had not seen the unedited take from the meeting but knew enough. Plus, Kate later admitted that she feared something would happen to Ben that day, at which point Charlotte realized her friend was in love.

"Of course, Kate," Charlotte said, sensing Kate's pain and not wanting her friend to have to answer the question. She could not bear to see her friend hurt, but she knew it was a hurt that Kate worked hard to bury. "This is relatively routine stuff, and I will get Julian to sign off, by hook or by crook." It really was nothing that serious, easily something the American Embassy Agency employees in Budapest could request. However, Kate was obsessed with the Iranians and was chasing these Immortals.

Privately, Kate would admit she was obsessed, because this reported group could explain how the Iranians were able to accomplish so many of their goals around the world. She had reports of Iranian members of this group assigned to different parts of the world. She believed there was one assigned to the Americas, one to Europe, one to Africa, and likely one to Asia. One person reckoned there were six in the group, led by a man believed to be one of the deadliest men in Iran.

"Thank you," Kate whispered, lost in thought about the Iranians and the threat they might pose to Ben.

"Okay," Charlotte said. She tossed the sheaf of papers on her keyboard, already having written the justification for sharing the information with her Langley counterparts in her head.

Kate admitted that senior levels of the UK Foreign Office would travel to observe the historic direct talks, which Charlotte knew meant the chief, Arthur Sinclair, would probably attend. Kate would certainly be there to observe the Iranians and lend her expertise, but also to watch over Ben.

"Shall I call that realtor we found, or will you?" she asked, already prepared to claim a semipermanent room in whatever property Kate and Ben purchased.

"**GRAND AYATOLLAH SHIRAZI**," the Teacher said, announcing his presence as he entered his boss's office, "thank you for agreeing to see me." Although confined to a wheelchair, the Teacher knew how to display appropriate respect and fealty to his patron.

"Tell me," the Grand Ayatollah commanded, setting aside papers to focus on the matter at hand. Although very busy with his role on the Expediency Council, his monetary investment from his family's fortune to create the Immortals paid off many times over the decades. Though originally a religious scholar, now, he pursued political control, which was the key to survival in today's Revolutionary Iran.

"Farrokh and Mahmoud detected surveillance on Ramin. Likely Mossad." The Teacher was not a man given to making up stories, the Grand Ayatollah reminded himself, but he permitted himself to appreciate that this could be a major problem.

"And how do you propose to resolve this problem?" the Grand Ayatollah queried, knowing the Teacher never approached him with a problem without a solution. It was one thing he respected about the man bound to the wheelchair before him, a man who did more than his fair share of killing during the turbulent times of the late 1970s.

"I am requesting permission from you, Grand Ayatollah, to remove the threat," the Teacher replied.

The Grand Ayatollah kept his face impassive, thinking back to the file he committed to memory. It seemed someone, perhaps an Israeli, at some point began following one of his beloved Immortals. He did not blame them, because they were bound to be noticed after so many decades of work, yet he would have to tread carefully.

"And I assume the plan we discussed previously will be implemented to ensure their safety?"

"Yes, Grand Ayatollah," the Teacher answered. "And if we handle this properly, they can also disrupt those planned negotiations. It might be advantageous for them to think the IRGC conducted this work, scuttling support from liberal government officials who seek peace with our main enemies."

"Let it be done, and may Allah protect my Immortals." *My sons,* he almost said but stopped himself.

CHAPTER

SIXTEEN

"IT IS GOOD THE WINTER IS FINALLY ENDING and the weather is getting warmer," Ramin said to no one in particular as he walked down the street. Mahmoud and Farrokh once again followed him from a distance, assigned by the Teacher to return and remain in Budapest until after the negotiations began. Farrokh drove in from Germany, while Mahmoud arrived from Bulgaria.

They were now in Mateszalka, a small Hungarian town near the Romanian border, to receive materials they would need to complete their mission. The administration officer's wife bought a Mercedes minibus, ostensibly for use to transport children they did not have, but in reality, for the three Immortals to use to transport what they needed undetected.

After receiving the materials, which they stored in the newly built compartments and inside metal-lined seats opened only with a magnetic key, they took their time driving back to Budapest. Now they were in Tatabanya, having driven around the capital to avoid approaching it from the east. They kept a selection of license plates at their disposal, able to produce diplomatic plates if pressed, but they hoped to keep those only in case of emergency.

This town is small and entirely too Western, Ramin thought, appreciating that since he was with his brothers, he once again thought more like an Iranian and less like an Eastern European. *That is dangerous,* he reminded himself, knowing his value lay in blending into the population. The Teacher routinely lectured them that they should not work together too much, though they changed their operations since Ramin required assistance carrying out the Grand Ayatollah's wishes to attack the Americans.

The brothers went to dinner at a Turkish restaurant with the most acceptable options and lingered over their meal to ensure they traveled the final distance under cover of darkness. Hungary remained a willing partner, or at least the police were willing to accept discrete payments to buy their silence.

"When is your next meeting with the Iraqis?" Mahmoud asked in English, refusing to speak Farsi in public, even when it was just the three of them. He never knew who might hear, and they would have a difficult time explaining the presence of three Iranians. *It would be so much easier if these talks were held in Turkey,* Mahmoud thought, knowing the Turks would never object to their operations.

"I will meet them in three days," Ramin said. With that timeline, the men knew they would kill anyone found to follow Ramin to the warehouse, desperate to protect the Iraqis who would carry out the direct attack.

We are not too old for such an attack, the three men each thought independently, *but the Teacher forbids us from carrying weapons in foreign lands.* They each knew the Grand Ayatollah treasured them, though only Mahmoud knew that each of the six was like a son to the great man himself. *We have been blessed by Allah,* Mahmoud thought and hoped Allah's blessings would continue to hold.

One more thing I must do, Ramin reminded himself. He was to speak again with the American. They continued to meet every two weeks, the American motivated by Ramin's threats against his children. Ramin warned the man against reneging on his promise.

"I AM TELLING YOU I DO NOT KNOW where the Iranian has been these past few weeks," Avi said into the phone, explaining once again to his supervisor in Tel Aviv on a secure line how the Iranian's movements had halted. "I believe he is going to ground before taking action."

"That you believe that means you are a more experienced field officer already," Jacob replied, sitting comfortably at his desk in Tel Aviv. He was a veteran Mossad officer and provided guidance to the young, new officers in the field. As he well knew, these men could not talk with just anyone, so Jacob would undertake these calls with a select number of field officers working on sensitive projects. Avi's case, of an Iranian sneaking around the site of next month's negotiations, was of the highest priority.

"I was afraid you would say that, *daad*," Avi replied. He treated Jacob like a respected uncle, able to trust in his advice and counsel while knowing that he would not be judged too harshly so long as he did not make mistakes while running an operation. "The community members reported that the Iranian surfaced again, perhaps alone, perhaps with others." He paused, deciding to be honest. "If the Iranian does have help, perhaps this is why I felt someone watching me that night in November."

Avi thought back to that encounter, recalling his failure to pinpoint which building the Iranian entered. He returned several times afterward to check various buildings, never able to find one that seemed to make sense. There was one being purchased by some members of the Iraqi community for use as a business center, but the transaction was still in process, so he hadn't yet bribed the official to get copies of the records. It seemed illogical that Iraqi refugees, mostly Sunnis seeking to escape the Shia-dominated government, would cooperate with a probable Iranian intelligence official.

Jacob shivered as he recalled Avi describing how he felt someone stalked him from the darkness. *There is a danger there.* Jacob felt it in his gut, but he knew he must trust the man in the field to make the best calls. Avi was a promising officer, part of a generation full of promise, and Jacob did not want to second-guess him.

Understanding that he faced a choice, Jacob let the line remain silent for a moment while he thought. He could, if truly worried, recommend that more officers go to assist Avi with this case. That would keep the young officer safe, but he feared the young Mossad officer would bristle at his protectiveness.

The second option was to trust the young man. He had graduated at the top of his class and seemed destined to lead Israel's intelligence service in the not-too-distant future. Making up his mind, hoping he would not regret his decision, Jacob spoke.

"Rely on your training, Avi, and continue reporting to me. That is the best way to stay safe."

On the other end, Avi felt a sense of relief, knowing from his training that Jacob could have chosen to protect him rather than take chances. As with any young intelligence officer around the world, Avi believed he was invincible, or as close to it as seemed possible in the twenty-first century. He had the training, the knowledge, and the tools needed to face any adversary. He was up to the task.

"Thank you, *daad*, I appreciate you trusting me." He hesitated, then added, "And I will check in with you every day, just to ensure you don't worry like my *savda*." He laughed, then disconnected the line before Jacob could respond.

Jacob shook his head, admiring the confidence of this young man, hoping he would not suffer the same gruesome fate as so many generations of officers before him.

RAMIN WALKED THROUGH THE STREET for everyone to see, hoping to draw out whoever seemed to trail him so they could take action and remove the threat permanently. If they did remove him, Ramin knew he would have to truly go to ground and would be unable to show his face in public again for years. The worst case would be an Israeli because the Jews were to be respected for their sophisticated technology and unlimited resources. He did not fear them but was wise enough to see his enemies' capabilities as greater than his own. Mahmoud and Farrokh, once again, were already ahead of him, Ramin's path into the warehouse district clear and predetermined.

Feeling eyes following his movements, Ramin made a half-hearted attempt at counter-surveillance, knowing he might alert those following him that something was wrong if he didn't follow the expected routine. He stopped at certain stores to check for tails, circled the block at irregular intervals, and even doubled back at one point.

The intelligence officer's classic move was to slowly pat his pockets as if looking for something and abruptly turn to determine if anyone was watching too closely. Good intelligence officers would continue following, willing to lose their target to avoid detection. Confident that he was not being too closely followed, and visibly relieved to find what he seemed to have lost in his pockets, Ramin turned back and continued into the warehouse district.

HE IS FOLLOWING TRADECRAFT *to determine if he has a tail,* Avi observed from a block behind the Iranian. He was pleased with the way he planned everything, though the monotony of the past week of waiting for the Iranian to appear grated on his nerves. It was the repetition that dulled his senses and made it difficult to focus. The adrenaline rush from the true start of an operation flooded his body, heightening his senses, and he felt truly alive.

Walking at a leisurely pace, he looked left and right, seeing the tip of caps, rustling of papers, and other signals from the watchers he stationed along the path through town to the warehouse district. Other watchers were stationed along alternate routes since there were plenty of aging Jewish patriots willing to take time out of their otherwise boring daily schedules to help their countrymen. Reaching for the left breast pocket of his jacket, Avi's hand swept downward, a motion all watchers on the street acknowledged by turning away or preparing to go home.

Thank you, all of you, Avi tried to communicate silently, sending these patriots home to their lives. He knew some would return home along prearranged paths while carrying newspapers or bags in a certain way, signaling to other watchers that they, too, could return home. From this point forward, Avi was on his own, tailing the Iranian, though hopefully today to the final destination. *I will learn more today,* Avi resolved, his training sharpened by a determination to achieve success with his mission. He ambled into the warehouse district, still more than fifty yards behind the Iranian but always keeping the man's figure in his sight.

RAMIN CONTINUED ON HIS PATH, THE SAME HE HAD TAKEN numerous times before. His body tingled in anticipation of action, though he willed his heart and breathing to slow. *I have done this hundreds of times before,* he assured himself, confident because he knew that Mahmoud and Farrokh were situated ahead on either side of the road.

Careful not to disappear from sight so as to not lose the man who he knew must be following him, Ramin continued on a steady path forward. He continued to feel eyes watching his every move, though he was unsure if those were the eyes of his brothers or those of his unknown stalker.

He moved with a purpose, thankful for the thick-soled shoes he wore, which protected him from the broken glass, discarded metal, and trash strewn throughout the streets. He walked past aging buildings, wondering absentmindedly what businesses used to operate here and where the employees worked now. He looked around now as if interested in the scenery around him but held tight to his training to never look back. He trusted his brothers to do that for him.

"THERE YOU ARE," FARROKH whispered to no one from his vantage point in a window above the street. His brother passed along the street, and he saw a man following nearly one hundred meters behind.

This man—*the enemy*—was ordinary in so many ways, dressed like a typical Hungarian in slacks, a button-up shirt, no tie, and a jacket. For all intents and purposes, the man was a prosperous businessman, except that he walked through the warehouse district, which was otherwise devoid of people.

His mistake is in continuing to follow, believing that no one will question his presence. Farrokh smiled, tapping once on the radio to signal Mahmoud that their target was in sight. One click to the radio in return confirmed that Mahmoud was also on the move.

Leaving his perch above, careful to avoid touching anything, Farrokh walked downstairs through the abandoned building to exit into an alleyway. He counted to ten, measuring the time and distance in coordination with Mahmoud. They arrived on opposite sides of the street at nearly the same time, as they arranged, and their eyes met. Having known one another for so long, despite not working operationally together as much as they would have liked, the men agreed with the slightest of nods to jointly track their quarry.

Carefully picking through rubble strewn about the alleyway, Farrokh doubled back through the system of back alleys that Ramin discovered when he first investigated this area. Between the buildings, built with service entrances to reduce the need for workers to walk along the main roads, Farrokh walked quickly to the next street, following the path he memorized days earlier. He once again arrived at the main road to see the same man still following Ramin, proving that the man was a foe who deserved the fate that was to come shortly.

RAMIN TURNED INTO THE EMPTY WAREHOUSE, accepting the risk he ran at using the Iraqi's building to catch the man who, for some time, tailed him. He signaled for the Iraqis to avoid the warehouse today, not wanting them to draw attention or create any challenges. Ramin would then find and eliminate the man following him.

Entering the warehouse, Ramin looked around and saw a sudden movement behind that confirmed someone had ducked out of sight just in time to avoid notice. *Or so he thinks.* He knew that, with his two brothers' assistance, he would deal once and for all with whoever was treading dangerously close to his operation.

THAT WAS CLOSE, AVI THOUGHT, thankful he hid behind the building as the Iranian approached the door. He would otherwise have been caught out in the open, obviously tailing the man ahead. After the door close, he looked around for a moment, taking stock of the situation. The weather was overcast and heavy. He listened for anything out of the ordinary but heard only the distant rumble of trucks.

The hair on the back of his neck rose. *What am I missing?* He paused to survey the landscape. Everything appeared quiet, yet alarm bells went off in his head.

Shaking off his fear and trusting in his training and the small firearm holstered in the small of his back, Avi left the safety and shelter of the building where he hid and set out across the expanse to the door. He reached it, his senses seeking the slightest movement or noise. Detecting neither, he opened the door and entered what appeared to be an abandoned warehouse.

Inside, his eyes adjusted quickly to the dim light. On the opposite side was a ring of chairs around a brick fireplace. Still alert for threats but curious as to why the location was empty, Avi scanned the large room. *This must have been some sort of building where they manufactured machinery,* he reasoned, seeing the dark outlines of machines long since removed on the concrete floor. Looking up, he noticed a light on in a room on the second floor. Backing up to the wall to stay out of sight, he carefully made his way towards a corridor, which he reasoned led to the stairs.

Avi reached the base of the stairs. *I do not see anything wrong,* he argued to instincts that told him to run. Ultimately, it was his desire to know, to verify what was happening with the Iranian. His gut told him that the Iranian was planning something. *If it benefits the Iranian regime, then it would hurt the Israeli state.* With that surety, he climbed the stairs, finding himself on the first floor, which housed offices for what would have been the company's managers and administrative staff. Numerous empty rooms had doors that were ajar, but he continued down the hallway to the lit room.

He approached the doorway and glanced around for threats. Seeing none, he leaned his head on the door to listen to the murmurs coming from inside. Concentrating, he blocked out the noises around him, such as the soft opening of a door behind him. As he strained to make out any of the words or decipher the language, Avi felt a sting in his buttocks and fell, and the world went dark.

WHERE AM I? **AVI THOUGHT AFTER** regaining consciousness. He lay on the floor in a room, perhaps the office where he heard voices. He was alarmed to discover that his arms and legs were bound with rope, and there was a cloth tied around his head, covering his mouth to prevent him from speaking. *And why am I lying on what feels like a hard sheet of plastic?* He tried to look around. He paused when he heard the sounds of scraping chairs and footsteps.

"Ah, our guest is awake," someone said.

Avi heard the man speak English and looked straight up to see three men standing around him. All were in their late forties or early fifties, give or take, and they watched him like a predator would watch its prey. The man who spoke stepped closer, leaning in to look more carefully, and Avi knew at once that he had failed to heed the instincts that told him to run. Slightly alarmed, he also noticed his firearm firmly in the man's hands.

After removing the bloodied gag from the man's mouth, Ramin stepped back, confident that he held the higher ground against the defenseless man at his and his brothers' feet. He held the man's compact pistol steadily pointed at him. He set the rag on the desk behind him, intending to dispose of it with the body. The rag tumbled to the floor under the desk, unseen by the three Iranians.

"Who are you?" Ramin questioned the man, his search of the man's pockets having produced only keys and money.

"I am a member of Hungarian intelligence," Avi lied, hoping to scare the Iranian. He knew trouble with the host country's intelligence agency might keep them from doing anything rash. He learned during training and countless discussions with his fellow officers to always play for time when possible and never give away too much information.

"I don't think so," another of the men said. "But I think we know where you work."

Why did that man just speak to me in Hebrew? Avi wondered. He felt groggy and was unable to focus. A voice in his head said he had been drugged, but analytically, knowing that truth was different than being able to do anything about it.

"So, Jew," the same man said, "why were you following our brother?" Farrokh stared at the man, willing him to answer but already knowing how this would go.

Twenty minutes later, Avi lay naked in numbed agony. "I don't know anything," he spat, struggling to remain in control but in so much pain.

The men, monsters from an unknown nightmare, methodically broke each finger and toe at the joint, intent on causing as much pain as possible. They sought information but also planned ahead with the tarp on the floor, ensuring they could clean up without leaving any blood.

"I believe him," Mahmoud interjected, speaking for the first time. He and Ramin let Farrokh ask the questions, knowing their brother's hatred of Jews outstripped their more neutral feelings. "No one could endure that much agony without saying something." That Farrokh's torture of the man was more personal and less business mattered little to him.

"How much do you know about me?" Ramin leaned over the man. "Have you seen me meeting anyone?" he asked, following up on the question left unanswered.

Rather than answer, Avi moaned in agony, never before knowing pain such as this. His hands and feet were on fire. The sadistic man who broke his fingers and toes with pliers and a hammer stared malevolently.

"I know nothing, nothing, nothing," Avi said, not knowing how to make these men understand that he did, in fact, know nothing. He began to shiver, in so much pain that he barely registered being naked.

"We will learn nothing more from this man," Ramin concluded, raising his hand to stop Farrokh from inflicting more pain on the man at their feet. *Perhaps he is telling the truth.* Though, really, he was just waiting and listening to determine whether anyone would come looking for the man. If anyone had come for the man, they would have had problems, but he appeared to be on his own.

"Farrokh, my brother, let us end this," Ramin said, seizing control of the situation. He held out his hand, offering the Israeli's pistol, and waited.

Swiftly, Farrokh took the pistol from Ramin and, in one fluid motion, shot the Jew in the top of the head, the way all Immortals were trained to deal with the enemy.

The bullet entered the top of the head, remaining inside the body so it wouldn't be found, yet it also emitted tiny particles of blood, which spattered outside of the plastic sheeting without any of the men realizing. They then gathered the plastic sheeting to wrap the body, making it easier to dispose of it as far as possible from the city. Before they left the room, Ramin grabbed a plastic trash bag filled with the dead Israeli's clothes, carefully following the Teacher's instructions.

As they each carried part of the plastic sheeting, Farrokh felt no remorse for torturing and killing the man they carried, nor burying the man where no one would ever find his body. He was confident that the Israelis tortured and killed enough Iranians, so this was just their opportunity to settle the score.

Ramin walked along, carrying the plastic sheeting with one hand and jingling the keys they found in the dead man's pockets with the other. He absentmindedly wondered what they would find at the address they managed to torture out of the man. Hefting the bag of the Israeli's clothes, he contemplated where to leave them, not vocally questioning the Teacher's instructions but also not understanding the full meaning.

Secreted inside Avi's jacket, standard issue for all Israeli Mossad officers, was sewn a transmitter with a battery life of at least two years. It was Bluetooth technology, adapted by an Israeli technology company to provide another way to track important assets or field personnel. The three Iranians searched the dead man before wrapping him in the sheeting, finding the cleverly concealed transmitter. Although only usable at a distance of less than fifty meters, it would continue to passively transmit its signal, waiting as long as its battery lasted for someone to find and retrieve it.

As they carried the bag to the van, Ramin searched his surroundings, confident that no one observed their movements. "The Israelis will find the clothes where we place them," he mumbled to himself, "but will they draw the conclusions we seek?" He knew they would never find the body, which they planned to place as far away from the clothes as possible. Even if someone found it in some weeks or months, by the time anyone determined this man's identity, Ramin would have left Budapest, not planning to return for at least one year. Perhaps longer.

CHAPTER
SEVENTEEN

"HE COULD NOT HAVE SIMPLY DISAPPEARED," Jacob reasoned aloud to the desk in his office, afraid of the worst-case scenario. Avi had not reported back in for two days, unusual because the young intelligence officer assiduously followed protocol.

It was his local partners, the people who looked out for him, who first raised alarms when Avi did not return after his operation to track the Iranian. Unfortunately for Jacob, and everyone else, the old helpers dithered for a day, unable to agree about whether to report Avi's disappearance. Eventually, they dialed the number they had memorized, and word reached Jacob.

The wheels of the Mossad began spinning quickly then, its officers not even waiting for visas to enter Hungary. Instead, they used European passports that did not require visas. They entered Avi's apartment and, finding it ransacked, initiated emergency protocols. Whoever searched the apartment was just a bit too good, too focused on appearing to cause damage without the randomness of criminals.

Luckily for them, Avi's training dictated that he kept all his files in his office safe, which the ambassador accessed. These redundancies were invaluable in situations such as this small, one-man Mossad shop where the officer operated without a safety net.

The files were now in Jacob's Tel Aviv office, the door closed, and his jacket tossed carelessly on the floor. He was taking this personally, and everyone knew because he had not acted prudently. No one blamed him. All his colleagues agreed that they would have made the same call in his shoes. *But what do I do now?*

The understanding that the Iranians likely targeted and killed a Mossad officer brought Jacob's blood to a boil, and he knew this would change how both intelligence services would operate for the foreseeable future. This was the kind of disaster that would disrupt the business of collecting intelligence, all because he, as a senior mentor, failed to properly protect his young officer.

Mossad's leadership already granted him absolution, though Jacob requested none and did not attempt to enforce one week of required leave from the office. Jacob's storied career spanned decades, and he knew where bodies were buried. Soon, he thought grimly, he would add more to that number.

As he tried to focus on seeking further clues to the identities of the killers, Jacob thought about the needle in the haystack. That Bluetooth device was their best hope of finding Avi's body, yet Hungary was a huge country; it would take weeks to scour it. He had already requested a drone to covertly search for the body, but leadership denied that as too brazen a violation of Hungary's sovereignty and unlikely to deliver success.

Screw their sovereignty, Jacob fumed, *that body deserves a proper burial.* Thankfully, he knew teams were driving the streets of the capital, hoping to get lucky. Jacob bowed his head silently in prayer, asking forgiveness and promising revenge.

"**WHEN WILL YOU NEXT TRAVEL** to Budapest?" Kate asked absent-mindedly, chopping vegetables in the kitchen. They cooked dinner together, an intimate act that gave them time to reconnect after long days at work. On Friday evenings, they went out for dinner, and when they had the opportunity during the week, they also made a point to spend time together.

"I leave on Monday," Ben replied, perturbed because Kate had asked the same question just minutes before. She was distracted—had been since returning from work—but he knew better than to ask. If it was something she wanted to discuss, he knew she would come out with it.

It is unusual enough that the Israelis are asking for help, Kate reasoned to herself, *but to openly suggest the Iranians made a Mossad officer disappear is tantamount to an act of war.* Kate knew the intelligence world acted according to a code, one that no one sought to violate. If intelligence officers began killing one another, then they could not engage in the art of collecting intelligence. The Russians understood this well, avoiding any possibility of roughing up opposition officers, even going so far as to protect some rival officers from random muggings. The Chinese also understood, though they were not above roughing up the odd intelligence officer just to set an example.

"Love," Kate said as she slid the chopped vegetables atop the shredded lettuce, "an Israeli intelligence officer from Mossad went missing a day ago, and no one has seen him."

Ben wondered why she was sharing this with him, but he knew her well enough to know she was not yet done speaking.

"It is indeed rare that they shared this with us," she said, answering his unspoken question, "but what troubles our people in London and at your Agency is that the body just disappeared." She did not tell him that the Israelis were out for blood, seeking anyone who might know anything and offering just about anything in trade for knowledge of their man. It was, she realized, the one thing that kept people like her going, knowing that their government would do anything to track down their bodies. She set that thought aside, knowing she was safe.

Ben was not versed in intelligence matters but was engaged in the trade, as it were. "I'm not sure how to respond," he admitted, then took a sip of wine before refilling her glass.

She leaned over for a kiss, both to confirm that he indeed was still there and as thanks for the wine. *I could really use a glass of scotch,* she thought as she looked at Ben's side table covered with liquor bottles. But she would wait until after dinner when she and Ben settled into the living room after their evening walk.

Following a dinner of steak salads—Ben had insisted on meat while Kate pressed for something healthier than pasta and pota-toes—Kate cleared the table as Ben loaded the dishwasher. After changing into exercise clothes for their walk, they departed the lobby of the building and set out for the Potomac, strolling quietly hand in hand.

After walking for an hour, giving them time to talk through their next day but never discussing any of their work in much detail, they returned to the apartment. Theirs was a comfortable schedule filled with time together. The apartment was not large but was empty save for them tonight. Charlotte was out of town for a week of work.

"Ben…" They sat comfortably with their feet intertwined. "I want you to be careful when you go to Budapest."

"Of course." Ben didn't look up from his book, forgiving her protectiveness because he felt the same way towards her.

Kate set down her magazine and leaned forward, then grasped Ben's book to get his attention.

"I am serious," she said, moving closer to straddle his legs and pin him to the couch. "There is something, likely someone, dangerous in Budapest who made that Israeli disappear. Plus, the Israelis will want revenge, and the whole city could become a powder keg. If this was the Iranians, it fits because they refuse to follow standard rules and practices."

He took her hand and kissed her palm. "I will be careful, my dear," he replied, meeting her gaze to convey how serious he was taking her concern.

His arrival in Budapest two weeks before the talks would require him to check in with her every day, until she followed a few days before the talks began, that is.

"That is all I ask," she replied, setting his book on the table and moving closer.

BACK HOME AFTER a full day in the office—his first since before Ludmilla's death—Robert contemplated the takeout Chinese he picked up during his commute home. He opted for a drink from his bar instead.

After dropping two ice cubes into the tumbler, Robert strode to the liquor table and selected a bottle, then poured a generous portion. He sat in his chair, next to Ludmilla's, and looked at his home. *More like prison,* he mused.

His eyes settled on his briefcase. In an inside pocket, guaranteed to be hidden from all but the most energetic, were three inches of copies of reports he deemed the most useful to the Russians. He imagined downing his drink, grabbing the briefcase, and emptying the contents into his fireplace.

But then how would the Russians react? He knew the answer to that question, and his eyes instinctively turned to photos adorning the wall, settling on the smiling photos of his sister's children. He felt true remorse that he never wanted children, but he always made an effort with his sister's kids. When he saw them, of course, which was not as often as he wanted.

Thinking about Sergei, Robert grimaced, knowing he would have to see the man again soon to deliver the documents. He read through some papers about preparations for the not-so-secret nuclear negotiations with the Iranians in Hungary, which were scheduled to begin in two weeks. He reasoned that sharing those documents wouldn't hurt anyone too much.

Not that anyone really cared about Iran, he thought as he drained his scotch and went to eat dinner. He selected a bottle of red to drink with his meal, then settled with his TV tray to watch television the rest of the evening. *All the action is in Europe, and anything that happens outside that continent does not really matter, at least not to people who matter.*

"IT IS HANDLED," FARROKH ASSERTED on the secure video call. He, Ramin, and Mahmoud huddled near the camera, knowing the Teacher watched them carefully. They used a secure chat function within a site dedicated for the discussion of Islamic studies, the sale of Qurans, and proselytization of the Shia sect of Islam. It was only accessible using multiple passwords and was reserved exclusively for the Immortals, so they knew exactly where to look.

The site, designed by a computer engineer educated at the Massachusetts Institute of Technology, was a veritable labyrinth of links, drop-down menus, and chat options. As an added security measure, Islamic scholars throughout Iran funded by the Grand Ayatollah were required to post on the site at least once per week, guaranteeing anonymity for the Immortals' network.

"As always, you have done well," the Teacher replied, uneasy with the situation yet secure in the knowledge that *his* men would be safe. *The ones who will suffer,* he reasoned, *will be the Revolutionary Guard and Etele'at intelligence officers, who the Mossad will target mercilessly.* That thought brought a smile because this furthered the Grand Ayatollah's plan and would disrupt the talks.

"How did you dispose of the body?" he asked. They explained in detail how they moved the body north from the city before burying it in a secluded, rarely visited forest.

"No one will find the body anytime soon," Ramin assured him, describing the secluded nature of the forest preserve and the untraceable method they used to transport the body.

"And the clothing and transmitter?"

Again, Ramin expertly described locating the appropriate apartment block in Budapest and then taking a meandering path away from it. Upon finding a suitable place, where the bag was sure to be ignored for at least several days, they quickly left.

They did good work. He was proud of teaching them how to account for every detail and never assume anything. The Americans had a proverb about assumptions, but he could not remember it just at that moment. Lost in thought, the Teacher stared at the screen, waiting for his men to speak further. Belatedly, he realized they had given their full report and looked to him for assurance that they acted correctly.

"I am proud of all three of you," he pronounced, seeing the relief on their faces. He knew he would have to relay this news to the Grand Ayatollah, but he remained confident his Immortals were still off the radar of foreigners. That meant any backlash would not directly hurt his men, so long as they were careful.

"And the Iraqis?" he queried, changing topics, to the relief of the men sitting in Hungary. "Are they ready to undertake the work?"

Ramin handled this brief, explaining that as a result of killing the Israeli, he changed their meeting location.

"It would be too dangerous to continue meeting in that location," Mahmoud interjected, "since we noticed a significant increase in activity at the Israeli Embassy since we killed their man."

The Teacher grunted his acknowledgment, assessing the situation and wondering if perhaps he should scuttle the plan to attack the peace talks using the Iraqis. The dangers mounted each day, and he was unwilling to risk the loss of these six men. They had, he realized, become like his children, boys he cajoled, trained, mentored, and shaped into killing machines with the goal of achieving anything the Grand Ayatollah desired.

"You are confident everything can move forward with no danger to yourselves?" the Teacher asked pointedly. These were *his men*, and he feared risking their lives. He accepted that he was getting old and had given in to the need for advanced training for the next generation of Immortals. The three men on the screen before him had already sacrificed enough for many decades and needed to come home to be with their brothers. He would convince the Grand Ayatollah.

These men meant too much, to him and the Grand Ayatollah, and could not be sacrificed. "I pray for your safety," he said, ending the connection. Then he whispered, "And a safe return home."

CHAPTER

EIGHTEEN

, and already things were not going well, Ben reflected. The Iran Desk sent several people to Budapest, just as the Senator sent Ben, and now all of them fought for limited resources. None of them operated from the embassy; they all avoided the wrath of the ambassador like the plague.

Ben sat in a restaurant, waiting for Brent, cajoled into meeting him for dinner with the promise of gossip from Main State. If there was one thing Foreign Service officers seemed to like more than anything, it was gossip about other members of their group. Ben was usually careful with his per diem, saving it for special occasions, but tonight he could justify spending all of it to buy Brent several drinks and relax.

The visiting Iran Desk officers were difficult, having gained no traction with Brent, so they only received what Brent sent back to DC. That meant Ben maintained the inside track on everything happening, which he transmitted directly to the Senator.

"I cannot believe they caught him cheating on his wife, with an intern no less," Brent laughed, downing the rest of his drink in one gulp and waving to the waiter for another. This was a small restaurant, out of the way, which gave Ben plenty of time to assess the man before him. The last time they spoke, Brent seemed full of despair but now was in much better spirits. He already confirmed that the ambassador mostly left him alone, concentrating instead on lobbying for a seat at the negotiation table with the Iranians. *As if,* Ben thought, knowing some senior folks would stop at nothing to gain an opportunity to get ahead.

Deciding to broach a subject he knew would be difficult, Ben took a sip of water and focused on Brent. *Here we go.*

"Brent," Ben started, having rehearsed what he was about to say, "I want you to know that I am worried about you, especially after everything you told me when I was last here in Budapest."

Brent smiled as he raised his new drink, then scanned the room before gazing at Ben. "My friend," he responded, feeling more relaxed and confident than he had since the ambassador arrived, "you have nothing to worry about."

Ben sat back, surprised at the turn of events, because he had prepared to confront the man before him about excessive drinking, anger issues, and the possibility of leaving himself open to blackmail. Before he could start, Brent took a swig of his martini and continued.

"Look, Ben, things were bad, really bad, in fact." He leaned back in his chair, seemingly without a care in the world. "But I have things under control. Stacey and I are back together, and we decided that we will curtail this assignment. I have not, and never will, do anything to endanger the safety of personnel here at the embassy."

As Brent described the endless conversations with his wife, Ben realized his fears about the man before him may have been misplaced. Still, he worried Brent was, and still might be, attractive to a foreign intelligence service whose agents would love to take advantage of an American Embassy officer unhappy with work and his personal life. Ben knew that any number of countries would kill to access the information contained in the brain across the table.

While speaking, Brent calmed his anxiety and reassured himself that things were going well. He had not heard from Radek in weeks, which was good news, though he had already provided most everything that would have been useful. His plan was to return with his family to Washington, where he could serve for several years, and put distance between himself and the distasteful time when he succumbed to Radek's friendship. The priority now was to move past his mistake and never tell anyone about it. He knew enough from short conversations with the Iran experts in town for the negotiations that the Iranians could not operate easily in America. *There, I will be safe.*

More relaxed after Brent's explanation, Ben decided to broach another topic, this one less personal.

"Brent, what do you make of my assertion that the Hungarians are cozying up to the Russians, and by extension, the Iranians?"

Brent stiffened. *Uh oh, here it comes.*

Dropping his glass to the table, Brent responded with a drunken wag of his finger. "There isn't anything to what you're saying, Ben," he retorted, leaning to stare into Ben's eyes. "You need to stop pushing this theory, it's making our embassy look bad."

Ben tuned out Brent's boozy response, leaning back to fold his arms protectively across his chest. *I know what I saw. The Senator accepted what I saw at face value and is still raising the alarm.* Despite his confidence, Ben knew it wasn't a battle worth fighting, not here in Budapest and not when the entire Department took the embassy's word over his. *It's just like Herat. The facts proved me right then, and I'm confident they'll prove me right this time.*

"On this issue, Ben, the ambassador and I agree completely. We accept the Hungarians are cozy with the Russians, as they've always been, but cozying up to the Iranians? That's too far even for them." He paused, picking up the glass and noticing ice cubes lying on the table. Picking at one, he continued. "The ambassador spoke with the assistant secretary, who agrees this doesn't merit any further action or our attention, not when we have so many other priorities to press in country."

Ben snatched his glass from the table and rattled it to get the waiter's attention. Catching Brent by surprise, Ben bent forward to whisper, "What've you heard about the missing Israeli?"

Brent fought to focus on Ben, startled out of his thought process, and leaned in to share the gossip he heard. In the back of his mind, he wondered if Radek, his *former* friend, had anything to do with it. The simple way Radek threatened his family made it seem likely, but so long as he cooperated, he would not be a target. "I know the Israelis are excited about something, but I'm not cleared for that."

Ben decided it made no sense to continue pushing, knowing he would never be able to get through the complicated mess that was Brent's life. He also understood that Brent would protect his embassy's equities, up to and including denying the Hungarians cozying up to the Iranians. He decided to ask Kate for her advice.

"Then, my friend"—Ben raised his glass, which arrived just as he drained the last of his previous drink—"I toast to your health and happiness, wishing you better days in the weeks, months, and years ahead. And may they find that missing Israeli."

"THERE ARE MORE AMERICAN, BRITISH, and other European officials here than ever," Ramin grumbled, knowing he would never again be able to get the weak American alone, at least not until after the negotiations were over. "Not to mention the hornet's nest at the Israeli Embassy."

The brothers sat around a table in a shared apartment, lost in thought. Ramin was no longer able to leave the apartment without a significant disguise involving makeup, fake hair, and rubber prosthetics to change the shape of his face, which typically took hours to apply; the risk of being sighted by an Israeli outweighed any possible benefit of going out. They would have to make an exception for tomorrow night, when he would meet the Iraqis one last time before the operation, if only to reaffirm their obligation to take action.

They knew reprisals had already begun, having heard from contacts that the Revolutionary Guard officer in Budapest fell in front of a bus on his way to work. He quietly thanked *Khoda* that Farid, the IRGC representative at the embassy who had grown suspicious of his activities in Budapest, was the one who died. That he left behind a wife and son was of no major consequence because Revolutionary Guard officers routinely harassed the Immortals when they traveled through Tehran, not understanding that their work was of any true consequence. It made little difference that each of the Immortals held Revolutionary Guard ranks; they still faced harassment and luggage checks when they traveled through the Imam Khoemenei airport.

In several other cities around the region, with larger Iranian embassies, they knew other Revolutionary Guard officers experienced similar mishaps, some fatal, others merely resulting in broken bones. *The Israelis must have found the bag of clothes,* Ramin thought grimly but did not question the Teacher's methods.

In response to the attacks, the Teacher reported that irate IRGC leadership ordered their people in the field to target Israeli spies and diplomats throughout Western Europe. The sudden death of an IRGC officer in Budapest, the son-in-law of a senior cleric close to the Supreme Leader, ensured a quick reaction. IRGC officers managed to target one known Mossad officer in Berlin but missed when targeting an Israeli diplomat in Madrid, instead killing his wife.

Despite knowing this was the Teacher's plan, the three men were accustomed to action, not to watching their fellow countrymen attacked one at a time. None blamed himself. Each acted under orders from the Teacher, who in turn received his direction directly from the Grand Ayatollah. As far as they were concerned, that was as good as coming from Allah. They briefly debated the merits of their actions, as they had many times over the decades, but they always deferred in the end to the wisdom of their elders. *Where was I before the Teacher, before the Grand Ayatollah?* they each thought, shuddering at the memories of their life before becoming Immortals.

I am bound forever, each knew, confirming in their hearts, minds, and souls their commitment to the cause. They would die for the men they served, willingly, but loved the men all the more because they knew they never went on suicide missions. Theirs was an existence of service but one that permitted them the knowledge that they advanced a mission that would one day bring the peace of Allah to the world, or at least to the great Middle East.

"HOW'RE YOU DOING, KATE?" BEN ASKED, sitting in his hotel room. He knew she was trying her best to get to Budapest but was fighting a system that was not designed for flexibility. In fact, it was her father who was displaying remarkable reservoirs of rigidity. He didn't want Kate in the middle of the Israeli-Iranian murder spree rampant throughout Europe.

Exhaling, Kate squeezed her eyes shut, blocking out her childhood room and concentrating instead on the voice on the other end of the line. "I am doing better now that I hear your voice, darling." She understood her father's protective nature but honestly feared missing out on the action in the streets, with Budapest being ground zero. She longed to see the Iranians in action, to be back doing the work she did in Afghanistan, yet she knew she could not go back in time. *I must attend those negotiations,* she fumed. *I can help!*

She ostensibly was in London trying to get to Budapest, but was also trying to apply some measure of sense to her Israeli contacts, with whom she met daily to discuss their desire for anything on Iran's operations. They learned from sympathetic sources that Kate was pulling on a thread that could lead them to the man who killed their operative.

Theirs was a barely contained rage, unbridled passion for revenge. They shared documents proving that their officer tracked an Iranian, a man who apparently led their officer into a trap but then disappeared off the face of the earth. *Their man had to turn up,* she reasoned, because bodies only completely vanished in movies or people's imaginations. In truth, it took serious effort to dispose of a body. It was difficult under the best of circumstances but would have been bloody difficult in a country like Hungary.

"What can you share about events in Budapest?" she asked, relaxing when she heard Ben's voice.

"Things are moving forward here, though our ambassador is being incredibly difficult, insisting that he must approve every arrangement." He exhaled, trying to release his frustration. "One problem I have," Ben admitted, unsure how to broach the subject, "is that I am worried about the pol/econ chief here, Brent." He thought through what to say, wanting to be careful but also trusting Kate enough to know she would have good ideas for how he should proceed.

"The fact is things are better for him, but I still see some really worrying signs about him, namely that he is in a very precarious mental and emotional state." He paused, then shared his fears. "It worries me that he could be a target for recruitment by a foreign intelligence service."

"Have you spoken with anyone at the embassy about your concerns? Perhaps the head of security?"

"No, I tried to raise it, but everyone here knows that Brent regularly experiences some shocking harassment at the hands of the ambassador. Did I tell you that Brent found the ambassador screwing his wife back in the fall?"

"Wow," she said, amazed things like that still happened. She heard stories of swingers at embassies, though that tended to happen primarily at smaller, more remote postings, usually in parts of Africa or Asia, where embassy staff were more secluded from local populations.

"Ben, that is really bad, because I can tell you that many foreign intelligence services are focused on the upcoming talks."

"Brent is doing better and getting his life back together. I would almost say he is back to the guy I vaguely remember from training."

"But is he back enough that his past will not return to haunt him?" She knew personnel turned by foreign intelligence services were extremely dangerous because they provided the type of insider information that was impossible for security officers to detect as a threat.

"No," Ben answered honestly, though it pained him. "I will make another run at the security officer and make sure he is aware of these problems." He paused, thinking before he spoke because he didn't want to sound like a fool while talking to Kate. "It could bring heat on Brent, though, and make my life more difficult." He took a breath before finishing his thought. "I've got to work with him."

"Isn't hurting his feelings worth keeping the entire negotiations safe?" she asked rhetorically, not to be judgmental, but she knew it was easy to overlook the vulnerabilities of friends and colleagues. During training, they forced her to read case files of men and women who spied on their countries, sometimes for money but more often because they were blackmailed into doing what the enemy wanted.

Seeking to soften the blow, Kate switched topics before Ben could respond. "Remember when I mentioned the missing officer from the friendly service?" She did not want to say too much, though by this point, the Israeli officer's disappearance was in the press, so she could speak freely when necessary, so long as she did not disclose sensitive information.

"Yes, I heard some rumors here in the embassy about that," he said, "and those folks are really freaking out, with a full complement of staff here." He remembered a rumor he wanted to share. "The most likely culprits, according to one of the regional security officers yesterday, are the Iranians. The RSOs are in regular touch with Hungarian authorities, who are investigating all Iranian nationals currently in country, focused on those affiliated with the embassy."

Bingo, Kate thought. She knew from her Israeli contacts that the Mossad officer was tailing a suspected Iranian intelligence officer when he disappeared. Under pressure from her leadership, she shared some information with the Israelis she collected on the mythical Immortals. Over the months, she collated a list of likely operations, all instances where the Iranian government benefitted directly from an action, though at this point, everything was circumstantial. That made her nervous because she preferred to report facts, not hearsay from unverified sources.

"We unfortunately can't discuss more on this line," she said, "and I simply cannot say any more right now." She added the last part quickly, not wanting to hurt Ben's feelings or exclude him. Her work as an intelligence officer meant she often had better access to information, and while the US and UK were allies, they each worked for a different country. For her, that meant that not all information could flow freely. She would only make an exception in case of a safety issue, which this was not. For now.

"I understand, babe," Ben replied. He knew the constraints on what Kate could and could not discuss. Ben knew he was not cut out for that level of absolute secrecy that intelligence officers had to adhere to.

"Thank you, darling," she whispered, "and I promise we will talk more when I get there."

"Absolutely, I love you and will speak with you before then."

In London, Kate set down her phone and looked around at her childhood room. It still bore posters from bands she loved when she was a teen. She stretched out her left hand, wondering what it would feel like to have a ring on her finger. Her father still asked when Ben intended to propose, since family traditions dictated that they inform relatives and eventually hold a party, and her mother regularly looked at her quizzically, as if she knew more than she said. *That makes sense,* Kate thought. Her mother always seemed to know more than she let on.

After leaving her room, she walked down the stairway, passing paintings of her ancestors. Some she secretly loathed based on stories she heard, and she could feel their eyes following her. It was the same when she was younger, though then the paintings kept her company whenever she did not want to interact with her sister or brother. Arriving at the base of the stairs, she heard her sister's voice from the drawing room and, by instinct, tried to escape to the kitchen.

"Kate, darling," her mother called, magically able to hear her soft footsteps from anywhere in the house. "Bea and I were just discussing a little outing this afternoon to look at dresses for your future engagement party." Kate reluctantly entered the room to find her mother sitting on an overstuffed armchair and Beatrix lounging on a leather couch.

"Yes, big sister," Beatrix said, sitting up to eye Kate with a mixture of envy and annoyance, "what on earth does one wear to an engagement party with an American? Speaking of, when will he propose?"

Kate stopped short of mentioning that Ben was from a middle-class background because she knew that would sound classist and draw a sharp rebuke from her mother. She did not want to start that fight. Not yet.

Kate eyed Beatrix cautiously, knowing theirs was a complicated relationship. So close when younger but now virtually estranged, they only saw one another on neutral ground and in the presence of their parents. Beatrix was shorter than her sister but equally as slim. Both wore stylish clothes, though Kate preferred clothes that were muted, while Beatrix sought to radiate her status. *The City changed her*, Kate mused. She knew Beatrix surrounded herself with wealthy men and women—*mostly men*—and so much wealth only brought out her more competitive characteristics.

Neither spoke of their brother, who they agreed was the most misunderstood member of their family, yet he loomed large because his was such a large personality. Rarely would the sisters set aside their differences, except when it came to their parents or him. Especially him.

She thought of her brother and asked, "Have we heard from—"

"No, dear, we have not," Angela replied quickly. It pained her not to have all three of her children in the house together. It had been several years since the entire family was together. *Perhaps a wedding will bring everyone back together,* she thought, *because there is nothing so grand as a new member of a family to create opportunities to heal.*

Leaning on the wall just inside the drawing room, Kate thought the same thing, as did Beatrix on the sofa. All three women missed the laughter and love of their brother. *If only he got along better with Father,* the three thought simultaneously, each staring at the same photo on the mantle.

When Beatrix rose from the couch, Kate reached out her hand. "I miss him too," she whispered loud enough for her sister to hear.

Startled, Beatrix awkwardly squeezed her sister's hand, struggling to hold back tears. "Me too," she whispered.

They loosely held hands, turning to stare at their mother, who sat focused, almost as if in a trance, on the photo of their entire family taken years before.

This closeness was unnatural for the two of them, but at that moment, they set aside their personal feelings and focused on their mother. They wanted to run to her, only just restraining themselves. It wouldn't do, they reproached themselves, to show too much emotion. It just wasn't done.

CHAPTER
NINETEEN

"**WILL THIS MAKE YOU HAPPY?**" Robert asked as casually as he could, setting his satchel on the ground between his feet. He sat at a picnic table at a park by the Potomac. *Sergei looks exhausted,* he realized, not really caring what steps the Russian took to ensure no one tailed him for their meetings.

He expected payment for his cooperation, yet he also remained angry at the man for killing his wife. He was still not sure how to rebuild his life but didn't want to return to a life where everything revolved around work. A few of his female coworkers were friendlier than in the past, all still feeling sorry for him. He wondered how long it would take before he would be ready to date again, knowing himself well enough that he could not live the rest of his life alone.

"Let us hope so, for your sake," Sergei retorted, though he was too exhausted to generate much anger after spending four hours driving around the Washington, DC, area to ensure he was clear. The tail cleaning process, known in the embassy as *uborka*, was used whenever an officer met with a sensitive American asset. The Americans were stretched thin, not as focused on him since he kept his schedule light in the week leading up to the meeting, so today's meeting was not as difficult to get to clean as in the past.

In truth, Sergei could bump into the American for a quick verbal exchange, but anything in writing required a much larger time commitment. His confrontation with the American in the forest near his house was dangerous, but it was a required step to solidify a nervous and reticent asset. The last thing he, or his Moscow supervisors, wanted was for either him or the American to be caught with such sensitive documents. He felt the bag slide underneath the table and didn't make any movement. He noticed the American looking at him, as if wondering about his matching case.

"You will be happy to know you can use your credit cards again," he said. The American must have known his cards stopped working as a threat after their discussion. It was meant to show that the Russians meant business. It would do no good for the American to grow too comfortable or confident.

"I want cash," Robert exclaimed, crossing his arms and pursing his lips. During the past several nights, alone in his house, he thought through a myriad of escape plans, none as elaborate as he wished. However, he knew he needed to build up a cash reserve to use if he needed to run. He stopped momentarily, wondering whether he would need to run from either American authorities or the Russians who had him by the balls, able to dictate what he could and couldn't do. He couldn't decide which would be more dangerous, knowing the Americans would put him in jail, but the Russians would kill him.

Staring absently at Sergei, Robert considered the few decisions he made. Confident that the Russians were not omnipotent and thus able to tail him everywhere, he opened a safe deposit box outside of the immediate DC area, where he began depositing cash on a weekly basis. In that box, he already had nearly $30,000, the initial $25,000 from the Russian, as well as what other cash he could collect in the past week.

Without his wife spending money like it was going out of style, he could save money. He never bought a large life insurance policy for his wife, but the little he would receive once those paper pushers finished asking questions would barely cover the cost of a decent vacation.

"And why do you need cash?" Sergei asked, not expecting an answer. He wondered how desperate the American could be. *Would he be willing to make a run for it?* Sergei judged not, because then he would have to leave his comfortable life. *Where could he go?* He did not think this man would be stupid enough to test his patience, secure in the knowledge that he did not make idle threats.

"I want to be able to give my sister cash so she can buy presents for her kids without having to argue with her husband about money," Robert lied, having concocted that story in advance. It was true, in a way, that his sister and her husband argued all the time about money. His sister also routinely asked for money, but in the past, Robert always refused, explaining that Ludmilla spent everything he earned. And more, if he was honest about his dead wife. Still, with extra cash from the Russians, he could begin sharing some with his sister, which would make her happy, plus he could build up his stash of cash.

That makes sense, Sergei reflected, having himself visited the town where the American's sister lived. She and her husband lived comfortably, yet with three children, they had little money for luxuries. He opted to believe the man sitting across from him, only to realize that he had no cash to offer.

"Regrettably, I do not have cash for you. But couldn't you draw from the initial amount of cash we gave you?" He found it difficult to believe the American could have spent $25,000, yet in his experience with men who sold their country's secrets, nothing was impossible.

"I spent it," Robert lied, deciding that saying as little as possible would raise the least suspicion.

"The next time we meet, I will have cash for you," Sergei promised.

"Fine." Robert focused on small victories, wanting to control every aspect of his life that he still could.

The weather remained chilly, which necessitated them keeping their exchange as short as possible. Sergei watched the road for signs of an impending convergence of FBI vehicles, which would spell doom for all that he and others within the Russian intelligence services invested. Unbeknownst to anyone but his supervisor in Moscow, Sergei arranged for two illegals to position themselves at the nearest entry onto the George Washington Parkway to alert him of any police or federal presence.

Both men lapsed into silence, neither with anything else to say. Sergei realized the documents would continue to earn him praise from Moscow, while Robert quietly seethed at the injustice of the situation that forced him to take orders from anyone. He considered his work in the Foreign Service quite a different thing because he maintained a level of autonomy, which would only grow when he earned his next promotion.

Robert rose from the bench, his hands empty, which he instinctively put in his pockets.

"Just so you know," Robert said in as even a voice as he could muster, given that his nerves were frazzled and on edge, "there are some interesting documents in there, proving that I will play ball."

He was thinking of one document in particular, some intelligence to do with Israeli threats to Iran, though he didn't see that as particularly important. He read through the summary, having read a TS/SCI version earlier, which seemed to have something to do with Israeli capabilities to conduct airstrikes against Iranian nuclear facilities.

What do I care if those heathens blow themselves up? The Israelis were an arrogant bunch, sensitive to threats but protected by their lobby on Capitol Hill. He worried about war in Europe, knowing any sort of conflict would destroy his beloved continent, but he did not care at all about the Middle East, particularly the arrogant Israelis and religious radical Iranians. They could kill themselves, and he might open a bottle of champagne to celebrate. The lower classification version of the intelligence was in there, still containing the essence, without any of the sources and methods of collecting the info. Anything classified as secret couldn't be that classified, could it?

Sergei fought the urge to open the satchel and read the documents, relying on his training to stay calm. His curiosity piqued, he hefted the case, which felt quite light. With nothing more to say, he nodded and walked off quickly to his car. Only after he entered the vehicle and saw the American drive off did Sergei's heart stop racing. He sat in the embassy vehicle, meaning no one could touch the documents safely placed in the back seat. Diplomatic protections worked to his advantage in this instance.

With that, Sergei pulled onto the Parkway to return to the Russian Embassy, first driving south, then north to flash his headlights at the two illegals who provided security. Having waited an additional twenty minutes after the American left and watching numerous other vehicles drive by, he avoided the natural human curiosity of his people, who often wondered what assets worked for the Russian government. People were people, he knew, and so oftentimes he engaged in operational security against his own people, telling effective lies to protect his sources. Yes, he told himself as he drove through Old Town Alexandria, even sources he could not possibly trust.

"WHAT WOULD YOU HAVE ME DO?" ARTHUR SINCLAIR asked into the secure phone, knowing he faced an impossible choice. His Israeli counterpart remained furious at the disappearance of one of their officers and demanded assistance from every friendly service. *Just what I or the Americans would do if in their shoes,* Arthur knew. He would provide what limited assistance he could. Intelligence services' main assets were personnel, especially highly trained field staff, and the loss of any member of their team was felt by every senior leader.

Arthur had served in Her Majesty's government nearly forty years, since he joined the Royal Marines in the early 1970s. Those years serving in uniform were the most thrilling for him. He looked fondly on those years when he was part of a unit, a team, something that intelligence officers often lacked. Sure, direct action teams worked as a unit, but more intelligence officers operated with their assets on an individual basis, not involving other personnel from their services.

"You can give me your support," his counterpart chided, "and help obstruct activities that threaten peace and stability in the region."

I truly doubt your allies see it that way, Arthur considered. "We shall of course offer every assistance available."

"Wonderful, thank you," the man responded. After a second's hesitation, he added, "Since you are being so generous, please send your officer who did in-depth research on the potential Iranian intelligence network." The intelligence chief knew the specialist was his counterpart's daughter yet also knew that bringing that fact into the open would not benefit his case.

Arthur was caught, secretly congratulating his counterpart for maneuvering him into being forced to send MI6's Iran specialist, *his daughter,* to aid in the search. It did not help that she was haranguing him every chance she could to get to Budapest to join the search and negotiations. *This would kill two birds with one stone.* He already considered capitulating to her, since she was his one child who followed him into the family business. Plus, having someone who everyone in MI6 trusted in Budapest would benefit his service, giving him extra insight into developments on the ground.

"Yes, I shall make the arrangements," Arthur replied, "though I ask you do your utmost to ensure the safety of my officer." He paused uncomfortably, unsure how to phrase his thoughts. "That officer is a valuable member of our team, as is every officer in my service. She will be on the next plane possible."

In Tel Aviv, Eliot Zakheim hung up and leaned back in his chair. The British were a friendly service, or at least not an adversary, one that warranted watching. Still, MI6, like the Americans, had considerable resources at their disposal, to include experts on Iran, which remained the most direct threat to Israel's continued existence.

Eliot looked down at the thick personnel folder on his otherwise immaculate desk. Opening it for probably the tenth time since he ordered it from the personnel office, he stared at the bright, excited face of another of Israel's youth, dead before he ever had a real chance to live. They held out hope of finding the body, but that faded when they found the officer's clothes stuffed behind a dumpster a mere two blocks from where the IRGC officer at the Iranian Embassy in Budapest lived.

He immediately authorized his officers to kill that IRGC officer, eliminating another threat to the state of Israel. He knew the fifty-meter range was proving to be a joke, and he ordered his technical experts to extend it for future models.

"But how are we supposed to find him using the Bluetooth device when they stripped him of his clothes?" he asked his desk. Eliot glanced over his office and sighed. Another young Israeli lost, and it was his fault.

Looking out his window, he remembered his call to Avi's family, knowing the pain they felt after losing his own child many years before. The pain of losing a child altered one forever.

He suddenly heard a crack and looked at his open hand, imagining the broken pencil in his palm was the neck of the man responsible for Avi's death. He squeezed the pencil and it broke, splinters flying across his desk. The sudden *crack* startled him from his thoughts, as he imagined what he would do if he caught the man responsible. *If,* he chided himself. *Why if?* He shook off the negative thoughts, unwilling to let go of the anger he felt.

He stared blankly at the wall across from him, covered by a giant map of the Middle East. Iran remained, and would remain, Israel's main threat. Until he took care of them.

IN MOSCOW, KONSTANTIN ALEXANDROVICH reviewed the reports provided by their asset, *Apollo.* The man's access was extraordinary, and he seemed receptive to tasking, despite his initial reticence. Unlike other men and women who spied for their country. The Russian government had fewer friends than ever, he knew, and so they needed ever more information to protect the Russian people.

His eyes sweeping his small office, Konstantin felt a sense of purpose, having dedicated his life to serving the Russian people. The son of a poor farmer, his aptitude for languages and natural charm brought him to the attention of party leaders at Moscow State University. He chuckled at the recollection of his parents learning that he was accepted to one of the most prestigious universities in the world. They both died a few years ago, having lived hard lives in their small village. Konstantin did all he could to make life comfortable for them, going so far as to bring in specialty medicine direct to their dacha.

Now responsible for monitoring Americans who appeared willing to betray their country, Konstantin had access to the crown jewels of Russia's intelligence empire. Such as it was, he mused. Back in the days of the Soviet Union, he recalled fondly, other countries feared and respected the Russian people. Now, however, the Russian economy ranked somewhere around that of Italy. The New Russia needed countries to stay in its sphere of influence in order to gain economic power but with NATO gaining ground on its periphery.

Flipping through the *Apollo* files, Konstantin stopped at the detailed itinerary and policy analysis ahead of the American's secret, direct negotiations with the Iranians. He set the report down, unimpressed by the Persian religious fanatics and unwilling to do anything to aid their apocalyptic fantasies. He should forward the intelligence on his desk to his friend, Nikolai, who dealt with the murderous Persians. However, he also sought to protect *Apollo*, whose intelligence confirmed the American president's plans for NATO expansion towards Russia's borders.

After several minutes of contemplation, he reached a decision on how to proceed without compromising his source. He picked up the phone and dialed the direct line to his old friend from memory.

"Nikolai Vladimirovich, *kak dela*?"

"*Ne plockha*," the veteran agent-runner said. His father had been a member of the Politburo for decades and ensured his only son reached the pinnacle of Russia's intelligence apparatus.

Konstantin felt bad for his *tovarisch*, who lost his wife to cancer six months ago so buried himself in work. *At least she received the best possible medical treatment and not Soviet so-called care, which would have killed her sooner.*

"You should come for dinner," Konstantin asked, not for the first time. "Marina asked again to bring you food. You cannot survive on black bread and vodka forever."

"What do you need, *tovarich*?" the man grunted, grudging kindness in his voice.

"Who are you sending to Budapest to monitor the Persian fanatics?"

Nikolai grinned, his first in months, at his friend's lingering hatred of the Iranians. Time would never heal those wounds, not after the years Konstantin Alexandrovich spent fighting the Afghans, losing troops to their attacks. He would never forget, nor would many of their generation who fought in that awful war.

"I am sending two men to monitor, aware the Iranians are more active in Hungary than we previously understood. The Persians want to learn all they can to help their economy. We are also monitoring open fighting between the Israelis and the Iranians, which is disrupting intelligence collection for everyone."

"What do you think started it?" Konstantin asked, as nervous as any intelligence officer around the world of open conflict between intelligence agencies. Neither the Israelis nor Iranians were true allies of the *Rodina*, but he remained apprehensive about other intelligence agencies being pulled into the fighting. Russia's services could ill afford such direct conflict, not after the West bought so many of their officers throughout the nineties.

"The best we know is that an Israeli Mossad officer went missing. It appears"—Nikolai looked at the folder on his desk—"that the Israelis blame the IRGC, though the generals we contacted absolutely deny any responsibility for the missing Mossad officer."

"What a mess they are creating, especially those damned religious fanatics." That he found comfort with his faith by attending Russian Orthodox services was beside the point, because after a lifetime of devotion to the state, he considered religion a personal matter, not a political weapon.

"I agree, but we need all the allies we can get, Konstantin Alexandrovich."

That made sense—those bastards would do anything against civilized nations. "I will also send a man," Konstantin said, "and I have some information I can share with you about what the Americans are thinking ahead of the negotiations." He paused, relishing the power afforded to him by the intelligence he controlled. "However, I cannot share anything until after I share it with the Palace."

"What kind of intelligence?" Nikolai asked, curious because at their level only truly useful intelligence would ever come to their attention. He could gain significant leverage over the Iranian government if he provided intelligence to aid them in their negotiations with the Americans, but only if his friend was willing to, and could, share.

"I must protect the source of my information, but I can assure you nothing will damage the security of the Russian state. This case has the attention of the big man himself."

"*Da, tovarisch,* I understand."

With that, Nikolai dropped the subject, knowing it would do no good to press further. After multiple scandals, to include losing sources in Western government due to Russians selling secrets, the one major rule in the SVR was to protect your sources. *Without sources, an intelligence officer is of less use than a reporter.*

Nikolai looked at the wall where the wooden board with that inscription hung. He was confident every student who attended lessons with that old bastard Ivan Gregorovich would remember that lesson so deeply it was instilled into their souls during the months and years of training.

"Will you come for dinner?" Konstantin pressed, knowing this was his best opportunity. "I will not take no for an answer." He paused, worried about his friend. "In fact"—he puffed up, ready for an argument—"Marina and I will arrive at your apartment tonight if you do not agree. Then you can explain to her why you have nothing more to serve than black bread, a bottle of nearly frozen vodka, and perhaps a tin of sardines."

Nikolai let out a loud bark of a laugh, surprised but gratified that his friend knew him, and his pantry, so well. His staff jumped at the noise, but did not disturb him. Nikolai missed his Ekaterina.

"*Da, moi brat,*" he responded, surprisingly excited at the

prospect of spending time with old friends. "Do not forget to tell Marina that I will bring the black bread, but I leave the vodka to you."

After he hung up the phone, Nikolai spun in his chair to face his desk, looking mournfully at the stack of reports that demanded his attention. He opened the top folder and began reading more about urgent communications throughout the Middle East and Eastern Europe originating from Israeli embassies about suspected retaliation for their missing officer. *Humph, they believe it was the Iranians, but I happen to know the Iranians only began ramping up their assets in Budapest a mere two weeks ago.* He wondered who could be busy disrupting a finely balanced situation. Balance was good, while unbalance without control could be very bad for Russia's interests.

He made a note to investigate, ordering that the two men he planned to send to monitor the talks in Budapest keep alert for more activity. Knowing how Iranians and Israelis felt about one another, he was certain the death toll would continue to rise.

CHAPTER
TWENTY

 " Ben said, shifting the gears of the rental car. They grinded a bit since he was out of practice.

Kate stared at the passing countryside, the windows down and the wind blowing through the small car. They sped out of Budapest, seeking refuge from the past days of activity in advance of the no-longer-secret negotiations.

"Yes, love," she said, glancing at him with amusement as he concentrated on driving. She knew she was a better driver, given her more extensive training, but she wasn't going to argue with his desire to drive them out of Budapest.

"There it is." She pointed, then folded the map and tucked it inside the glove compartment. After charming the concierge, they received a list of seldomly visited Hungarian national parks. After days of the Israelis asking questions about potential Iranian intelligence operations, she needed a break. She couldn't possibly answer even her own embassy's questions about Iran's likely negotiating position. *I need a break from people. Except Ben.*

Kate had listened patiently to Mossad officers decrying the loss of their man, shuddering at the thought of losing a colleague under such mysterious circumstances. She knew those visiting Mossad officers canvassed the town searching for clues, increasingly frustrated at finding no body. The Israelis were out for blood, unwisely killing the IRGC officer at the embassy. It was fuel to an already roaring fire that threatened to spread throughout Europe.

"Park here," she directed, seeing the signs to the trailhead they wanted. A walk through a quiet forest with Ben, without hearing the mindless chatter of people, was all she wanted right now.

Exiting the rental car, Kate noticed numerous tire tracks. None appeared new, yet one set must have been a larger truck that visited shortly after a rainstorm, having left deep tracks in the mud. There were also footprints everywhere, rendering the dirt lot a compact patch of hard surface after baking in the sun.

"It is so lovely and quiet here." After walking for half an hour, they stopped for water.

Eyeing him over her bottle, Kate noticed Ben scanning their surroundings. She loved that he was as alert to his surroundings as she was, or nearly as alert. It enabled her to relax, even slightly.

Kate replaced the cap on the bottle before putting it in Ben's backpack next to a travel medical kit, granola bars, and a flashlight. "You are something of a Boy Scout at times, Ben."

"Always be prepared, that's what my scout leaders always said." He looked around, seeing the trail wind through the trees, but then noticed what appeared to be a break in the woods off to the left.

"Let's try this path."

"I don't know if this is a real path," Kate said from behind, wishing she had on sturdier shoes. She easily kept up with Ben but hadn't expected to venture this far from a path.

"Ben, what was that?" Kate shouted a minute later, startled by movement out of the corner of her eye. She saw Ben busy climbing a hill towards a peak that held his interest.

Turning and unable to see Kate through the trees, plus hearing her shout in fear, Ben bolted down the hill, leaping through the fallen branches cautiously. He rushed to find her walking through the trees, pushing limbs to the side as she stalked towards a bunch of crows atop a mound. She approached slowly, the birds eyeing her malevolently.

"You should probably be careful as you approach that flock of crows," Ben cautioned, wanting to enjoy a quiet morning in the forest rather than needing to find a doctor to deal with injuries from angry birds.

"It's called a murder of crows," Kate said absentmindedly. She stared at the birds, trying to figure out how to move them.

"Oh, yeah, I think I heard that once," he lied, staring at the birds.

"For a Yank, you are remarkably well-educated," she teased.

They stood still, and their lack of movement seemed to put some of the crows at ease enough to resume pecking at the mound beneath their claws.

"Can you see what's below the birds?" she asked, cautioning herself that she could be wrong. "It looks like they're eating something." *Just what are the chances?*

"If you want to move the birds," Ben said, selecting a large branch from the ground, "let's move the birds."

Kate watched, amazed, as Ben swung a large branch from a fallen tree and, brandishing it like a lance carried by knights of old, he charged at the birds. For effect, he screamed as he charged.

Nonetheless, his trick worked. The birds screamed their irritation as they flew to branches not far away.

As Ben and Kate approached, both paused, gagging at the strong stench. "This pile of dirt smells awful," Ben said, reaching out to feel plastic sheeting under a layer of dirt.

"What is it?" Kate asked.

"A plastic sheet?" He began sweeping leaves and dirt off the mound and found a hole the birds were pecking through.

Kate approached the mound from another angle, leaning down to help brush leaves and dirt off.

"This side is lower," she mumbled to herself, moving around to stand near Ben. "What'll we do?"

"Let's figure out what's under this plastic sheeting. I see something dark inside that hole." He pointed, shuffling to the other side.

After uncovering most of the sheeting, Kate and Ben positioned themselves at either end of the mound. They recognized the shape of a body beneath the sheeting.

"Let's try to flip it over," Kate suggested, leaning down to grab hold of the mass.

"One, two, three."

"Holy Christ," Kate exclaimed, stepping back in shock but quickly recovering her composure.

"Who do you think it is?" Ben asked.

Everything appeared black, but they could see through the opening in the plastic sheeting that it was, in fact, a giant pool of dried blood. In the center of the mass, they saw a naked Caucasian male. Kate leaned towards the head, seeing a gaping wound with remarkably little blood around it at the top of the man's head.

Ben felt a chill as he looked down at the dead body, eyes open to the sky. The mouth was otherwise a mask, the features set in a grimace. It pained him to consider the man's last moments, which must have been horrendous for such a look to remain fixed on his face. Resolving to do something, if only to calm his conscience, Ben stooped down to try to close the eyes. They wouldn't budge.

"Rigor mortis set in. His eyes won't close." Kate wasn't prone to emotion, but she choked up at the sight of the dead man at her feet.

Looking closely at the man's face, she registered a familiarity with his features.

"Ben, I think I know this man," Kate whispered.

Ben was busy examining the body, hoping to find some clue. *In the movies, the body always has a clue of some sort,* he thought. He noticed that the man's fingers and toes were all at odd angles, but the sight of the naked man lying at their feet stunned him to silence.

Suddenly, Kate realized where she had seen the man's face. Wordlessly, she pulled her phone from her purse and, walking a few steps up the hill, checked for a signal. She selected a number from her recent calls and hit dial.

"Hello, may I please speak with outreach?"

Ben heard Kate speaking and, wondering who she called, stepped to stand near her.

"Good morning," she said, speaking with a confidence she didn't entirely feel but seizing control of the conversation. "We spoke at length yesterday."

"YES, I REMEMBER YOU." STEPHEN REMEMBERED the British intelligence officer well, frustrated that she so closely guarded her research on the Iranians. He didn't say anything else on this unsecured line, set up so people could provide information on Avi's case.

"Would you be able to come out to a location to investigate something?" he heard from the other end of the line. He stopped tapping his pen on his notebook and focused on her voice.

"Can you send me a photo?" He needed confirmation of some sort before he went anywhere. He believed the British would not want to waste their time, but he needed to protect his limited resources.

"I'll send a photo. You can call me for the location, or not. One second," she said, then the line went dead.

"Everyone," Stephen called out to the team, "we might have

something." He knew the conversation with the British intelligence officer was brief and nonspecific but held hope they would find Avi's body.

The others gathered around the table, all leaning over in exhaustion. Stephen felt guilty pushing the three others so hard, but they were under the gun from Tel Aviv and were expected to provide updates every eight hours.

Running his hand through his hair, Stephen looked at the ceiling of the conference room as he waited near his phone.

Ding. Staring down at the photo, Stephen felt a lurch in his stomach. He set the phone on the table, and all four of the others leaned in for a better look.

"That's him," Sarah whispered. She was there because she and Avi had attended training together. Unable to control her emotions, and knowing he was truly dead, she began to weep.

Hitting the necessary buttons to dial the number, Stephen called the Brit back, leaving the phone on the table and hitting the speaker button.

"Where are you?" he asked, fury in his voice.

CHAPTER
TWENTY-ONE

BEN AND KATE STOOD TO ONE SIDE, neither willing to leave the body but for different reasons.

Kate replayed the conversation with her Israeli intelligence contact. After giving him their location, she placed several calls to the British Embassy and then to London. She was still on the phone nearly thirty minutes later, giving details to her operations center about their discovery.

Ben stood listening to Kate, lost in thought. *Who could have done this?* He witnessed death and destruction in Afghanistan, but this felt different. He once again thanked God for not having chosen a life or career in the intelligence field, though he commended the Israelis for pursuing their man's body. Curious about the man, Ben turned to the body.

Ending her call, Kate walked to stand next to Ben. When she first saw the body, she focused entirely on the man's face, but now she examined it further and stared in horror at his extremities. She covered her mouth with her hand, turning to look at a tree, and took deep breaths. "Ben, look at his hands and feet," she said with as little emotion as she could muster. "They tortured him."

"Oh my God," Ben exclaimed, having observed the mutilation, but not fully comprehending that the man was tortured. He stumbled several steps away from the body, leaning against a tree while he emptied his stomach.

Kate opened her phone and placed another call to report her new findings that the man's fingers and toes were broken and at unnatural angles.

"Another update we just discovered," she spoke into the phone calmly, knowing it would do no good to lose her composure on the line with her headquarters. "The fingers were broken. I suspect he was tortured for quite some time before they executed him. They also appear to have broken his toes."

After she ended the call, she walked to stand by her fiancé again. He spat out the remains of his sick, careful to lean his shoulder against the tree so he did not get any vomit on his shoes or clothes.

"There is no shame, darling," she whispered, rubbing his back. She didn't want him to feel alone. They stood silently for several minutes, both lost in thought at the senseless nature of the execution of the man whose body lay just meters from them. She moved closer to Ben when she heard footsteps in the distance, steeling herself for the new arrivals.

CRASHING THROUGH THE FOREST, Stephen tried to move in as straight a line as possible, only to discover that the terrain worked against him and forced him to move with the contours of the forest. Finally, after what seemed like hours, he crested the hill and saw a man and woman standing meters from a plastic sheeting and naked body.

He rushed down the hill, struggling to keep his footing, but he arrived ahead of his younger colleagues. Stephen slowed to catch his breath.

Viewing the scene, Stephen felt as though he were in a dream. He saw the two people, the man leaning against a tree after likely having thrown up. Standing near him, in what could only be defined as a protective gesture, was the British intelligence officer. He approached the body.

"That's him," Stephen said. Behind him, he heard the footsteps of his slower colleagues.

Samuel, the medic who accompanied them in case they found their comrade alive, immediately went to the body and began examining it with a flashlight. Stephen heard a gasp from behind him, knowing Sarah must have arrived.

Stephen saw the man stand from his leaning position against the tree, wiping his hand with his mouth as he walked towards them.

"We were walking along the path over there"—Ben pointed—"when we saw a group of crows over here, pecking away at a mound."

"When we approached," Kate continued, "we discovered plastic sheeting. Unsure what we had, we turned it over and discovered the body."

"I tried to close his eyelids," Ben interjected apologetically, unable to stop thinking about the indecency of the corpse with eyes open. It seemed so wrong to him, even worse than his death. He lapsed into silence, unsure what else to say. He knew words could do no justice to what the four Israelis in front of him must be feeling as they looked at the dead body of their colleague.

Anger welled up inside Sarah. "Did you touch his body?" she yelled, rushing towards Ben.

Stephen watched as Kate quickly stepped in front of Ben when Sarah rushed at him. Snapping out of it, he realized he needed to seize control of the situation and ordered Sarah to stop. Stephen was surprised when Sarah collided with Kate, twisting in fury as she rolled to the ground.

Stephen rushed to Sarah and held her to the ground. "He didn't do anything wrong," he yelled, pinning her to the ground and forcing her to look him in the eyes. Her eyes burned with fury, seeking a target for her emotions.

"They found him," he reasoned, relaxing his grip when she stopped fighting him.

"We treated him respectfully," Kate said, still on guard, though Ben now stood next to her, his arm around her in a show of solidarity and protectiveness.

"God dammit," Sarah screamed into the forest as she jumped up, letting out her aggression the only way she knew how.

They stood uneasily, none of the five sure where to look, though they could all feel the tension dissipate as Sarah began crying and crumpled onto the forest floor. Stephen rose from his crouching position and cautiously walked towards her, prepared to intervene if she lashed out again. He would not allow her to strike anyone but another Israeli.

When Sarah's sobs finally slowed, and Stephen saw her look up at him in apology, he turned to look once again at Avi's body. "We need to get him out of here and back to Budapest." He didn't speak to anyone in particular but more seemed conditioned to telling everyone his plan. As he and his team approached the body, Ben and Kate stood back, not wanting to get too near the grieving Israelis.

The Israelis unzipped a field stretcher from a canvas bag. Not wanting to leave any evidence behind, Stephen ordered the medic to fold the plastic sheeting and place it by the body's feet. After joining them, Sarah helped them place the body onto the stretcher, then Avi's jacket before zipping the bag over his face.

Ben watched as the four Israelis positioned themselves at the corners of the stretcher. Thinking back to his training before and during his assignment in Afghanistan, he examined the six carry loops, knowing that carrying from the ends would be more difficult on the mourning Israelis.

Stepping forward assertively but not in a threatening manner, Ben approached the group leader.

"Excuse me, but could we help?"

"We can carry our man out of this wretched forest," Sarah spat out, realizing she was lashing out at a man who meant her no harm.

"I never said you couldn't carry his body, but there are six carry loops on that stretcher. We want to help."

The four Israelis stared at Ben, surprised at his insistence on helping, and each looked down to discover that there indeed were six carry straps.

"Thank you," Sarah said, calming down. "We appreciate and accept your help."

Ben and Kate each grabbed one of the middle carry straps, and the six of them filed out to where their vehicles were parked by the side of the road. They drove the winding roads leading out of the forest. Ben and Kate listened to music to pass the time, neither sure what to say.

The drive was speedy, with virtually no traffic. Ben and Kate followed the Israeli's van. Upon entering the city limits, their two-vehicle caravan seamlessly folded into a motorcade of two other vehicles from the Israeli Embassy. With minimal trouble at the airport, the four vehicles drove onto the tarmac, navigating to a waiting El Al plane. *They must have some amazing resources,* Ben thought.

Ben and Kate watched as the four Israelis, along with a security officer and the ambassador, gently carried the body from the van to a lift vehicle near the plane. A casket sat waiting, enabling the six Israelis to reverently place the body inside. Ben saw bags of dry ice nestled against the side of the casket. *It seems the Israelis don't overlook even the slightest detail.* As the flight crew oversaw the casket's loading, he heard a click of heels, turning to see the six Israelis laser-focused on the casket. Ben stood straighter, showing respect for the dead Mossad officer and the Israelis.

Ben watched as the four members of the team approached them.

Sarah extended her hand to each of them, starting with Kate. "I want to thank you both for your help. I will accompany Avi's remains back to Israel so his parents can bury him properly."

Sarah paused, then leaned in to embrace Ben. Kate watched as Sarah kissed Ben on both cheeks, straightening as she held Ben's shoulders with both her hands. "I am sorry for attacking you." She smiled, a genuine smile that momentarily showed her true beauty beneath her devastated outer shell. She then reached out to grasp Ben and Kate's hands, stepping closer. "I owe both of you a debt of gratitude."

Sarah disengaged, first releasing Kate's hand, then unexpectedly hugging Ben again before turning on her heels and walking quickly to the plane.

Ben felt her tears on his cheek, realizing she must have been exorcising some demons. He moved closer to Kate, grabbing her hand tightly.

"Will there be an autopsy?" Kate asked, raising her voice as the plane started its engines.

"Yes," Stephen responded, looking to the medic at his side. "Our medical personnel in Tel Aviv will examine him." He stood erect, looking more like a soldier than an intelligence officer.

The medic nodded and spun, walking to scale the stairs and enter the plane. Ben saw Sarah looking out a window at them. *I wonder if she loved him?* Ben didn't know and would never be able to ask, though her strong emotions hinted at more than just the loss of a fellow officer. *I wonder if I will ever see her again,* he thought as he watched the plane before turning to look at the two remaining Israelis.

"Are you staying here in Budapest?" Ben asked, surprised they hadn't boarded the plane. They all backed away from the plane, covering their ears as the pilots revved the engines of the plane to taxi away.

"Yes, we are staying here to continue our investigation into Avi's death," Stephen said after the plane taxied for takeoff. "I will help, if you let me," Kate offered, knowing that if the Iranians were involved in killing an Israeli Mossad agent, MI6 would want someone on the inside to track progress.

"My supervisors requested your partnership. I will work with you," Stephen answered, then he and his colleague stepped towards their van.

Ben watched the other Israeli, a man who had not yet spoken but whose penetrating gaze analyzed everything. Inwardly shuddering at the thought of what the silent man before him would do to an enemy, Ben was thankful the Israelis were on their side.

"Okay, I must call London to report and coordinate, but then we can meet you in two hours. Where shall we meet?"

"We have a safe house at an address I will send you shortly." Stephen stopped, turning to appraise Ben carefully. "You should consider reporting to Washington, but I can tell you now that we will only share information with you. I don't need one of your Virginia Farms Boys tagging along on my operation."

Ben paused, understanding this could be a problem. "I'm not an intelligence officer," Ben replied.

"No." Stephen smiled in a grim and tight manner. *His smile is similar to Johann Schenk's, as if the simple act of smiling caused him pain.* Ben wondered what Schenk would make of this predicament.

"Yet you are engaged to a British intelligence officer, or at least appear to be so. Plus, you helped recover the remains of our friend." He shook Ben's hand. "You are a *mench*, and in our book, that counts for a lot. It means I owe you a debt of gratitude."

With those final words, Stephen and his colleague withdrew to their van and drove away, trailed by the two vehicles from the Israeli Embassy. Ben understood that the ambassador and other staff returned to their vehicles, never joining their conversation. *Compartmentalization at its finest.*

"How am I going to explain this?" Ben asked after he and Kate entered their rental car. He got behind the wheel and followed the Israeli convoy to exit the tarmac, noticing the Hungarian security officers padlocking the chain-link fence after the four vehicles departed.

"I would recommend slowly, in great detail, and consistently," Kate teased, "because your station folks are not going to like your involvement when they are blocked access."

Kate took the phone from her jacket pocket, and while Ben navigated back to their hotel and contemplated how he would explain this, Kate called London to explain the situation.

Ben listened closely, taking mental notes on how Kate explained the series of events to use during his calls. *I'll call the Senator first and then figure out who at Main State to call.* He knew Diplomatic Security would have a field day with his involvement in this, though he would no sooner be left out than not stay for the upcoming negotiations.

"TEACHER, BASED ON WHAT YOU SHARED, everything is unfolding according to the Grand Ayatollah's and your plan." He provided more details for several minutes while Mahmoud and Farrokh listened quietly from a nearby table.

Ramin and his brothers were on edge, hearing just minutes before from the Teacher that the Hungarians were in a frenzy after the Israelis found the body of their missing intelligence agent. The Teacher read them a dispatch from the Iranian Embassy in Budapest, relaying details from a Hungarian official that two unregistered passengers boarded the flight, as did a casket containing remains that the Israeli Embassy described as diplomatic cargo.

"The worst case is that the Israelis found the body," the Teacher concluded after hearing Ramin's report. "It is disappointing news that they found it so quickly, but I cannot fault you. This is merely bad luck."

At hearing the Teacher's assessment, the three Iranians relaxed. They knew the Teacher would report to the Grand Ayatollah, which would be embarrassing, but operations were complicated, and sometimes their adversaries got lucky.

"*Khoda* remains on our side, I believe that truly," the Teacher continued. "You cannot send anyone out to confirm they found the body." They knew he was thinking out loud, a teaching technique he long used so they knew how he processed information.

"We considered that," Mahmoud interjected, "but the Hungarians will consider it a crime scene, while the Israelis, perhaps even the Americans, will have the site under surveillance."

"You are prudent, my Immortals," the Teacher said. *All these years of training have made them perfect, though now we must contend with how the Israelis will continue their response.*

The Teacher had additional reports on his desk detailing three deaths already, though he did not trouble himself with the death of Revolutionary Guard officers. *They are easily replaced, whereas my Immortals are irreplaceable.* Senior Revolutionary Guard generals were demanding information.

"Can you confirm, my Immortals, that the IRGC officer Farid Hashemi died in the bus accident?"

"*Bale,*" Ramin confirmed.

"Then that is a loose end tied up, as Westerners say," the Teacher said. He did not tell his Immortals that he heard from IRGC sources that Hashemi had grown suspicious of the three Immortals' presence in Budapest, only a well-placed call to the ambassador stopping Hashemi from further action that could have complicated his Immortals' efforts.

"We will let events run their course," the Teacher concluded, ending further discussion.

The three Immortals were glad to put that behind them.

"For now, I want you to focus on the major operation. May *Khoda* go with each of you, my Immortals, and I will report all progress and successful developments shortly to the Grand Ayatollah."

After hanging up, the Teacher swiveled his wheelchair and decided to make his report to Grand Ayatollah Shirazi in person. *He will require a full readout, and I must be prepared to answer as many questions as he has.* As he rolled through the compound, the Teacher knew other parts of the Iranian government would feel pain due to his Immortals' activities. But, he reasoned, there is no growth without some pain.

TWENTY-TWO

"MARTY, I SWEAR THAT'S THE WHOLE STORY," Ben said into the phone, tired of repeating himself. After arriving back in Budapest, he wisely decided to visit the embassy to brief the regional security officer, Trevor Robinson, who called in the Regional Affairs chief. They sat in the Regional Affairs office, Ben speaking into a secure phone while the regional security officer and the Regional Affairs chief listened.

Peter Murdock arrived in Budapest a year earlier and headed up the small Regional Affairs office in the embassy. Since they did not view the Hungarians as a threat, they primarily cooperated with their host nation counterparts and monitored the activities of unfriendly foreign nationals. His hands were full monitoring the activities of the Russians and Chinese, though the Iranians would, on an irregular basis, pop up on his radar when they scored a foreign policy win with Hungarian politicians.

Astounded at the turn of events but taking Ben's word for it that the Israelis would only include him in their investigation, Peter decided not to antagonize the FSO, seeing there was little else he could do. He wrote up a full report and sent it back to Washington as a secure message, awestruck at the turn of events, and waited for guidance. Perhaps the folks in Washington could pull strings and get him in with the Israelis, but until then, he was unwilling to waste his energy.

"Yes, I know the Senator will arrive tomorrow, which makes this all the more complicated," Ben replied after listening carefully and taking notes. "The best we can hope for at this point is that the Israelis wrap up their investigation quickly, share everything they can with us, and I can pass everything on to State and others."

Ben thought through his next steps, understanding that he was in a tricky situation. Technically, he was on a fellowship with the Senator's staff, yet he remained a Foreign Service officer. He reported to the Legislative Affairs Bureau at the State Department, but neither the office director responsible for FSOs assigned to Capitol Hill nor the principal deputy assistant secretary knew how to handle this situation. Completely unprecedented was how the situation was described by PDAS Tucker, a career FSO who served on four continents and who genuinely liked Ben.

After reporting to his bosses at State, Ben fully briefed Marty, expecting to also brief the Senator but had forgotten that the statesman was on his way to Europe. Ben's work phone was not syncing with the server, so he couldn't get to his email to check the Senator's schedule, and he didn't want to waste half a day sitting at a computer. He had the Senator's arrival information but couldn't tell where they were on their trip to Budapest.

Ben knew McKenzie accompanied the Senator, so at least he had someone available to arrange things. As a living legend, every embassy fell over themselves to care for the Senator.

"Yes, of course I'll explain everything to the Senator," Ben promised, "but now I need to get going to meet up with the Israelis and, uh, my date." He set the phone down, looking up to see two sets of eyes staring at him.

"A date? Who else are you meeting?" Peter asked. He tried to make it sound like an offhanded question, when he knew virtually nothing about this officer. Ben visited the office when he first arrived, making the rounds to meet everyone, but Peter's schedule didn't allow him to sit down and speak with every visitor unless they demanded his attention.

"My girlfriend," Ben responded curtly, not feeling the need to share that he was actually engaged. He had already filled out more than enough paperwork with Diplomatic Security to declare his relationship with Kate, which was extremely complicated because she was a foreign intelligence officer. Luckily for them, the Brits cooperated and agreed that they would jointly approve of their relationship so long as each notified them when things progressed further. Which Ben did, of course, the Monday after he proposed to Kate at O'Connell's.

Kate, meanwhile, told Ben that she notified her personnel department, confident in their assurances they would not share details with the chief until she and Ben could make it official.

"And your girlfriend is?" the regional security officer asked, taking notes for his detailed report back to Washington.

"Her name is Kate Sinclair. She works for the Foreign Commercial Office." Wisely, and according to their agreement, Ben left out Kate's true affiliation, though he assumed it would take Peter only a phone call or two before he realized Ben's omission. He took a deep breath, sensing the questions from previous experience, and continued over their questioning looks. "Before you get too worried, I declared my relationship with her back in Washington to *everyone* and their mother, so no one at State or elsewhere will be surprised."

"Why is your girlfriend here in Budapest?" Peter asked, writing out Kate's name and underlining her last name. He was sure he had seen it somewhere before. A quick call to the British Embassy would surely clear up all his questions, but he didn't want to get ahead of himself.

"She's helping out at the embassy in advance of this weekend's negotiations." Trying to be helpful, he added, "She's an expert on Middle East issues." Ben knew he was walking a fine line. He didn't want to share Kate's expertise on Iran with these men he barely knew, but he owed them some details.

"This just keeps getting better and better," Trevor grumbled, writing down everything to report to Washington. When Peter looked over, he saw that the RSO misspelled Ben's girlfriend's last name. Knowing his hunch might be correct and knowing the phonetic spelling would be corrected by folks back in DC with the right clearances, he decided to forego the rest of his questions.

"Well, I know you were due to meet the Israelis half an hour ago," Peter said, standing up to end further questioning and get Ben out of his office. He scribbled a few notes and ripped a piece of paper from his spiral notebook. "Can we give you a ride over there?" Peter asked, grabbing his keys and coat. It seemed less like a question and much more like a demand.

Ben stood, seeing that it would do no good to argue with either of the men. As they filed out of the secure office and made their way through the embassy, Ben sensed the increase in activity, seeing the flurry of visitors running to and from conference rooms to confirm meetings, deconflict schedules, and ensure everything was in place before their principals arrived the next day. He also noticed Peter stop to hand a piece of paper to one of the people in the office, but Ben didn't think too much about it, reasoning that Peter needed to check something with DC.

Outside, Ben climbed in the back seat, Peter in the driver's seat, and the regional security officer in the passenger seat. Ben was still dressed in his hiking clothes, never having an opportunity to change, though he was thankful he returned to the embassy to deal with this situation. News such as this never kept well, and he knew asking forgiveness later would not be welcome, not with a dead Israeli intelligence officer.

Peter expertly navigated the streets, weaving the Land Cruiser past double-parked cars and dodging pedestrians crossing the street wherever they wanted. Ben sent Kate messages on the drive, not wanting her or the Israelis to be surprised when he arrived with company.

"SENATOR, WELCOME BACK TO LONDON." Arthur Sinclair stepped forward from his phalanx of bodyguards to meet the Senator at the end of the jetway. He saw a young lady following behind, dragging two carry-on bags. "Greetings, I am Arthur Sinclair, and you are?"

"My name is McKenzie Jackson, the Senator's assistant." She set down her bag and offered her hand, which Arthur shook.

"Policy guidance on the talks?" Arthur asked, curious about the pecking order.

"McKenzie focuses on domestic issues, while I rely on Ben to fully understand the foreign policy implications of the talks," the Senator responded for McKenzie. She was slightly older than his granddaughter and someone he trusted. Unlike many other members of Congress, the Senator never slept with his staff. He was still happily married to his wife of four decades and blessed without a roving eye.

Arthur filed that information away, always eager to understand the role of everyone around him. He knew negotiations with Iran were an issue with the Americans, a political football he believed they called it, so it made sense that the Senator would bring a domestic policy advisor. The Senator also further confirmed Ben's foreign policy expertise, not that Arthur questioned it, but more data was always better than less.

"I understand, thank you for explaining. This way, please." Arthur's head bodyguard, Mark, took the position behind his principal. Arthur gestured for one of the younger men from his security detail to help McKenzie with the bags, and they continued as a group through the terminal. He watched as McKenzie offered two checked luggage claim tickets to a security officer, who raced ahead to collect their bags.

"Are there any major updates?" the Senator asked, unaccustomed to being out of contact with staff or news for so long.

"You already likely heard about Ben and Kate finding the intelligence officer's body in the woods outside Budapest," Arthur responded. "I spoke with Eliot, who complimented both our people." He permitted himself a smile, proud that his daughter helped earn his service praise from the Israelis. Now they owed him a favor.

"And the negotiations are still on?" the Senator asked tersely. *Despite confirmation the Iranians likely killed the Israeli,* he didn't say. He urgently sought any excuse to scuttle the talks, never believing the Iranians would keep their word about anything. It didn't help that the *mujahideen* fed him the information about the Iranian mullahs. After what he went through with the Carter administration wonks in 1979, he could never trust the radical Iranian government.

Speaking quietly so only the Senator could hear, Arthur said, "Our government leaders suspect that it will take more than the death of a foreign intelligence officer for your president to cancel the talks."

McKenzie heard the Senator's bark of laughter, humorless after decades as a member of Congress, and wished she could hear their conversation. She dutifully followed, enjoying her talk with the young security officer, who already shared his disappointment that she would not be able to stay in London longer than one day.

They turned off to inside hallways, the security personnel accustomed to the route. They avoided steps, not wanting to force the aging Senator to climb or descend stairs, and took ramps at a slower pace. Eventually they reached their waiting convoy of vehicles, the security men relaxing slightly as they neared bulletproof vehicles.

"We will drive directly to work meetings," Arthur explained. "Then you can visit your hotel to freshen up before a working dinner." He walked to the rear passenger door, which Mark opened quickly, before adding one more thought as the Senator entered the other side. "We are trying to organize a call with Ben and Kate so they can brief you on developments on the ground since there may not be much time when we arrive tomorrow, but they are caught up in a series of meetings."

Ignoring the last comment, the Senator relaxed in his seat. His stop in London, which should have been simply a layover, would extend until tomorrow because Arthur Sinclair and UK officials wanted to hear his thoughts on the upcoming talks. *I have Ben to thank for my newfound working relationship with Arthur,* he mused. He always enjoyed his visits to London, especially when he did not have to fight traffic or worry about logistics.

AS THEIR LAND CRUISER PULLED UP in front of the address the Israelis provided, Ben watched as Kate, Stephen, and the silent Israeli stood waiting for them. Exiting the vehicle, Peter checked his phone, a single message confirming his assumption. He exhaled, knowing he had to tread carefully because operating without instructions was dangerous, though expected in his line of work. The Agency hired him for his judgment.

"Good afternoon, gentlemen," Stephen said, stepping forward to bar the stairs leading to the apartment building's entrance.

Trevor, who had served in the Marine Corps for ten years before opting for a career that would allow him to spend time with his wife and two children, sized up the three people before him. The woman,

Kate, stood to the side and reached out to grasp Ben's hand. *If those two are just dating,* he thought as he analyzed their body language, *then I served in the Chair Force.*

"My name is Trevor Robinson." He held out his hand to the two men barring his way. "I'm the regional security officer at the American Embassy."

The man on the right, who exuded confidence and command, looked like he killed people for breakfast and then sat on the beach in the afternoon. Trevor looked over the man on the left, a foot behind the other, and decided he never wanted to meet him in a dark alley. Roughly the size of a commercial freezer, Trevor knew the silent ones who were that large were usually deadly. The man had forearms the size of his legs. He wore a jacket that had to be specially made. His proportions were not God-given but earned from thousands of hours in the gym.

Stephen shook the American's hand, using the time before they arrived to confer in detail with his supervisors in Tel Aviv to talk through a variety of potential scenarios. Jacob, an intelligence wizard who seemed to have a fortune teller on retainer and a crystal ball in his back pocket, predicted this as the most likely scenario. *Except he didn't foresee Avi's death,* Stephen thought ruefully, *which would have saved us all this hassle.*

After hashing it out with the director's senior staff, a plan blessed by the boss himself, they agreed to include one additional American but to keep Ben involved. He, they reasoned, helped find Avi's body, earning their respect, but was another intelligent mind. They needed all the support they could get to track down Avi's killer.

"My name is Stephen," he said, shaking Trevor's hand, both sizing up the men before them, ignoring Ben and his girlfriend.

This feels like a Mexican standoff, though we will lose if we go against these two, Peter thought.

Both Trevor and Peter looked to the man to Stephen's right, expecting him to say something. He merely stared at them, ready at any time to crush them beneath his size twelves.

"Ben briefed us on developments. We're here to help," Peter explained, churning over details of how Ben found the missing Mossad officer. *Dead Mossad officer,* he corrected himself, thankful he fired off a message to that effect before leaving. He was on a roll, delivering late-breaking intelligence to his headquarters, which he knew would earn him a couple extra points with his supervisors. *That's good because I bid for my next assignment soon and need all the help I can get.* His wife wanted a posting in the British Isles, preferably in London or Dublin, somewhere she could pursue her hobby of genealogical research.

"I have authorization from my headquarters for one additional American," Stephen replied. He held up his hand to halt any protests. "But if you demand I take Ben off the team, we shut it down and no one gets anything." He looked at Ben and Kate, who held hands and waited patiently. "We believe he will bring a unique perspective to this, plus he helped find our comrade." He made the final statement with a finality that suggested arguing was pointless.

Sensing the reality of the situation and knowing this was more an intelligence operation than anything else, Trevor relented, but not before first laying down a marker.

"Peter will serve as our embassy's representative," he said, "but if there is any hint of threat to members of the American diplomatic community, especially as it relates to senior visitors arriving for events tomorrow, then I must know immediately." He delivered his monologue with the force of his position and authority as the senior law enforcement officer for the American Embassy. He didn't know that the four intelligence officers around him had little time for anyone in law enforcement, preferring more direct ways of removing threats than arrest.

"We agree to that just as we provided the same assurances to the British Embassy," Stephen said.

Facing Trevor, Peter held out his keys. "You can take my car back to the embassy. I'll call for a ride later."

"No need," Trevor said, pointing behind him at a vehicle with diplomatic plates rolling towards them along the street. He turned to the others. "I knew both of us couldn't get in on the action, as much as I wish otherwise, but so long as Peter is involved, I know our equities are covered."

Pointing at Ben, he continued. "But the last thing I need is for one of my Foreign Service officers to get hurt during a foreign intelligence operation."

Speaking from the back, surprising everyone but Stephen, the silent Israeli interjected. "I think he is a man who can take care of himself," he said with a thick Italian accent. He looked approvingly at Ben, who stared, astonished that the silent Israeli spoke.

Trevor simply patted Peter on the shoulder and quietly confirmed they would check in with one another later before entering the idling black Chevrolet Suburban. He drove off, leaving the five of them standing in the street.

"Let's head inside," Stephen insisted, leading the way while the no-longer-silent Israeli followed, his eyes sweeping the street.

They ascended three flights of stairs, bypassing the ancient elevator. Inside the sparsely furnished apartment, they settled into a rundown but clean living room. The chairs and couches appeared older than any of the occupants, the fabric threadbare and colors muted from years of use.

"I like your décor," Peter quipped. "Perhaps your decorator could come by and lend us a hand at one of our safe houses."

Stephen smiled, ever so briefly. He had encountered two Americans in one day he didn't instantly hate. Ben carried himself with a relaxed self-assurance, while Peter displayed a sense of confidence that came with seasoning in the intelligence world.

"Let us search through our officer's final weeks, at least according to reports he sent to Tel Aviv," Stephen began. He pointed to one pile of file folders and papers on a rickety dining table, which appeared ready to give out under the weight. "We will also look through lists we received from the Hungarians of Iranians who entered the country in the past two months." He pointed to a second, much smaller pile of folders.

Kate walked to the second set of folders, far more interested in tracking down the Iranians, and was joined by Stephen. Ben, Peter, and the mostly quiet Israeli focused on the files that detailed the Mossad officer Avi's final weeks.

Seizing the initiative and wanting to do more than just watch the action, Ben analyzed the pile.

"This looks like about a third of the pile," Ben said, grasping the first third of the paper.

"I'll take that," Peter lunged, eager for the opportunity to see how another intelligence agency conducted business. He hefted the papers in both hands and, looking around the room, settled on one end of the lone couch that looked like it could bear his weight.

"Would you prefer the next portion or the last?" Ben asked the enormous Israeli.

"My name is Gideon," the Israeli offered, extending his hand. Ben gripped it tentatively, sure the giant of a man could easily break his hand. Surprisingly, the handshake was warm and gentle.

"Ben," he said, unsure of himself, "but you knew that already." He chuckled inwardly, uncomfortable with the entire situation but determined to stick with it for as long as possible.

Gideon, obviously a man of few words, removed the second portion of documents and walked to the kitchen table. Ben watched as the man settled tentatively on the chair as if afraid his weight would break it. Taking the remaining documents, Ben grabbed a lone cushion from the sofa and settled on the floor near the window. He saw Kate leafing through papers, laser-focused and oblivious to everyone else.

Shaking his head and willing himself to focus, Ben began reading through the papers. He picked up the thread a week before Avi's disappearance, reading about clandestine preparations for the purported Iranian's return to the warehouse district.

Two hours passed with no one speaking and minimal movement except for the shifting in chairs or rustling of papers. Ben found blank pages interspersed among the reports, so he used them to take notes. He found the level of preparation, including scouting, to be somewhat excessive, though the man whose files he read had died, so perhaps he hadn't prepared enough. *That isn't fair, and I need to remember that I'm looking at all of this through a different lens.*

After what seemed an eternity, Ben finished reviewing all the documents. Some names he couldn't track easily, so he assigned letters of the alphabet to Avi's helpers, who he discovered numbered in the dozens. *What would it be like to have so many people available to help, all because they were fellow countrymen?* Ben didn't completely comprehend the challenges the Israeli state faced. Uncle Sam, his employer, seemed to have limitless resources at its disposal. Would Avi still be alive if his government had given him more help? He read the Israeli's description of the man he suspected was Iranian. Avi had described a man who could likely blend in almost anywhere.

As he let his mind wander, Ben realized someone was calling his name.

"Yes?" he responded.

"I said that we planned to order food and then compare notes. Are you okay?" Kate asked.

"I'm fine." He placed the files, his notes, and the pen to the side, then stood and stretched. He was stiff after not moving for so long, and after several twists, he felt his back crack back into a looser state.

"I could devour an entire chicken right now. Or a burger. Really, any food in front of me," he told Kate.

"That's good, though I already ordered a selection of food from a local restaurant down the street," Stephen said. He took a closer look at the American. *He is most definitely not an intelligence officer.*

Returning to the dining table, the only place where all five of them could fit, they selected chairs and placed their files back in the center of the table. Seeing that there would be nowhere for them to eat, Stephen stood and dragged the small oval kitchen table to just behind him and transferred the files from the dining table.

"Okay, what do we know?" he asked, seizing control of the conversation and looking to Peter.

Peter succinctly summarized the portion of files he read, to include discussions with observers, the Iranian's likely destination within the warehouse district, and preparations to scout out the location in advance of the Iranian's return.

Next, Gideon relayed what he read, to include approximately two weeks' worth of the timeline. He spoke softly, head bent to read from his notes. Ben looked at the tight cursive, unable to read the language but amazed that such a large man could write such beautiful script.

"My turn," Ben quipped when Gideon finished speaking, and he detailed the preparations, to include conversations about potential routes. "The one emotion I felt in his writing was a sense of frustration at waiting for the Iranian to return," Ben concluded. Everyone nodded and concluded that this must be typical in intelligence operations.

Just then, Stephen's phone pinged. He checked it and, excusing himself, went to pick up their food. He returned wearing a hat and sunglasses despite it being well after sundown.

After handing out packaged meals, all identical, Stephen tossed each of them a plastic fork and then tore into his grilled chicken skewers. Chewing, he nodded at Kate.

"Ah, yes, my turn, I suppose." She set down her untouched meal and picked up her notes.

"The one thing I will say from my half of the files was that the Hungarians kept remarkably good track of Iranians entering and exiting the country, but there are inconsistencies." She walked over to retrieve several files stuck out at perpendicular angles from the pile. "These three men arrived in the past month, but I have no record of them exiting the country despite their stated intention to stay only for a week." She laid three files on the table, open for the others to examine.

"Those are similar to what I found," Stephen said, setting his meal aside and pulling out a piece of paper. "I noted two men who entered the country, claiming to visit for a short period, yet there is no record of them leaving." He turned to pull two files from his pile of folders and laid them on the dining table.

Between them laid five folders, each containing a photo of the man at the point of entry. Ben stood to get a better look, only to begin laughing. He stopped when everyone looked at him.

"None of these men are likely to be killers." He picked up three files. "Look, these men list their professions as imams, while these last two are jewelry and precious metals traders." He dropped the files on the table for the others to see. The others stood to stare down at the photos, disappointed because all five men allegedly still in the country were well over the age of sixty, hardly the age of a killer.

"Is there any chance," Ben asked, spearing a piece of grilled chicken with his fork and popping it in his mouth, "that who we're searching for entered on a different passport?"

A lightbulb went off for Kate, and she began leafing through the dozens of sheets of her notes, both sides of each piece of paper covered in handwriting.

"Just because Avi mentioned in his notes that the Iranian was likely affiliated with but didn't work at the Iranian Embassy doesn't mean he entered on an Iranian passport," she announced. "Which would track with some of the chatter we have on the group of Immortals who we suspect work for a senior Iranian official."

Peter leaned in, realizing he would learn something close hold from Ben's girlfriend. He wished he could take notes but knew his job at this moment was to pay attention and commit everything he could to memory.

"I don't have my files here," she said, "but what I can tell you from memory is that we heard about a group of six or so Iranian assassins who dub themselves the Immortals. They each appear to have a geographic region, though none are assigned to the Middle East itself. Their goal appears to be killing opponents of the Iranian regime, but only those who oppose certain policies."

"How long have they operated?" Ben asked, his notes forgotten on the table as he listened to his fiancée detail the part of her job that he knew was her virtual obsession.

"At least since the nineties." She smiled. "Which is a good point because it means we're probably not looking for young men."

"Or so you conclude," Stephen pointed out. "Wouldn't it make sense that they would bring in new, younger members in place of a bunch of older men?"

"Perhaps," Kate admitted. "There is much we don't know about them, and I am the only one tracking them for now."

"We know more than we did before," Peter said, standing to stretch after he finished his meal.

"I think we all agree that we are tired," Stephen observed, looking at his watch, "and each of us must report back to our superiors."

Everyone nodded and mentally calculated the time difference to their headquarters and preparing a draft report. "Many thanks for leaving your notes on the table," he said, watching as Peter reluctantly stopped folding the sheaf of papers and placed them on the table. "Information sharing only goes so far in our line of work." He was pleased to see that neither Ben nor Kate touched their notes, which lay on the table.

Ben offered his hand to Kate to help her up, and they walked to the door together.

"Should we all plan to do some digging on our side and touch base late tomorrow morning?" Kate asked the assembled group. Finding whoever did this was only one part of the equation. Taking action would involve a step in which she could not easily be involved.

"Agreed," Stephen said, then bid them all farewell. He and Gideon stayed in the apartment while Ben and Kate, trailed by Peter, walked down the flights of stairs to exit onto the street.

"Would you two like a ride?" Peter said, nodding to his official vehicle. "I can drop you off easily."

"We prefer to walk," Kate replied, offering her hand and then gently pulling Ben away.

"Are you sure I can't convince you to join me?" Peter asked. He wanted in on their discussion, suspecting they would talk through details and knowing it could raise valuable intelligence to produce a lead.

"No, thank you," Kate said, "but I am confident Ben will share anything we discover with you when he sees you tomorrow." She waved and walked off, engrossed in talking with Ben.

"I'll hold you to that," Peter called to their backs, not shouting but loud enough to be sure they heard him. He unlocked his car and drove back to the embassy, prepared for a long night on the phone with folks back in DC to fill them in on everything he heard and saw.

IN MOSCOW, KONSTANTIN ALEXANDROVICH sat facing Nikolai Vladimirovich, who grasped his teacup with both hands and smiled.

"So, the religious fanatics are pleased with our information you shared with them?"

"Da, Konstantin Alexandrovich, they are most pleased." He set his teacup down, eager to get to the bottom of his friend's source of information. "Tell me, from what source did you get the information?"

Konstantin stiffened, protective, as always, of his directorate's sources, even against inquiries from other directorate chiefs. "We have a source inside the American government who provided the report that so fascinated the fanatics."

You are being clever and not answering my question, Nikolai Vladimirovich thought, though he knew the palace would have asked the same question and received a truthful answer.

"What is so useful about the document that we passed?" Konstantin asked. He never troubled himself to learn about the Middle East. He hated all Muslims, but especially those who supported the Afghan *mujahideen*, who fought like cowards. He knew this was his blind spot yet still made the snap decision to share the information with Nikolai's directorate right away, ensuring the Iranians would learn of the intelligence.

"As you know, *tovarisch*, the Iranians are in a corner, surrounded by threats. While the Americans continue to sanction their country, the Israelis are the most likely to actually follow through on their threat to carry out a targeted attack on Iranian nuclear facilities." He paused, choosing his words carefully so as not to offend his host. "This intelligence"—he held up a Russian translation—"confirms that the Americans are tracking Israeli planning and drills to attack Iranian facilities. The IRGC general who read the report thanked me, for the first time ever, and immediately drove off with a copy of the document."

"Wait, you gave them a copy of the document?" Konstantin asked. *That is a violation of protocol,* he didn't say, but his accusation carried that implied theory.

"*Nyet, tovarisch,*" Nikolai responded calmly, knowing that would be a concern. "I permitted the Iranian general to read the actual document, but the document he took with him was transcribed using modified language." That some specific names could not be changed was of no great concern to him because the Iranian general called later to thank him again, saying that the intelligence he provided was of greater value to defend against Israeli attacks than anything given in years. *Hence, why am I here?*

"Okay," Konstantin said. "Our asset is named Apollo, and he works for the American Foreign Ministry. He is an expert on European affairs and seemed not to have understood the importance of the document he provided, I now understand, thanks to your explanation."

Nikolai considered the bare facts his colleague shared, knowing he would get no further. "And if your Apollo shares something pertinent to my directorate again in the future?"

"I will, of course, authorize my people to share a sanitized version with your directorate right away." Konstantin raised his hands as if surrendering to some invisible enemy. "I do not have to like the religious fanatics to share information with your directorate, which I know you will then share with them. Everything we do is to protect the *Rodina,* is it not? That must include aiding the enemies of our enemies." He leaned forward, hands on his knees. "Should we drink to that?" Without waiting for a response, he stood and walked to his desk to retrieve a bottle and crystal glasses, as he often did when his friend visited.

Satisfied that his friend would be true to his word, Nikolai Vladimirovich stood as Konstantin returned with two ancient glasses and a bottle of *nastoyaschi* Russian vodka, not the garbage the workers bought at corner markets. He absentmindedly wondered what the IRGC general would do with the information. Was it a secret that the Israelis threatened to bomb Iran's nuclear facilities? Not even a bit. Still, the confirmation from American documents made the Iranians happy, so he decided that he served his country, just as his colleague did. Indeed, his friend.

"To the *Rodina, tovarisch*," Konstantin roared as he toasted their country. Their glasses clinked, and they each downed their shots before pouring another and toasting to their friendship.

"THE TIME HAS COME," HASSAN SAID, "FOR US TO PREPARE for the attack. We will get the final word from Radek about the timing very soon."

The men sat in the same warehouse, though since first moving in, the space was unrecognizable. Those windows they had not yet replaced, they covered with plastic sheeting, ensuring the space was less drafty and making it easier for them to maintain a comfortable temperature. They maintained the brick oven that Abdullah created but moved it to the side, nearer the stairs that led to the second floor, where the warehouse's offices were. The five of them sat upstairs in what used to be a conference room but was now their meeting room. They stared out at the open space where their families congregated.

After locating the owner of the facility, they combined their money and purchased the property, turning it into a facility that produced many different goods. In one corner, two of the Iraqis used traditional tools to build furniture by hand, while in another, they set up a makeshift mechanic shop. Finally, in the last corner, they operated a clothing shop, employing several female members of their families. It was not perfect, but now each of the men provided for their families comfortably.

They stared down at the plans of a large compound, though, as yet, they didn't know where it was located. From their general wanderings in the city, they had an idea that the house was likely somewhere in the diplomatic quarter of the city. Abdullah suggested it could be an ambassador's house or perhaps the American Embassy because it looked positively palatial from the drawings Radek permitted them to keep. They dismissed outright the idea of their target being a Hungarian government facility because they recalled from their first meeting that the intent was to strike at the Americans.

Since they were men of some means now and thus able to afford proper newspapers and news magazines, they devoured the news. They all knew of the reported negotiations involving the Americans occurring in the city in the coming days, though the specific location of the talks remained a closely guarded secret. Still, they readied themselves for action they knew must be taken.

Almost as one, they shuddered at the thought of their pitiful state when the Iranian first encountered them, especially the terrible living conditions for their families. At that time, the men didn't know how they would put food on the table; now they were investing and building wealth.

"The most important thing," Aref, the mechanic, said, "is to ensure no one catches us, or there will be repercussions for our families."

The men contemplated that reality, knowing they could no more back out of their agreement with the Iranian, who was likely to treat them in the harshest possible way, than they could to abase themselves before an unbeliever. They were stuck, a fact they each accepted, but at a minimum, each provided a better life for their families than they had back in Iraq.

They stared out onto the warehouse floor, each lost to his own thoughts. Smiles crossed their faces as children ran from place to place and their wives talked. Slowly, they relaxed, making peace with not knowing what the days ahead would bring. They trusted their skills and their brothers and that Allah would see them through to the end. Then it was time to concentrate on their discussions and go through the plan again until they knew the steps of their attack by heart.

CHAPTER

TWENTY-THREE

"THIS AIRPORT IS A ZOO," BEN REMARKED TO KATE as they stood in the arrival terminal. The parking lot was at capacity, with official vehicles double- and triple-parked while waiting for their dignitaries to arrive.

"No one is quite sure who they chose to process through the VIP passenger terminal," Kate replied, having spoken at length with the UK Embassy's leadership about the arrival of several senior members of the British government to attend or observe the historic negotiations. She only learned last night that her father was one of those coming to attend, along with other senior MI6 officials.

"God, I hope my mother doesn't come too," she whispered to Ben, thankful that the British Embassy booked a large enough block of rooms. They should be able to accommodate any surprise visitors.

She didn't know how wrong she could be.

"There they are," Ben pointed, seeing a large group of passengers exiting the baggage claim area, a porter with a large cart of bags trailing behind.

"Oh my Lord!" Kate exclaimed so only Ben could hear. Her mother walked along behind her father, who chatted away with the Senator. Even further behind were senior members from the Foreign Commercial Office, all attended to by aides.

"I think we're going to need more vehicles," Ben said with as straight a face as he could muster. McKenzie, the Senator's traveling aide for this trip, waved from a distance and rushed up to say hello, drawing stares from Kate and her family.

"Hi, Ben!" she exclaimed. She leaned in for a hug, but Ben used the railing between them to give her a perfunctory hug and kiss on each cheek.

Kate stared impassively at McKenzie, mentally reminding herself to discuss this with Ben.

"Hi," Kate said, putting her hand out to McKenzie. "I'm Kate, and Ben is my boyfriend." Ben never knew Kate to be jealous, but she obviously didn't know McKenzie, who loved and hugged everyone.

"It is so nice to meet you too," McKenzie exclaimed, hugging Kate with a reckless abandon that shouted her American-ness.

Kate smiled, amused that she felt even moderately threatened by McKenzie, yet she would never admit feeling that way to anyone, especially not her family. *Thank God Beatrix is not here!* Walking around the barrier, Ben trailing an instant behind, she rushed to greet her parents and the Senator.

After greetings all around, they moved towards the line of cars. Out of a large, very American-looking passenger van, she saw Mark hop to open the door to the rear compartment.

Kate stood back, watching as the chaos quickly resolved itself with the myriad of passengers folding into seats throughout the twelve-passenger van. She picked a seat next to her mother, but near Ben, mindful that he would need to answer the Senator's questions.

Out of the corner of his eye, Ben spied the ambassador looking around expectantly for the Senator, but rather than help the bully, Ben quickly ducked inside the van and took his seat. McKenzie settled into the back, Kate's father engrossed in conversation with the Senator, and Kate sat in a middle seat, patting a space for him to sit.

"On to the hotel, shall we?" Kate called out. The van shot forward, leaving the gaggle of other vehicles behind and racing towards the city center.

"Mother, what on earth are all of you doing here?" Kate asked.

"My darling," Angela replied, "you do not even know the half of what we have planned for the coming days." She smiled mischievously, and Ben felt a mixture of intrigue and pity for how crazy the next few days would drive Kate.

"How could there possibly be more?" Kate whispered to herself. "You do realize that I am here for work, don't you, Mother?"

Ben could tell Kate was annoyed with the situation, so he threaded his fingers between hers, squeezing tight. He relaxed when he felt her squeeze back.

"You'll see," Angela said, looking out the window to see the passing scenery while maintaining a permanent half smile on her lips.

"YES, THE RESULTS FROM THE AUTOPSY are back, and they confirmed that every one of Avi's fingers and toes was broken," Stephen reported in the lobby of the hotel. He paused to let that sink in, then added, "Most likely with pliers and perhaps even a hammer, based on the fractured bones."

They stood in a corner of the lobby, Ben and Kate having hastily agreed to meet Stephen and Gideon there when they could not escape their visitors.

"Stephen," Kate whispered, "who is that man who just entered? Is the director of Mossad here in Budapest?" She pointed to the delegation that just arrived, breezing through the entrance of the Grand

Hotel Budapest. Opened in 1971 as the Inter-Continental Budapest, the building served as a landmark for tourists and was fully booked by the Hungarian government in coordination with the American, British, and French embassies.

"I just learned he was coming an hour ago, as his plane landed." As if to punctuate his arrival, a ten-man team of giant security officers cleared the way for Eliot Zakheim, who seemed diminutive in comparison. They stopped when they encountered Arthur Sinclair, who sat to one side of the lobby, taking tea with Angela and the Senator.

In an observably unplanned dance, they shifted the seating to permit Eliot to join. With Ben and Kate watching in fascination, first a French and then an American delegation swirled through the doors. The French Deputy of the Directorate General for External Security approached the group amassed for tea and settled himself on one side of the Israeli director, while the American Deputy Director of Operations at the CIA approached Arthur Sinclair with a hand extended. Throughout the procession, Stephen and Gideon appeared mesmerized by the presence of their director.

"I count more bodyguards than hotel staff at this point," Ben commented, trying to count men and women with guns.

Kate observed the various functionaries matching up with their counterparts and seizing what seating remained in the lobby. All of them, security and functionaries, appeared on edge at such an inviting target.

To one side, Kate saw a man, appearing in his sixties, enter with the director of the Mossad, but he stayed in the background and moved around the edge of the room as he headed their way. He observed them from a distance, almost imperceptibly nodding his head in her direction before turning to watch the spectacle of intelligence officials in front of him.

"Anything else you can share?" Kate asked, averting her eyes and blocking out the avalanche of sound from the assembled men and women enjoying tea, as well as those guarding their periphery. The man she suspected of being a Mossad officer, probably a senior one at that, stood less than ten feet from them.

Before Stephen could reply, Peter approached their group, expanding their circle slightly. They searched for a quieter space, eventually finding one near the empty bar. Kate noticed that the older Israeli followed them, observing that Stephen and Gideon tracked his movements with respect, which struck her as interesting. *Who is this man?*

"What I am about to say is very close hold, but I choose to trust you." Gideon checked to see that no one else was nearby other than the older man.

Ben, Peter, and Kate all leaned in. Ben felt a sense of anticipation, as if he was going to learn something that could lead them to the Israeli's killer.

"All our operatives in the field carry transmitters and recorders designed for a situation like this, but it didn't help us find the body immediately because they stripped the clothes off the body."

Peter was ecstatic learning this, knowing he could provide insight into how the Israelis operated and wondering if this was something perhaps the Agency should do.

Kate had heard this previously but knew the Israelis depended more on technology because they were such a small service, with nowhere near as many staff as most services.

"Without getting too far into technical issues, we recovered the recording from Avi's device and listened to it. In essence, much of the conversation was in English, but parts included his captors speaking Hebrew to Avi and Farsi to one another."

"You said captors?" Kate asked.

"Yes, our voice analysis concluded there were three different voices."

"That means there are three probable Iranian killers on the loose in this city?" Ben asked. He shuddered, especially after yesterday's realization that they likely didn't enter on Iranian passports.

In unison, the four of them turned to look around the spacious lobby of the Grand Hotel Budapest. It remained a chaotic environment, with people entering and exiting seemingly at will. The older man approached their group, Stephen and Gideon making space, and he spoke before anyone could say anything.

"I suspect you are Kate." He smiled politely at her, then turned to grab Ben's shoulders. "And you must be Ben, the only diplomat in our midst." He gave a genuine smile and then spun to acknowledge Peter, who stood stunned at the man's appearance and the respect both Stephen and Gideon afforded him.

"My name is Jacob. I was Avi's mentor, the one who permitted him to undertake his operation alone. And his blood is on my hands, so I must ask for your help in capturing his killers." He looked at each in turn, pausing an extra beat when he stared at Ben, as if searching his soul.

"What's our next step?" Kate asked, deciding then and there that she would work with this man because the talks were truly in jeopardy. This was personal for her, with her parents in town, and she resolved to do anything to keep them safe.

"For starters," Jacob whispered, "our chief is telling everyone to cancel these negotiations. They are a ticking time bomb. We have no idea who will die if they continue."

Isn't that a hell of a conclusion? Ben realized. He knew there wasn't a playbook for him to follow, so he remained quiet, steeling himself for the next steps.

FOLLOWING THE AMBASSADOR DEJECTEDLY, Brent realized he was well and truly screwed.

The ambassador had not met the Senator at the airport as he desperately wanted, and now he faced questions from the senior US negotiator over where everything stood. Nothing at work was going well, and he knew the ambassador would take his frustration out on anyone nearby.

Keeping Paul between him and the ambassador, Brent trailed behind as they rushed along the sidewalk towards the Grand Hotel Budapest, where they discovered, after numerous calls, that several senior foreign visitors were staying. *God, I hope we find the Senator there.*

Brent wondered what had happened to Ben, whom he had called numerous times to inquire about the Senator's itinerary. *I should be pissed that Ben never got back to me, but he dropped off the grid so completely, so he must have something else happening.*

As he followed his boss, Brent looked around, privately amused at the ambassador's annoyance that his limo couldn't drop him off in front of the hotel and instead stopped at a security barrier that prohibited vehicles from nearing the hotel.

Oh my God. Radek.

For as long as he could, Brent avoided any of his usual haunts, either staying home or at the embassy, rarely going elsewhere. As a result, he hadn't seen the man he suspected was an Iranian for some time, leaving him hope that he could put those interactions behind him. However, there stood Radek across the street, staring at him in broad daylight. Brent felt that little bit of hope turn to dread.

Brent averted his eyes and walked forward, holding up his badge as their small group from the embassy entered the Grand Hotel's lobby. He didn't want to cause a scene, but he knew he could never properly explain the stranger. He scanned the room, searching for familiar faces, and spotted Ben off to one side with a small group.

They nodded to one another, Brent holding up his right hand in the shape of a phone, to which Ben responded with a thumbs-up. *I hope he calls, because it seems he knows more of what is happening than I do.* Brent knew he needed information, both to feed to the ambassador and to have ready for Radek. Both men were dangerous, but in very different ways.

HE IS AFRAID, RAMIN REALIZED AS HE TURNED and walked away. The hotel was something, a true local monument. He'd observed the Hungarians installing surveillance cameras around the area in the previous days, so he carefully stuck to what he hoped were the camera's blind spots. That made it dangerous for him to show his face, so he wore one of his disguises.

Ramin concluded from his observation that the American did not confide in anyone. His mere existence here, not in custody, assured Ramin that his plans were safe. This was not the type of man who changed overnight, that much Ramin knew.

However distasteful his threats to the American's family had been, he knew they struck a nerve and kept the American on edge. That worked to his advantage and bought him time, for soon enough, the Iraqis would stage their attack and he could disappear from Hungary for the indefinite future, once again able to spend time at the Immortals' headquarters in Tehran.

"Our delegation arrives tonight," Mahmoud said, joining him on the sidewalk as Ramin strolled through downtown Budapest. Both men wore hats and sunglasses, as well as ill-fitting light overcoats, like poor visitors from a small town in the region. Nobodies, and thus invisible.

"The Teacher does not want any of our nationals hurt."

Mahmoud said nothing because he knew this was Ramin's method for processing the next steps. In any event, he was privy to all of Ramin's plans and knew tomorrow's attack was set to occur at the American Ambassador's residence. He considered the schedule another of Ramin's sources provided, noting the American Ambassador planned to host a reception. If they attacked at the end of the event, after most guests left, they could kill their targets and catch the embassy's security officers when they were tired and less alert.

"It will all work," Mahmoud agreed, "so long as nothing changes before tomorrow night."

THAT EVENING, BEN SAT AT A TABLE in a private restaurant rented out for the occasion by the Hungarian government's intelligence service to entertain the myriad of senior intelligence officers who arrived from the various parties and observers to the negotiations. He suspected, correctly though no one confirmed, that he was the only nonintelligence officer at the dinner.

He managed to speak with Brent between finishing at the hotel and departing for dinner and could tell the man was nervous about something. It all seemed so odd, yet Ben knew there were so many things he still didn't understand.

Brent seemed on edge and evasive when Ben asked a few simple questions. Though Ben knew the ambassador continued to give Brent a hard time, he suspected there was more happening. No matter with whom he raised the subject, no one at Main State would listen to Ben's complaints about the ambassador's behavior.

The Senator also raised the issue with his colleagues on the Hill, promising Ben that the next time the man appeared before the Senator for confirmation, they would question him about his interpersonal skills. *Too bad I can't share that news with Brent,* Ben thought, yet he didn't trust the Foreign Service officer not to gloat to his boss, messing up the backroom favors the Senator called in to deal with the bully.

Though he was uneasy about Brent, Ben knew that every FSO underwent rigorous background checks and screening, which were designed to weed out people with problematic behaviors. Then there was also a periodic reporting requirement, requiring every FSO to report their contacts with foreign government officials, particularly those from specially designated countries unfriendly to US interests.

Is it possible that the man I saw following and then speaking with Brent could be a foreign official? He racked his memory, trying to remember the man's features, but it was plain that he would need to see the man again to recognize him. *In all likelihood, Brent spoke with a work contact, someone who, as political and economic chief, he could easily justify speaking with at any time.*

Ben felt stuck. He already tried to get people to care about the way the ambassador treated Brent, but no one seemed to care about the man's reputation for rampant bullying. Although the Senator found the ambassador sleeping with Brent's wife particularly distasteful, given his high moral standards, that happened often enough in corridors of power, in and out of government, that few viewed it as a major topic of concern.

Additionally, Ben finally gave up trying to convince people at State that the Iranians were actively courting the Hungarians. They offered him all manner of excuses, defending the embassy's assertion there was nothing to worry about. Even Kate didn't fully believe Ben, and he had stopped talking with her about it. *You're on your own.*

"Are you okay, love?" Kate asked, grasping Ben's hand to get his attention.

"Yes," Ben replied, grateful for Kate reaching out to him. "I'm just thinking through things. But it still feels like I'm missing something important." *At least I'm not as alone as I thought.*

CHAPTER

TWENTY-FOUR

THE NEXT MORNING, BEN MADE HIS WAY BACK to his seat behind the Senator in the Hungarian Foreign Ministry's main meeting hall. *This is a beautiful room,* Ben thought. The Hungarians were hosting the Iran nuclear negotiations in a grand style. During the first session, the Hungarians greeted everyone, and then representatives from each participating country in the negotiations spoke briefly. Ben tried to adopt a mien of studied indifference, taking notes as necessary for the Senator but otherwise hearing expected remarks from each delegation's head.

Ben and Kate agreed that, for the purposes of the negotiation, they would try not to spend too much time together. Kate poured over the list of members of the Iranian delegation, comparing the photos of each to their combined memories of Avi's description of the Iranian he trailed. They agreed that the Mossad officer's description, while useful to narrow down characteristics, applied to far too many men of Middle Eastern or Eastern European descent.

Ben saw Kate following the chief British representative, Lord Christopher Spencer, to the talks from the Foreign and Commercial

Office. For the purposes of these negotiations, Kate's cover was as an analyst for the FCO. It seemed to Ben that everyone in the room hid their true identity.

"Ladies and gentlemen," the Hungarian Foreign Ministry official called in slightly broken English, "please to take to your seats." Ben found it odd that the foreign minister decided to attend today's negotiations since he was absent during the plenary yesterday, but he suspected the man wanted to attend one day for the photos and to claim credit for making these talks a reality.

Looking across the table at the senior representatives of each participating country, with assistants behind them, Ben observed the mix of nationalities. Chinese, Russian, and Iranian delegations were all spaced somewhat apart, not to appear too close. Ben knew well, however, that though all three may view themselves as having common global enemies, divisions between each mitigated against the full alignment of their interests.

Through his translation headphones, Ben half listened to the brief statement from the Hungarian foreign minister, more interested in hearing what the Iranian official would say. Time that morning crawled by slowly, European delegations taking turns speaking until, at last, the Iranian representative stood to speak.

Ben thought through the man's biography. Saeed Raisi served as the current secretary of the Supreme National Security Council, leading the body tasked with giving advice to the Supreme Leader on all national security aspects for the Iranian government. Ostensibly an advisor to the Iranian president, Raisi's Basij background and experience fighting the Iraqis during the eight-year war branded him as an idealogue who would defend Iranian interests to the end. The man wore a jacket over a collared shirt and sweater vest, looking more an academic than Iran's lead negotiator.

"In the name of Allah, the Most Merciful," Raisi began.

Ben sat a little straighter to take in the entire room. He considered listening directly to the speech but instead relied on the earphones he wore for simultaneous translation, neither relying completely on his rusty Farsi language skills nor wanting to attract the attention of the Iranian delegation for being one of those *jasus* who spoke their language. He knew the Iranians believed every American who spoke Farsi but was not ethnic Persian must be a spy. Ben didn't want that kind of attention.

Leaning forward in his chair, paying close attention to Raisi's words, Ben noticed the folks around him scribbling furiously, trying to take down every word. He didn't even try, knowing he was no stenographer and therefore couldn't be expected to get the speech word for word.

"We condemn actions taken by the Israelis," Raisi said, "especially the preparations for Operation Barak they are undertaking even now to strike at Iranian nuclear sites from the Ramat David Airbase."

Ben felt people around him tense, not quite knowing the consequence of everything he said but implicitly understanding that this was history.

"Israeli F-16 military aircraft of the Scorpion Squadron are, even now, on standby to strike at targets throughout Iran, specifically targeting peaceful Iranian facilities near Isfahan, Natanz, and Arak."

Ben was confused as Raisi went into details that even he didn't know. He stared into space as if in a daze, then saw the Senator waving from his seat directly in front of him.

"Ben," the Senator whisper-shouted, keeping his voice calm, but he was visibly flustered. "Are you taking notes on all of this?"

Looking around, Ben saw the collective American delegation staring in disbelief at Raisi, no one taking notes, and realized he needed to handle this quickly.

"Yes, Senator, of course I am tracking." He sat up a bit more, not wanting to cause a disturbance but also needing to get a sense of the room.

To his left, sitting in the back, were several people he knew to be nuclear experts carefully taking notes. Those folks, Ben knew, were technical experts, rarely interested in policy. To his right were several people leaning in, speaking as quietly as they could, while in front of him was the American Under Secretary of State for Policy, Orvill Johnson, passing notes to her staff as quickly as she could write.

"What the hell is happening here?" Ben mumbled before he saw Under Secretary Johnson raise her hand to interrupt. Raisi looked perplexed, as if he could not believe an American, much less a woman, dared to interrupt him. Silently, he turned to the Hungarian foreign minister.

"Yes, Madame Under Secretary," the foreign minister said into the microphone.

"My apologies, *Agha* Raisi," she said, nodding to the lead Iranian negotiator, then staring directly at the Hungarian foreign minister, "but I received a note that there has been an emergency in the United States that requires mine and my entire team's focus. I request your permission to adjourn and offer that *Agha* Raisi can begin the next session after lunch anew, if he desires."

Everyone, especially the European diplomats, stared at the brazen lie the Under Secretary told, realizing this was some sort of stalling tactic.

"With your permission, Mr. Raisi, we would not want to stand in the way of an emergency, would we?" the foreign minister said, unable to hide the surprise in his voice.

Saeed Raisi leaned to listen to one of his staff, who quickly translated, then straightened to respond. "Of course not, Mr. Foreign Minister. We agree to the American request."

Though simply spoken words, they may as well have been the starting gunshot that propelled nearly every American to stand. Ben quickly stuffed his notebook in his suit jacket pocket, reasoning that whatever the Senator did, he should do too.

While most Europeans gawked at the American delegation, with a nod from the lead UK negotiator, that delegation stood and also made their way out of the room. Ben saw Kate looking ashen-faced and startled, though he maintained his distance, following the Senator out of the room and to the waiting vehicles.

Ahead of him, he saw a tight group of American personnel surrounding Under Secretary Johnson, talking quickly until finally he heard her voice. "Everyone just shut up, now. The next person who says a word will be on the next plane back to Washington. We will all return to the embassy to discuss this." She turned to lock eyes with the Senator. "All of us."

The Senator nodded and grabbed Ben's arm to propel him forward. Ben followed quietly, quickening his pace to keep up with the group. The lead UK negotiator approached the group and called out the Under Secretary's name, stopping her momentarily to confer. After less than thirty seconds, they shook hands and parted, the entirety of the American delegation exiting the palatial building and rushing to enter waiting vehicles.

"Senator, what on earth is happening?" Ben whispered.

The Senator leaned in so close Ben could smell his cologne. "Not here, my boy."

The next twenty minutes of driving, their convoy of vehicles escorted by Hungarian police with sirens and lights flashing, were in silence until they unloaded in front of the embassy and poured inside. Ben noticed that security personnel quite literally corralled them all into the building, with the DC delegation leading the way. He expected them to navigate to the secure conference room but was surprised when Peter rushed ahead to open the door to his space.

They all packed into the small room, someone perched or sitting in every available space.

"Okay, everyone," the Under Secretary said, quieting the room with a wave of her hand as the most senior US official present. "You all just heard what Raisi said."

"I don't think everyone should be in here," someone called, standing and looking directly at Ben. Susan, the director of the Iran Desk. "I happen to know that this man is working for the Senator and doesn't have the required clearances for this topic." She smiled at him, the meanest smile he had ever seen, and then added, "For that matter, I think this conversation should be limited to the executive branch and not include everyone currently in this room."

Ben wasn't sure what to say, so he stood to leave, but then felt the iron hand of the Senator force him back into his perch.

"Madame Under Secretary," the Senator started. Ben could tell by his tone that he was gearing up for a fight, one he certainly would not lose. "If you throw my Pearson Fellow out of this room, then I will leave too." His voice, though soft, thundered through the room.

"Senator, I have no intention of asking either of you to leave," the Under Secretary responded, standing to respectfully address one of the most powerful men in Washington. Ben exhaled and relaxed. "In fact, I insist that every person who listened to Mr. Raisi remain in here to be indoctrinated into a special compartment of classified intelligence." The Under Secretary then turned to Susan and said, "Any questions?"

Susan quailed at the attention on her, while Ben focused on not smiling.

"Now that we all understand that everyone stays," the Under Secretary continued, "let me explain. The fact of the matter is the Iranians just spoke about a highly classified operation, and we must get to the bottom of how they got this information."

Ben recalled Raisi mentioning Operation Barak, the Ramat David Airbase, F-16s, and attacks on Iranian nuclear sites in Isfahan, Natanz, and Arak. He wondered how the Iranians had such detailed intelligence but could tell by the panicked looks on everyone's faces that this could only have been based on US intelligence.

"Madame Under Secretary, either that intelligence came from a remarkably well-placed Iranian source, or we have a mole in the US government," someone on the other side of the room said. People around the room began speaking in hushed tones, all visibly terrified of even the possibility of a mole.

"That will be a much larger and more dynamic conversation," the Under Secretary responded, "but for now, we need to decide how we respond to this new information." She paused, looking around the room. "How do we advise the president? I am inclined to end the talks today because the Israelis will go ape when they discover the Iranians learned of their attack plans against Iranian nuclear facilities."

So it's true. Ben was astonished that the Under Secretary allowed him to stay. Battle plans were one of any government's closely guarded secrets. He considered Israel's position in the Middle East, surrounded by countries threatening to wipe that nation off the map. Shaking his head, Ben knew it all boiled down to religion, particularly the inability of two of the world's major religions to coexist. Though he never studied other religions that closely, he knew the fundamental differences were large enough that there would be no peace for the foreseeable future.

Listening as people shared ideas, Ben sat quietly without anything major to share. Then an idea occurred, one he couldn't restrain himself from sharing, so he leaned over to whisper.

"Senator, if the Iranians have such excellent intelligence that they know about these Israeli battle plans, wouldn't it stand to reason that they may have detailed intelligence about these negotiations?"

"Yes, I suppose so," the Senator whispered in reply.

"You know, Senator," Ben said, "during my first visit to Budapest, I witnessed Russian and Iranians entering the same hotel where I stayed. I reported the observation immediately, but no one believed me. Does it make sense for the US delegation to host a reception at the ambassador's residence tonight? I mean, couldn't we logically assume a greater threat?"

"An increased threat—" the Senator stopped speaking, then added, "because the intelligence the Iranians shared in that speech originated in the US."

"Do you mean that there must be a mole within our government?" He sat back, stunned. He wanted to go back to his observation of the Russian and Iranian delegations, the ones *he* observed but no one believed. *This could be my chance to raise this issue.*

"Is there something the Senator and his aide would like to share with the group?" the Under Secretary asked. All heads turned to them.

The Senator stood to beam at the Under Secretary and said, "Madame Under Secretary, Ben pointed out that since the Iranians appear to have procured intelligence from a very sensitive source, one that I am concerned could be American, then tonight's reception at the ambassador's residence could be a target. Does that about sum it up, Ben?"

"Ma'am," Ben began, "the assembled group of dignitaries, including yourself and the Senator, would be a very inviting target for the Iranians, especially in light of their remarkable access."

He considered raising the issue of the Russians and Iranians, understanding such a connection with the Hungarian government raised even more questions. However, as he looked around the room, he searched for people who would side with him or at least offer support for his theory. *I forgot I'm surrounded primarily by intelligence analysts who make their living by offering options, whereas taking a stand entails a real risk of being wrong.*

Ben wasn't surprised when the first person to speak up disparaged his idea.

"I think it would be a mistake to even postpone, much less cancel, this important reception in honor of these historic talks all because a junior officer shares an unqualified opinion about security. I mean"—Susan looked around the room, eliciting tentative nods from some staff—"the ambassador went to tremendous effort to organize this party, and it would be unseemly to waste all that effort because of an uneducated security assessment. And we have worked for months to bring everyone together, and I would hate to see the president's Iran policy derailed by a misguided opinion." She took her seat, smiling when she saw people nodding and muttering agreement.

Unqualified. Uneducated. Misguided. Ben almost felt those words floating in the air, directed at him, and he hated having to sit there and take her abuse. He wanted to scream at her, *What did I ever do to you?* But he knew Susan was acting at the behest of Marsha Hunter, who still bore a grudge from Afghanistan. Would he ever be able to get beyond her enmity?

"As the regional security officer," Trevor interjected, "I believe Ben makes excellent points about the increased threat. It would be prudent to delay the reception pending a further security assessment, and I will put that recommendation in writing to the ambassador." His words hung in the air, a stinging rebuke to Susan. It was one thing to criticize Ben, but few would dare to directly contravene the RSO, who held unmatched power and authority over security issues.

People began speaking to their neighbors, Trevor's statement causing those who supported Susan to rethink their positions. Meanwhile, others who until then had remained silent began sharing their opinions, opining that *perhaps* it would be *prudent* to merely delay the reception rather than cancel it.

"But these talks are so important," Susan said, "and the perception of any delay or cancelation could jeopardize these critical talks."

Ben realized Susan sought to make her career on the success of the talks, damn any associated consequences.

Through it all, the Under Secretary sat listening to the discussion, wanting others to field thoughts, and waiting for a general consensus. However, on the issue of security, she never wavered. Before she could share her opinion, someone spoke from a chair near the station chief's office. Every station around the world was the same, Ben knew, and usually the one person guaranteed a private working space was the chief, which was a standard observed in bureaucracies around the world. The boss always got more privacy than any of the worker bees.

"It is worth noting," a senior CIA official from Washington said, "that the Senator was absolutely correct that the information shared by the Iranians likely originated from Washington." No one said a word, the undisputable reality crashing down on them. "I will not go into extremely sensitive sources and methods"—he reached for a printout, which Peter handed him—"but the wording the Iranians used was lifted almost exactly from a CIA report released several weeks ago." He paused, adjusting his glasses in obvious discomfort at speaking to so many people. "I believe it would be prudent to reevaluate the security situation."

"I want to thank Ben for sharing his opinion," the Under Secretary said. "It takes moral courage to put forward an opinion with which others disagree, but I commend you for putting the safety and security of American and other delegations' personnel ahead of all other considerations." She eyed Susan, daring her to disagree, but the director of the Iran Desk wisely stayed silent, her mouth opening and closing.

"I will inform the ambassador, as well as personnel back in Washington, of my recommendation that we postpone tonight's reception. Let us now adjourn and plan to meet again in three hours, giving everyone time to consider our best path forward."

Everyone knew the Under Secretary's recommendation carried more weight than any other US executive branch opinions in the country, given her position as the fourth most senior State Department official in the world.

Ben tuned out the rest, content to know that not only was his idea accepted but the Under Secretary singled him out for praise.

"Ben, my boy, thank you for speaking up," the Senator said. "Both privately to me and more broadly to everyone." He looked at Ben with pride, knowing this FSO had a bright future, so long as the State Department's bureaucracy didn't discourage him or set too many obstacles in his path.

"Thank you, sir," Ben said, grabbing his obligatory notebook. He was prepared to take notes, but he didn't want to write anything down in this space because of classification concerns. "But where do we go from here? How do we begin informing our allies that we are postponing tonight's reception?" *Particularly the Brits,* he thought but didn't say.

"That is for others to worry about." The Senator paused in thought, then continued with a wink. "But I doubt it would do any harm to tell your Kate in advance."

ACROSS THE DANUBE IN BUDA at the UK Embassy, Kate sat listening to everyone, her mind still spinning from the revelations in Raisi's speech. The UK government had access, through the Five Eyes program, to this very sensitive information. What most people did not know was that the sources were Israelis who spied *for* the American government *against* the Israeli government. That made it some of the most classified intelligence in the American government. While everyone understood the need to spy on enemies, few allies admitted to spying on their friends.

How could the Iranians have gotten ahold of such intelligence? That was the question the group discussed, yet she knew the Iranians were nearly world-class when it came to intelligence. Whether the Americans admitted it or not, the Iranians were a far more formidable enemy than almost any other in the world, given the Supreme Leader's stated intent to spread their version of Iran's Shi'a theology throughout the Middle East region, then on to the rest of the world.

"Kate, do you have anything to add?" The assembled group looked to her, and much to her surprise, Kate realized she had not said anything throughout their discussions.

"No, Ambassador," she addressed Sir Charles Harper, the UK Ambassador in Budapest, who held the unenviable responsibility of providing on-the-ground expertise. She felt for anyone who dealt with multilateral affairs, which were infinitely more complicated than bilateral affairs with its multitude of viewpoints and national interests.

"Come now, as an expert on Iran issues, you must have some insights."

"Well, Ambassador…" Kate adjusted her notebook, collecting her thoughts. She hated to speak off the cuff but decided to share some of her thinking. "I unfortunately do not believe we will ever learn how the Iranians procured the intelligence about the Israeli operations." She looked down at her notes, formulating her next thoughts carefully, knowing they would be hyperanalyzed. "However, I assess that the Iranians must have received it from a third party because the access is too good, and their intelligence penetration of the Americans cannot possibly be that complete. Otherwise, they would have been more successful in their Middle East operations."

"Are you confident of that assessment?" Lord Spencer asked from his seat at the head of the table. All heads swiveled from Spencer to Kate, scrutinizing her carefully as they awaited her response.

"Lord Spencer, if you will permit me to interject," Arthur Sinclair spoke. He knew Kate could stand up for herself but did not want her to have to face a senior government official on her own.

"MI6 fully concurs with our Iran expert Ms. Sinclair's assessment. Let me explain. Had the Iranians such an amazing source as this within Washington, it is unlikely this would be the first revelation that they shared publicly."

"Are you sure, Lord Sinclair?" a man from the UK Foreign and Commercial Office asked. "What if this is a new source?"

"The reason that would not make sense," Kate said, "is because this information is code-word intelligence. Any intelligence officer who secured this information would understand the importance of obscuring the details, not pulling directly from American reporting." She reached to the center of the table, where an MI6 document lay. "This document does not even give *us* insight into the American's source of intelligence. And we are arguably the Americans' closest ally." She slid the document to Lord Spencer, the head of negotiations of the UK delegation.

Lord Spencer collected the document, opened it, and sat back in his plush leather chair, deep in thought. Arthur Sinclair turned to look at Kate. *Her response was spot on.* He couldn't have been prouder of her.

The FCO diplomat, who Kate knew from previous conversations as someone more interested in protecting his reputation than finding real answers, served in Tehran but seemed a bit too oblivious to the realities of Iranian intentions.

How will American intelligence agencies respond to this leak of their information? Kate wondered. Feeling a slight chill despite no draft in the secure room, she understood. *Is there any way the Israelis could track this information back to the Americans?* Without knowing the source of the intelligence, which she assumed must have been from a well-placed Israeli official, she could only make educated guesses.

Kate didn't realize Lord Spencer stared in her direction, contemplating her assessment, which he considered very grave. He knew her expertise on Iran was renowned within MI6. Having also forged his own career separate from his family's name and centuries of political activity, he recognized in Ms. Sinclair a desire for individuality. When she sat up, Lord Spencer raised his hand for silence.

"Ms. Sinclair, what are you thinking?"

"Excuse me, my Lord," Kate responded, looking at Lord Spencer, "but I comprehended that although the number one question this group is discussing appears to be how the Iranians procured this intelligence, I argue one significant question is how the Americans will respond to its disclosure." She let that hang in the air for several seconds, then continued. "But the second, perhaps more important question is how the Israelis will respond *when* they learn of this leak of their planned military operations and whether they will blame the Americans."

Everyone blinked hard, catching up to Kate's line of reasoning. Each reached the same conclusion: Israeli's response could provoke serious regional conflict.

Lord Spencer considered this and asked, "What do you suggest is our next step, Ms. Sinclair?"

RAMIN SAT OUTSIDE the Hungarian Foreign Ministry, having tracked the departure of the American and British delegations more than two hours ago, while the other attending delegations stayed around for some time after to confer and discuss their positions. He knew from reporting that the Teacher shared that the session was scheduled to last all day, with the preliminary session in the morning, followed by direct negotiations in the afternoon.

Sitting at a café within shouting distance of the Hungarian Foreign Ministry, Ramin checked his watch and thought through the next steps. The Americans would host their reception tonight, meaning the Iraqis needed to be ready. He trusted that they would, because their honor depended on them following through on their promises to conduct the operation. Raising his hand to order another cappuccino, which he preferred to Iranian tea after years of living overseas, he considered the sequence of events, ready to adjust as needed.

Just then, as Ramin contemplated ordering lunch to justify keeping his table, he saw motorcades descend on the foreign ministry building. The first motorcade was British, with the flag fluttering on the hood of the luxury vehicle revealed, followed immediately by the American delegation. The Suburban he knew from surveillance and the license plate to be the American Ambassador's personal vehicle. There were three trailing vans full of people. *Don't the Americans ever go anywhere in small groups?*

BEN STEPPED FROM THE VAN and walked away to stretch his legs. The Under Secretary's staff arranged by phone to rejoin the negotiations after the next break, so he had some time to sit outside and get fresh air. He looked around for Kate, having heard over the radios that the UK motorcade had been two minutes ahead of the American motorcade. Not seeing her outside waiting to say hello, he assumed she went inside with her delegation. Nodding to the Senator, who walked straight into the foreign ministry as they agreed he would in the van, Ben began walking a short distance away before withdrawing his work phone from his pocket.

He leaned against a tree just off the sidewalk, with his head down and distracted by email on his phone, Ben felt as rush of air as someone hurried past him. He looked up and caught sight of a man dressed in a business suit nearly running away. He realized it was Brent.

Ben had only about fifteen minutes before he needed to return to his seat to observe the continuing negotiations. But his curiosity got the better of him, and he walked away from the foreign ministry building, keeping Brent in sight.

Wondering how far he would have to go, Ben was surprised when he saw Brent head for a café directly across the street from the foreign ministry. He watched his colleague walk up to a table where a man of medium build sat.

"YOU ARE HERE, RADEK, as promised," Brent said but almost also asked as he approached the table. Ramin/Radek spotted the American leaving the foreign ministry, noticing other people following him, but none of them appeared to be directly tracking his agent. *Yes, he is my agent, a man who will do whatever I ask.*

"Yes, I am here," Ramin responded curtly. "Sit."

Brent sat uncomfortably, looking around for anyone he knew in the café, but decided to dispense with all caution. "They are canceling tonight's reception, but perhaps it'll be rescheduled, maybe even for tomorrow night."

Ramin stayed quiet, willing the American to say more.

"I don't know everything they discussed because even the ambassador wasn't invited in. Only people who attended the negotiations were in there, but once they finished, they used the bathrooms and then piled back into their vehicles to return here. I only just got a seat, after the ambassador ordered me to learn what I could. I saw you here so rushed over to share everything I could."

Brent felt as if he had run a great distance, exhausted from sharing so much.

"You did well telling me immediately." Ramin churned over the details. The American already admitted he didn't know much more than what he heard. Was there any other useful detail he could ask for?

"I don't want my family's life in danger because you don't think I am sharing with you," Brent said morosely, slouching in his chair. A waiter approached, and he ordered a cappuccino.

Ah, Ramin thought, *fear is now the greatest motivation for this man.* He smiled inwardly, his face a mask.

"I can tell that you came right away, and your family is safe." He counted to ten before continuing. "For now." He willed the man across from him to say more, letting his final threat hang between them.

Brent stared at him, transfixed, then began speaking without thinking. "In the car, no one really said much, but I overheard that the visiting British delegation might host a reception tomorrow night. Perhaps that will take the place of our reception?" he offered hopefully, not wanting to appear to hold anything back, which wasn't difficult because he didn't know what else to say. The people in his van had been quiet, almost morose, and he didn't know much else.

"Very well, that is good information." He didn't want to heap too much praise on this man for merely sharing what he knew, but he knew this man's actions would force him to reschedule with the Iraqis and give them new, detailed information on likely British facilities. "If you hear anything else, I will be here or down the street waiting for more information." He pointed to a red awning.

Brent nodded, knowing he now took orders from this man as much as he did from the ambassador. "I'll go," he said. Leaving his cappuccino untouched, he rose and walked from the table.

Ramin withdrew his phone and began typing a message.

ACROSS THE STREET, BEN WATCHED the two men meet, unable to hear anything they said but able to read their body language. Having found a good place to watch, he took several photos of Brent and the man who looked like a local Hungarian.

Ben turned to the side as Brent crossed the street, but he knew with sunglasses on, it would be difficult, nearly impossible, for Brent to recognize him. Turning back to the café, Ben decided to take one last photo of the man sitting at the table, zooming in with his phone's camera and snapping a photo that caught the entirety of his face.

Not wanting to push his luck and risk someone noticing him, Ben turned to walk back to the foreign ministry building, walking an extra distance to ensure he did not follow directly behind Brent. He needed to approach the foreign ministry from the other direction.

As he entered the main gate, he held up his pass, and the Hungarian guard waved him into the meeting. Inside, Ben saw Brent talking with Hungarian officials, so Ben walked quickly to enter the main hall, finding his seat near the Senator.

"You cut it close, my boy," the Senator chided Ben softly.

"My apologies, Senator." Ben flashed his smile. "I enjoyed being outside and saw something of interest, so needed an extra couple of minutes." He settled back in his seat, withdrew the notebook from his suit jacket pocket, and prepared to take notes.

To the side of the American delegation, Kate observed Ben entering late, wondering why he hadn't looked around to at least make eye contact with her. Where had he been? She knew the entire American delegation entered as one. No one even stopped to use the bathroom. But luckily for Ben, the Iranian delegation had taken a few extra minutes during the break. She made a mental note to speak with Ben, wanting to know what the Americans discussed but also to ensure that Ben knew that UK Ambassador Harper and her father would host a reception at Harper's residence tomorrow night.

CHAPTER

TWENTY-FIVE

"**WELL, THAT WAS QUITE THE DAY,**" Ben said, holding his drink at the British Ambassador's residence, where he was invited for a light meal and after-negotiation drinks. The Senator sat chatting with Lord Spencer in the corner. Under Secretary Johnson left half an hour before, and Ben observed that besides himself and the Senator, everyone else in the room worked for the British government.

"Ben, how are you?" Arthur Sinclair asked, approaching while Kate walked away to refresh her drink.

Ben rose. After Arthur took a seat directly next to where his daughter sat a minute before, Ben sat back down, comprehending that he would never be able to relax. *I'm even still in my suit, more than twelve hours after putting it on,* he thought, cursing his inability to have any downtime.

"I am quite well, sir, especially with a drink in hand." He raised his glass in a toast. He chuckled inwardly that he and Kate's father never again discussed how he should address the Peer of the Realm, who would one day be his father-in-law. "Did you get the full briefing on all discussions at the negotiations today?"

Kate returned with her drink to find that her father had followed through on his promise to buttonhole Ben to get more of a sense of everything that happened. The American Under Secretary had already briefed them all in their discussion at the American Embassy, noting their cancelation of Ambassador Richards's reception scheduled for this evening. They obliquely referred to the Iranian's intelligence slip, citing highly classified information, but agreed that so far, the Israelis were in the dark about what Raisi said. Even the French, they felt sure, seemed unaware of the significance of Raisi's words.

"Father," Kate said as she skirted around and sat next to Ben. "Scoot over, love," she half suggested, half ordered. Ben lazily adjusted to the side to make space on the loveseat.

"I was just chatting with Ben," Arthur drawled as the two of them adjusted to make space for one another. He could see their relationship was still young, in the way that they were not yet fully comfortable around one another, but he knew that would change. When would Ben propose to Kate? He knew that would set off a flurry of events but secretly looked forward to the first of his children getting married.

"Father, Ben and I have not seen one another alone all day," Kate said.

I'm not leaving, her father's expression communicated clearly.

"No, it's always nice to spend time with your father," Ben said. Having judged Kate's relationship with her father during their limited interactions, Ben knew their bond enabled them to communicate nonverbally.

"Thank you, Ben," Arthur said, smiling and deciding that he would no longer give this young man a hard time. "To your question before Kate arrived, I believe I have a good sense of the negotiations but welcome your thoughts and insights." He took a sip of his drink.

Ben took a swig of his gin and tonic, deciding this step up in his lifestyle was one he liked. Being a diplomat entailed socializing with people, but this was with a different level of society. It intimidated him slightly because he still saw himself as a small-town Minnesota boy, but he tried to suppress that feeling of unease.

"I don't know if there is much else to say beyond what the Senator and others said." He hesitated, then continued. "The Iranians obviously got that information from somewhere, but until we find out where, the Under Secretary plans to stall for time."

"Yet the challenge is that the Iranians actually appear to be offering some measurable concessions, such as independent UN verification of their enrichment activities," Kate offered. "Perhaps the most interesting thing is that they offered no preliminary objections to any guaranteed American insistence that US representatives be allowed on the UN team."

"The Iranians can and will block their visas at a later date if they want to make things difficult," Ben offered offhandedly. "But what I find most interesting is that Raisi and supporters appear to be offering real concessions, all in hopes of winning relief from sanctions." He decided to press further. "This could represent a shift in Iran's strategy, perhaps that they're willing to give up more than we thought because sanctions are really hurting their country."

"What are the chances that your Congress will lift sanctions?" Ambassador Harper asked as he approached, selecting a seat near Arthur.

Ben began to rise, but Harper waved him down. "Ben, whilst we are in the confines of my residence, encircled by friends, please address me as Charles and refrain from standing on ceremony."

"Yes, Charles," Ben responded, raising his glass. He smiled, knowing he seemed to have joined a very particular club where his relationship with Kate would open doors he never knew existed. "I would guess that members of Congress will want assurance from the administration that the Iranians will follow through on their promises, not simply removing sanctions before seeing results."

He didn't have to add that they'd all seen the Iranians agree to anything to see sanctions against them lowered but then never held up their end of the bargain. *Congress won't stand for that,* Ben thought, not saying it aloud because that might be going too far.

Kate watched as Ben held his own, discussing the finer points of US foreign policy, and she knew that despite her reservations, Ben's assignment on Capitol Hill gave him insight most American diplomats never considered truly important. She knew that some UK diplomats could secure similar postings working on parliamentary committees, but it never occurred to her to consider doing something similar, because MI6 didn't second its staff to Parliament.

"Have we any news about Israeli activities?" Arthur asked, placing a firm hand of control on the conversation.

"Nothing we have seen," Kate responded.

"Would anyone like me to freshen their glass?" Charles asked. Kate saw the question as an invitation for her and Ben to leave, but she deferred to her father and Lord Harper.

"Not for me, thank you, Charles," Arthur said as he stood. He walked across the room to his wife, who was speaking with Charles's wife, who showed off the residence and solicited thoughts for the next evening's reception.

Ben and Kate rose as one, offering their thanks as they made their way to the door. Ben saw the Senator and Lord Spencer speaking in the corner, neither seeming in a hurry to leave, so Ben approached.

"Senator, is there anything you need?"

"Not at all, Ben, thank you for asking." He turned and introduced Ben. "Chris, I would like to introduce one of my team, Ben Brownwell."

Lord Christopher Spencer extended his hand and grasped Ben's firmly. "It is a pleasure to meet you, Ben, and I understand that you and Miss Sinclair are something of an item?"

Kate, who stood beside Ben, blushed at the comment. Just then, the Senator excused himself, walking away quickly.

"It seems that the two of you are hiding a secret," Lord Harper nearly whispered, just loud enough for the two of them to hear. Kate and Ben stared at the UK's lead negotiator in disbelief.

"My Lord," Kate whispered, "I'm not sure what you mean."

Christopher Harper chuckled, watching as the two of them stood so close to one another, trying to avoid touching.

He smiled. "Your secret is safe with me, but I absolutely insist on attending the wedding ceremony." With that, he patted Ben's shoulder and walked off to join the Senator, who was speaking with Charles Harper.

"We have to get out of here," Kate said as she grabbed Ben's hand and pulled him out to the waiting vehicles. She was gratified to see that her father and mother were already in one vehicle, so she waved for Mark to close the door and leave them standing outside.

"It appears the Senator and Lord Spencer intend to stay later tonight," Charles Harper commented as he appeared behind them, almost as if by magic.

Kate turned, not letting go of Ben's hand. "We, of course, defer to them," she said, "but intend to return to our hotel. It has, after all, been quite a long day, and tomorrow promises to be another full day."

"I am not holding you up," Charles said, smiling as he gestured behind him, "but I arranged for another of our vehicles to take you home rather than waiting for your father or the Senator."

Ben was exhausted. He was so grateful to return to his hotel and wanted nothing more than to fall asleep, though he knew in the fog of exhaustion and liquor, there was an issue he wanted to discuss with Kate.

"Thank you so much, Charles, that is kind of you," Ben said, offering his hand in thanks. Kate was about to say something about how she only wanted to take a taxi back to their hotel, but Ben pulled her to the vehicle.

"Have a good night, you two, and we will see you in the morning," Charles Harper said, then closed the door.

In the vehicle, Ben slumped in the seat and closed his eyes in exhaustion.

Kate surveyed her surroundings, noting that the vehicle had a divider that could close between the driver and passengers in the rear. Searching the vehicle, she found the likely button and pushed it, giving them privacy from the driver.

Ben heard the sound and opened his eyes just as Kate turned to him and smiled, realizing that the two of them were alone at last as she leaned to rest against his chest.

"How are you feeling?" she asked as innocently as possible, snaking her hands up until she ran her fingers through his hair.

"I wanted to talk through something with you," Ben said, relaxed as he enjoyed being so close to Kate.

Before he could say anything else, Ben felt Kate draw his face to hers for a passionate kiss. He twisted to embrace her, focused on the intensity of her kiss and quickly losing track of all other thoughts. Countless minutes later, their vehicle slowed, and the driver knocked on the divider before lowering it, never saying a word or looking in his rear-view mirror.

Kate nearly pulled Ben out of the vehicle, waving thanks to the driver as they strolled into the hotel together. The lobby was deserted, and the hotel elevator opened right away. Once inside, they fell again into a passionate kiss.

As they approached his room, located closer to the elevators and therefore the most convenient place to stop, Ben fumbled with his room key before properly swiping it on the second try. He never let go of Kate's hand, which made it difficult for him to use his left hand to search his various pockets. They entered the room and embraced, falling onto the bed.

Half an hour later, Ben dozed, turning to his left as he cuddled up against Kate to get into a comfortable position.

"Was there something you wanted to discuss with me?" Kate asked.

"Nothing I can remember," Ben responded sleepily.

THE NEXT MORNING, BEN AND KATE sat at breakfast in the hotel dining room. They enjoyed nearly fifteen minutes of silence, planning to talk through several things. However, first Peter arrived, grabbing a chair with no invitation. Then Stephen and Gideon arrived with plates from the breakfast buffet, wordlessly expanding their table with three chairs to confer about the day ahead. Although Peter's arrival meant they were forced to tread carefully with what they said, the Israelis' arrival meant that they had to completely avoid the disclosure of information by Raisi.

Ben marveled at Stephen and Gideon's ability to pile so much food onto one small plate. *How can they eat so much?* He moved his foot carefully to rest against Kate's, taking comfort in her touch despite the intrusion of the three additional men at their table.

"Is there anything in particular you guys want to discuss?" Ben asked the three men, "or did you simply not want to eat alone?" Ben waved his arm around the nearly empty dining room, about to keep asking questions when Kate leaned forward to interject her own thoughts.

"Stephen, is there a reason you and Gideon brought three chairs to the table, especially placing the empty chair next to me?" Kate asked innocently, then sipped at her tea.

Stephen looked around as if conjuring a wordless response and pointed with his fork to turkey sausage and eggs over his shoulder to the restaurant's entrance and the start of the buffet. Expecting someone to have appeared and looking very annoyed, Stephen turned and waved his free hand vigorously.

As if reacting to a summons, a woman appeared carrying a plate and wearing a frown. She approached the empty chair and seated herself after meeting everyone's eyes and nodding. Ben recognized Sarah.

Settling into her seat and carefully placing the cloth napkin in her lap, Sarah smiled thinly first at Ben, then at Kate. "Good morning," she said in her accented English. She appeared to want to say more but instead focused her attention entirely on her plate, which contained small piles of food. It was carefully segregated and piled so nothing touched anything else.

"Good morning," Kate responded, shifting to focus on Sarah. "When did you return to Budapest?"

Sarah appeared to contemplate her answer, staring at Kate with the same thin smile and willing her to look away. *Little does she know,* Ben observed, *that Kate would win a staring contest with a sphynx.*

After nearly a minute of silence, during which Peter watched everyone, taking in the exchange, while Stephen and Gideon merely continued eating through their plates laden with food, she responded.

"I returned last night, feeling that I was needed here." Sarah ended further conversation when she grabbed her fork and began picking at her food.

Ben watched as she would eye a piece of food, separate it from everything around, and then spear it with the fork in her right hand. Whatever item she picked out, she mercilessly used the knife in her left hand to keep it in place, as if prepared for the food to make a hasty run for the door.

"I think I'm going to get more food," Ben declared to the table, rising to make a break for the buffet. As he reached down to get his plate, Stephen looked up and, with a fork over-laden with food hovering near his mouth, called out, "Come back quickly, we have much to discuss."

Ben met Kate's eyes, unsurprised to see her wink at him. *There she sits,* Ben thought, *surrounded by people who are her natural competitors in their search for information, yet she appears to be the most relaxed.* Ben turned to walk away, catching a glimpse of Kate drinking her tea in a way that proclaimed she was in control of the table filled with intelligence agents from a multitude of countries.

As he approached the buffet line, Ben sensed and felt rather than saw someone step up behind him. He spun to see Peter picking up a fresh plate, then raise his hands as if showing he was unarmed.

"It's okay, sport. I'm on your side," Peter said, then stood next to Ben and scanned the array of foods, randomly selecting items to pile onto his plate.

Ben thought about how Sarah must have so carefully placed items on her plate so no item touched another. He wondered at the psychological implications of each of these methods for loading plates with food but set that aside, understanding that he couldn't get that caught up analyzing other people.

"I see it isn't your or your girlfriend's first time meeting Sarah," Peter observed in a low voice, obviously not wanting anyone to hear him speak.

When Ben moved to the next station to study the assortment of honeys and jams, Peter followed, though not before tossing still more items on his laden plate.

"I mentioned before, I recall," Ben responded in an equally low tone as he leaned over the breakfast buffet to scoop more food onto his plate, "that she was the one who attacked me when she was emotionally overcome at the sight of Avi Cohen."

Peter nodded acceptance, confirming that Ben indeed was not lying. "Did you know that she is one of Mossad's most capable assassins and snipers?"

Ben snapped his head up, bumping his head on a glass flower pot hanging from the ceiling. The dirt flew across the floor and miraculously missed the food. Restaurant staff scurried to clean the mess, apologizing and asking if Ben was okay.

Ben turned to walk to his table, unsurprised to find Peter carrying not one but two plates loaded with food. They took their seats to find only Sarah still eating, still carefully selecting pieces of food to eat one at a time.

Stephen and Gideon appraised first Ben's, then Peter's plates, nodding their approval at Peter's selections. Gideon rose slightly to get a better look at Ben's plate.

"I see you managed not to get any dirt on your food," Gideon said, displaying a broad smile as he vigorously stirred his coffee.

After a long silence, punctuated only by the waiter arriving to refill their coffee cups, teacups, and water glasses, Stephen conceded defeat and spoke.

"Unfortunately, our nation does not have any representatives in this ill-fated negotiation," he began, then launched into a soliloquy about how the Iranians could never be trusted.

"Stephen," Ben said, "I don't think anyone at this table trusts the Iranians on anything."

Gideon smiled, as if privy to some private joke, and Ben could tell this was something the great bulk of a man did sparingly, though with real emotion.

Stephen merely grunted his assent, then nodded for Ben to continue.

"I dealt with the Iranians in Afghanistan—"

"As I did, in different contexts," Kate said.

"I doubt anyone here has any sympathy for the clerics who so ruthlessly rule Iran," Ben continued, looking at their faces for disagreement, "or feels anything but sadness for Iran's youth, who are systematically being robbed of their futures."

Again, no one disagreed, surprising Ben because he expected one of the Israelis to come up with some retort. Ben forged ahead.

"It was really nice of everyone to accept the invitation we never sent to join us for breakfast, but if no one has anything, then Kate and I are going for a walk before we change and leave for the negotiations."

Sarah wiped her mouth with her napkin and said, "I felt I was needed here because we intercepted telecommunications traffic that exposed two pieces of relevant intelligence to our experts, which they asked me to share."

Ben noticed Stephen and Gideon sat relaxed, as if they had already heard the intelligence. Only Peter seemed to lean forward ever so slightly, betraying a curiosity that everyone else concealed so carefully.

Sarah went on. "First, yesterday we learned that the Iranians exposed intelligence information extremely detrimental to our nation's security, making allegations about alleged plans of efforts by us to attack Iranian nuclear facilities."

Though she dropped that bombshell without emotion, Ben suspected the Israelis must have lost their minds when they learned the full extent of the intelligence breach.

"We are confident that the Iranians could not have learned that on their own, so we suspect another foreign power likely acquired the intelligence and traded it to the mullahs."

Peter listened carefully so he could report this conversation in full to Langley the moment he got to the embassy. That meant he would miss part, potentially all, of today's negotiations, yet his hunch that joining Ben and Kate for breakfast would pay off felt like a prescient call. It made up for not seeing his children before they woke that morning.

"Second," Sarah continued, "we learned that there is an as yet undetermined threat against the American and British delegations." She leaned over to pick up her small leather satchel and carefully opened it to withdraw two manila folders. These she held up, handing one to Kate and the other to Ben.

Knowing this was far beyond his expertise, and noticing Peter literally fidgeting, Ben handed the manila envelope to Peter.

As if confirming a bet or resolving some discussion, Stephen's face tightened, and Gideon smiled broadly and rapidly spoke Hebrew. Sarah shot Gideon a sharp glance, but Ben could see he was not a man easily cowed. Nonetheless, he stood and reached across the table, ruffled Ben's hair and said, "I see you are an honorable man, one who reveals what he knows and understands his limitations. You deserve our respect and friendship."

Sensing Stephen was ready to speak, Gideon resumed his seat. Seemingly oblivious to the world around him, he busied himself with pouring sugar and milk in specific quantities into his coffee, almost as meticulously as Sarah ate her breakfast but just as effortlessly.

"We do not question why you did not share the Iranian disclosure of Israeli government secrets, knowing that everyone at this table reports to someone else," Stephen said. "However, we are trusting you with some part of the security of our country."

Ben met Stephen's eyes, seeing respect and an intensity marking a professional asking for help.

"Thank you for this information," Kate interjected. She didn't want Ben to feel the need to respond because this was decidedly not his area of expertise. She thought about the recording device in her purse that she activated when Sarah approached. Kate would share the recording with Ben, but Peter should have come prepared with a similar audio device. If he arrived unprepared, he would remain distracted and struggle to remember everything while wondering as she did about the folder's contents.

"I suggest, pending approval from my organization's leadership here, that you set people up outside of the venue," Sarah said. "If there are any developments we are authorized to share, I will bring the information out to one of you directly, assuming, of course, that I can do so without attracting our adversaries' attention."

Stephen relaxed, yet his face remained stoic. Ben understood that Kate offered something of an olive branch of cooperation, one cloaked in uncertainty and stipulations that she could never begin to control. Still, Ben took it as a mark of Kate's self-assurance that she was confident enough to make such an offer, one the Israelis would expect her to negotiate. That meant she thought it through and believed she could negotiate successfully.

"We agree," Stephen muttered, ending what he had thought would have been a lengthy argument. He sat back, adopting a more relaxed pose, and carefully analyzed Kate Sinclair. All they said about her back in Tel Aviv was that she was an Iran expert who performed well enough that she never needed her father's help to gain attention. *And yet,* Stephen wondered, *how would her relationship with her American boyfriend change her future career trajectory?*

Looking to Gideon and Sarah, Stephen nodded imperceptibly to each, signaling that they got what they came for. Mossad always cooperated with other intelligence agencies, but only when their interests aligned. The three stood as one and prepared to take their leave.

"You're leaving so soon?" Ben asked humorlessly. *They must have gotten what they wanted.*

Peter wondered, *What will the Israelis accept?* He was thankful he hadn't been in the spotlight, yet glad for the ringside seat to watch the sparring between the Brits and the Israelis. He figured he would write up two pages about this and send it off to Langley. Peter didn't envy the analysts who read through every report because many case officers around the world were often terrible writers. Often, those officers relied on other staff to rewrite their reports. Luckily, Peter knew his writing style was quite good based on his classical, humanities-focused education.

"We should also be going," Kate declared, standing to place her hand on Ben's shoulder. In turn, Ben finished his coffee and rose, then checked his pockets and looked around to ensure he didn't forget anything. The two waved to the three Israelis as they paid their breakfast bill and left Peter to finish eating.

"Oh my, we only have twenty-five minutes before we must leave," Kate said, pressing the button again to call the elevator.

"It won't take me long to shower and get ready," Ben said. He knew Kate would take longer.

Up in his room, Ben remembered there was something he wanted to discuss with Kate. He resolved to raise the issue about Brent when he and Kate ate lunch together, preferably alone. *What are the chances anyone lets us eat lunch without interruption?* Ben wondered as he laid out a suit, shirt, and tie, careful that everything matched.

CHAPTER
TWENTY-SIX

RAMIN SAT AT HIS USUAL TABLE. *One positive of the West is that if you leave a generous tip, you are buying their future cooperation.* He could not leave too large of a tip, as he would be remembered too well. But a generous tip meant that staff would give him any table he requested, provide attentive service, and then leave him alone. *Just so they don't remember me weeks from now.* Though by then he would have accomplished his mission and left this city, not planning to return for at least a year.

Earlier, numerous motorcades arrived. Ramin observed them all and made careful notes in the margins of his newspaper.

Straining to see the Americans trail out of their vehicles, Ramin thought he identified Brent among the group before everyone entered the ministry. Were he not an experienced intelligence officer, he would be nervous about the American avoiding him. However, Ramin knew the American would never forget the threat against his family. *I just need more information, but at least the Iraqis are standing by, readying to conduct their attack.*

STEPHEN, SARAH, AND GIDEON arrived in the vicinity of the Hungarian Foreign Ministry, parking their vehicle several blocks away. All three carried a weapon under their jackets in the small of their back. The average Hungarian did not own a firearm, so they had to be careful. However, they suspected the Russians and potentially even the Iranians stationed their people outside to surveil the entering and exiting diplomats, and some of those adversaries might carry weapons.

Surveying the area, the three split up and each took a table at cafés and restaurants within eyesight of the foreign ministry building. Stephen walked towards a café and saw approximately half of the tables full, mostly Hungarians enjoying tea or coffee while reading their papers. A trained observer, he wound through the tables and mentally noted the language of the newspaper each person had.

No Iranian intelligence officer in their right mind would bring a Farsi language newspaper on an operation, Stephen thought, but he played for the other side to make mistakes. One man had a Hungarian newspaper laid out before him, but it had notations in the margins written in another language. *What language is that?* He was careful not to turn around but made a mental note to try to get a better glimpse when he next walked past the man.

BRENT FELT RESTLESS. The ambassador ordered him to stay in the lobby to monitor things, and even worse, there wasn't anywhere good to sit. But the Hungarians provided a steady supply of strong coffee. The server regularly brought him a fresh cup. *I need to pee,* he thought, *but I also need to get outside and provide Radek the details of the British reception tonight.*

Only upon arriving at the embassy that morning did Brent see the full details of the night's reception from the invitation waiting in the mailbox outside his office. The local staff made their morning rounds, delivering newspapers and mail, the latter usually diplomatic correspondence from the Hungarians but also from other diplomatic missions. After photocopying the invitation, Brent left the original on his desk but carefully folded the copy and placed it in his inside jacket pocket, for Radek.

Checking his watch, Brent saw that the negotiation's morning session should break up soon. He finished his coffee and decided to use the bathroom. He took his leather satchel with him, not trusting the Hungarian staff with watching over it.

Two minutes later, feeling much better, the first of the delegations left the meeting hall. The ambassador was looking around, and Brent quickly approached and explained that everything had been quiet out in the hallway. He noticed that Ambassador Richards looked pleased with himself for finally getting into the negotiations. Still, with that distracting him, Brent knew the man would not go out of his way to torture him. *At least not too much.*

Knowing he had at least twenty-five minutes before the ambassador would look for him again, Brent hefted his satchel and headed to the building's main exit. Outside, he sidestepped numerous people speaking in front of the doors and turned right to head to the main road. Brent was in such a hurry he didn't look around. He was completely focused on speaking quickly with Radek, making a phone call to cover his absence, and then returning to spend the next several hours in the waiting area.

BEN PACED OUTSIDE, HOLDING HIS PHONE while breathing in Budapest's fresh, cool air. The inside smelled of stale smoke. Looking up from his phone, Ben noticed as Brent Paulson walked quickly from the main entrance. *Where on earth is he going now?* Ben thought, belatedly recognizing a pattern.

Ben followed Brent for quite some distance.

Watching Brent studiously walk towards the main road, Ben kept a slow pace, easily able to follow as Brent crossed the street. Hungarian drivers weren't terrible, nothing compared to crazy Afghan drivers. He saw Brent heading towards a particular café but then suddenly lost track of the political and economic chief as he went behind a large group of tourists who stood directly between the café and the street.

WHO IS BEN WATCHING? Stephen wondered as he tracked the American's movements from the right side of the foreign ministry building to the left. *If I didn't know Ben was a diplomat and not an intelligence officer, I would suspect he was tailing someone. And doing a good job of it,* Stephen thought. Just then, a large group of Asian tourists walked along the sidewalk and obscured Stephen's view.

Inside the café, another American—judging by the tailoring of his suit, plus the color of his shirt and tie—entered and scanned the tables. Stephen looked down at his newspaper, today's edition of the International Tribune. It marked him as a foreigner, though not necessarily as someone from anywhere other than the United Kingdom, which matched the passport he carried in his coat pocket. The British would not have been amused to find that the Mossad forged their passport, but then the Mossad employed some of the best forgers in the world to provide cover identities for their officers.

The American approached the table of the man Stephen passed earlier, taking a seat directly next to the presumed Hungarian. *Bad luck,* Stephen thought as the American sat blocking any clear view of the Hungarian, leaning forward so the Mossad officer could not clearly see either of their faces. The two spoke intently, but Stephen was several tables away and was unable to hear their conversation. He did notice some movement, which appeared to be the new arrival giving something to the other man.

"**YOU DECIDED TO COME OUT** and speak to me," Ramin said brusquely, frustrated after waiting. Mahmoud and Farrokh were stationed not far away, moving around to maintain visual contact.

"You made very clear the consequences if I didn't cooperate," Brent replied.

"Do you have anything for me?" Ramin simultaneously loathed the American and wished the Teacher would authorize him to kill the man.

"The Brits are hosting a reception tonight," Brent said, then shared the details he knew.

AFTER THE LARGE GROUP OF ASIANS DEPARTED, Stephen watched as Ben appeared unexpectedly on the café's side of the street. *Who is he searching for?* Stephen wondered as Ben scanned the café, stopping to stare before seeing him at his table. Although he briefly considered waving to Ben, Stephen kept his hand down and instead watched as Ben withdrew his phone, answering a call.

Turning to glance at the two men huddled at the table, Stephen watched Ben holding his phone out, as if trying to get a signal. Just then, Ben turned and slowed, aiming the camera directly at the two men speaking intently to one another.

Is he photographing those men? Stephen wondered. *Did I misidentify Ben? Could he, in fact, be an intelligence officer? Or does he just have good instincts?* Stephen felt he had observed something important but knew he was missing too many pieces of the puzzle to understand the importance of the events that unfolded.

"ARE YOU SURE EVERYTHING YOU TOLD ME IS TRUE?" Ramin asked, grabbing the American by the arm.

"Yes," Brent said.

Realizing he had heard all the information he needed to change his plan, Ramin leaned in close to the American and whispered, "If you are lying to me, your children and wife are dead."

JUST AS BEN TURNED AROUND AGAIN, Stephen saw the man he assumed was American stand up from the table and take a defensive position. *What are those men discussing?* He wished that rather than splitting up from Gideon and Sarah, he would have insisted that one of them sit in this café. Belatedly hoping the likely American would stay put a few more seconds, Stephen withdrew his phone and snapped several photos before the probable American walked away.

On the street, Ben walked down the sidewalk, away from the café's entrance. At the same time, the American exited the café and nearly broke into a run as he rushed across the street, barely making the crosswalk signal before the cars started driving. Then, as if everything happened all at once, the man with notes in the margin of his paper donned oversized sunglasses and a brown hat that he pulled low, fully obscuring his face. The man then rose from his table.

Stephen quickly studied his menu. The man he assumed was Hungarian turned a full 360 degrees to scan all around him. Stephen used his peripheral vision to see the man apparently taking note of everyone around him. Obscuring himself in plain sight, Stephen signaled the waiter that he was ready to order, earning himself a scrutiny from the supposed Hungarian. *Is he surveilling the café? If not, what else is he doing?* The waiter approached Stephen's table, and the man watching him continued looking around, then turned to scan the street.

After loudly declaring that he wasn't hungry, Stephen asked for the check in British-accented English, handing the waiter double the cost of his coffee. He counted to ten, carefully folding his paper as he watched the man he thought was Hungarian exit the café, and quickly stood to follow him. Wherever he was going, this was unusual behavior, out of the ordinary enough with Ben's focused attention that he wanted to know where the man was going. Stephen assumed the man who left the table went to the foreign ministry building, while the one he thought was Hungarian walked the opposite direction.

After looking around to give the impression he was momentarily disoriented, Stephen locked eyes with Sarah at the restaurant across the street, motioning her with his head to follow him, then did the same with Gideon, who was standing near a newsagent. Both began moving, but Stephen turned to see the likely Hungarian farther away than he expected. *Is the man running?*

Momentarily losing the Hungarian behind several people, Stephen regained sight of him still walking in that same direction, wearing the same color hat he donned at the table. The Hungarian appeared to be walking slower now; he took out a map and stopped as if to look around to orient himself. Knowing he risked attracting notice if he turned away, Stephen continued straight ahead, only to realize that this man was of the same build and wore a similar jacket but wasn't wearing sunglasses.

Reaching behind him, Stephen splayed his fingers wide, knowing Gideon and Sarah would understand that they needed to slow down to observe the man Stephen would pass next. With that, Stephen walked with purpose and only looked out of the corner of his eye at the man reading the map. He could have sworn the man had a slightly different haircut.

What is happening here? I studied that man from the back, only seeing his face as I walked past, but it was a grossly ordinary face, one almost designed to not be memorable.

Exactly the face of a spy, a voice inside screamed to Stephen.

This isn't the man I saw at the café, yet he is wearing the same hat, unless two men with matching hats just happen to be walking along the same street. Stephen knew he missed something important and cursed his luck at not understanding it soon enough. But he knew this was the way the intelligence game was played. Sometimes you caught a break, but more often than not, you didn't.

He looked around, hoping to recognize the face he saw for only a moment, but it was a lost cause.

WATCHING THE MAN WALK PAST, Ramin analyzed his face, wondering why the man followed him so quickly. He knew he wasn't being paranoid.

In just two minutes, Ramin exited the café and quickly walked down the street, taking off the large sunglasses and handing his hat to Mahmoud, who donned the hat and assumed his identity for anyone who might be following. Ramin also took off his coat before going to a table, where Mahmoud sat just seconds before, and donned a pair of reading glasses, further changing his features.

Praise Allah for the procedures the Teacher insisted we put in place, Ramin thought as he read a paperback and sipped at the mineral water Mahmoud left on the table. Although their features were different, by styling their hair in similar ways and wearing similar clothes, even with different styles and colors of shirts, the two could switch places as if by magic. In fact, Ramin carefully unbuttoned the shirt he wore at the café and took that off at the same time as his jacket, revealing what appeared to be a completely different outfit to any but someone carefully studying him.

The man continued walking down the street. Ramin could not see anyone with him, but if there was another team of intelligence officers in the area, they would be formidable opponents. The man did not look Jewish. *Could he be from the Hungarian intelligence service?* Ramin was not worried about the Hungarians, seeing the Jews as his biggest threat, followed closely by the Americans.

Still, he felt in his pocket for the piece of paper the American gave him. The British were hosting an event at their ambassador's residence, which was problematic because the Iraqis never studied that as a target location. He considered the time, deciding to wait just ten more minutes and then conduct a surveillance detection route to ensure no one followed him. Then he would go directly to prepare the Iraqis for their new mission.

Tonight, the Iraqis will earn their money, Ramin thought. And if all went well, they would never meet again. As far as he knew, only the men saw his face, though it was possible some of the men's wives or children also could have seen him. Not that it would matter, because he and his brothers would depart immediately after the attack, putting significant distance between themselves and the successful terrorist incident.

BEN DOUBLED BACK AFTER WALKING to the end of the block, never seeing Stephen or the exit of the man who Brent visited. He slowed as he approached the crosswalk and waited for the signal to cross. After surviving a year in Afghanistan, he refused to jaywalk. He survived a war zone. Why get taken out by a car?

Resisting the urge to look at his phone, Ben compared the images in his mind, reasoning that in three separate incidents, Brent met a man of average height and features. *Could the three men all be the same?* Perhaps, but Ben wouldn't know until he examined the photos side by side. Luckily his phone time-stamped when each photo was taken, so if his hunch proved correct, he could prove beyond a reasonable doubt that Brent was acting suspiciously.

I should take this to the RSO, Ben thought, but it was dangerous to accuse a member of country team of acting improperly. *Perhaps to Peter?* Ben thought about that but knew his hunches would not impress anyone, not given the high burden of proof he would have to overcome.

Crossing the street, Ben thought through everything he knew about Brent, deciding then and there that he needed to voice his concerns to Kate. *Now.* He showed his badge to the Hungarian official at the door, who compared his name to the list and waved him through the inner doors and on in to join the delegation as it prepared to reenter the negotiation room. Ben scanned the room and met eyes with Kate, who looked at him quizzically, to which Ben merely shook his head, indicating that everything was okay.

Everything is not okay, but I need more proof before I can accuse Brent of something. Having taken annual security trainings since joining the Foreign Service, Ben knew State Department culture didn't trust outsiders, but once someone was inside, it seemed to give them leeway to do whatever they wanted.

In another part of the room, Ben found Brent standing with his back against the wall, looking as bored as usual. He was only half a dozen steps from Ambassador Richards. *What if I approached Brent and asked him why he keeps speaking and meeting with the same guy?* Ben knew Brent would have an explanation, probably sufficient to convince Ambassador Richards. Though the ambassador hated his political and economic chief, Ben knew he would accept that his senior reporting officer needed to meet people to do his job.

No, he couldn't accuse Brent that easily. The fact was he needed Kate's advice because acting too hastily would merely make everyone question him and attract attention, which he could not afford. That would make the Senator look bad. Realizing he hadn't checked on his boss in some time, he scanned the room again and, not seeing the man, entered the cavernous negotiation room to find the Senator looking down at his phone.

"How are you, my boy?" the Senator asked as Ben took his seat.

"Not bad, I just needed some fresh air after sitting in the stale air in this room for hours."

"Well, no one ever accused the Hungarians of designing their buildings for comfort, right?"

Just then, the Hungarian foreign minister stood and addressed the crowd. Ben and the Senator donned their translation headphones and listened intently as the next session began.

"WHAT ARE THE CHANCES THESE NEGOTIATIONS will be successful?" Kate asked Ben over lunch. They exited the foreign ministry building separately when the negotiations broke for lunch. Ben explained to the Senator where they would go, while Kate merely exited to find them a table.

Scanning her environment was as natural as breathing to her, and she immediately noted Stephen at a café across the street. Though her face remained a mask, she smiled at the thought of identifying the Israelis, knowing they were masters of intelligence because they played in a world where mistakes meant death. It was the same for her, though she played with more protections.

"I don't know, Kate," Ben said, putting down his menu and reaching for his phone.

"I mean," Kate started, but then she noticed Ben wasn't paying attention to her. Instead, he scrolled through photos on his phone. "What are you doing?"

"I meant to talk with you about this yesterday. I really need your opinion," Ben started, edging his chair closer and putting his arm around Kate's shoulder to get her to focus on the phone.

Kate leaned in and listened as Ben told her details about Brent.

"I saw Brent meet a man when I first came here to scout out the location, remember?" He held up his phone. "Here is the first photo I took when I saw Brent talking to a man yesterday."

Kate nodded, seeing a photo of two men, one who Ben identified as Brent, the chief of the political and economic section at the

American Embassy in Budapest, the other an average-looking man.

"Here is the photo I took this morning. I am willing to bet that the man I saw following and then speaking with Brent before I got on the plane is the same man in these two photos."

Kate switched between the two photos, comparing the other man's features.

"I agree that this is the same man." She looked around the room, sensing that someone was watching them. "And I believe you when you say that the man in the two photos is the man you saw Brent meet when you first were here." But then she turned the phone over and sat up when Stephen entered the restaurant and made a beeline for their table, trailed a dozen paces behind first by Sarah, then Gideon.

"Hello, you two," Stephen said. He took a chair at their table, while Gideon and Sarah went to tables on either side of theirs and took seats.

"Stephen, this is not a great time," Ben said.

"I want to discuss why you exited the foreign ministry this morning and followed someone I believe was an American into a café," Stephen said. His attention was focused on Ben until Kate protectively placed her hand over Ben's downward-facing phone.

"Have you been following me?" Ben knew the Israelis did not play by the rules, viewing them as things to be broken. But following him would be too much. "If so—" he began, but Stephen cut him off, leaning in so no one could listen. Ben noticed that as Stephen leaned in, Sarah and Gideon looked outward, both ready to protect against anyone eavesdropping or approaching their tables.

"We positioned ourselves outside the foreign ministry building, as agreed," Stephen said. Then he told Ben and Kate how he observed Ben approach the café. He mentioned that he sat behind the man at the table but that Ben didn't see him because he was so focused on tracking his quarry.

Ben listened quietly. *Can I trust them?* Ben decided he would share partial information. He started by describing Brent and his position in the embassy, then retold how he observed Brent speak with a man last fall. Kate seemed to support his plan, flipping Ben's phone over and handing it to him to unlock. Ben handed over the phone, showing Stephen the two photos, first yesterday's and then the one he took that morning.

"This is the man I saw speaking with the American," Stephen said. He examined the photos, confident after comparing the photos that they were the same man. He then explained that he followed the man, who appeared to have switched hats with someone else.

Stephen just admitted that someone successfully switched places just meters ahead of him, Kate realized. Mossad officers were some of the most highly trained intelligence officers in the world, after the Secret Intelligence Service. Pulling a fast one over on them would be no easy feat.

"You suspect the man in these photos to be an intelligence officer," Kate said.

"I do, given his excellent tradecraft." Stephen was reluctant to admit a weakness, but then said, "He ditched me and my team, which I assure you is not a task easily accomplished."

Ben thought about that admission, having heard tales of Mossad's professionalism. "Do we have any idea who this guy works for?" Ben asked, reaching for his phone.

Stephen seemed reluctant to let go of Ben's phone, then released his grip. "I think our first decision is whether we can justify putting a tail on this man Brent," Stephen said.

"You cannot tail an American diplomat without first getting permission from the Americans, or you risk backlash when they discover what you did," Kate said.

Stephen nodded thoughtfully, still gazing intently at Ben's phone.

"I suppose you are correct, assuming the Americans ever detected our surveillance. Or either of you told your embassy authorities."

"While I am happy to offer the cooperation of Her Majesty's government, I cannot allow Ben to jeopardize his career by even responding to that statement," Kate replied. She moved closer to Ben, instinctively protecting him.

Eyes full of mirth, Stephen chuckled. "I think you have things the wrong way round." He glanced to Sarah and Gideon, who appeared relaxed. Neither looked his way, their postures conveying their focus on external dangers.

"The last thing I would do is permit Ben to jeopardize his career." He looked at Ben and added, "You would make a formidable intelligence officer, and with proper training on top of your instincts, you could rival our best officers."

Kate was taken aback by Stephen's praise of Ben, especially following Stephen's admission that his team lost track of someone they tailed. She knew the Mossad were proud of their intelligence officers. One of their senior field officers would not offer praise lightly. Kate had not seen Ben in the field since Afghanistan, when she admitted he displayed remarkable skills when dealing with the Iranians during their meeting at Minister Bashiri's residence. She moved even closer to Ben to show her support.

Ben felt Kate, interpreting it as a comforting presence, and leaned against her, drawing strength from her unspoken support.

"Those are kind words, but I don't know who we could ask for permission to surveil Brent," Ben said.

Before either Kate or Stephen could say a word, Gideon whistled. He was looking intently at the door, where Peter entered discreetly and made his way to join them.

"Jesus Christ," Ben exclaimed loud enough for just the six of them to hear, "are we transmitting our location to everyone?"

Everyone except Kate chuckled at Ben's outburst, but Stephen quickly answered Ben's query. "We tailed you here, Ben, then messaged Peter to join us as quickly as he could."

"Thank Christ," Ben grumbled. "I thought someone surgically implanted a transmitter in my ass." He knew Kate would have noticed their surveillance but admitted he just didn't have the training to defend against professional intelligence officers.

"You definitely have a way with words, Ben," Peter said, taking off his coat and draping it over an offered chair before taking a seat.

"I don't have the energy to describe this all again," Ben complained. But he needn't have worried because Kate immediately launched into a fully accurate description, leaving out no details.

Stephen took over to describe the sequence of events he witnessed, then Kate opened Ben's phone and showed the photos.

Examining the pictures, Peter asked, "Ben, is this your work phone? If so, you should probably change your password given that a foreign intelligence officer memorized your unlock code."

"That is my personal phone." Ben laughed.

"And I haven't once tried to access his work phone," Kate responded defensively, though she correctly recognized Peter's joking tone.

"So, the question you are all probably asking yourselves is, who can tail Brent?" Peter said after some thought, surprising everyone by cutting directly to the chase.

Stephen stared at the phone. Ben took staring at an inanimate object to be the Israeli's way of thinking things through.

"It would take far too long to get authorization and resources to begin investigating Brent Paulson," Peter said. "However, I will return to the embassy shortly to brief Trevor and start the process." Everyone seemed to hold their breath, unsure what he would say next.

"That said, if any *friendly* service were to begin following Brent and provided a full, cooperative, and continuous report of his movements"—Peter stressed his words as if he were reading from a legal contract—"I can assure them we would welcome that information."

Peter knew he was shooting from the hip, but with this level of detailed information, he could make a case to begin investigating Brent for having developed ties with a suspected foreign intelligence officer, whether on purpose or not.

Slowly and quietly, Stephen said, "I need to speak with my superiors." Everyone at the table strained to hear him, as he mentally constructed his plan to track Brent Paulson. He had already decided to task Gideon and Sarah to begin after they left the restaurant. In his line of business, it was always better to ask forgiveness than permission.

CHAPTER
TWENTY-SEVEN

NEARLY AN HOUR LATER, Ben stood in the atrium of the foreign ministry building, having joined a small group of mid-level European diplomats. Kate was among them, on the other side of the circle. The American and European diplomats who would undertake negotiation with Iranian officials wore grim, determined expressions on their faces. Meanwhile, Russian and Chinese diplomats observed the proceedings.

"There is fundamentally no trust between the United States and Iran, because the Iranians are the only government to have ever held American diplomats as hostages," Ben said to the German diplomat beside him. The Senator approached from the other side of the room, with McKenzie trailing behind. "People like the Senator especially will never forgive the Iranians."

President Reagan had threatened strikes on Iran, while the revolutionary Iranian regime sought the unfreezing eight billion dollars in funds in Western banks. The Islamic government announced the release of the fifty-two men and women they held for 444 days on January 20, 1981, mere minutes after President

Reagan was sworn into office. The next day, the hostages arrived in West Germany. Ben knew the hostage crisis, including the failed rescue attempt, overshadowed all other issues and cost President Carter the election.

Ben left the group to join the Senator. "Ben, it looks like this catastrophe will continue as scheduled," his boss grumbled as he approached. "Let's go find our seats and prepare for an afternoon where we hear more lies from foreign diplomats."

"Yes, sir," Ben responded.

Under Secretary Johnson entered with her delegation, and they took their seats at the table, the myriad of advisors settling into predetermined seats. The closer each person was to the Under Secretary, the more power they displayed, both within their circle and to all other diplomats in the room.

Surveying the room, while the Senator stared daggers at the Iranian delegation, Ben saw the British, French, and German delegates, all equivalent to the Under Secretary. To the side, listed as observers on the placards were deputy foreign minister equivalents from China and Russia, along with their delegations. Having previously served in Russia, Ben understood something of that culture, but he had no experience working in East Asia.

The Chinese delegation appeared nearly as large as the American delegation, though they were there simply as observers. The Russian delegation strutted around the rooms, chatting amiably with their Hungarian hosts, as well as the Iranians and Chinese, but were rebuffed, politely or not depending on the level, by their European and American counterparts.

Hearing the Hungarian foreign minister again start the meeting, Ben grabbed his headphones and took out his notepad.

HALFWAY ACROSS TOWN, THE IRAQIS STOOD around their gear, checking it in the afternoon gloom of their warehouse. The evening before, the Iranian called off the attack, so the men collectively decided to treat their families to an evening out for dinner. Their wives were shocked at the extravagance of the meal, but the men explained that they were due a treat as families. In the afterglow of the nice meal at a Persian restaurant, the couples enjoyed romance, their wives understanding the men needed comfort ahead of a big planned event.

Unbeknownst to the others, each of the men confided to his wife the nature of their planned operation, trusting their spouses and knowing they deserved to understand the risks involved. Still, their families were so much better off because of Radek's help, so they were ready to pay the price.

Nasser checked and rechecked his weapon, having spent days cleaning it. He knew any chance he and his brothers had of returning to their families depended on their weapons working well. Ali and Abdullah, the most nervous around weapons, self-consciously shifted their weapons around their bodies, trying to find the most comfortable way to carry the rifles.

On the other side of the table, Malik twisted to stretch his back, gratified that he no longer felt physical pain each time he moved. And yet he felt a constant pang of emotional pain, his heart still broken from the loss of his beloved daughter. "Narisa," he whispered so quietly that no one could hear him. Even the night before, after he lay with his wife, he wept for the loss of his Narisa. Although his eyes were now clear and bright, he still felt a hollow pain in his chest every minute of his days, one he knew would never fully go away.

"My brothers," Hassan said as he joined them after walking Radek out of the warehouse, "our Iranian benefactor is gone. Do we all understand what we must do tonight?"

Looking from face-to-face, Hassan knew the men were prepared, just as he knew they listened as Radek changed plans on them, first yesterday and then again today. The five men would leave early for the new location, the better to scout it out.

"Then let us prepare ourselves before we must depart this place," Hassan said.

Without a second thought, each of the men turned from the table, on which lay their dark clothes, weapons, and piles of ammunition, and went to pray. Gone were the days when they knelt on threadbare carpets. Instead, each man spread a thick, plush carpet, facing in the direction of Mecca, and began their devotion.

Hassan thought of his recent communication with his cousin, Muqtada, who confirmed that the Iranians provided the promised financial support to each of the men's families still in Iraq. He hoped their detailed planning and preparation would enable them to succeed, but in the pit of his stomach, he wondered how many of their number would die during their attack tonight.

Abdullah concentrated, steeling himself for this task. He knew he was not the bravest but resolved to fight with as much ferocity as he could muster. He knew only by killing as many people as possible could all of them survive the upcoming battle.

Nasser contemplated how his job as the largest of the men would be to carry as many extra rounds as possible, plus to barrel into the location and scare people as much as possible. He tried not to think about not seeing his wife and three children again. It scared him to think he would not be there to care for them all their lives. They all had bright futures, with their mother's brains, and hoped he would return after tonight's operation. He still longed for his old job at the bank but knew moving his family from Iraq was the right decision.

Ali, who seemed to have adjusted the best to life in Budapest because of his language skills, firmly pressed his palms against the ground to mask his trembling hands. He no longer wanted to keep his word, because he didn't want to die. However, the times he expressed any misgivings, the men sternly warned him of the consequences of not honoring his commitment.

His wife, Sahar, was now pregnant, so early that no one else knew. The hotel where he worked already gave him one promotion, the owner seeing past his Iraqi heritage and valuing his skills. The manager gave him a letter of introduction and instructions where to apply in Germany. *Do I dare go?*

Unbeknownst to the other men, Ali had a plan to sneak away. His wife prepared to flee with what money they collected, just to be together. But he didn't know if he could build up the courage to leave his brothers to fight on their own. *Which matters more,* he asked himself for the thousandth time, *my obligation to my brothers or to my family? Or is that question a distinction without a difference?*

Malik repeated his daughter's name while he arranged his weapons, his Kukri knife in one hand and the Kalashnikov in the other. He agreed with Aliyah that they must trust to Allah's will, knowing that whether he would return or not depended more on fate and luck than anything else. His time in Saddam's army showed him that battle was confusing, none save Allah truly understanding how things flowed from one moment to the next.

He wept silently when Aliyah admitted that she would kill herself if he died, realizing that he, too, saw this operation as a suicide mission. While hugging his wife extra tight, she whispered, "I will see you tomorrow in heaven, reunited with our Narisa." Drawing his strength from his wife's convictions, Malik took a deep breath, trusting he would not live to see tomorrow's sunrise.

The five men prayed, each experienced enough to hide their emotions from their brothers. Privately, they knew what lay in store for them, but each sought to apply their own frame of understanding.

The room around them was still, their wives and children back in their large home they rented. Each man knew his wife was waiting for word on the success of their mission.

They knew the hours ahead would be the longest in their lives, with some hoping for safety, one steeling himself to abscond, and the bravest among them ready to reunite with his wife and daughter in the afterlife.

RAMIN POUNDED DOWN THE ALLEY behind the row of warehouses, desperate to get away from the building where he dropped the bombshell of a change in the plan with the Iraqis. Predictably, they reacted with anger, then resignation, recognizing their inability to change the course of events. "One enemy is as good as another," he told them, still desperate to achieve success in his mission but knowing the lack of careful preparation would result in more casualties.

Confident no one could have followed him after twenty minutes winding through the warehouse district, Ramin stepped onto the street and headed directly towards a main artery, where he knew Mahmoud and Farrokh waited with a car. He felt self-conscious, even after his decades of work in the field, but was confident in his training.

As he wound through the alleys, he expertly altered his appearance, turning his coat inside out, donning glasses that changed the shape of his face, and lighting a cigarette. He slowed his pace when he saw other people, projecting to them the air of a man on a walk with nowhere important to go, a practiced indifference that belied his emotions.

Farrokh merged with traffic after Ramin took a seat in the back of the sedan.

"You're clear," Mahmoud said as his eyes swept for static surveillance. All three men continued to analyze their surroundings.

Once in traffic, Farrokh spoke. "On to our next destination?"

"Yes, we follow the plan," Ramin muttered. He knew the Iraqis would carry out their task because they gave him their word. He trusted their word, as much as any man could trust other men, because he had changed their lives. More importantly, he changed the lives of their children, so they owed him a debt. Still, he felt an uncertainty.

After several minutes of silence, Ramin spoke. "As per the Teacher's instructions, we will station ourselves not far from the British Ambassador's house." He scanned the passing cars and scenery, searching for threats but finding only ordinary Hungarian landscape. "Once the gunfire starts, we will quickly exit the city and drive north to Slovakia."

"It will take us not more than ninety minutes to get to Nove Zamky, depending, of course, on traffic," Mahmoud said from the passenger seat, having analyzed the various routes.

"The roads will be clear that time of night," Farrokh declared, responsible as the driver for analyzing traffic patterns. "It might be faster if we take the toll roads."

"We shouldn't take the toll roads," Ramin said. "Wouldn't it be too easy for them to track us on the toll roads?"

"Our rental car is just one of hundreds on the road," Mahmoud said, "and the toll road will save us fifteen minutes."

"As you say," Ramin said, unwilling to press further.

The three of them would then drive northwest to Bratislava, catching flights out of Europe and disappearing entirely from everyone's radar.

As he looked around the city that had been his home for many months, he knew he would miss the coffee shops, but also knew it would be safe for him to visit again after twelve to eighteen months.

"All must go according to plan," Ramin whispered as he relaxed slightly. Farrokh drove, and Mahmoud kept vigilant watch of their surroundings.

BRENT STOOD WAITING FOR THE AMBASSADOR to finish speaking with UK Ambassador Harper, expecting the inevitable tantrum in the car but not caring. He was beyond worrying about Richards's childish behavior. His conscience nagged at him after he passed information along to Radek about the reception at the British Ambassador's residence, but he knew that failing to provide the information could have meant repercussions for his wife and children. It was better, he reasoned, that Under Secretary Johnson canceled last night's reception at Ambassador Richards's, but he didn't know why. *I still don't have any solid evidence of what Radek plans to do with the information, so there's no use worrying so long as me and my family are safe.*

Knowing that all he did was pass information, Brent reasoned that the direct threat against Stacey and the kids remained but lessened after he rushed out to share what information he had about the UK reception and Ambassador Harper's residence. Brent felt a chill as he realized the Iranian could make just about anything look like an accident, after reading threat reporting over the past few weeks about Revolutionary Guard capabilities. He shuddered at the thought of his family in danger, knowing that talking with Radek was a mistake, but he had to see this through.

Thinking back, Brent understood that trusting Radek at the bar was a mistake, but not his first one. No, that had been working too long, leaving his wife to the powerful clutches of Alan Richards. He believed Stacey when she said that relationship never meant anything to her and knew she was trying to patch things up. They ate dinner as a family again. They enjoyed family game nights. In fact, they were a happier, more complete family now than they had been for many years.

Brent listened as the British Ambassador explained the evening's planned events. Richards maintained his composure when surrounded by people who did not work for him, then took out his frustrations behind closed doors on his subordinates.

"That makes sense, Charles, I suppose, though I am disappointed because we put so much effort into arranging the reception last night at my residence, only to have Washington cancel it." He could not hide his disappointment or frustration, but he could vent to his peers.

"Bad luck," Charles Harper said, not truly meaning it. Few in Budapest's diplomatic community respected Alan Richards, especially after hearing of his penchant for sexual innuendo that went beyond what even most British politicians would accept. "We have multiple senior visitors here from London who decided that they want to host an event, so embassy staff are scrambling to make arrangements." He checked his watch, reasoning that all was on schedule.

"Will you extend invitations to all participants in the talks?" Alan Richards asked, almost afraid to hear the response.

"Yes," Charles Harper responded, uncomfortable with the conversation but under strict instructions to notify the American at the first opportunity. "You naturally are invited, as will be all members of the American delegation. The reception will begin a seven." He paused, building up to the next part.

"We understand that the Iranians will likely send a representative to attend our reception and are making preparations to accommodate all guests." By that, Ambassador Harper meant he would have to ensure sufficient space between the American and Iranian delegations, not wanting to offend either party. The United Kingdom continued to maintain cordial diplomatic relations with the Iranian government, despite challenges and the continued perception that the British government only ever sided with American foreign policy.

"I understand, and thank you for telling me," Ambassador

Richards responded. Inside, he was fuming at hearing this news so late. He excused himself, not seeing the relieved look on Charles Harper's face, and rushed to pass the news to the Under Secretary. He didn't want her to hear it from someone else.

Brent trailed behind his ambassador, stuck staffing the man he detested. He also didn't want to speak with the multitude of Hungarian officials at the event. It was his job to know all the officials, but this event was focused on the proposed Iran nuclear deal, so his role was minimal. Lost in thought, he looked towards the door, wishing he could find an excuse to escape.

Sensing movement nearby, Brent saw the Under Secretary and her entourage leaving, Ambassador Richards left behind. He approached, sensing the man's seething anger and preparing for the man to scream at him, whether right here or in the car.

"What do you want?" Ambassador Richards snapped, annoyed because the Under Secretary already had the full guest list. *Why didn't I have the god damned guest list by now?* he fumed. He wanted to lash out at someone but knew this wasn't the place to do it.

The day before, the Under Secretary counseled him on some of his behavior, saying that while Washington wasn't planning to recall him, he would not get another ambassadorship unless he treated his people better.

That wasn't a comfortable conversation, but if they knew I was screwing this guy's wife, even in the past, I would have been on the next plane out. He was glad at least that wasn't a widely shared secret. Collecting his thoughts, Richards took a deep breath.

"Brent, my apologies, this is all happening so quickly."

Brent almost fell down. *Did he just apologize to me?* Then he realized Richards was still talking.

"… It's just a nightmare, dealing with so many delegations. Multilateral diplomacy isn't for the faint of heart."

Brent tuned Richards out, not really caring what he said. Alarm bells were going off in his head, and he wondered why this man, who for months treated him and others like shit, was suddenly being nice to him.

"This reception tonight," Richards said, "you will, of course, be there."

That wasn't a question. "Yes, sir, of course."

"Are you planning to bring Stacey as your date?" Richards asked as benignly as possible.

Brent stiffened, as if struck in the face by hearing Richards say his wife's name. *This man screwed your wife! Tell him to fuck off!*

"No, sir," Brent replied as evenly as possible. "She'll be busy grading papers and doesn't enjoy formal events." *Plus, she never wants to see you again.*

"Too bad," Richards replied, wishing for another go at Brent's hot wife. Ignoring Brent, Richards looked around and, seeing the German Ambassador to Hungary, walked to speak with him.

Brent felt confusion, anger, and relief all mixed together. He didn't know what to make of Richards being nice to him. He was livid that the man dared say his wife's name and yet also felt relief that he didn't yell at him. Brent no longer really cared and so headed for the door, deciding he needed to get out of there before Ambassador Richards changed his mind and screamed at him.

CHAPTER

TWENTY-SEVEN

"**I RECOMMEND YOU DO NOT ATTEND** the event this evening," Stephen told the Israeli Ambassador, standing on the carpet in front of the man's desk, while Jacob sat silently near the door. It was the largest office in the Israeli Embassy, with a fine view of the garden and the roses that the ambassador's wife would soon plant.

"The British lead negotiator *personally* invited me to attend the reception this evening, fully endorsed by the American Under Secretary. Should I risk offending them?"

"We have serious concerns about your safety," Stephen retorted, then read the ambassador's mind and continued, "even with your capable *local* bodyguard."

The ambassador sat, startled by the Mossad agent's mindreading skills. Budapest was not a major city, so he didn't rate more than a driver who also doubled as a bodyguard.

"You will have two bodyguards tonight," Jacob said, speaking for the first time since entering the room. Although phrased as a suggestion, both Stephen and the ambassador knew that Jacob's words carried the weight of authority. Only the most foolish person in the world would interpret what he said as anything other than an order.

Momentarily uncomfortable at the thought of two bodyguards following him around the reception, the ambassador brightened.

"Well, that is settled, then, isn't it?" The ambassador smiled. "Is there anything else? If not, I would like to make a few phone calls before we leave for the reception."

"Will you bring your wife tonight?" Jacob asked, not moving.

The ambassador was perturbed that the two men hadn't yet left, but he was under strict instructions from Tel Aviv to listen carefully when Jacob spoke.

"I planned to. Why?" He didn't know where this was going but was ready to argue for his wife to be allowed to go.

"You will also bring your niece to the party," Jacob suggested, turning to leave. "Sarah is a beautiful girl, and she will provide extra protection in case anything goes wrong." Jacob opened the door, and Stephen followed at his heels.

"It is a pity you also cannot attend the party," the ambassador called out, smiling. "I am confident I can bring you if you want to go."

Turning to look at the ambassador, an experienced diplomat yet still his junior in age by twenty years, Jacob replied, "Someone needs to stay here to mind the store, Ambassador."

He also knew that going would be too great a gift to Israel's enemies, who would sacrifice many of their officials for the opportunity to kill the man who spent so many decades defending Israel against its enemies, to include organizing targeted attacks on Iran's nuclear infrastructure and other strategic facilities years before.

Stephen trailed behind Jacob as they walked to Avi's office. Though mostly clean by now, the dead officer's personal effects boxed up and ready to ship back to his family in Israel, the desk was still untidy.

"Nothing yet on the American?" Jacob asked as he took Avi's seat, relegating Stephen to a seat on the other side of the desk.

"Gideon and Sarah are following him, but it is too soon," Stephen said.

Looking around the office, his eyes settled on a giant map of Budapest, pins placed in various locales around the city. Although he never knew Avi, Stephen recognized the tell-tale signs of a young officer who put his training to good use. Killed prematurely at the hands of an enemy. Like far too many good, young Israelis.

"He hasn't yet done anything out of the ordinary," he said, his eyes following the roads on the map from the Israeli Embassy to the UK Ambassador's residence. "But it has only been a few hours." He repeated himself now, more focused on the map than their conversation.

"Do you think I should attend the reception, perhaps to keep an eye on things?" Jacob offered.

"There will already be three of us there with the ambassador, which is enough." Stephen moved his eyes to Jacob but saw nothing but studied indifference, honed after decades in the field. "Plus, you are an Israeli national treasure. I don't want you anywhere near the Iranians at the reception."

"Are you saying I am too old to look after myself?"

"Not at all, but we don't need to present the Iranians with an inviting target."

Jacob prepared to argue but could see Stephen was analyzing the situation properly, not jumping to conclusions or making false assumptions. *But I long to be back in the field, doing something useful, rather than simply sitting on the sidelines and watching the young ones do the real work.* That he defended Israel's very existence for many decades, fighting in the Yom Kippur War and killing dozens of Arab soldiers, didn't matter. He was tired, and anyway, he promised his daughter he would not willingly put himself in danger.

Suddenly, Stephen's phone rang. Jacob tried to hide his annoyance at Stephen bringing his phone into Mossad's office in the embassy. It wasn't their secure communications center. *Still,* Jacob groused, *why do they rely so much on these damn devices?*

"Well?" Jacob asked as Stephen busied himself typing, ostensibly replying to the message he received.

"The Americans want me to attend a meeting at their embassy." He stood, grabbed his coat, then turned to again face Jacob. "With your permission?"

Jacob nodded, watching Stephen walk out the door, then carefully closing it behind him. Jacob stared at the spot marked as the UK Ambassador's residence.

"YOU STUPID LITTLE PRICK. Who the hell do you think you are?"

They stood in the American Embassy, outside a conference room where Trevor briefed the American delegation on the emergent but unknown threat. Trevor carefully had not mentioned anything about Brent, because Brent was in the room already, until the ambassador demanded to know who they accused of meeting with someone outside of the Hungarian Foreign Ministry building. As the story unfolded, the Senator and other senior delegation members listening intently, Ben explained his suspicions and how he followed Brent to the meeting.

Seeing the hurt in Brent's eyes when he recounted how he followed Brent to the café, Ben decided this was business, nothing personal. *Sure, smokey,* Ben told himself, *and Brent won't take this personally.*

Peter added his observations, refusing to divulge his sources on orders from Langley and the Legal Attaché. This was now a counter-intelligence matter that Washington was handling externally, so they didn't yet want Brent or the ambassador to know how far things had developed. Peter did not mention that the Israelis witnessed Brent's meeting or had begun following Brent around town, though DC officially approved surveillance on Brent.

After listening to Brent defend himself to the panel against Ben's accusations, the ambassador stomped out of the room into the corridor to confront Ben, far enough that no one would hear. Or so he thought.

"He claims that he was meeting someone from Hungarian protocol to discuss preparations for ongoing peace negotiations, which as you know are the major priority." He clenched his fingers, flexing them into and out of a fist, and Ben thought at that moment the man wanted nothing more than to punch him. He wondered how Trevor as regional security officer would respond if the ambassador hit him, though he felt certain Peter would side with him.

"When have you ever believed him, or defended him, for that matter?" Ben asked, his temper up and rising to the ambassador's bait. He understood this was one of his major failings, his inability to control his temper, but no one was perfect. "You fucked his wife, in your office, and tried to have him assigned to a war zone so you could continue screwing her. You destroyed a good officer!" He saw a mean grin on the man's face, realizing that he had walked into the man's trap. *God damn it,* Ben fumed, *I let my temper get the best of me again!*

"You'll be on the next plane, tonight," the ambassador said, turning his back and walking towards the conference room, oblivious to the short distance and their raised voices.

"I don't think so," Ben said, standing his ground. "I'm here working for the Senator, a member of the legislative branch of the US government. You'll have to convince him to send me home."

The ambassador faced Ben, clenching his teeth.

God, that must hurt, Ben thought, thankful he at least did not give voice to the running commentary in his mind.

"In fact," Ben unconsciously took a step towards the ambassador, giving in to his rising anger, "I think this is more about you wanting to be at the center of attention, even though you're about as useful in these negotiations as a third nipple."

Ben immediately regretted his vindictive tone. He decided that rather than stand there and get yelled at, he would leave the space. When he entered the room, all heads swiveled towards him, the ambassador on his heels.

"Get out of my embassy, you little shit," the ambassador spat, pointing to the door and not paying attention to anyone else around him. Tunnel vision blocked out all other sounds.

"Yes, sir, Mr. Ambassador," Ben responded, forcing himself to maintain composure and simply walking to grab his bag.

The Senator raised his eyebrow. McKenzie sat next to him with her mouth open, watching in awe as a US Ambassador screamed.

"Senator, with your permission?" Ben asked.

The old man read the room and waved him out. Before the start of the meeting, with Kate, Trevor, Peter, and Lionel in attendance, Ben laid out the details for the Senator in the station's secure space. In an unusual step, Peter arranged for Stephen to join them to brief the Senator, calling him over from the Israeli Embassy. After their initial discussion, Stephen, Peter, Kate, and Lionel slipped out the back. Peter was careful to ensure no one else noticed their presence.

"Get out of here, Ben," the Senator said, rising to stand while simultaneously winking at Ben, the only one who could directly see his face. "We *will* discuss this more later at the reception," he said quietly.

Ben walked tall past the ambassador, focusing all his concentration on maintaining a mask of his emotions. The Senator warned him that the State folks would not want the negotiations interrupted for any reason, especially without hard proof, and Peter even suggested that Brent would have an explanation for who he met.

He exited the chancery, waving as he passed the Marine in Post One, and walked outside into the courtyard, striding quickly to the main embassy entrance and exit. As he stepped out onto the street, he took off his badge and stuck it in his bag, satisfied that he played his part to perfection.

"Hey, stranger, you look like someone just kicked you out of a meeting." Ben smiled as he rushed to kiss Kate. He noticed Mark, Kate's father's driver, standing near their vehicle.

"You usually frown on public displays of affection." She smiled and responded to his kiss with her own. "But I appreciate this development."

"Pardon the interruption, lovebirds," Mark said, "but we need to stick to the timetable to make this work."

After withdrawing from their embrace, Ben held Kate's hand and followed her to the waiting Land Rover, a UK Embassy vehicle with bright blue diplomatic plates. "Get in." Kate shoved him in first. "And don't drool on the seats."

They drove to the British Ambassador's residence, arriving to a flurry of activity, all controlled by visible and invisible layers of security. With agreement from the UK Ambassador, who pronounced his counterpart as "a daft prick," he authorized increased security, tempering due to the sensitivity of the wide range of invited guests from across the diplomatic community.

"Tonight will be a bloody pain in the ass, having all those arseholes in there," Mark said, slicing expertly through the afternoon traffic. "There are too many threats we cannot anticipate, but I agree that we should, at minimum, cancel tonight, or at least reduce the number of invitations to the biggest assholes."

"Mark, tell me again what you did in your diplomatic training," Ben said.

"Sod off, yank," Mark replied, waving a finger towards Ben, a faint smile on his lips.

"Don't tell me you actually enjoy this banter with an American." Kate laughed.

"Sod off, the lot of you," Mark grumbled, though his grin widened. "He gives as good as he gets, which is not the norm for the ungrateful former colonists."

"LET THAT CAR IN!" LIONEL FAIRFIELD YELLED at the man guarding the gate to the British Ambassador's residence. A retired lieutenant colonel, Lionel was accustomed to men jumping at his commands, especially his Hungarian security staff. *They're all lazy bastards.* He never forgot his early days in the British Army, when they expected you to do *anything* they ordered.

Ben stood outside Ambassador Harper's residence, watching as vehicles arrived to disgorge occupants for the reception. Though put together seemingly at the last moment, everything came together quickly. *Must be British efficiency.*

Kate stood several feet away, chatting with the Ukrainian Ambassador and her husband, who had arrived minutes before.

Ben watched as Gideon exited the front passenger seat of the next vehicle, followed by Stephen from the door behind the driver. Both stood near the rear passenger doors, opening them only after scanning the area. *A bit theatrical,* Ben thought. But he knew many others also watched this show of strength. Inside the extended vehicle, Ben glimpsed additional armor that increased its bulk. Out came the Israeli Ambassador and his wife, trailed by Sarah, who Stephen told him would act as their niece for the evening.

Stephen nodded to Ben and Kate, signaling that all was going according to plan, and they approached the residence front door.

"Excuse me, but we would prefer no weapons inside the building," Ambassador Harper said, "since we will have so many different delegations mixing this evening."

"Of course," the Israeli Ambassador responded. He directed Stephen and Gideon to return to their vehicle, and neither attempted to hide their resentment as they deposited their weapons with the driver.

"And you won't mind if I ran a quick scan, will you?" Lionel asked, not waiting before he began waving a wand over first Stephen, then Gideon, and identifying each piece of metal before continuing. After he finally declared them cleared, the two men skulked into the residence after their principal, Ben trailing several steps behind and once again trying not to laugh at the theater.

Behind them, a line of drivers and security personnel in diplomatic vehicles watched the procession, mutters of amazement as the British subjected the Israelis to such an invasive search. Some muttered their agreement, others decried the loss of security, but they all agreed that it was nice to see the Israelis brought down a notch or two.

The French Ambassador was next, followed by the Russian and Chinese Ambassadors, who consented to their guards staying outside rather than relieving themselves of their weapons. When the Iranian delegation arrived, carefully placed in line to observe British security relieve the Israelis bodyguards of their weapons, they consented faster than expected. Mahmoud and Farrokh followed Saeed Raisi and the Iranian Ambassador into the residence's main hall.

Mahmoud remained impassive. He was not excited to go into the hall with a man he despised so deeply, yet the Teacher ordered the last-minute change in plans. The two assigned IRGC officers fought their being replaced, but a call from Tehran quickly put the matter to rest. He and Farrokh were inside because Ramin had spent the past months entering and exiting Budapest, so they agreed he could too easily be recognized, potentially endangering the operation.

As people filed into the residence, purposely built for entertaining large numbers of guests, they accepted drinks from trays. Mahmoud watched as Raisi selected a fruit juice, careful to avoid the trays laden with forbidden alcohol. A true believer who supported the revolution, Mahmoud still did not believe alcohol should be forbidden but instead should be a choice each person made. If he learned anything from his time in the United States and Canada, it was that people were stronger than the Supreme Leader and others would admit.

The Iranian Ambassador nodded in Mahmoud's direction, the precoordinated signal that he needed to find a restroom. Mahmoud met the eyes of a British security officer, one of the few people he knew would be permitted to have a weapon on the premises. *I don't have to like it, but this was why we made a backup plan, wasn't it?*

LIONEL MOTIONED THE IRANIAN SECURITY OFFICER, along with his charges, towards the bathrooms. *Jesus, does everyone need to use the loo the moment they enter?*

The flow of people continued uninterrupted, aided by Hungarian police controlling traffic in the area outside the residence, though Lionel remained annoyed that they provided no armed security. He fumed at their notion that he should have informed them in advance of the British Ambassador's intention to host a party. *How am I supposed to know the scheduling for an impromptu party!* There was little he could do to control this situation, though he reasoned once the Americans arrived, he would have sufficient armed, trained personnel he trusted to keep the place safe.

He heard an argument behind him and turned to see the Israeli delegation with their two bodyguards facing off against the four Iranians. *A good old Mexican standoff,* the Americans would say. He couldn't have a fist fight in the residence, especially not when he knew he shouldn't have sent Israelis and Iranians into the loo, or the general vicinity of the loo, at the same time.

AS BEN OBSERVED THE TENSE EXCHANGE, scenes from Westerns he remembered watching with his father did not do justice to the tense nature of the confrontation. Stephen was ready to start throwing punches, and Ben recalled that the Iranian's head of delegation, Raisi, was, in fact, a senior member of the Basij, having also worked to found Hezbollah in Lebanon. He knew most Iranian Ambassadors were IRGC, due to their revolutionary zeal, which made both Iranians dangerous. Seeing the Iranians facing off against the three Israelis by the bathroom, Ben set down his drink on a table, ready for anything.

As a condition of the Israeli's Ambassador's attendance, Stephen and Gideon found weapons hidden inside the bathroom. It was a prudent precaution against potential threats, Stephen argued, given the multitude of delegations attending the party. The British Ambassador personally authorized the peculiar arrangement, reasoning that it would not do to offend the Israelis. Shockingly, Ben was the only American to learn of the arrangement. No other Americans were present during preparations for the evening reception. *I guess that means dating Kate gives me a ticket to the British side of the pond,* Ben thought wryly.

Lionel quickly moved to stand between the two groups, but there simply wasn't enough space for the two groups to pass. And neither wanted to back down. Making a split-second decision, Ben stepped forward.

"Good evening, *Agaye Raisi*," he addressed the lead negotiator. "*Agaye Safir*," he said, then nodded to the Iranian Ambassador. He stayed back several paces with his hands out but continued to address the men in Persian. The four of them turned as one to stare at Ben, the lead negotiator glaring suspiciously.

"Good evening," he responded in the same language. "Do I know you? Are you from the British delegation?"

"No, General," Ben said, focused on the four Iranians. "But I had the honor to study your beautiful language before I served in Herat. Persian poetry has no rival in the West for its beauty."

"Are you the spy who was honored enough to meet Grand Ayatollah Shirazi?" the Iranian Ambassador asked, but he didn't wait for a response. "I heard that you brought back the weapon that killed Behzad Bashiri's grandson, a cowardly act committed by one of your murderous soldiers. You seem to have impressed the Grand Ayatollah enough that he mentioned the existence of one American who spoke our language with such fluency that he must be a spy."

Smiling to ease the tension, Ben relaxed, hoping the Iranians would as well. He noticed the Israeli Ambassador, Stephen, Gideon, and Lionel's eyes glued to him as he addressed the Iranians.

"I always have been, and always will be, a diplomat, Mr. Ambassador." He hesitated before continuing. "But I will not argue the point with you, understanding that you will see in us that which you understand in yourselves."

WATCHING IMPASSIVELY, MAHMOUD WAS AGAIN surprised, this time by the quick thinking of Ben Brownwell, the American for whom the Grand Ayatollah held grudging respect. He realized the young American was playing a dangerous game, and playing it well, to reduce tensions.

Snatching a quick glance around, he observed that if he stepped forward slightly, appearing to approach Ben, then the Israelis could walk away from the confrontation, giving them a way out that would avoid losing face.

Mahmoud hated the Israelis as much as any other Iranian, but he knew a confrontation at the British Ambassador's residence would have far-reaching implications. *It must not appear that the negotiations break down because of us,* the Teacher warned, knowing the world always sought to cast the Iranian government as the enemy.

Deciding he could play a role in deescalating tensions in the room, Mahmoud stepped forward, speaking more harshly than he intended but justifying it as focusing all attention on the American.

"Only a spy could lie so easily," Mahmoud accused, "and I believe this American is being disrespectful to address each of you, General, Ambassador. In fact, it appears that he accuses us of being spies, just as we know him to be."

Ben studied the Iranian's features. *Do I recognize him? He looks familiar, but I cannot place him.* He realized he could easily be assuming that all Iranians looked the same. He saw in the men's features before him a combination of Asian, European, Middle Eastern, and even some North African features, a result of centuries of conquest aimed at controlling the crossroads between the ancient world.

Sensing anger from the Iranian security guard, who could never pass as an aide, Ben took a step back, hoping that by doing so, he could reduce tensions further. However, retranslating the last statement from the security officer, Ben realized this was not merely a dumb bullet magnet but an intelligent man who understood Ben's veiled criticism and responded in kind.

WATCHING THE INTERACTION AND KNOWING BEN BRAVELY stepped in to deflect attention from their actions, Stephen grabbed his ambassador's arm and pulled him away from the restrooms. *I did not retreat but took an opening to extricate my ambassador from a tense situation.*

As Gideon followed, the two men felt the weight of the weapons tucked inside their suits, safe in the knowledge that any danger directed towards their delegation would be met with force. They carried an extra weapon for Sarah to use, but her outfit wouldn't currently accommodate anything, not in the dress the ambassador's wife selected.

In the distance, he saw the British intelligence officer, Kate, watching Ben's exchange with the Iranians. She looked ready to jump into the fray, but he tried to convey to her with his eyes that he was capable of handling the situation on his own.

Once away, the ambassador casually approached a senior Hungarian Foreign Ministry official, raising his voice to be heard above the silence and intense focus on Ben facing off against the four Iranians.

The Israeli Ambassador addressing the Hungarian officially broke the spell that seemed to hold occupants in the large room, though it wasn't until the Iranians spoke that people relaxed.

"YOU ARE VERY BRAVE," SAEED RAISI commented, reaching out a hand to Mahmoud to stand down and stepping forward. "Your name is?"

Ben felt tension washing away and registered that the Israeli Ambassador was now speaking with someone behind him. Offering his hand, Ben stepped nearer the Iranian.

"My name is Ben Brownwell, sir, and it is a pleasure to meet you."

Raisi seemed at a loss but gripped Ben's hand firmly, taking his measure of the man. He thought back to what he heard in Tehran about the encounter, which people retold because it was so rare that an American would learn to speak Persian so beautifully. He had verbally sparred with one of the most influential Grand Ayatollahs in Iran, Raisi recalled being told, remaining respectful throughout, but supposedly he argued with the Afghan official.

So strange that he showed respect for an Iranian, America's enemy, yet argued with an Afghan, whose government currently serves the interests of the Great Satan's government.

"You may claim to be anything else," Raisi remarked, releasing Ben's hand, "but I see that you distracted all of us enough to defuse the situation and permit your Israeli lackeys to run away."

The Iranian Ambassador approached and laughed, enjoying his superior's joke. "Only an intelligence officer would be cunning enough to control such a situation so well," the ambassador agreed.

Farrokh coughed behind them, seeking to get their attention to conduct their business. "Ambassador, did you say that you wanted to wash your hands?"

"Yes, I did," the ambassador said, seeking to learn more from the American for his report to Tehran. "Ben Brownwell," he said, offering his hand, "your Persian is quite good, for a spy."

"Your diplomatic skills, Mr. Ambassador," Ben responded, shaking the extended hand, "are quite good for a member of the *Sepah Pazderan*."

The ambassador momentarily looked furious, but Raisi smiled, seeing the American clearly for the first time. Before the ambassador said something they might all regret, the general responded.

"One day I hope we can welcome you to Iran, young Ben Brownwell."

"*Isfahan nesfe jahane*," Ben replied. The ambassador appeared startled, and he added, "but I prefer to plan my visit for a time when I will not travel directly to Evin prison. Good evening, Agaye Raisi, Ambassador."

Ben chided himself for not just keeping his mouth shut and turned away from the group. He saw Kate watching from ten feet away. He kept walking, feeling the eyes of the Iranians on his back, until he turned a corner.

"You bring the idea of an American cowboy into the twenty-first century, my love," Kate said, grasping his arm and pulling him through the residence towards the rear balcony.

Ben looked up at the sky, took a deep breath, and turned to face his fiancée.

"I diffused the situation, didn't I?"

CHAPTER
TWENTY-EIGHT

HALF AN HOUR LATER, BEN STOOD LISTENING to Kate recount the confrontation, from start to finish, to the Senator. She had followed the Iranian delegation inside, watching to see who they spoke with and how they responded, when they nearly walked into the Israeli delegation.

"Several people from State will not be amused," the Senator warned, though he laughed as he congratulated Ben for diffusing the situation without any problems.

Stephen grasped Ben's shoulder. "That was a foolish," he said in mock anger, but then changed his tone, "but a very brave thing you did for us, Ben." He reached for a one-armed hug, showing a level of appreciation that made the Senator stare at the arriving Israeli.

"It is my pleasure to see you again, Senator," Stephen said, offering his hand, "and I am sure you are just now hearing about Ben's exploits." The Senator shook his hand, turning to meet the Israeli Ambassador, while Ben listened to their analysis of his performance.

Just then, the rest of the American delegation entered the large main sitting room, having remained outside for several minutes after arrival for official photographs with Hungarian officials.

Ben studiously avoided glares from both Susan and Ambassador Richards, who each appeared furious but unwilling to approach while Ben stood so near the Senator. *Obviously, they heard about my little performance.* Ben wondered why he always seemed to get into these situations.

Despite the anger directed at him, Ben looked for signs of the Iranian delegation. He knew from an earlier briefing that they would stay with Russian and Chinese diplomats on the other side of the residence, farthest from the American and Israeli delegations. Longing to know more, he moved toward the Senator, who prepared to circulate in the room.

"Everyone, may I have your attention, please?" Ambassador Harper called as he stood near the front of the large room, purposefully near a doorway to a separate sitting area. "If you would please join us in the back garden, we have more refreshments and food so you can enjoy the beautiful Budapest evening."

Everyone murmured their approval and took stairs out the rear of the residence to an expansive garden, tables laden with Hungarian foods and desserts. Ben watched as the event settled into a comfortable détente, with the Iranian, Russian, and Chinese delegations finding places to stand near the right side of the back yard, the British and French delegations staying mostly in the middle, the Americans slightly to the left, and the Israelis as far from the Iranians as possible. All agreed they did not want a replay of the washroom standoff, as people jokingly called it.

Ben and Kate stood together, while her parents sat at a table with the Senator, Under Secretary Johnson, and the British Ambassador. Facing the house, Ben noted the Israelis warily eyeing the Iranians across the yard. He decided that they looked particularly lonely, so he wandered over to ask Stephen a question.

HASSAN AND HIS FOUR COUNTRYMEN walked the several blocks as quietly as they could. They were careful to stay out of the lights because they carried bags with their Kalashnikovs safely inside, as well as extra ammunition. They all wore black clothing, and they parked their van far enough away from the British residence that no one would connect its occupants to the upcoming attack.

The men remained startled by the change in plan, having studied the map of the American residence over and over, confident they could have staged that attack and gotten away. Now they were forced to rely on a quick survey report from the Iranian, who, during his brief visit, promised them more money to conduct the attack with no preparation. Not that they could have walked away at this point, because they were now honor-bound, but the additional money ensured the men would be able to improve their families' lives considerably.

Ali felt the most ill at ease. He already regretted his decision and hoped to pull off his plan. Without telling anyone, he arranged for his Sahar to leave with their belongings and hide only two blocks from the UK Ambassador's residence. Though he felt guilt for not supporting his brothers, he knew in his heart that living to protect and provide for his unborn child was his destiny.

The Iranian would never find him, not with the plans he put in place, especially the job offer awaiting him at a hotel in Frankfurt. The journey would take days, but with the money he saved, as well as what Sahar earned by selling their few major belongings, they had enough to afford real bus tickets. Crossing the border into the European Union would be difficult but not impossible, especially now that each of them was more respectably dressed than when they first arrived in Budapest.

None of them spoke as they walked, each of them wondering whether any would survive the night's events. Nonetheless, they would apply their skills as demanded by the Iranian. Abdullah, the quietest of their group, wondered aloud whether they would see their families again. All agreed that it would be better to die than go to jail, though they feared their families would be punished for their actions. The Hungarian authorities already did not like immigrants, especially Muslims, and harassment increased of late as the police sought to root out any threat.

Hassan led the group, accepting the inevitability of the attack. He knew there remained a chance for them to escape if all went well. Their best chance, the Iranian told them, was that none of the guests would be armed, so they would all be easy targets. Stressing to the men that they needed to walk away alive, Hassan told them to shoot as many people as possible, killing Americans, if possible. Then get away immediately. *No heroics, brothers, because we all want to see our families again.* He replayed that phrase in his mind, praying to Allah the Merciful that they would survive. *Even just one of us,* he thought, his mind immediately going to Ali, the youngest of their group.

Examining the crude map in the starlight, Hassan led the men to the rear of the British Ambassador's residence. As the Iranian promised, there was a small path leading behind that went through the yard of another large house. *This is a mansion, if I ever saw one,* he thought, but suppressed those feelings and concentrated on the task at hand.

Noises that seemed distant at first grew louder, and Hassan turned to motion for the men to be quieter still as they approached, with Ali at the back. *Where did the Iranian get his information?* Hassan wondered, realizing that without that detail, he and his men would be blind.

The Iraqis wouldn't have known that Iranian intelligence officers around the world sought details of the residences of enemy countries' ambassadors, reasoning that, at any given time, they could be a target. Ramin accessed the embassy intelligence officer's records using the Teacher's connections, ensuring he could be prepared for every contingency.

"Enter near the left side of the house to find the rarely used service door," the Iranian had stressed, having conferred with Mahmoud and Farrokh, who steered the general and ambassador to the other side.

Damn the man, Hassan fumed, *is it left looking at the house or from the house?*

"THIS CHAMPAGNE IS EXCELLENT, thank you, Ambassador," Angela Sinclair declared. "But I am afraid the night air is much cooler than anticipated. Will you please excuse me?"

She rose from her seat, needing to find a restroom. She was also tired of the games played between the men in the expansive yard. She searched for Kate, sighting her near Ben where they were speaking with the Israelis. Their eyes met, and Kate understood that her mother could play diplomatic games with the best of them but often needed a break from monotonous discussions.

"THIS IS THE DOOR INDICATED on the map," Hassan whispered, approaching to hear voices on the other side, though it did not appear they were too close.

"Abdullah, come and open this lock as quietly as you can," he whispered with less fear in his voice, as noise from the other side of the tall brick wall blocked out any noise he and his countrymen could make.

Their expert in all things mechanical, Abdullah crept to the lock, stopping to examine it by starlight. He did not dare risk using a flashlight, for fear it could shine through and alert anyone on the other side of the door. He was relieved to see the key used to open it was bulky, but then he noticed rust on the hinges.

"I can open this lock," he whispered for the other four men to hear, "but we will have to enter quickly to avoid anyone hearing us."

Reasoning there could only be one door, Hassan nodded for the engineer to get to work, while the other men holstered their pistols, unzipped their bags, and withdrew their Kalashnikovs.

After a mere thirty seconds, Abdullah delicately tested the lock and stepped back. "The door is open."

"Before we enter," Ali interjected tentatively, "should we not listen to ensure we hear English?"

"Bravo, young man," Hassan whispered, grinning at their youngest member's insight, and pressed him toward the door to listen.

Ali crouched near the door, hearing a variety of voices but unable to make any of them out clearly.

"MR. AMBASSADOR, good to see you again." He paused. "Ambassador Richards. You remember me, of course!" Alan Richards walked across the yard, extending his hand to the Russian Ambassador. He spoke English so everyone could see him conversing with the ambassador from an opposition country. He cleared the approach with Washington in advance, as well as with the Under Secretary, who stood watching from the other side of the garden.

Alan was a man to be respected. He was the first in his Foreign Service class to make ambassador, all the result of hard work, determination, and a willingness to put forth as much time and effort as the job required. Perhaps he should be nicer to the people who worked for him, but they were all peons and deserved to be abused, just as senior staff had abused him when he first joined the Foreign Service.

"We last saw one another at the Chinese New Year celebration, correct?" He shook hands, then turned to speak with the Chinese Ambassador, who stood nearby.

"THE MAN I HEARD SPOKE ENGLISH is likely the American Ambassador. But I don't know who he addressed." Ali slowly backed away from the door, returning to his position at the rear of the group.

Hassan weighed the risk of waiting versus the opportunity of catching the men and women on the other side of the door by surprise.

"That is good enough for me," he declared, and the men in unison stood with their weapons, flipping off the safeties.

"Aim for the Americans, kill Jews if you can, but most importantly, watch out for one another, and let's all come out this same door alive so we see our families."

He saw the grim determination on each face. *I am responsible for these men, but we are all doing this for our families.* Each of the men closed their eyes, whispered a silent prayer, and turned to focus all their attention on their task.

At the rear of the group, sensing his moment of opportunity, Ali waited quietly, willing his body to stop breathing as if the world would ignore him if he was sufficiently quiet.

The men raised their weapons and burst through the door. Four of them did, at least. The fifth member of their group carefully laid his weapon on the ground and, as quietly as possible, retraced his steps the way they'd come. While his four brothers ran to danger, Ali ran toward his future.

"*ALLAHU AKHBAR!*" BEN HEARD, followed by gunfire piercing the night and drawing everyone's attention. He saw a gap in the wall overgrown with vines, through which at least two men rushed.

Reacting instinctively, Ben rushed forward for cover behind a table while the men dressed in black sprayed those directly in front of them with gunfire.

Grateful to feel Kate land next to him, he turned to ensure she was not hit, then looked to where Stephen and Gideon held the

Israeli Ambassador's head down below a table, weapons drawn and prepared to engage any nearby enemy.

Just behind them, Sarah was protecting the Israeli Ambassador's wife. The most surprising thing was the men appeared on the other side of the garden, near the Iranian, Russian, and Chinese delegations, firing indiscriminately at every human near them.

FARROKH FELL TO THE GROUND, taking a bullet to the shoulder before he could react. He was near the small door, which the British security officer assured him was impassable. *Not so impassable, why did they enter on the wrong side!*

Mahmoud, meanwhile, grabbed Raisi and pulled him to safety nearer the house, shielding the important man with his body. Deciding he could justify the weapon the ambassador smuggled into the reception, Mahmoud withdrew it but did not take immediate action. He wanted the Iraqis to kill as many of their targets as possible.

As Mahmoud watched, Lionel and Mark drew their weapons and began firing, but not fast enough to prevent the immediate deaths of seven men. Each fell to the ground, screaming into the evening as their plans for the future ended with bullets piercing their bodies, collapsing their lungs, and pouring blood into the green grass.

ALI SAW SAHAR WAITING FOR HIM at the intersection carrying two bags. He took the heavier, not wanting his pregnant wife to carry anything too heavy. In the background, he heard the echoes of gunshots, discerning the difference between the clatter of the Kalashnikovs and the retort of other, likely Western, weapons. After he quickly embraced his wife and put his backpack on, they ran, screams of pain ringing out behind the mansion just blocks behind them.

"MADAME UNDER SECRETARY!" BEN CALLED, seeing her crouching behind a chair and realizing she was unlikely to move. He also saw Arthur Sinclair, who stood behind Mark, searching for an escape route. He half wondered where the Senator was but could only focus on one thing at a time.

Just then, Ben saw one of the attackers turn to fire at Mark, who fired back, but not before being struck with at least two bullets to the chest. Without thinking, Ben rushed toward his future father-in-law and pulled the man down just before the large attacker in black sprayed his automatic weapon where they both just were.

Searching frantically, Ben found Mark's handgun, which dropped to the ground just two feet away from his reach. He saw Kate thankfully followed as he pulled her father to cover, relief evident on her face that her father was out of harm's way. Ben thought he heard the Senator's voice somewhere behind but fixed his concentration on the threat ahead of him.

Chancing a look up at the large attacker approaching with a weapon pointed in his direction, Ben saw Kate grab at Mark's handgun and act without thinking. She started in a crouched position, raised the handgun with both hands, and began firing.

The first bullet caught the large bear of a man in the stomach, the second in the chest. The man crashed to the ground, no longer firing. No longer an immediate threat. Kate turned, sweeping the area for other targets, then dropped to crawl to her father, desperate to make sure he was okay.

Ben popped his head up to scan the area.

STEPHEN WATCHED IN ADMIRATION as Kate's two shots hit their mark, then watched Ben pop his head up and shout observations to Kate. Seeing a man from Ben's left raising his weapon, Stephen reacted by raising his weapon, blocked by two people rushing past him to safety. *I don't have a shot,* he fumed, desperate to fire before the man killed anyone else.

Gideon saw the same events unfold, but he crouched farther to the left and had a clear view. He rose and aimed his weapon in a fluid, practiced motion, squeezing off three rounds in succession, all head shots. His target didn't even fire in his direction.

After Hassan fell to the group, he stared unblinkingly, mourning the senseless loss. *How many did we kill?* he wondered. He felt life ebbing out of his control, felt his eyes closing, and his last thoughts were of his wife and children. *I hope they remember how much I loved them,* he thought, after which he closed his eyes for the last time.

FROM THE OTHER SIDE, with his weapon concealed, only for use if the Iraqis attacked their group, Mahmoud watched as one last, lone man crouched with his weapon, prepared to fire. He scanned the area and saw a young ostensibly British woman rushing from the middle of the yard, noting the young American Ben also there with one of the older British officials. Somewhat farther away, on the other side, Mahmoud observed a man who had just shot and killed another of the Iraqis. Only one Iraqi remained. *He must be a Jew.* Though from this distance, in a split second, he could not tell the difference. *They don't all wear the Star of David, you fool.*

Will he aim at the Jew, whose death I will not mourn, or at the young American?

All those thoughts flashed through Mahmoud's mind as the lone Iraqi turned to fire at the standing targets.

Damn you, Mahmoud raged, though he understood that the Iraqi would want to kill the nearest target rather than risk trying to aim at a farther threat. *Exactly what I would have done.*

Raising his weapon in a motion he had repeated tens of

thousands of times before, Mahmoud pulled the trigger three times, though he could have sworn he heard at least six gunshots.

BEN TURNED AT THE SAME TIME, seeing the man swing to fire at him, and screamed for everyone to get down. A distant part of his mind heard Kate screaming his name behind him, but he tuned that out, wishing he had a weapon.

However, just as Ben thought the man would kill him, he saw Lionel jump from behind a table and shoot three rounds into the last attacker. Ben swore that he heard six shots.

After the man in black dropped, three men stood with weapons outstretched in the back yard of the British Ambassador's residence: one British, one Iranian, and one Israeli. They looked at one another, then, after scanning the bodies, they each raised their weapons to the sky, palms open, hearing the shouts from security personnel pouring from the rear of the house.

Among the shouts, injured men moaned while others merely lay on the ground, dropped where they stood just minutes before drinking cocktails and laughing over the trivialities of diplomatic problems that seemed so important.

Hearing moaning near him, Ben cautiously walked towards the man Kate shot, finding him lying on the ground in a pool of his blood.

NASSER FELT SEARING PAIN IN HIS STOMACH and chest, knowing he would die. *My family,* he wanted to cry out. All at once, he recalled when he met Aisha, courted her, and fell in love. He saw the births of his three children, saw them growing up. Tears welled in his eyes as he realized he would never again see his children learn, or laugh, or hug his beautiful and intelligent wife. *It is so unfair,* he wanted to scream, but he couldn't muster the breath.

More sensing a presence than seeing one, Nasser turned to see a young Westerner standing over him, while another man rushed forward, standing just outside his vision. He felt as if he were staring into a tunnel, only able to see the man hovering above him.

"I THINK HE IS STILL ALIVE," BEN SAID. He saw Lionel approach and scoop up the attacker's Kalashnikov, then noticed Kate's rounds, which had pierced the man's stomach and chest. *That is a sucking chest wound,* Ben thought. In any other circumstances, he should have tried to provide medical aid, but at that moment, Ben didn't feel much charity.

"Is he trying to talk?" Ben asked incredulously. He saw the man's mouth moving and instinctively took a step forward.

"Ben, don't!" Kate said from six feet behind, but she approached too and stood just behind Ben to peer at the man bleeding at their feet.

"TAKE . . ." NASSER SAID, his arms following his commands as he withdrew his great-grandfather's prayer beads from his pocket.

It hurts so much to move, to breathe. His body screamed, struggling to obey. Nasser felt his arms shaking as he struggled.

Obey my command! he roared in return, his iron will quickly overcoming his body's weakness.

"Please give these to my wife," Nasser whispered in English, remembering the language from his years working at the bank. *Perhaps I should have kept my family in Iraq,* his mind raged, doubt rushing in beside the fear that swept over him like a blanket. He raised the prayer beads and, through an act of mercy that only Allah could have granted, placed them into the man's hands the first try.

"BEN, BE CAREFUL," KATE SAID.

Ben knelt on the ground. "Please be quiet. He is trying to speak."

Ben leaned in to listen to the man.

"He asked me to give these to his wife," Ben said, never taking his gaze from the man. He held up the beads.

"Where is your wife? How can I reach her?" Ben asked. If he could, he would try to grant the man's dying wish. He recalled his father telling stories of his time in Vietnam of being given letters from his own troops for mothers and girlfriends back home. *This is different, but it's my time,* Ben understood, and he pressed for information more urgently, repeating his questions.

"Green warehouse," Nasser whispered, thankful that the man understood his English. *I can die in peace, knowing and trusting this man will deliver these beads to my family.* "Industry park, many factories."

Ben, somehow without thinking about it, knew that delivering this man's beads to his family would be important.

Watching as the man's lips stopped moving, Ben stood, secreting the beads in his pocket.

CHAPTER
TWENTY-NINE

STANDING NEXT TO KATE, Ben suddenly felt so tired, as if he had run a race. He wasn't bleeding, though his entire body felt bruised from crashing to the ground multiple times. Kate held him in a hug, while Lionel returned to grab the weapon Kate dropped.

Ben heard the distant yells of the British security officers approaching men on either side of the yard. On the one side, near where he remembered seeing Saeed Raisi standing, Ben saw a man toss his weapon to the ground and raise his hands in surrender. Behind him, he heard a voice that sounded strangely like one of the Israelis offering to lower his weapon but only after ejecting the magazine and flipping on the safety.

Moving slowly to the stairs to the house, Ben turned to see Kate's father, his jacket smeared with mud. "My apologies, sir, for pushing you to the ground," Ben said.

"He appears delirious but otherwise unhurt," Arthur drawled, then stepped forward and stooped down to examine Mark. He stirred, attempting to sit up, but rubbed his chest where the bullets had slammed into his hidden Kevlar vest.

"It appears that did the trick," Kate quipped, eyes sweeping the area to see others standing from prone positions behind tables, chairs, and toppled tables that previously were laden with food.

The Senator approached from behind, and he stood near Ben and Kate, looking down in admiration. "You did a fine job, Kate," he bellowed, pride evident at the woman who dispatched one of the attackers. "And you, Ben, were cool under fire." Nearby, McKenzie wept uncontrollably, her body shaking as she trailed a short distance behind the Senator.

"How in Christ's name did so many people get weapons in here!" Arthur demanded. He looked first to the Iranian delegation, where one man lay bleeding while the ambassador lay dead, then to the Israeli delegation, where the ambassador stood behind the two men who Arthur assumed to be Mossad officers. A younger woman stood at the ambassador's wife's shoulder, looking more someone meant to protect rather than be protected.

"I authorized the Israelis to have weapons," Charles Harper responded, not bothering to approach, merely calling from his place near his wife's side. She lay on the ground with a sprained ankle after trying to run from the gunfire but was otherwise unhurt.

"We will discuss that later," Christopher Spencer added as he approached from the stairs, attempting to seize control as the most senior lead of the delegation. "But how did the Iranians get weapons in here?"

Several men advanced on the Iranian delegation, including Arthur Sinclair, to see three men clustered around the dead body of the ambassador. The lead Iranian negotiator, Raisi, raised himself to his full height and began shouting.

"You call this security! You British. Our ambassador is dead because you did not provide security!"

Soon, a chorus of other voices—some Russian, others Chinese— rose up, all screaming at the dead in their delegations.

Arthur looked back, seeing Kate with Ben. *That boy will fit in to the family nicely,* he realized. Turning toward a sound near the house, Arthur saw his wife peering out a window, as if frightened that one of those they loved was injured—or dead.

"Mark, can you stand?" he called out, only to see Mark approaching, rubbing his chest but otherwise alert and appearing unharmed.

"Yes, sir," Mark responded, reaching absentmindedly for his weapon, which he knew Lionel must have confiscated in the aftermath. He would need the full story because he apparently missed the best parts.

Arthur left the screaming Iranian, Chinese, and Russian official, and approached Ben. "Your future mother-in-law is over there waiting for us. Shall we go together to allay her fears and confirm we are all safe?"

Ben looked at the man before him, disoriented from the rush of events. He held tight to Kate's hand, and the three of them walked carefully toward the back of the residence, Mark following from only a short distance, ushering them inside to safety. The Senator and McKenzie followed several steps behind, in a daze, eager to leave the chaos.

As they walked, Ben kissed Kate's hand and whispered, "I have never loved you more than now. You are amazing."

Kate beamed at the compliment, knowing she would soon feel a rush of nausea after firing the first gunshots ever in anger. *Intelligence officers aren't supposed to shoot people.* She knew from her childhood that MI6 officers didn't engage in gun battles. Still, she acted on instinct, protecting Ben and her father. *Why would I need to protect Ben before my father?* She knew this was the man who she would spend her life with. *Yes,* she thought, *I would do it again, anything to protect my family.*

At the same time, she desperately wanted to know what Ben heard from the dying man, who gave Ben something. *Now isn't the time to draw attention.* She trusted the man holding her hand, as her father embraced her mother, relief evident on both their faces. She surveyed the scene in Charles Harper's back garden, knowing it would take days for all details to be understood about everything that happened in a span of minutes.

TWO VEHICLES SPED THROUGH the late-night traffic, the drivers weaving expertly around slower cars. Two British citizens and one American in the back of the British Embassy's largest vehicle, while two Americans and one Brit sat in the follow vehicle. Each of them quietly relived the events that somehow permitted them to all leave unscathed.

Arthur sat in the seat behind Mark, his wife in the middle, and the Senator near the other door. Trying to allay her fears and recounting what he remembered of the attack, Arthur detailed how Mark absorbed the bullets that otherwise would have struck him. He reached forward to pat the head of his security detail on the shoulder, then described how Ben rushed up to drag him to the ground after Mark fell, saving his life in the process.

Mark turned in his seat, wanting to ask more questions, but he saw two versions of his boss in the rear seat: one was a man clinging to his wife's hand and the other the head of Britain's Secret Intelligence Service, whose death would have caused tremors in London. Arthur then recounted how Kate had picked up Mark's service weapon and fired at the approaching attacker, bringing him down.

In the follow vehicle, Ben lay his head in Kate's lap. They hadn't bothered to buckle up.

McKenzie sat contemplating her life. *What do I need to do to get my life on track and make it mean something?* She watched with envy as Ben and Kate nestled close to one another, jealous that they had one another. *What do I have other than a job that demands all my time?* The young Congressional staffer grew up at that moment, deciding she would prioritize her personal life and seek someone who could give her the comfort she so craved, the comfort in abundance in the seat ahead of her.

Meanwhile, Kate stroked Ben's forehead, whispering softly to him about their return flight to Virginia.

"We must take a road trip so I can see more of your country," she whispered, promising herself that they would discuss everything the moment they were in their room together. *Not the first moment though.* She smiled. In the aftermath of the attack, more than anything, she wanted to take a shower. Smiling, she decided that Ben would have to join her.

ARRIVING AT THEIR HOTEL, the six passengers disgorged from the vehicles and walked to the entrance, Mark trailing just behind after bidding good night to the driver, still rubbing the points of impact. *I really should call for someone else to provide protection,* he considered, but like any good British subject, he refused to abandon his duty.

Just as they approached the front doors, a vehicle sped towards the hotel. Mark reached for his pistol, which Lionel gave him before they left Harper's residence, and prepared to fire.

As Mark raised his weapon, two men and a woman jumped from the vehicle and stood with their arms in the air. Then he heard a noise to his left and feared it was another attacker, so he quickly began to back away. He wasn't quite ready to fire, not until he saw a direct threat, but he also didn't know any of these people.

"Ben or Kate," Stephen called out, "could you please tell him that we mean no harm?"

Ben turned from the front door, in the back of the line of people with Kate as they struggled to rush her parents, the Senator, and McKenzie into the hotel, and looked behind him. He walked towards

Mark, Kate immediately on his heels, and saw Stephen, Gideon, and Sarah standing with their hands up, while Jacob stood to the side, cautiously watching like a referee at a tennis match.

"Mark, those are our Israeli colleagues," Ben said, unsure why he called them colleagues, because friends felt a bit too odd to say about Mossad officers.

Mark half turned his head, identifying them out of the side of vision. "Kate, do you confirm that these are not enemies?"

"Yes, Mark, I confirm," she called out, recognizing the professional desperation in the bodyguard's voice.

Mark lowered his weapon, cautiously at first, then fully when he saw that the three Israelis kept their hands up while walking very slowly towards them. He recognized that they sought to dispel any notion that they were a threat, though he knew that as likely Israeli Mossad, the three of them posed no direct threat to his boss or his boss's family, much less to him. He also watched as the older man who stood to the side approached, joining his three colleagues, but without raising his arms.

INSIDE THE HOTEL, THE FOUR ISRAELIS approached to shake hands. Jacob kissed Angela's hand after introducing himself to Arthur, while Stephen, Gideon, and Sarah nodded respectfully to her and Arthur.

The Senator suggested they go to the side bar for a drink, the better to get somewhere safer, and they all agreed. McKenzie excused herself, explaining that she was tired and needed sleep.

"Poor girl," Angela said, having wisely sheltered inside the residence during the shooting, trusting that her husband, daughter, and future son-in-law remained safe. "I also am dreadfully tired," she said, kissing first her husband and then daughter each on the cheek, then hugging Ben, before she went to her room.

Sitting in the bar, they arranged themselves around a table. Ben ordered a double Manhattan, and Kate ordered a gin and tonic. Mark sat at the nearby table at first and only joined them after Arthur insisted, saying Mark earned one drink. "Surely we will all be safe at the hotel," he exclaimed, "what with the legions of police out looking for additional perpetrators in the attack." He looked around impatiently, feeling he earned a drink, then added, "Though I'm certain they'll have more questions for us to answer in the morning."

After the drinks arrived, they began exchanging views on the attack, all marveling that none of their number was seriously injured. Throughout, Stephen stared at Ben, who remained conspicuously quiet.

After speaking quietly in one corner with Jacob, the Senator and Arthur stood, expectedly announcing how tired they were, then leaving after tossing some bills on the table. Arthur Sinclair ambled up to his room, taking the time to order a bottle of champagne to his room with two glasses, while Mark followed behind. The Senator took a separate elevator to his room to call his wife.

Just the six of them remained—one American, one Brit, and four Israelis. Stephen unexpectedly leaned forward, the table in front of him threatening to buckle under his weight. "What happened with the man who was dying on the floor?" he asked, curiosity getting the better of him.

Sipping lazily from his glass, Ben remained calm, feeling very relaxed and looking forward to his second drink, which sat on the table before him. He knew he would crash that evening and wake in the morning with a hangover, but at least he was alive to wake with a hangover. With his other hand, he reached for Kate, reassuring himself that she was still there, and then set down his drink.

"If you must know…" Ben considered how much they knew or suspected. He met four pairs of eyes, all scrutinizing him. *Jesus, I would hate to play them in poker!* "Okay, I found the guy still alive."

He told the story for the first time, not having even had time to recount everything to Kate, who leaned forward and listened carefully. As he explained what the man said, he withdrew the beads from his pocket and laid them on the table in front of him. Everyone stared at them, knowing they belonged to a man now dead for at least two hours. He was also one of the men who tried to kill them all.

Jacob was the first to break the silence, reaching tentatively to grab the beads, which he examined carefully in the light. "These are old beads." He fingered each of them, noting the worn edges. "They look to be very worn down from years, perhaps decades, of use."

"The man asked me to return them to his wife," Ben explained, retelling the details about the green warehouse in the industrial district.

Nodding thoughtfully, they passed the beads around the table. When they got back to Ben, he put them back in his pocket, feeling an immense sense of responsibility with their weight.

"Now that we've all touched the evidence, making it useless for forensics," Gideon said, "what's our next move?" He set down his half-finished beer and looked curiously at Ben.

"In the morning, Kate and I plan to find the warehouse the man described and return these beads," Ben said, then took yet another drink. He didn't have to say that he decided not to share these same details with Peter or Trevor at the embassy. *They'll just go back to Washington for guidance, likely entering this green warehouse with guns blazing.* Ben trusted himself, as well as Kate, to handle this, after which he would share all details with the personnel at the embassy.

"Can you wait that long to return them?" Sarah asked, then sipped her juice. She still grieved Avi, the man she was destined to marry, yet she had been too stupid not to make the first move. She blamed herself, even though that was foolish.

"How are we supposed to find this green warehouse at night, when it is so dark outside?" Kate asked in a clear, sober voice, despite starting on her second cocktail. No one responded to her logical assertion, so she continued. "In the morning, we can drive out there, but right now we could drive by the warehouse and miss it completely." She knew Ben's independent spirit, which didn't always like to play by the rules, would rankle his superiors at the State Department. However, it would be easier for the two of them to visit the warehouse, then report to their organizations whatever they learned.

No one had a good response. Jacob looked down at his hands, while Stephen and Gideon stared at the table before them. Ben realized these were all people accustomed to action, not sitting around, yet he agreed with Kate.

Standing abruptly from his seat, Ben finished his second drink, set the glass on the table, and reached for the third. "I don't know about everyone else," he said to the assembled Israelis, "but I plan to go upstairs and thank God I'm alive."

"Are you four going to stay down here all night?" Kate asked, genuinely confused, but confident in the knowledge that they would solve their accommodation problem without any challenges. She then walked out with Ben, stopping to sign the bar bill, and they went to his room, hanging a Do Not Disturb sign on the door.

EIGHT HOURS LATER, KATE RUSHED to her room to shower and change. Ben stayed in his room to do the same. He didn't know what the day would bring. He selected slacks and a sweater to ward off the chill in the morning air, then stopped by Kate's room. She made him wait a minute and then walked out to give him a morning kiss before they rode the elevator down to the lobby.

They entered the restaurant for breakfast, unsurprised to find the four Israelis sitting at the same table as if they hadn't left since the night before. Jacob read an international newspaper, which bore no reports about last night's carnage in Budapest. Stephen and Gideon wolfed through plates piled high with food, and Sarah sat drinking a cup of tea. Ben and Kate each selected plates of food, took their seats from the night before, and thanked the waiter when he brought them coffee.

After several minutes of silence, during which Ben managed to eat most of the food on his plate and Kate picked at her eggs, Ben pushed back and looked inquiringly at Jacob, who continued to read his paper.

"Well?" Ben asked, unsurprised that the Israeli ignored him.

"I am sorry to say at least ten men are dead, including the American Ambassador, two senior Russian officials, the Iranian Ambassador, and three Chinese officials who died protecting their chief observer." He drank noisily from the cup of coffee at his elbow, then set the cup back on the plate. "The other dead men were serving food when they were caught in the crossfire. In addition, many more are injured. At least one Iranian shot in the shoulder, but they rushed him and the other wounded to the hospital."

He looked at the group, all of them concentrating on his next words.

"As you may expect, today's talks"—he checked his watch—"or shall I say *today's proposed talks* are canceled until further notice."

"I guess that means we should probably start our search for the green warehouse," Ben said, getting a nod from Kate, who he saw had finished her breakfast and was nearly done drinking her tea. He knew it would do no good to object to the Israelis joining them, so he waited patiently for them, tapping his foot in anticipation of what they would find.

CHAPTER

THIRTY

AS THEY DROVE THROUGH BUDAPEST'S LUSH tree-lined streets, they approached the industrial park district. "Slow and pull over here," Jacob ordered from the back, the chase car with Stephen and Gideon stopping behind. Only seconds later, the two men appeared, one on each side of the rear windows.

"Avi left me his notes," Jacob began, his voice cracking with emotion yet controlled as he spoke.

Ben looked at the man, whose decades in service to the Israeli government he imagined involved significant sacrifice, especially of fellow officers.

"As I was saying," Jacob started after he took a breath, his voice stronger this time, "Avi left me his notes and described how he followed the Iranian he observed many times entering an industrial park. He never was able to follow the man all the way to his destination. If he did, he only did it once…" He paused to light a cigar, then exhaled out the window. "In the past days, I sat with the helpers who served as lookouts for Avi, men and women who remember things."

Jacob recounted with details the routes the Iranian took into the industrial park, recounting from Avi's notes when he lost the man each time.

"My guess is that, after the attack, we likely don't need to worry about encountering this Iranian," Jacob said.

Just then, Ben snapped his head when he heard four weapons cocked. Stephen, Gideon, Sarah, and Kate each checked and holstered their pistols.

"Why does everyone get a gun but me?" Ben asked no one in particular.

Jacob pointed down the street. "While it is possible there may be other industrial parks in the city of Budapest, I believe it likely that we will find the warehouse the dying man described in this area."

All four exited the vehicle, joining Gideon and Stephen in the deserted street. On this particular morning, the entire street seemed eerily silent, as if everyone remained sleeping even after eight o'clock in the morning.

The six of them walked down the street, observing the dilapidated state of the buildings and general infrastructure. Ben saw that few of the buildings could possibly be inhabited by businesses since most windows in the surrounding buildings were broken.

Jacob admitted they had already passed the point into which Avi penetrated the industrial park, so from that point on, they were on their own.

"We should split up and cover more ground," Ben half-heartedly suggested.

"Your desire to get away from us is admirable," Jacob said dryly, "but only you have the beads, so we will all stay together."

The six of them spread out, not bothering to stay on the broken sidewalks because they hadn't seen a vehicle since entering the industrial park. Ben noticed small alleyways that ran between some of the buildings, wondering where they led. He was aware that in the maze of the giant blocks of warehouses and other industrial buildings, it would be easy to get lost if one didn't know their way.

After exploring for twenty-five minutes, just as they reached an intersection, Ben thought he heard a sound. *Are those children playing?* Trusting his instincts, which had always served him well in the past, he reached into his pocket and felt the prayer beads. Taking a deep breath, he turned to his right and followed the sound of the noises in the distance. Everyone else followed just steps behind.

As they neared the next intersection, Ben approached and saw a number of children playing soccer outside. *Football, they play football here in Europe.* He briefly hesitated but forged ahead, and the children noticed him at last.

"Good morning," he said cheerfully to the children but received no response.

"*Jo reggelt*," one of the children said.

Another repeated "Good morning" in a small voice.

"Do any of you speak English?" Ben asked, his mind churning through the options.

No response to that. Ben was unsure what he expected. The children all giggled and observed them. None of them got too close, but they also didn't run away.

"*Sob be-kher*," Ben said. He was greeted again by silence, though one of the children stared at Ben intently.

"*Sabah al-khayr*," Ben said next, and the children stopped speaking.

"*Hal tatahadath ale-Arabia?*" one of the older children asked.

Ben looked down at the child, willing himself to remember the Arabic he learned before he served in Jordan years before.

"*Aywa*," he replied tentatively, and the children as one rushed towards Ben, all speaking at once.

Just then, Ben heard a voice that commanded all to listen, including the six adults. Ben turned to see a woman in her early forties wearing a headscarf standing outside the door to a large green warehouse. Unlike all the other warehouses, dilapidated and broken-down things, this one was clean and maintained, with complete windows and a working door that wasn't boarded up.

Ben walked towards her, hands up to show no threat, but did not approach too close. Kate approached from behind, standing near but not next to Ben.

"*Hal tatahadath ale-Arabia?*" Ben asked the woman. She appeared slightly shocked at Ben speaking to her in Arabic in the middle of an industrial park in Hungary.

"Your Arabic is not very good," Aisha said in halting English, smiling and relaxing at hearing her native tongue.

Ben approached closer, pleased the woman spoke English far better than he spoke Arabic, and noticed she looked exhausted, with puffy bags under her eyes. "I don't think she has slept in days," Kate whispered from behind.

"What do you want?" Aisha asked. She didn't seem afraid at the appearance of four men and two women, all foreigners, outside her door. She wondered where her husband was, fearing the worst but judging these six people to be less of a threat than the Hungarian police. They visited many times, sometimes demanding bribes but more often amused by the prospect of Middle Easterners making a better life for themselves.

"Can we speak inside?" Ben asked. He wondered how many more people were inside the warehouse. He didn't want to disclose the deaths of the men in front of the children. Without thinking, Ben turned to look at the children, who alternated their gazes between Ben and the woman, one commanding their respect and obedience, the other drawing their attention as something foreign.

Aisha eyed him carefully, looking from Ben to Kate, then back to Ben. She hadn't heard any news reports since yesterday, after the children broke the radio while playing, so she felt anxious.

"I promise we will not hurt you," Kate said, addressing the woman cautiously, "but we have something important to discuss with you."

Seemingly undecided about what to do, the woman scrutinized Kate. *Why do I feel like I'm being analyzed by someone used to judging other people?* Kate asked herself.

"You women come, And you." She pointed to Ben. "But you stay outside." She pointed to Jacob, Stephen, and Gideon. Sarah stepped forward, arranging her jacket around the gun at the small of her back. She didn't want the woman to see that she was armed. Kate already did that earlier, unaccustomed to drawing her weapon against anything other than a target. *Except for the two shots I fired last night.*

The three of them followed the woman inside. Jacob, Stephen, and Gideon stepped away from the warehouse.

Just then, the children all began to follow, but Ben stopped. "It would be better…" he began, but Sarah spoke rapidly in Arabic to the woman, so fast Ben could barely comprehend.

"I think Sarah is telling her that it would be better if the children didn't go in," Ben whispered to Kate.

The woman in the headscarf seemed pleasantly startled by the woman speaking Arabic fluently. She yelled to the children in Arabic, and they returned to playing outside, obviously accustomed to taking orders from this woman.

Inside the warehouse, Ben's eyes adjusted to the large but poorly lit space, seeing what used to be a large factory floor but was now a space subdivided into various work spaces. On the far end were two women in headscarves huddled around a brick stove that was built into the side of the warehouse. It had an exhaust vent designed to keep the smoke out of the space. *That is quite some craftsmanship,* Ben observed, impressed that they invested so much in this space.

The women in headscarves stood as they approached, Sarah and Kate in the lead with the woman they met outside, while Ben followed two paces behind, not wanting to appear threatening. The first woman they met began speaking, and Ben realized how out of practice he was with his Arabic. He wished he practiced as much as with his Farsi.

Sarah entered the conversation, the women eyeing her warily at first, but they seemed to appreciate hearing the sound of their native tongue.

Waving Ben forward, Sarah positioned him across the fire from the women. None of them looked like they had slept in days. Ben looked around more carefully, realizing what this space lacked. *Where are the men?* Then he realized these women's husbands were the ones who attacked the party the night before.

"Who are you and what do you want?" Aisha asked in English for the other women, who looked at her anxiously at being cut out of the conversation.

"If you like," Sarah offered, "you are welcome to speak Arabic, and I will translate."

"*Shukran,*" Aisha said, smiling with relief for the first time. She spoke quickly, and when she finished, Sarah translated for Ben and Kate.

"She says her name is Aisha. And she asked what you want here."

"Where are your husbands?" Ben asked, getting to the point, because it made no sense to waste time.

Sarah translated, and the women all looked at one another, anguish clear on their faces, before Aisha spoke again.

"They have not seen their husbands since they left their home in the middle of the night, two nights ago. And they are worried."

"Are you missing any other people?" he asked, having counted the chairs and realizing that with ten places around the fire, it made sense that four people were missing, especially since four men attacked the party. *There must be at least two missing.*

Sarah translated again. "Two people, the youngest in our group, went missing, the wife and her husband." Sarah paused to listen to one of the other women speak, then translated. "She wants to know why you are here."

Not knowing how else to break the news, Ben withdrew the beads from his pocket, raising them and asking in the best Arabic he could remember, "*Hal hadha yakhusu 'ahad rijalika?*"

"Did this belong to one of your men?" Sarah translated for Kate, impressed with Ben's rudimentary Arabic. "My respect for Ben is growing, given how he continually surprises me with his skills," Sarah whispered to a quiet Kate. But she didn't have time to respond.

Aisha stood, her mouth open in a voiceless scream, but then she found her voice. "Where you find that?" she screamed in English, then switched to Arabic and rushed at Ben.

Momentarily alarmed, Ben wondered if she intended to attack him but decided that standing his ground made the most sense. He wasn't about to punch this woman. Luckily, she stopped just inches from him, Kate having grabbed at her clothes to keep her from touching Ben.

"*Qafa!*" Sarah yelled, all four women turning to face her.

In the next seconds, the women returned to their seats, speaking rapidly while Sarah translated quietly for Kate. Ben kept his distance, realizing that pulling out the prayer beads was definitely not the right decision, yet he wasn't sure what else he should have done.

"That was foolish," Kate whispered to Ben. But then she smiled. "Yet the shock got the women talking quite freely." She took the prayer beads and gave Ben's hand a squeeze.

Ben watched as Kate took the beads and placed them in the hands of Aisha. She cried as all the women spoke over each other.

With no apparent role to play in that conversation, Ben began walking around. He went to the back of the warehouse and found a hallway, which he followed to a set of stairs. Curious, he climbed the flight of stairs to find what must have been the offices when the factory still operated. He found many doors, though the people using this space hadn't gone as far as to clean out every one of them, only a few that they used for additional workspaces. At the end of a hallway, where he saw more dust gathered, he found a room with a closed door and a sign pasted onto the cracked glass in Arabic. He thought the sign looked familiar, but he couldn't understand it.

After he opened the door, Ben entered to see surfaces covered in dust, with the exception of the middle of the room, where it seemed someone had cleaned, or at least cleared away the dust. He flipped the light switch, but that didn't work, so he pulled out his phone and used the flashlight function to look around.

As he circled the room, starting in the center and working out from there, he found the space orderly, as if someone cleaned it up before they closed the factory. *It doesn't appear they've used this space in quite some time.* Having seen everything that he could after just a few minutes, Ben turned to leave when a piece of white cloth caught his eye. It was under the desk, tossed carelessly aside and hidden in the shadows. Had someone not looked carefully, or had a light, they would have missed it, just as Ben missed it when he first walked near the desk.

After stooping down to pick up the cloth, he nearly dropped it when he discovered it was covered in blood but instead adjusted his grip to hold it by a part that was still white. He carefully folded it, knowing it could be important but not wanting to alarm anyone by walking around with a blood-soaked piece of cloth. Placing it carefully in his jacket pocket, he closed the door and retraced his steps, arriving downstairs to find Kate and Sarah speaking away from the women.

"Ben, where were you?" Kate asked.

But Ben didn't have the chance to respond, because Sarah began speaking.

"These women are Iraqi, originally from Baghdad, and the children outside are theirs." She looked at Ben curiously, as if sensing he had something to say, but she wanted to share what she learned first. "They explained that five families left Iraqi, encountering unimaginable suffering during their trip here, to include losing a child. Their destination was Germany. She said sometime after they arrived, a man approached the five men in their group, offering them money if they would undertake a mission for him."

Ben raised his eyebrows, as if ready to ask a question, but didn't interrupt.

"The man, who the women initially claimed they never saw, gave their husbands money that helped them not only survive the winter but also thrive in this city. The women finally admitted that they saw the man, plus each of them admitted that their husbands confided to them that their task was to attack and kill Americans. In exchange"—Sarah looked around—"the man promised them enough money to get them all safely to Germany. But they cannot describe the man."

Just then, Kate looked at Ben, stepping to close their circle of three. "Ben, give me your phone," she demanded, stretching out her hand.

Ben pulled out his phone and handed it to her. In response, Kate grabbed Sarah by the jacket sleeve and pulled her to approach the three women, unlocking the phone as they walked. The women looked up as they approached. Ben couldn't exactly understand what they said, but less than a minute later, Kate and Sarah returned, excited.

"They say this is the man who visited their husbands," Kate said, returning Ben's phone.

"And two of them admitted that their husbands confided that the man was Iranian, likely connected to the IRGC," Sarah finished.

Kate was thinking quickly, Ben observed. As he was about to say something, the door they came through opened. Stephen and Gideon entered, with Jacob trailing several paces behind.

"What is going on in here?" Stephen demanded, looking around the space to see three women in headscarves crying near a brick stove.

Sarah and Kate began speaking quickly and quietly, filling the three men in on everything they learned. Meanwhile, Ben thought about the bloodied cloth in his pocket and approached the huddled five.

"There were five men, yet only four attacked," Sarah said. "But they still haven't explained where the one couple is, or where the fourth woman is."

"That's the short of it," Kate said, turning to make space for Ben as he joined their group.

"I explored while Kate and Sarah spoke with the three women," Ben explained and told them about the space above. He pulled out the piece of white cloth covered in blood from his pocket. "What are the chances?" Ben asked the group, already feeling as if he knew the grim answer, "that this Iranian who set these men to attack last night's party could have used this space to kill Avi?"

Jacob went white as a sheet as he stared down at the bloodied cloth.

Seeing the four Israelis start to grow angry, Ben spoke quickly. "I could be wrong," he admitted, yet he suspected they made the leap to draw the same conclusion.

Jacob stepped forward, putting one hand on Ben's shoulder and reaching for the cloth in Ben's hands with his other hand. In what appeared very paternalistic, he held Ben's gaze, speaking after a pregnant pause.

"I want to thank you, Ben," Jacob said, emotion threatening to break through his wall of willpower, "for everything you have done for us." Ben felt Jacob take the cloth and hand it carefully to Gideon, who withdrew a plastic bag from his cargo pants and carefully placed the cloth in it. After that, Jacob cupped his hands around Ben's face, then drew Ben into a bear hug from which Ben couldn't have escaped if he wanted. *The old man is stronger than he appears.* Ben was surprised by the man's embrace.

After a minute-long hug, Jacob kissed Ben on both cheeks, then withdrew two steps to reform their circle. "We will need to conduct blood tests on this cloth," Jacob said, regaining full control, "but first, please take Stephen and me up to explore that room."

Ben led Jacob, Stephen, and Gideon to the stairs and then up the one flight.

Meanwhile, Kate and Sarah returned to speak with the women. They found them weeping uncontrollably, inconsolable at the realization that their husbands were dead.

Kate and Sarah approached slowly, gaining their attention before crouching down to speak with them.

"Will you please ask the women what happened to the fourth woman?" Kate said, shuddering at the realization of the death pact the fourth woman and her husband made. The women explained that they found the woman dead in her bed the night before, an obvious poisoning.

"After they found her dead, they wrapped her in bedsheets, then brought their children here to wait for their husbands," Sarah translated. "The women feared the worst, though they said that Aliyah, who killed herself, and her husband Malik never recovered from their daughter's drowning."

Kate almost began crying at the realization of the pain each of these women must be enduring. She turned to look for Ben and wondered how she would respond if anything happened to him. *I'm not yet married to Ben, and I already know I would be devastated if anything happened to him.* She thought about the grief the woman who committed suicide must have suffered, having lost a daughter and then knowing that her husband went on a suicide mission yesterday.

That man knew he was going to die, both women simultaneously understood, it dawning on Kate that after losing his daughter, the Iraqi must have welcomed death. *I hope the three of them are reunited in heaven,* Kate thought. She was thinking more like a person than an intelligence officer, but she didn't care.

"What will they do next?" Kate asked Sarah. The British and Israeli intelligence officers quickly formed a plan to help these victims.

RETURNING AFTER EXPLORING EVERY INCH OF THE ROOM, Ben marveled at the Israelis' thoroughness. They found scuff marks made by several different men. Gideon pointed out that at least three men must have walked in that room, plus there was a tarp or some other large piece of plastic covering the floor, which Stephen explained likely swept away the dust when it was put on the ground.

Back down in the main room, Ben saw Kate and Sarah talking seriously with the three women. With time to spare, he pulled out his phone and began checking messages, unsure what else he could do. He saw multiple messages from the Senator, and he had several missed calls. *If I don't report in soon, I'm going to be in trouble with everyone,* Ben thought, though he knew the information they collected this morning would go a long way to answering many questions left from last night's attack.

Simultaneously, Ben saw Jacob leading Stephen and Gideon towards him, while Kate and Sarah withdrew from the three grieving women to join their group.

"We found flecks of blood on the floor," Stephen reported grimly. Ben was surprised, not having seen anything, but he reminded himself that he wasn't a trained intelligence officer. "We took samples, and will compare them with the blood-soaked cloth you found."

Before Stephen could continue, Sarah began explaining everything they learned from the women. Ben was astonished by all that the women shared, especially the harsh news that one of the women committed suicide.

"What about—" Stephen began to ask, but Kate cut him off.

"We have a plan," she began. She detailed how she and Sarah wanted to enlist the aid of Israeli contacts in the community to support the three women and their children. "I think I know people who could help them get to Germany, where they will find a community."

Why should we help these widows and children of terrorists? Ben thought but didn't say. He wondered why the Israelis would ever want to help families of terrorists. At the same time, he admitted that the women were not at fault for their husbands' choices. *The West doesn't believe in collective punishment,* Ben knew, seeing the justice in what Kate and Sarah proposed. He even thought he might know some people in the NGO community who could help these women.

Ben felt eyes staring at him and turned to see the three women standing some distance, looking directly at him. Aisha held the prayer beads Ben brought with him, reminding Ben of his conversation with her husband the night before.

"Sarah, would you please translate for me?" he asked and began telling Aisha of her husband's final thoughts and words, Sarah translating throughout.

The women cried even more, with grief on their faces, as Ben, Kate, Sarah, Jacob, Stephen, and Gideon bade farewell and went outside. They saw the children stopped playing when the adults exited, knowing that the women needed to tell their children their fathers were dead. Not wanting to witness that event, the six of them quickly retraced their steps to find their vehicles.

CHAPTER

THIRTY-ONE

ARRIVING BACK AT THE HOTEL, Ben entered the lobby to find the Senator eating lunch with Kate's parents. Ben approached to explain, but Kate took his hand and, with her grip, urged restraint when it came to the details.

Over the next hour, the Senator and Kate's father asked clarifying questions, which Ben, Kate, Sarah, and Jacob attempted to answer, while Stephen and Gideon made calls and received a steady stream of people who exited almost as soon as they arrived.

"So, it was definitely an Iranian who communicated with your American political chief Brent and coordinated the attack by the Iraqis. Bloody industrious fellow, isn't he?" Arthur said with a hint of admiration in his voice, realizing he underestimated Iran's intelligence services. "I only wish we knew who he was."

With a photograph, they would be able to put a lookout with the Hungarian police and friendly intelligence services, guaranteed to get cooperation for the man who sought to kill a host of foreign dignitaries and diplomats.

Once they finished answering questions, Ben asked for an update, learning that the regional security officer arrested Brent for espionage while the negotiations with the Iranians were scuttled.

"It appears the Iranians went to great lengths to stop the talks, or at least one faction of the Iranians did," the Senator said, "but at a terrible cost to participants in the talks, including our ambassador, Alan Richards."

"Well, I won't miss him," Ben muttered so only Kate could hear him.

Just then, Peter and Trevor arrived, followed by Charles Harper. They approached their table, but Ben suddenly felt exhausted.

"Senator," Ben whispered, "do I need to be here for all of this? I don't know if I have the energy to retell everything all over again."

"No, my boy," the Senator said gently, "and I suspect your Kate also doesn't need to stay." "Thanks ever so much," Kate responded, feeling exhausted as she rose from her seat to confer quickly and quietly with her father.

"Ben, where are you going?" Peter asked.

Trevor exclaimed, "We have questions!"

The Senator broke in. "I think you will get better answers from Ben after he rests, even for an hour, and you could start by interviewing others first."

Without even waiting, Ben walked away from the table, grateful that the Senator supported his need for a moment away. Kate finished speaking with her father and, after giving a quick kiss on her mother's cheek, joined Ben, holding his hand as they walked across the hotel lobby.

They walked toward the bank of elevators, but then Ben stopped in the middle of the lobby. He looked at the assembled people gathered around two tables, discussing and processing the myriad of information they learned that morning. Plus whatever actions others undertook.

Kate didn't see Ben stop and kept walking, nearly yanking Ben's arm off, but spun to see Ben rooted to the spot. "What is it, Ben?" she asked, perplexed. There wasn't any danger she could detect, feeling protected with a virtual army of Hungarian police controlling access to major tourist sites, which included their hotel. Only because they drove diplomatic vehicles had they been able to park at the hotel.

"I'm just wondering…" Ben said. "Who leaked that information about the Israeli plans to attack Iran?"

SITTING IN HIS OFFICE AT MAIN STATE, Robert looked at the neat stacks of documents for him to clear, arranged on his desk based on who submitted them, their priority, and the country of interest. He looked at the various action memos that Tammy printed for him, all destined for the secretary's desk, some even for the White House. *This is important policy work,* Robert thought. He knew he needed to focus on advancing these important priorities that related to broader European security.

Half an hour later, after marking up each of the documents and calling Tammy in to apply edits to the electronic versions, then returning them to the drafting officers, Robert checked his email. He read through cable traffic to get updated, seeing the reporting coming out of Budapest about the attack that killed nearly a dozen foreign diplomats, including the American Ambassador to Hungary. *Alan never treated any of his people well.*

Though he should have felt remorse at the death of a colleague, Robert instead wondered how the eternal shuffle of career Foreign Service officers would create an opening that would enable him to climb the ladder at least another rung. *Perhaps two, if I play my cards right.*

While Robert mulled that over, he thought about how he needed to continue feeding information to his Russian handlers. Although he had some cash saved, it wouldn't be enough to escape. *Plus, why would I ever want to leave the career I love?*

Understanding that the only reason he ever considered leaving was because of Ludmilla, Robert knew he would stay in the Foreign Service as long as he kept getting promoted. He felt a hole in his heart every time he thought of Ludmilla or saw a photo of her. That was why he put all photos of her away in drawers, only pulling them out when he wanted to get drunk and speak with her ghost. During those times, he locked the doors and closed the drapes, and begged her forgiveness, knowing she died because the Russians sought to control him.

Still, I am a realist who must keep living. Therefore, the man entrusted with secrets by the State Department and trusted by his colleagues at the National Security Council, the Department of Defense, the Department of Energy, the Defense Intelligence Agency, and the Central Intelligence Agency, continued noting documents he would provide to his Russian handler. He would do this because not to was unthinkable. If he didn't give the Russians what they demanded, he would die. *Who would benefit from my death?* he reasoned, knowing that despite any other activities, he would carry out his job.

"HOW DID THOSE MEN, Iraqis according to reports, gain access to such weapons?" the general asked. He spoke in Tehran two days later in front of the Grand Ayatollah. Farrokh, Ramin, and Mahmoud were present, as was the Teacher, who sat in his wheelchair to the side.

Farrokh's shoulder remained bandaged under his shirt, but he appeared as mobile as any of the others. They were in Grand Ayatollah Shirazi's apartment, high above the busy streets of Tehran.

"As my Immortals told you already," the Grand Ayatollah said sternly, "they were there to observe and report. We will investigate, of course, but we have no plausible idea who could have orchestrated such an attack." He stared daggers at the IRGC general, an insolent young pup who was still in school when the revolution happened. *How dare he accuse me? Even if it is true,* he noted with satisfaction.

"Our country needed more oil revenue," the general asserted. "More than we receive from your efforts through Afghanistan." That the Grand Ayatollah's pipeline of dollars increased his power and prestige throughout the country was not in question, but the IRGC objected to any entity vying for control of the Iranian state, especially the ear of the Supreme Leader.

"You can be assured," the Grand Ayatollah said, "that I have no wish to disrupt the IRGC's control or influence throughout our great country, or your regional efforts to spread revolutionary influence."

What witchcraft is this, the General thought, *that he knows my thoughts precisely?* He reasoned that he needed to tread carefully, because the man before him not only had the ear of the Supreme Leader, but now he understood the true reach of the Grand Ayatollah's private army of these so-called Immortals. *Time to neutralize that threat.*

"I believe the guards would benefit from leadership of your Immortals, men who could convey their skills and experience to the younger generation."

"While I would welcome promotions for each of them, perhaps to colonel"—the Grand Ayatollah looked to the Teacher, who nodded assent to the idea he suggested earlier—"I am loath to lose the services of men who are like sons to me."

The three Immortals stiffened at hearing that, each then staring straight ahead, struggling to control their feelings.

"I would never intrude on control of your Immortals—" the general began.

"We will redouble our efforts, shall we?" the Grand Ayatollah looked to the Teacher, who promptly spoke.

"We can triple the amount of hard cash that enters Iran every month, guaranteeing the IRGC alone receives the additional funding."

The general stared in amazement, unable in the immediate moment to comprehend the power and influence that much money would buy. It would further cement the IRGC as the preeminent power in Iran, provided the Grand Ayatollah held up his end of the bargain.

"And in return, you ask?"

"In return, you will instruct your men to be"—he paused, as if searching for the word—"*amenable* to my Immortals recruiting from your ranks for our tasks. Both in and out of Iran." He stared for a second, then continued. "Plus, you will no longer obstruct our efforts when we need logistical or equipment support."

The general nodded his assent, knowing that much money could buy him whatever he desired. Plus the guarantee of increased attacks against the Israelis in the coming months. He longed to fund more research on drones, the better to carry out remote attacks, and here was the funding he required.

"Done," he said, relaxing as he looked around the apartment, noticing movement behind him in the form of a young girl wearing a loose-fitting headscarf carrying a tray.

"Is this a member of your family?" the general asked, unable to hide his tone of displeasure that the girl's headscarf did not fully cover her hair.

The three Immortals tensed as one, intensely protective of the little girl who referred to each of them as uncle, while the Grand Ayatollah unexpectedly stood. The little girl did not appear to notice these actions, intent as she was to carefully place the tray on the table beside the Grand Ayatollah. She then turned as he approached, standing to one side while he turned her to face the general.

"This is my granddaughter, Homeira Shirazi, who upon my death will inherit all my possessions and control of the Immortals."

The little girl stared unblinkingly at the general, as if objectively analyzing his worth in a market. Her impassive face showed her verdict: *worthless*. He felt a chill, realizing that he went too far. "My apologies, Grand Ayatollah, for offending you."

"If you truly seek penance," the Teacher spoke from his wheelchair as he approached, "then you should also apologize to Homeira."

"Abase myself before a woman." He spat at the cripple in the chair, shocked at the request. Before he finished his sentence, he felt three sets of hands grab him, all far stronger than he was, pinning him to the floor. "Let me go!" he screamed, writhing on the floor but unable to move in their grip.

"I said apologize to her," the Teacher repeated.

"Or you will have no deal," the Grand Ayatollah finished, approaching while holding the girl's hand.

"I... I... I..." he stammered, unaccustomed to losing control of any situation. The small girl child stared down at him, with men as vicious as wolves on the edges of his vision. "I apologize if I offended you."

Homeira continued to stare at him, appraising him to determine whether he was worth permitting to live. "I accept your apology," she replied in a Tehran accent, which she always adopted when she spoke with anyone she did not know.

The Immortals hauled the general to his feet, then picked him up and set him down as if he were a particularly large sack of flour, but with less effort.

"Then our deal stands," the Grand Ayatollah said, patting the girl on the head before returning to his seat. "And we are happy," he finished, watching with pitiless eyes.

The general withdrew, all eyes on him, but the eyes that lingered in his dreams were those of the small child, Homeira. He decided he never wanted to meet her again.

"**THANK YOU FOR YOUR HOSPITALITY** the past days," the Senator said, offering his hand to Arthur as they stood in the VIP departure lounge. The Sinclair family, joined by Ben, the Senator, and McKenzie, flew from Budapest to London on a private government plane after exhaustive debriefings, answering repetitive questions.

Finally, Arthur wielded his power to demand they be permitted to provide answers to requisite questions from the comfort of London rather than in the presence of nosy Hungarian officials who might have demanded more details, and frankly, honesty.

Ben learned during questioning that the FBI took Brent into custody, transferring him to stand trial in federal court for espionage. Suspecting that with the right lawyer and cooperation Brent would reduce his jail time, Ben remained shocked that the man he was friendly with admitted to cooperating with a man he suspected was a foreign agent, all to pursue revenge against Alan Richards. *I still cannot believe Richards was the only American who died.* Though Ben knew the Russians, Chinese, and Iranians remained mad as hornets from the losses they suffered.

"The Israelis are quietly helping the three women and their children to build their lives in Budapest. They've secured permits for them to stay after calls to UNHCR." Ben knew the women's cooperation with the investigation guaranteed they would be permitted to stay in Hungary, though he wondered how long it would take before they either continued to Germany or began attracting other Iraqi families, building a community in Budapest.

"And we still have no idea who leaked intelligence about the Israeli's plans?" the Senator asked. This forced the Israeli government to reconsider their plans, but even they admitted this was not a catastrophic loss because they could always formulate a new plan. Or two.

"We still don't know who disclosed that sensitive information, Senator," Ben said. He heard from Marty that FBI agents in DC, likely including Jenny, were starting a full review of all personnel with access to that information.

Holding Kate's left hand, he smiled at the thought of how he proposed to her in front of her family. The day prior, they attended a small ceremony in the presence of Her Majesty, in which she congratulated Ben on not only interrupting the attack on the bridge but also both him and Kate acting during the terrorist attack. Without telling anyone else, Ben got down on one knee, officially proposing to Kate and giving her a ring her grandmother provided earlier that day.

Surprising even Her Majesty with his impromptu proposal, the Queen remarked that she looked forward to attending the wedding, earning looks of gratitude from Elizabeth and Angela Sinclair, who excitedly contemplated an upcoming social event.

Arthur Sinclair wondered how many of his friends he could invite, before Kate reminded Her Majesty that she remained active in the Secret Service and would not be permitted a public wedding. "I never said I wanted to attend a public wedding, dear," Her Majesty responded with a smile, "but even a private affair can offer an opportunity for celebration without too many photographs."

As Kate stood holding Ben's hand, watching her father speak with the Senator, she heard Ben's phone ping. "What's that?" she asked as Ben opened his phone and began reading.

"Folks in DC denied my request to extend for a second year with the Senator," he whispered, knowing this was retribution for having served the Senator more than he served the State Department. Ben also heard that security personnel in Washington were angry with him for not having checked in with them before he went to the warehouse district, claiming that Ben was too much of a cowboy and needed to serve in a more typical Foreign Service assignment.

"What will that mean for us?" Kate asked, realizing this would complicate their lives. She understood this change called into question the house she planned to buy for them in Alexandria, her planned assignment to stay in Washington.

"As a backup, I asked if they would consider assigning me to London." Kate's face lit up. "But they denied that request, saying they have an urgent vacancy they need me to fill." He handed her his phone, which she quickly scanned, only to read they would provide the *to be determined location* soon.

Disappointed and frustrated, Kate resolved to set to the side that which they couldn't control. "What's next, darling?" she asked, longing for a nice break but fearing a near-immediate return to work, albeit with Ben's unknown new assignment hanging over their heads.

"I thought," Ben responded with a smile as he pulled two tickets from his pocket, "perhaps you could show me around Scotland so I can learn more about your country." He was upset at the change, but dwelling on that would only cause friction with Kate.

She pulled him into an embrace, whispering in his ear as she planned where to go first. "Soon it will be yours too."

AUTHOR'S NOTE

TO MY FELLOW READERS, MANY THANKS FOR ENJOYING this work of fiction, *Diplomatic Tangle*. I hope you appreciated the adventure contained within these pages, as well as the unexpected plot twists I included to keep the story interesting.

Many readers asked me about the origin of the Immortals in my first book, complimenting the details and depth of characters. To my knowledge, there is no Iranian organization similar to the Immortals, nor has there even been since the Persian army of the Achaemenid Empire from 550-330 BCE. The group in my books was entirely a construct of my imagination, representing a formidable force operating on behalf of the Iranian regime.

This book focuses on a group of characters who fled Iraq to Europe seeking a better future for their children and themselves. I wrote based on news reports, conversations with some people I met, and details shared by friends who specialize on migration issues. I will not delve into the right or wrong of varying opinions, but will say that I sought to add depth to these characters, as I do for all who inhabit the world I've created.

For me, it is not only the protagonists who deserve depth and substance, but also antagonists, as well as those who dwell in the gray area between. I assert that were most of us in the positions of others around the world, we would make many of the same decisions they do, motivated by a desire for a better future. No characters in my book are perfect; indeed, protagonists and antagonists alike benefit from character flaws and gifts that make them unique, just as these flaws and gifts make each of us inimitable human beings.

Writing my second book was a labor of love, albeit one that took more than a year of writing, a year of re-writing based on comments and suggestions from people who read the text, and then nearly a year of editing. I acknowledge that I'm a novice published author, so learned from mistakes I made while publishing Proportional Response. Many thanks to Mike, Sonja, Susan, Rhino, and Emily for reading my first drafts and providing edits, all strengthening my story.

One process that I undertook with my second novel was to seek professionals who could improve my writing skills. For that I give thanks to Mark S and Nay, both of whom made structural and grammar improvements to my manuscript, increasing the readability of this novel. Many thanks to them for their focus, partnership, and professionalism.

Thanks also to those who provided input as I reached the final steps of publication, to include designing my cover and other sundry details. Thanks to Victoria for her creativity and ability to provide the support without which this book never would have been read.

Through it all, my family and friends supported me. I would love to list the names of all I thank for their support, but fear I would exclude names. If you've spoken or messaged with me in the past three years, suffice it to say you've provided invaluable support to me. Thank you.

In the end, my children and wife deserve the most credit for supporting me. They gave me time to write, enabling me to focus and weave together the plotlines into a tapestry that you hold in your hands. Each of my children served as inspiration for characters in my book, as did many of my friends. Emily, especially, encouraged me throughout my writing journey, offering "tough love" in the form of plot rewrites that improved this story by leaps and bounds. Emily, you are my partner in every way in my life and all success I have is due to your support.

To my readers, thank you again for your continued support. With the publication of this, my second novel, I now begin writing my third novel. I look forward to seeing how characters continue to change, as well as introducing new characters. Adventure awaits!

ABOUT THE AUTHOR

TIM ENRIGHT is a State Department Foreign Service Officer who has served in Iraq, Russia, the United Arab Emirates, Afghanistan, Nigeria, and Albania, as well as on extended temporary duty in Sudan and at the U.S. Mission to the United Nations. He is married with four children, hails from  Minnesota, and currently calls Virginia home, although he and his family wander the world seeking adventures.